THE HIGHLANDER'S HOLIDAY KISS

"May I kiss you?"

She took in the suddenly roguish gleam in his gaze, and something else—desire, strong enough to jumble her thoughts like a puzzle thrown askew.

"You may," she replied.

Braden's smile flashed for a moment, but then his rogue's expression became tender. Carefully, as if she were a piece of porcelain, he cupped her chin. Samantha instinctively rested a hand on his chest, her fingers curling into the fine wool of his coat as if bracing herself. She hadn't been kissed in such a long time, and her insides fluttered with nerves and anticipation.

He bent his head and his warm, firm mouth touched hers, carefully at first, as if testing her response. Then he began to truly kiss her, slowly but possessively, with deliciously teasing caresses. His tongue flickered along the seam of her lips, not pushing or rushing her, but simply tasting.

Samantha found herself sighing as she leaned into the kiss. His mouth on hers suddenly seemed like the most natural thing in the world.

As if sensing the change, Braden's other hand came up to cradle the back of her head, holding her gently as he deepened the kiss. Beneath the fabric of his coat, she felt the firm beat of his heart against her fingertips. Her senses sparked and desire rose, a sensation she'd thought buried forever.

Oh, how wrong she'd been . . .

Books by Vanessa Kelly

MASTERING THE MARQUESS

SEX AND THE SINGLE EARL

MY FAVORITE COUNTESS

HIS MISTLETOE BRIDE

The Renegade Royals
SECRETS FOR SEDUCING A ROYAL BODYGUARD
CONFESSIONS OF A ROYAL BRIDEGROOM
HOW TO PLAN A WEDDING FOR A ROYAL SPY
HOW TO MARRY A ROYAL HIGHLANDER

The Improper Princesses
MY FAIR PRINCESS
THREE WEEKS WITH A PRINCESS
THE HIGHLANDER'S PRINCESS BRIDE

Clan Kendrick
THE HIGHLANDER WHO PROTECTED ME
THE HIGHLANDER'S CHRISTMAS BRIDE
THE HIGHLANDER'S ENGLISH BRIDE
THE HIGHLANDER'S IRISH BRIDE
THE HIGHLANDER'S HOLIDAY WIFE

Anthologies
AN INVITATION TO SIN
(with Jo Beverley, Sally MacKenzie, and Kaitlin O'Riley)

Published by Kensington Publishing Corp.

The Highlander's Holiday Wife

VANESSA KELLY

ZEBRA BOOKS
Kensington Publishing Corp.
www.kensingtonbooks.com

ZEBRA BOOKS are published by

Kensington Publishing Corp.
119 West 40th Street
New York, NY 10018

All Kensington titles, imprints, and distributed lines are available at special quantity discounts for bulk purchases for sales promotion, premiums, fund-raising, and educational or institutional use.

Special book excerpts or customized printings can also be created to fit specific needs. For details, write or phone the office of the Kensington Sales Manager: Kensington Publishing Corp., 119 West 40th Street, New York, NY 10018. Attn. Sales Department. Phone: 1-800-221-2647.

First Printing: October 2022
ISBN-13: 978-1-4201-5453-5
ISBN-13: 978-1-4201-5454-2 (eBook)

10 9 8 7 6 5 4 3 2 1

Printed in the United States of America

CHAPTER 1

Edinburgh
November 1826

For the space of a few breaths, Braden Kendrick contemplated the idiocy of taking unnecessary risks.

Should have listened to Logan.

He shifted his leather satchel to his left shoulder and pulled a knife from his right pocket. It was a dandy little blade, but laughably inadequate for facing two hulking brutes, one armed with a club and the other with a machete.

Only yesterday, his older brother had lectured him on taking proper precautions in Edinburgh's Old Town. "What you need is a pistol. The criminals down there will gut you without hesitation, because it's a damn sight easier to rob a dead man. You've got to properly arm yourself."

Braden had pointed out that he'd never once been robbed while attending an emergency call. Logan had tartly replied that he'd be damned if he had to explain to the family why he'd allowed their little brother to get himself murdered in some backwater alley. Braden had just rolled his eyes and not given the matter another thought.

Well, regrets wouldn't save him now, when he had to think his way out of an ignominious death.

"Gentlemen," he said, adopting the tone he used on fractious toddlers and nervous patients. "Violence is completely unnecessary. I am more than willing to allow you to rob me. I'll just extract my billfold and you can—"

"Shut yer yap," snapped the one with the machete. He carried a small lantern in his other hand. When he raised it high, it cast a dim, ghoulish light on his face. "It's other business we have with ye tonight."

With full cheeks and a rounded chin, the man looked somewhat cherubic—but for his nose. That mangled feature resembled a grisly chunk of beef.

"I've got a good memory for faces, especially ones like yours," Braden said. "But I don't believe we've ever met."

"Nae, but we know *ye*, Kendrick," snarled the other man in a guttural rasp. "Bloody interfering bastard that ye are."

Now *that* voice was familiar. The rasp was a result of a childhood injury, according to the man's wife.

Braden's odds of survival grew slimmer by the second.

"You're Dougal Parson, Naomi's husband. Or, former husband, should I say?"

"Thanks to ye," the man bitterly replied. "Ye put ideas in her head, ye stupid nob. She were satisfied with her lot until ye told her to kick me out of my own bleedin' house."

"Actually, it was her father's house. And I don't regret suggesting that Naomi divorce you, since you beat her and shoved her down the bloody stairs. You almost killed her."

Tragically, though, the evil bastard had killed Naomi's unborn child. While Braden had been too late to save the unfortunate babe, at least he'd been able to save the mother.

And though he'd been unable to convince Naomi and her elderly father to go to the police—both were too frightened—Braden *had* convinced the girl to obtain a divorce made possible by Scotland's more lenient marriage laws.

He'd also made a point of hunting down Parson, finding him hiding out in a tavern near Tanner's Close. That time,

Braden had armed himself with a pistol. He'd told Parson that if he ever bothered Naomi again, he would ensure that Clan Kendrick would mete out their own brand of justice for the lass, the kind that didn't involve courts or tidy prison cells. The threat had done the trick, and Parson had disappeared.

Or so Braden had thought.

Now, the unrepentant thug aimed a gob of spit at Braden's boot. Thankfully, it fell short, since Parson's dental hygiene left much to be desired.

"Clumsy little bitch fell, is all. She was always fallin' and hurtin' herself. But ye wouldn't listen, now would ye, doc?"

Braden's fingers instinctively tightened around the handle of his blade, and he fought the impulse to charge. "I don't make a habit of believing wife beaters and liars."

"I can't get no work in Old Town, 'cause everyone's too scared of ye and yer bloody family. I'm flat broke."

"How sad. Frankly, I'd rather see you dangling at the end of a rope than sneaking around Old Town like a diseased rat."

Mangled Nose elbowed Parson. "Oy, ye gonna let him talk to you like that?"

"Of course not, ye stupid shite. I'm gonna kill him."

"Well, get on with it. I reckon he's got a pile of blunt stowed in them pockets, not to mention a gold watch."

Braden chuckled. "Oh, I never wear my gold watch into Old Town. That's just tempting fate."

When the two thugs exchanged a perplexed glance, he took advantage of their hesitation.

"Finally," he said, shifting to look past his moronic adversaries. "It's about time you arrived."

Proving they were indeed morons, both men glanced over their shoulders into the stygian gloom. As they turned back to him, Braden hurled his satchel at Parson's face.

Hit squarely by the bag heavy with medical instruments, the man roared and staggered back. Braden bolted, dodging between the men and slashing with his knife. The blade caught Mangled Nose in the arm. He bellowed, stumbling aside and clearing a path.

Braden took off into the dark. Skidding around a nearby corner, he bashed his elbow into a brick wall. Ignoring the pain, he ran as fast as he dared over the uneven cobblestones. His attackers were already in hot pursuit, their heavy footsteps pounding behind him.

Dark tenement buildings loomed over him like decrepit giants, blocking out the pale light of the moon. He couldn't risk twisting an ankle on the uneven stones, or tripping over a doorstep. Fortunately, his assailants had to deal with the same problems. And since he was both younger and fitter, he just needed to keep on his feet until he reached safety.

Finally.

Light shone at the end of the seemingly endless alley, with Cowgate just ahead. There'd be at least a watchman or constable nearby, and a few taverns would still be open. Braden had friends in those taverns, people he'd doctored over the years. They'd never—

His thoughts splintered as his boot slid through something wet and slimy. He pinwheeled his arms but went completely off-kilter, landing hard on his right hip and arm. The knife flew, clattering somewhere off in the dark. Though pain lanced through his body, he forced himself to scrabble up just as his pursuers appeared out of the murk, like demons loosed from the pits of hell.

Well, huffing and puffing demons, anyway. Mangled Nose was cradling his injured arm, and Parson's mouth was bleeding.

But they were mobile and furious. Like the boy who'd kicked the hornet's nest, Braden was now about to get thoroughly stung.

"Think yer so clever, don't ye?" growled Parson, raising his club. "We'll see how smart ye are now."

Braden put his hands up, as if in apology. With a little luck, he might be able to deflect the club before it bashed in his skull.

"In all fairness, I did manage to get past you."

"Only because ye sliced me up good," Mangled Nose complained. "Ruined my arm, ye did. And I thought ye were a doctor."

"I am a doctor, and I'd be happy to stitch and bandage you up, free of charge and no questions asked."

The man frowned. "Ye would?"

"Fecking hell, but yer an idiot," Parson snapped.

"That's nae way to speak to yer best friend," his companion sulkily replied.

"It certainly isn't," Braden said. If he could just keep them talking. "In fact, I think—"

"No one cares what ye think," bellowed Parson, brandishing his club. "I'm gonna shut that gob of yours once and for all."

He moved in for the kill. Braden curled up his fists, and—

Boom.

Plaster exploded from the wall behind Parson, showering chips and dust down on his head. He staggered sideways, crashing into his friend.

Mangled Nose howled. "Dougal, that's my bad arm!"

"Who gives a shite about that? Who the hell is shootin' at us?"

Braden peered toward the end of the alley. "I believe they did."

Two figures garbed in black advanced silently toward them. One was a tall, broad-shouldered man swathed in a greatcoat. He was carrying a pistol, so had obviously fired the shot. It had been an excellent one, too, stopping Parson dead in his tracks by barely missing him.

But the other figure? Braden shook his head, as if to clear his vision. That person was slender and not very tall.

"Dougal, that be a girl," Mangled Nose said.

No, a young woman, Braden guessed.

Dressed in a black riding habit, her hair tucked under a brimmed cap, she carried a walking stick and matched her companion's steps with easy, confident strides. The mystery man and woman both wore dark scarves wrapped around their lower faces, effectively disguising their features.

"What the hell?" Parson growled, facing the pair.

Braden snapped out of his astonishment. "Tough luck, old man. Good Samaritans have come to my rescue."

Parson threw him an ugly sneer. "Some doxy and a bloke who just shot his bolt? I'm ready to piss myself with fear."

He began to stalk toward the pair. As the silent man reached into his pocket, the woman darted forward, whipping up her walking stick.

Except the stick was actually a long, lethal-looking blade. When she deftly slashed it across Parson's cheek, he roared with pain and reared back, clapping a hand to his face.

"Oy," yelled Mangled Nose, charging forward, machete held high.

Another shot boomed out, fired from a second pistol the man in black had pulled from his coat. Shards flew up from the cobblestones, directly in front of Mangled Nose. With a shocked cry, he turned on his heel and staggered back up the alley. Quickly, he disappeared into the night.

Parson was made of sterner stuff. He held his ground, holding his bloody cheek and glaring at the woman, who slid over to stand beside Braden. Her companion joined them, a silent, threatening guardian.

"I should kill the whole lot of ye," Parson snarled.

Braden cocked his head. "I just heard the night watchman blow his whistle. He probably heard the shots and is calling for a constable. You'd be wise to follow your friend, Parson."

A string of truly vile oaths ensued as the bastard shot a final glare at Braden. Then the man took to his heels, following his partner in crime.

For a moment, Braden and the others stood frozen in a silent tableau, listening to Parson's footsteps fade away. Then Braden reached to doff his hat to his rescuers before realizing he'd lost the bloody thing in the bloody alley.

He smiled instead. "Thank you. I'm hoping you didn't save me just so *you* could rob me."

The big man simply shook his head, while the woman huffed an impatient breath from behind her black silk scarf.

"Then you have my sincere gratitude for your excellent timing," Braden said. "I doubt my skull would have survived the encounter with Parson's club."

The man shook his head again before gesturing toward the lights of Cowgate. He and the woman then strode off in that direction, leaving Braden to both mentally and physically catch up.

"Can I know your names, so I can properly thank you?" he asked, coming up behind them.

The woman didn't even glance back.

Braden almost laughed in disbelief. This was turning into the most bizarre night of his life. And given his family's history, that was a very high hill to climb.

As he followed close behind them, a flicker of movement caught his attention. The woman's gloved hand moved in gestures that looked practiced and precise. Braden's amazement grew as her companion responded with a few sharp motions of his right hand.

They were communicating with some sort of sign language.

"So, I take it you are not going to talk to me," he commented.

The pair continued to ignore him as they gained the entrance of the alley. The woman reached out and grabbed something. She slid her blade into the slender wooden sheath that she had leaned against a wall. Instantly, her lethal weapon was transformed into a genteel walking stick.

Braden felt as if he'd fallen into a dream or some sort of

upside-down fairy tale, one where the mysterious princess did the rescuing.

They led him out into Cowgate, and Braden had to blink against the flare of gas lanterns lining the street.

His silent escorts stopped and turned, calmly perusing him from behind their extremely effective disguises.

Now that he could finally get a good look at her, Braden saw that the lass had a trim, neat figure, dressed in a close-fitting wool jacket over a matching skirt. Her walking stick appeared to be of polished ebony with a carved brass handle. As for the man, who towered over her by a good foot, Braden had the impression that he might be a servant. He stood a few inches behind the woman, patiently waiting, as if taking his cues from her.

Fascinating.

If not a fairy tale, then Braden felt he might have stumbled into a corking-good adventure. Unlike his brothers, he never fell into corking-good adventures.

"If you won't tell me your name," he said, "then allow me to—"

A shrill whistle cut him off. They all glanced up Cowgate to see a sturdy watchman, lantern and long staff in hand, trundling toward them in the distance.

The woman glanced at her companion. He twirled a finger by his head and then pointed back to the alley. She nodded, and they turned in that direction.

Braden made a grab for her. "Wait, you can't go back in there."

As she gracefully eluded him, the man stepped in front of Braden, his stance all but yelling, *back off.*

He quickly put up his hands. "I just want you to be safe."

The woman huffed out a ghost of a chuckle. Then she tapped the brim of her cap, saluting him before disappearing into the night, with the tall man at her heels.

Braden was still peering down the alley, his brain spinning

with astonishment and questions, when the watchman finally arrived.

"Is that yerself, Dr. Kendrick?" the fellow asked in a worried tone. "Did I hear shots? Are ye all right?"

"You did, and I am. A pair of thugs tried to bash my head in. Fortunately, a warrior princess and her trusty companion came to my rescue."

The watchman snorted. "Now yer pulling my leg, sir. But who were them two that were just with ye? And where did they go off to?"

Braden shook his head. "On both counts, I'm afraid I have no bloody idea."

CHAPTER 2

Stifling a yawn, Braden descended the center staircase to the entrance hall of the house. Tangling with murderous thugs was bound to stimulate one's system and prevent sleep. So did questions about his mysterious rescuers—especially a woman who seemed perfectly comfortable wielding swords.

And that sign language? Pondering that had certainly kept him awake. Braden had seen something similar before, and he'd be following that up later this morning.

Their butler emerged from the back hall to greet him. "Good morning, sir. Mr. Kendrick and Joseph are having breakfast in the dining room, if you care to join them."

"Thank you, Will. I mean, Macklin. Now that you're a proper butler, I'll have to observe the appropriate protocols."

Will flashed him a wry smile. "It seems just as odd to me as it does to you, Dr. Kendrick. I hope I don't disappoint."

"You won't. You've been helping to keep us in line for years. When I was racketing about this place on my own, I tended to let things slide. I'm sure you and Mrs. Kendrick were properly horrified at the state of affairs."

Will Macklin had been with the family for as long as Braden could remember, originally hailing from the village attached to the Kendrick ancestral estate, Castle Kinglas. Eventually working his way up to under-butler at Kendrick

House in Glasgow, he'd recently been promoted to butler at the family establishment in Edinburgh.

Braden had taken up permanent residence in Edinburgh several years ago as a student. Subsequently, he'd accepted a position at the Royal Infirmary and the medical college. He'd have been satisfied with a small set of rented rooms near work, but the rest of the family had been appalled by that notion. Nick, Braden's oldest brother, was Laird of Arnprior, and had insisted on purchasing an elegant townhouse in New Town as a home for Braden and a port of call for various visiting Kendricks.

Major changes had recently come to the house on Heriot Row. Logan, the second oldest Kendrick and owner of a booming shipping company, had decided to move his family from Glasgow to Edinburgh. Thanks to the recent completion of the Forth and Clyde Canal system, Logan's Glasgow offices now had steady access to the nearby port of Leith. So, along with his wife and two children, Logan had decided to settle into Heriot Row for as long as needed to establish another thriving branch of Kendrick Shipping and Trade.

Logan, who was fourteen years older, had been away for much of Braden's youth, building up his trading company in Canada. Since his return to Scotland had coincided with Braden's permanent move to Edinburgh, their paths had only occasionally crossed.

While Braden might sometimes regret the loss of his peace and quiet, it was a good and necessary opportunity to spend time with Logan, Donella, and the two bairns. As much as he might be inclined to forget it at times, he was still a member of Clan Kendrick. That meant family came first, even if that family could sometimes be downright nosy and interfering.

"The house was in prime condition, sir," Will politely protested. "It needed nothing more than a good airing out."

It had needed more than that, since Braden had closed most of the place up, making do with one maid and a cook.

"Hmm, I'm quite sure I heard my sister-in-law shriek with horror at the state of the attics."

Will struggled to repress a smile. "Mrs. Kendrick never shrieks, no matter the provocation."

"I'll try to keep provocations to a minimum, regardless. Speaking of which, no one heard me come in last night?"

"I don't believe so, sir."

"Let's keep it that way. And if any of the servants should ask about the battered state of my clothes, just say I slipped and had a fall in the muck."

Thoroughly used to the wide variety of Kendrick antics, Will nodded. "Of course, sir. And I'll see to your coffee and breakfast immediately."

"Just coffee, please. I'll grab a roll to take along with me."

As he turned to head to the dining room, Braden didn't miss the butler's sigh. Everyone from Logan on down to the kitchen maid thought him underfed. At home, someone was always trying to shove cakes, scones, and assorted delicacies down his throat. It was nonsense, since he was perfectly fit. But he was used to being compared to his older brothers, who were exceptionally brawny men who looked more like Highland warriors than men of the city.

He quietly stepped into the elegant dining room, its formal nature softened by the view out the bay windows to the city gardens. Although it was a bit grand for Braden's taste, Donella insisted they eat their meals together there as a family, on a regular schedule. When Braden had objected that his work defied scheduling, his sister-in-law countered that he needed a more orderly lifestyle, more rest and food, and more leisure time with family. Any attempt he had made to explain the average physician's day had been firmly refuted, which was typical Kendrick behavior. Wayward family members were to be alternately cajoled and bullied into line. All in their best interests, of course.

But Kendricks also excelled at ignoring each other when

it suited. Over the years, Braden had become a master of that family attribute.

Seated at the head of the table, Logan glanced up from his copy of the *Caledonian Mercury*. "Glad to see you slept in this morning, lad. I'm sure you needed it. What time did you get in last night, anyway?"

"Oh, sometime after midnight," Braden replied as he perused the generous breakfast laid out on the mahogany sideboard.

"It was just after two o'clock, Uncle Braden," said Joseph, seated to the right of Logan.

Braden mentally sighed. Logan's son was thirteen. But he was exceptionally bright and incredibly observant, sometimes inconveniently so.

Logan frowned. "Son, were you reading late again? Staying up half the night isn't good for you. Besides, you read so much during the day."

"Yes, but that's for my studies, Papa. And I'm reading *Robinson Crusoe* right now. It's a bang-up adventure, you know."

"Yes, I know, but—"

"And you gave it to me, remember? It was your favorite book when you were my age. You said I should read it."

"Ouch. Hoisted on your own petard," Braden said as he took a seat on the other side of the table.

"Lad runs rings around me," Logan ruefully replied.

Joseph gifted his father with a beatific smile. "Mamma says it's because I'm so smart."

"Smartest one in the family," Braden added.

"No, that would be you, Uncle Braden. Mamma says that, too."

"Och, not true. You're the smartest Kendrick of all."

Joseph was greatly advanced in his studies, and when not studying, the lad was usually found with his nose deep in a book. Braden had recently started tutoring him in chemistry, at the boy's request. Given how ably his nephew picked up complex formulas, Braden suspected he would grow up to be a scientist, or even a physician.

Logan adopted a comical expression. "Hang on, what about me? I do run a rather large and successful business. Can't be a dummy and do something like that, you know."

Joseph patted his father's hand. "Of course not, Papa. But everyone knows that Uncle Braden is the smartest of the brothers. Uncle Nick and Grandda always say so."

"Splendid. Well, I hope I'm good for at least something around here," Logan said with mock complaint.

Joseph went back to slathering butter on his scone. "You're good at bashing heads. Uncle Nick says you're the best when it comes to that."

Given that Logan was a veritable giant whose fighting skills had been honed in the wilds of Canada, that statement wasn't an exaggeration.

Logan snorted. "Thank you, son. I'm also very good at sticking to the point, which is that you stay up half the night reading."

"I wasn't just reading last night, Papa. I was waiting for Uncle Braden to get home. He's usually not so late, so I was worried."

Smart as a whip *and* sensitive, Joseph tended to worry too much about the safety of his family. It stemmed from long separations from his father when he was just a tyke.

"You know I sometimes have to make emergency calls late at night," Braden gently said. "There is never any need to worry."

"I'd like to think that's the case," Logan said. "But where were you last night? Not Old Town again, I hope."

Braden repressed a groan. "I was perfectly fine, in any event."

"But you weren't," Joseph said with fatal candor. "I think you might have been robbed. You were very dirty, and you had a big rip in your coat. I saw it when you tried to sneak down the hall to your bedroom."

Good God. The lad would make an excellent spy.

Logan threw his son a startled glance. Then his gaze transferred to Braden, his eyes narrowing to slits as cold as the North Sea.

"Care to explain?" he asked in a mild voice.

Braden wasn't fooled. If he didn't think fast, a volcanic eruption was imminent.

Fortunately, the door opened and Will came into the room, followed by a footman carrying a coffee service.

Logan transferred his ire to the butler. "Macklin, why the hell didn't you tell me that Braden was robbed last night?"

"I wasn't robbed," Braden interjected.

Joseph frowned. "But you were in a . . . a *fracas*. I heard you say that to Macklin last night, when you came in."

Logan slammed down his coffee cup, slopping the brew onto the starched tablecloth. "And why the hell am I only hearing about this now?" He stared daggers at Braden, then at Macklin.

"It was nothing, really," Braden said. "Very minor."

His brother pointed a finger at him. "Now, look here, Braden. You may be—"

"I said it was nothing," Braden firmly interrupted.

Logan swept an irate gaze around the room. Since that gaze had been known to cause grown men to whimper like babies, it wasn't surprising that the footman, new to the household, almost dropped the coffee service. Will deftly snatched it and placed it on the sideboard.

"Can I pour you a cup of coffee, Dr. Kendrick?" he asked, unperturbed by his employer's glare.

Braden flashed him a grateful smile. "Yes, please."

"Macklin, this is not the end of the conversation," Logan said. "When someone in my household gets attacked, I want to know about it."

"Of course, sir. Can I freshen up your coffee?"

Looking massively annoyed, Logan continued to scowl at their butler before holding out his cup. "Deranged, the lot of you."

"Do stop blustering, dearest," Donella said as she entered the room. "It's much too early in the day to be terrifying your family, much less the staff."

"I'm not terrifying anyone," Logan grumbled. "Unfortunately."

Braden grinned at his brother. "Losing your touch?"

Donella patted her husband's shoulder. "Of course he's not losing his touch. Why, poor Ryan looks like he's seen a ghost."

Their new footman now looked mostly bewildered. Braden couldn't blame the poor fellow.

"I apologize, Mrs. Kendrick," Will said. "I'm still in the process of training the new staff."

"I'm afraid no amount of training can fully prepare anyone for our rather demented family," Braden commented.

Donella took the empty seat on the other side of her husband. "That's certainly true. I'm still getting used to them, even after several years."

"Says the woman who was kicked out of a convent, and then followed that up by triggering a kidnapping and a clan feud," Logan dryly said.

"Thankfully, you rescued me by throwing several men off a bridge into the River Tay," Donella replied as she reached for the teapot.

"Only two men, love," Logan corrected.

"True. You shot the rest of them."

Ryan, who'd been clearing empty plates from the sideboard, knocked over a tray of scones.

"You may return to the kitchen," Will told him with heavy disapproval. "Immediately."

The poor footman almost tripped in his haste to get out of the room.

"It'll be a miracle if the fellow doesn't give his notice forthwith," Braden commented.

Donella sighed. "And I was so hoping that Ryan would work out. Really, Logan, you simply must stop growling at everyone."

"How is this my fault?" her husband protested. "Besides, I only growl at family members who get themselves into dangerous situations and then try to hide it from me."

"Possibly because you kick up such a fuss?" Braden said before taking a gulp of coffee.

"Papa does get fashed when any of us gets attacked," Joseph said.

"No more getting attacked," barked Logan. "I forbid it."

Braden smiled at Joseph. "I was perfectly fine, lad. I promise."

Thanks to a mysterious young woman and her equally mysterious companion. That detail, however, was not something his family needed to know.

"But Papa can help protect you," Joseph earnestly replied. "It's his job."

"Exactly right, my boy," his father said with an approving nod.

"I cannot disagree," Donella said. "I saw your coat, Braden. The rip is quite beyond repair."

"Well, that's a bother," Braden replied.

At that observation, Logan looked ready to explode.

Donella glanced at her husband's face. "Macklin, perhaps you might bring us some fresh tea," she said to the butler.

When Will tactfully retreated, Braden looked at the clock on the mantel. "Good Lord, the time. As delightful as this discussion has been, I'm off. Already late for work."

Logan jabbed a finger at him. "Don't even think about it.

You were attacked, Braden. And how was your coat ruined? Perhaps by a knife?"

"Och, don't be silly," Braden said.

Donella wrinkled her nose. "Truly, Braden, we're not trying to be busybodies. We just worry about you."

Braden eyed the faces studying him with obvious concern. They were all so different—his brawny older brother, who had the strength and courage of a giant, his lovely sister-in-law, whose kind heart had rescued Logan from a lonely life, and his nephew, whose gentle nature was complemented by a maturity beyond his years.

What united them was their steadfast devotion to each other and to every member of the family. Behind all the bluster and nonsense was love—and worry. Kendricks were champion worriers. Given all the tragedies they'd suffered over the years, it was hardly surprising.

Now that the cat was well out of the bag, trying to dismiss their concerns would only fash them more.

"It was a bit of a sticky wicket," he admitted. "But it wouldn't have been a problem if I hadn't slipped and fallen arse over teakettle."

"It happens to the best of us, lad," Logan said in a sympathetic tone. "That's why it's best to be prepared for every contingency."

"What *did* happen, dearest?" Donella gently prompted.

After a quick glance at the clock, because he really *was* going to be late for his meeting, Braden gave a highly expurgated version of events.

Logan nodded his approval. "Throwing your bag in the bastard's face was quick thinking, lad."

Donella tapped her husband's arm. "Language, dear."

As if on cue, father and son rolled their eyes in identical fashion.

Braden repressed a smile. "I would have been well away from the bast . . . er, idiots, if I'd not slipped in some disgusting muck. Fortunately, my would-be attackers spent most of their time issuing empty threats instead of getting down to the business of robbing me."

Joseph frowned. "Then how did they manage to wreck your coat?"

"Er, that happened when I slipped and fell. I hit the cobblestones quite hard."

"Now this is starting to sound like a fish tale," Logan said with disapproval. "Pursued by two armed villains, you go down in the muck, and yet somehow you return home basically unharmed and unrobbed. Please explain how you managed that feat."

"We were just off Cowgate at that point, so I raised bloody hell calling for the watch. There's a watch booth right near there, you know. As soon as the watchman heard me, he blew his whistle and came running."

Logan crossed his arms over his chest. "I have never seen a watchman come running in my life."

"Well, this one responded promptly. Clearly, the pair that attacked me last night were short on courage, since they took to their heels when they heard the whistle."

His brother narrowed his eyes, obviously still suspicious.

Donella poured her husband another cup of coffee. "Thank goodness for the watch, then. But perhaps you could be a bit more careful, Braden. Try to avoid some of the more dangerous parts of Old Town."

"I'd be happy to comply, if only my patients wouldn't insist on living there."

She wrinkled her nose. "I'm sorry. I didn't mean to sound callous. We are so fortunate to be up here in New Town, while so many live in those dreadful tenements."

Logan leaned over and gave her a kiss. "Good thing you're doing a bang-up job of giving away half our fortune to charitable causes, love."

"We can afford it," she pertly replied.

"Aye, we can." Logan returned his attention to Braden. "I'm afraid I'm going to insist that you carry a pistol from now on, old man. I know you're not fond of them, but I'm even less fond of the idea of you getting carved up like a joint of beef."

Braden snorted. "A distinctly unappetizing thought."

"Then we're agreed. You will start carrying a pistol with you at all times."

"I will at night, but I hardly think pistols are appropriate for the Royal Infirmary or the classroom."

His brother leaned forward. "You'll carry one at *all* times, or I'll start going with you on these night calls."

Braden snorted. "That is certainly not happening."

"And you work hard enough, darling, without taking on bodyguard duty," Donella said. "If Braden is properly armed and takes precautions, he'll be fine."

"This isn't new for me, you know," Braden added. "I've been dealing with patients in Old Town for several years."

Logan tapped a finger against his chin. "That's actually an excellent idea, Donella. The best solution might be to hire Braden a bodyguard."

"Good God, Logan," Braden said, exasperated. "This is literally the first time anyone has tried to rob me. And that's because almost everyone knows who I am, and that I'm there to help them."

His brother shook his head. "A bodyguard is the best solution. I'll speak to Macklin about it. Maybe one of the new footmen."

"Perhaps Ryan?" Braden sardonically asked.

"I can go with you," Joseph chimed in. "As long as it's not *too* late. Papa taught me how to shoot, and I am very good at noticing things. Plus, I think I want to become a doctor, so I can see how you work."

Braden smiled at him. "Well, thank you, lad, but I think your papa might have ideas about that."

Logan snorted.

"Perhaps next year, Joseph," Donella tactfully said. "You're still a bit young to be making house calls, especially at night."

"Oh, rats," the boy said, sighing. "You always say I'm too young to do the fun things."

"Let's be clear. My son is not going anywhere near the stews, not this year or next year, either," Logan sternly added.

Joseph eyed his father with disapproval. "I'm not a little boy anymore, Papa. I'm getting very tall."

"You are rather shooting up like a weed," Donella said with a smile.

Braden stood. "Look, I really must—"

"Sit down," Logan rapped out. "We have not finished this discussion."

"Sorry, I have to go. I'm already miles late for my meeting with Blackmore."

His brother adopted his most intimidating glower. "Braden Kendrick—"

"We'll pick it up later, old man." He strode for the door, and then turned to face his brother. "I promise."

"That is an entirely empty promise, because you always make sure to evade the blasted subject."

"How clever of him," Donella said with a twinkle.

"I thought you were on my side," Logan tartly said to his wife.

Donella simply widened her eyes at him.

"You do tend to yell when you're fashed, Papa," Joseph said. "No wonder Uncle Braden avoids you."

"I forbid anyone avoiding me from now on."

His son snickered.

"No one will avoid you, my love," Donella said in a soothing tone. "Let me get you one of these orange scones. They're so delicious, aren't they, Joseph?"

"Papa should definitely have one, and probably some plum

cake, too," Joseph said. "Plum cake always makes him feel better."

"I feel perfectly fine," Logan protested as his wife starting piling food on his plate.

Once again, Braden's big, tough brother had been rolled up. He found it all rather hilarious, but it simply confirmed for him how complicated families—and especially wives—could be.

Braden had been rolled up by a woman once before, one he had truly loved. And how had that ended?

In a trip to hell.

It was an experience he had vowed never to repeat again.

CHAPTER 3

Braden took a hackney to the university, telling the driver to crack on. His colleague, Dr. John Blackmore, was giving a lecture on the latest developments in managing difficult pregnancies, and now he'd be lucky if he caught the tail end of it—thanks to Logan reading him the riot act.

He paid the driver and hurried upstairs to the east side of the university, a three-story building with massive columns framing the doors. Although most of his day was usually spent at the Royal Infirmary, Braden kept a small office at the college for study and meeting with his students. He also assisted John, a senior professor with specialties in midwifery and infectious diseases. John had taken Braden under his wing, and in those four years, he'd taught Braden as much as almost all his professors combined.

He'd become a damn good friend, too, and probably understood Braden better than his own family did.

He sidestepped a rush of black-gowned students coming out of the lecture hall, enthusiastically discussing the lecture they'd just heard. Then he made his way down the narrow center aisle, past rows of writing tables and chairs, to meet John.

"There you are," his mentor said as he packed away his

instruments. "I'm sorry you missed the lecture. We had quite a lively discussion afterwards."

"My sincere regrets, but I had my own lecture and discussion at Heriot Row. And there are no short discussions in my family."

John's incisive gaze flickered over him. "About another late night in Old Town, I suppose, and your brother didn't approve. You're looking rather worn around the edges, Braden. Was it a difficult case?"

"Actually, no. It's what happened afterwards that was tricky."

"Ah, a mystery, then. You can tell me all about it as we walk to my office. You look like you could use a strong cup of tea—or coffee."

"I wouldn't say no to either."

They headed down the long corridor toward the professors' rooms, Braden keeping pace with the older man's long stride. Although well into his forties, John had as much strength and energy as a man half his age. Unlike many other successful physicians, John refused to *go soft*, as he dismissively called it.

John's devotion to his patients and his work was superseded only by his devotion to his wife and daughter. As a mentor, Braden couldn't have picked a better man. As a role model—one who easily seemed to manage both his personal and professional lives—he found John a bit daunting.

Now that he thought of it, he was rather like Braden's older brothers, who were equally successful in work and in love. It was a formula he'd never been able to crack.

"What's wrong?" John quietly asked.

Braden dredged up a smile. "Nothing. Just a bit tired."

"You know, it won't do your patients any good if you fall ill from lack of rest."

"Nonsense. I have the constitution of a sewer rat."

His friend snorted. "I'm not sure that's a good thing."

"It is for a doctor who works in Old Town."

John put out a hand to stop a passing college porter and ordered coffee. Then he unlocked his office door and waved Braden in.

As a dean and supervising physician at the Infirmary, John had one of the largest offices in the college. Sturdy book-shelves, packed with hundreds of volumes as well as glass jars containing medical specimens and botanical compounds, lined two of the walls right up to the wood-paneled ceiling. A polished oak table, piled high with books, stood in front of a tiled fireplace, and a large writing desk, cubbyholes stuffed with papers, was positioned in front of the window for maximum light.

John quickly stirred up the banked fire while Braden sank into the leather club chair in front of the desk. Foggy tendrils weaved through his brain. He straightened his spine, refusing to give into the urge to let his eyelids drift shut.

"Coffee should be up in a few minutes," John said as he settled behind his desk. "That'll put some life into you. I'm afraid you look rather like hell."

"You'd look like hell, too, if you were set upon by one idiot with a machete and another idiot with a club."

His friend jerked upright. "Good Lord. Did they actually get a hand on you?" He leaned forward over his desk. "Do I need to examine you for injuries?"

"Och, you're as bad as my family. I escaped, and I'm fine."

"So, it was a robbery attempt?"

Braden shook his head. "Only in part. Do you remember Naomi Parson? It was a near thing with her, as I'm sure you recall."

"Yes, a miscarriage. It was a very distressing situation. Her husband blamed you for encouraging Naomi to go to the—"

Understanding dawned, and John's gray gaze turned

stormy. "Bloody hell. Don't tell me the villain tracked you down for revenge?"

"Yes, and he brought a jolly friend with a machete along with him."

"Were you armed?"

"Only with a knife."

John's frown turned disapproving. "Braden, I think it's time you carried a pistol with you in Old Town, especially at night."

"Yes. That oversight will be corrected forthwith, I promise."

"See that it is. So, how did you manage to escape?"

"I whacked Parson in the face with my medical kit and then ran like hell."

John choked out a surprised laugh. "Thank God for quick thinking."

Braden tapped his skull. "Unlike my brothers, I prefer to use brains over brawn."

"I find that's usually best."

After knocking on the door, the porter entered with a coffee service and a plate of scones.

"You may leave it on my desk," John said. "I'll pour."

"Aye, sir."

"Just coffee, thanks," Braden said, after the porter left. "Sugar and cream will do nicely."

"You should eat," John said. "You're beginning to look like one of the skeletons in the anatomy classroom."

"Thank you for that charming comparison. And while I might not be a brick wall like my brothers, I'm lean and I'm quick. Which does come in handy when running away from armed morons."

"That's one advantage, I suppose." John frowned. "You're fortunate to have been able to get away from them."

"Yes, but there's more to the story," Braden replied after a gulp of the hot brew. "That's what I wanted to speak with you about."

John let out a sigh. "So there is trouble. I do believe you're as bad as your brothers, after all."

"That is literally impossible, at least according to any normal law of nature."

John twirled an impatient hand. "What happened?"

"I only escaped because I was rescued by a young lady."

"One of the Old Town girls?" John shot him a quizzical look. "I know a number of them carry knives, but against two armed men?"

His friend often provided free medical services to the prostitutes who plied their trade in Old Town. He and his wife, Bathsheba, made a point of helping vulnerable women who were forced to support themselves on the streets.

"No, this woman had an armed manservant with her, and she also carried a very lethal blade concealed in a walking stick." He shook his head at the memory of her impressive skills. "And let me say that she knew how to use it."

"Good God."

"That's not even the oddest part. Neither she nor her companion uttered a single word at any time. They simply rousted the villains and quickly escorted me back to safety."

John had been about to take a sip from his cup, but put it down. "They said nothing at all?"

"Not a word. They did, however, communicate using hand gestures."

"You mean like sign language?"

"That's what I wanted to ask you about."

John's sister-in-law, Rachel Compton, was an accomplished young woman of twenty-four. She was also profoundly deaf. Rachel was part of the reason John had accepted the position in Edinburgh in the first place. One of the first schools for those who were deaf had been founded in the city, run by excellent teachers who'd helped develop a standardized language of signing. Rachel had proved such a capable student that she'd recently taken up a position as a teacher at a new school in London.

"Describe their signs," John tersely said.

Braden mentally frowned at his friend's odd tone, but then he gave a quick run through of events, and as much detail as he could remember about the mystery couple's communication.

"So," he said when he'd finished his description, "does that sound like the system taught at the school in Edinburgh?"

John spread his hands flat on his desk and stared at them for several long moments. "Possibly. What happened after your attackers fled?"

"My rescuers escorted me out to Cowgate. When the night watchman approached, they promptly retreated." Braden held up a finger. "Back the way we came, I might add."

John's eyebrows shot up. "Back into the slums?"

"Yes."

"Good God," his friend muttered.

"Yes." Braden waited for several seconds while John stared down at his hands. "So, what do you think?"

John's gaze flickered up. "About what?"

"Was it sign language or not?"

"Obviously, since they were using it to communicate. When Braden raised his eyebrows, John grimaced. "Sorry, but you have to admit that it's a bizarre story."

"That's putting it mildly, especially since they were clearly disguised and ready for trouble."

"Or looking for it," John said in a thoughtful tone.

Braden snorted. "And they found it."

Again, John seemed lost in thought—and not happy ones, from the looks of it. Then he seemed to shrug it off, and he reached for the coffeepot.

"I can't say if it was a system of signing that they invented themselves, which is entirely possible, or if it's a standardized form. I know that's not very helpful, but there it is."

As Braden studied his friend's austere expression, he was unable to shake the feeling that his friend was . . . lying? But that didn't track. That man was all but incapable of lying, and was sometimes blunt to the point of rudeness, if necessary.

Something was definitely off.

John calmly sipped his coffee, as if they'd just been discussing a mildly interesting medical case and not a bizarre and dangerous encounter in the slums.

"I suppose it will have to remain a mystery, then," Braden finally said.

"Apparently. By the way, I've got an interesting proposal for you."

The abrupt transition confirmed that something indeed wasn't right. But if John didn't wish to talk about it, applying pressure would be fruitless.

For the moment, Braden decided to let it go. "A proposal about what?"

"You know of my work with the Penwith Philanthropic Foundation."

"I do. I've always wondered how you fit it in on top of all your other work."

"About the same way you fit in your free clinic on top of your other duties," John noted.

"I don't run two university departments, nor do I have your schedule of duties at the Infirmary. Not to mention a wife and a daughter."

John smiled. "Bathsheba and Mary make everything better, but your point is valid. I do need help."

"Do you need me to squeeze some blunt out of Logan for you?"

"No, although I will keep that in mind during our next round of fundraising."

"What, then?"

"As you know, the foundation runs an orphanage for boys and a charity school for girls."

Braden nodded. "It was founded by the Penwith family some years ago, was it not?"

"Correct, although only one member of the family is currently involved—Lady Samantha Penwith."

Braden rifled his mental files. "She's a widow, isn't she?"

"Yes, she's Roger Penwith's widow. He set up the foundation and ran it until his unfortunate demise. Have you ever met Lady Samantha?"

"You know I'm not one for socializing."

Braden was all but allergic to the Edinburgh social scene. Parties bored the hell out of him, unless there was another doctor or scientist lurking behind the potted plants. That's where he was generally to be found whenever he allowed a random family member to drag him to a party.

"Neither is Lady Samantha," John said. "She devotes most of her attention to her charitable work. And to Roger's younger sister," he added, almost as an afterthought.

"She sounds like an admirable person." Braden still had no idea where this was headed.

"Braden, we wish you to join the board of the Penwith Philanthropic Foundation. You would be a great asset, I feel sure."

He tried not to grimace at the invitation. "Endless meetings, gruesome social events, hitting up dowagers for money. John, I have to say no, thank you. Again, if you need a contribution—"

"I'm perfectly capable of fundraising, as is Lady Samantha," John bluntly interrupted. "That's not what we want you for."

"So, why do you want me, then?"

"There have been disagreements amongst the board members. While Lady Samantha's vision for the foundation is outstanding, most of the others see her ideas as too progressive and rather alarming. It certainly doesn't help that she is a young woman. With a few exceptions, the other board members tend to dismiss her, even though she's a great deal smarter than they are."

"How old is she?"

"Twenty-six. Why?"

Braden put down his empty coffee cup. "She's young to be running a foundation. Most won't even tolerate a woman on the board, much less allow her to set the guiding vision."

"Which is exactly why she needs allies."

"Why not just get rid of the lot of them, and start over?"

"It's complicated, unfortunately."

Braden snorted. "You'd be far better off with Logan on your board. He'd terrify everyone into compliance."

John waved a dismissive hand. "I don't need another businessman. I need a physician and scientist, someone who will know exactly what we're trying to accomplish." He hesitated for a moment. "Braden, I believe it would be good for you to expand your horizons. Meet some new people, do a bit of socializing, attend a few gruesome parties. And did I mention that Lady Samantha is a very lovely and intelligent young lady?"

Braden rolled his eyes. "I don't have time for socializing or lovely young ladies. I've barely enough time to cover both my regular practice and my clinic."

"But that's just it. Working on this board could be an excellent way to garner support for your clinic. Possibly even fold it into the foundation at some point. Just think how many more patients you could treat with the support of the Penwith Foundation."

"You've been thinking this through, haven't you?" Braden wryly said. "Wait until I'm tired, not thinking very clearly . . . and then you pounce. Sorry, old fellow, but I'm not *that* out of my head."

John chuckled. "All right, I'll stop pestering for now. But

please promise that you'll consider it. Especially the part about helping your free clinic and your patients and how much good you could accomplish."

Braden shook his head. "You're bloody relentless, you are."

"Me? Never." John drained his coffee cup and stood. "I'm off to make my rounds. Care to join me? There's an interesting case I'd like you to see."

Braden rose. "I thought you'd never ask."

That was the world he was most comfortable in, that of science and medicine. It was a world where intellect and talent held sway, not emotions. And it was definitely where he could do the most good.

As for socializing and getting involved with lovely young ladies? It would be a frosty day in Hades before he made that mistake again.

CHAPTER 4

Samantha buttoned up the cuff of her sleeve as she hurried down the staircase. Bathsheba Blackmore was her closest friend, but she was not one to make an early morning visit. Something was surely wrong to bring her to Samantha's doorstep when the day had barely begun.

Mrs. Johnson, Samantha's housekeeper, awaited her in the hall.

"I put Mrs. Blackmore in the family parlour," she said. "I thought that would be a wee bit cozier on such a cold day."

Samantha smiled at her steadfast confidant, whose round figure, pink cheeks, and snowy-white hair gave her the appearance of a cheerful grandmother. Yet underneath that appearance was a quick mind and the fierce devotion of a tigress protecting her cubs. Mrs. Johnson had served the Penwith family for years and had been exceptionally dedicated to Samantha's husband. She'd stayed on after Roger's death, helping Samantha, as well as Roger's younger sister, Felicity, navigate their way through tragedy and challenge.

Like every other staff member in the small household, Mrs. Johnson was devoted to Samantha's mission. The woman would face down a firing squad before betraying her secrets.

"Thank you, Mrs. Johnson. Is the tea tray coming up?"

"In a twinkle."

"Is Felicity about?"

"She's with Mrs. Blackmore. The two of them be talking up a storm."

Samantha smiled at the description, since there was nothing but silence from behind the closed door.

"Felicity loves Mrs. Blackmore. She'll be excited to see her."

They had so few visitors, and whenever Samantha thought about Felicity's isolation, her heart grew heavy. Still, it was the only way to keep her sister-in-law safe. Trying to give the girl a normal social life would bring down her grandfather's stern hand with stunning swiftness.

Not that Samantha was one for parties or fetes on her best day. From the day she'd arrived in the city from her family's remote Highland estate, she'd been considered an awkward country bumpkin. For Roger's sake, she'd done her best to fit in. But she'd never truly caught the trick of getting on with Edinburgh's finest, not like the other women in their social circle seemed to do.

Thankfully, her husband had never cared about any of that. And his love had more than compensated for every snub and cutting remark Samantha had ever endured.

When he was ripped away from her, nothing was left behind but black loneliness.

"My lady?" Mrs. Johnson quietly asked. "Can I get ye something?"

Samantha opened the door to the parlour. "Tea will be fine, thank you."

Bathsheba sat with Felicity on the floral-print settee in front of the fireplace, where a crackling blaze poured forth heat and good cheer. The pair carried on their silent conversation, hands moving in quick, precise gestures as they occasionally mouthed words in response to each other.

Not for the first time, Samantha sent up a prayer of gratitude for John and Bathsheba Blackmore. Felicity was adept at reading lips and the household staff had all learned to sign, but communicating with others was a chore for the girl. Constantly reading lips was exhausting. Even worse, most people chose to ignore Felicity, assuming that because she was deaf, she must also be stupid or mentally defective. It didn't help that Lord Beath, her grandfather, felt much the same and did everything he could to prevent the girl from leading an active life.

But John and Bathsheba, both accomplished at communicating with those who were deaf, were true friends to Felicity and maintained a steadfast support. Samantha would be lost without them, too. After Roger's death, there were few in the city she could rely on for help and encouragement.

But even that steadfast friendship could only take her so far. Only Samantha could truly protect Felicity and find Roger's killers.

Bathsheba broke into a laugh and held up her hands.

"You must slow down," she said to Felicity, clearly enunciating. "I cannot keep up."

The girl rolled her eyes with all the drama of a sixteen-year-old.

Samantha joined them. "I see my sister is talking your ear off."

Bathsheba glanced at her, lifting her expressive eyebrows. "Ah, there you are, Samantha. Yes, we were having quite the chat, but I'm afraid Felicity was talking too fast for me."

"You must slow down," Samantha said as she signed to her sister-in-law. "You're too quick and smart for us."

Felicity flashed a grin as she tapped the edge of her right hand against her left palm.

True.

Samantha chuckled. "Cheeky, too."

She smoothed Felicity's glossy auburn curls. The girl was an echo of Roger, with her bright blue eyes and ruddy Scottish complexion. She was both a lovely and heartbreaking reminder of the cherished past.

"Sorry to keep you waiting," Samantha said as she settled into a needlepointed wingchair. "I was still dressing when you arrived."

"Did you oversleep?" Bathsheba asked. "You look a bit peaked, love, almost as if you were out very late. Up to no good, perhaps?"

Samantha mentally stumbled. Her friend's teasing smile was at odds with her sharply penetrating green gaze.

Felicity pointed at her and then brushed her palms together.

Samantha shook her head. "No, I did not go out last night."

When Felicity's gaze narrowed, Samantha forced herself not to react. She and Donny were always careful when they left the house at night, waiting until Felicity was asleep.

But had the girl been awake when they returned home two nights ago, earlier than their norm? Their usual pattern of search had been disrupted by the need to rescue Dr. Kendrick and then subsequently avoid the watch. Samantha had recognized the doctor almost immediately, of course, and had been tempted to break her silence and deliver the dratted man a lecture on the risks of wandering about the slums unarmed.

She was indeed tired, but her fatigue wasn't the result of their late-night searches of Old Town. It was worry that had kept her awake the last few nights, worry that their surprise encounter with Kendrick might put them at risk of discovery. The doctor was known to be an exceedingly intelligent man, and if he put—

"Here's tea, my lady," said Mrs. Johnson, coming in with the tray of tea and biscuits.

"Thank God," said Bathsheba. "I'm famished after such a lively discussion."

"What were you talking about?" Samantha asked.

Two fingers extended, Felicity wriggled her hand down her body.

Schoolwork.

"Are you having a problem with your studies?" Samantha asked, puzzled.

Felicity snorted, disdainful of the question.

"Apparently, you're not giving our girl enough to do," Bathsheba said. "She wants John to start teaching her anatomy, in addition to Latin."

Latin was Felicity's favorite subject. John had volunteered to teach her, partly as a necessary distraction from the tragedy of Roger's death. Samantha had initially objected, knowing how busy he was, but they'd reached a compromise. Sunday afternoons he would teach Felicity Latin, while Bathsheba and Samantha went for a drive or visited friends.

"We already take up so much of John's time," Samantha protested. "We couldn't possibly ask him to take on another subject. I'm sure you barely see him as it is."

"Not to worry. John always gives me the attention I deserve." Bathsheba winked. "And plenty of it, too."

Mrs. Johnson made a choking noise as she handed Bathsheba a cup of tea.

"Sorry," Bathsheba said, not looking sorry at all.

Samantha hesitated. "I'm not sure Lord Beath would approve of the subject," she said to Felicity.

Her sister-in-law, closely following her words, snapped her brows together in a fierce scowl. It was her usual response when her grandfather was mentioned. She couldn't stand the man, and Samantha didn't blame her one bit.

Bathsheba tapped Felicity on her arm, drawing her attention. "Let me speak to John. He will think of something."

Felicity visibly relaxed and gave her a nod.

"Good," Bathsheba said. "Now that we've got that sorted—"

She paused when Samantha waggled a hand.

"I still need to speak with you," Bathsheba continued in a firm tone.

Drat. So, there *was* a specific reason for this early morning call.

Samantha glanced at her housekeeper. "Mrs. Johnson, I understand Cook is making pies this morning. I think Felicity would enjoy working with her."

The older woman nodded. "Aye, my lady."

Samantha caught her sister's attention. "Can you help Cook with the pies?"

Felicity rolled her eyes again, but stood without further complaint. The girl enjoyed the precision and challenge of the baking process, as well as the delicious results.

After giving Bathsheba a quick hug, Felicity followed Mrs. Johnson to the door. Then she turned and signed to Samantha, both index fingers briefly touching her cheeks before she pulled her hands down to her chest and curled them into fists.

Watch out.

Samantha blinked, too startled to reply. By the time she collected herself, Felicity had closed the door.

Bathsheba cocked her head. "What did your sister just say to you?"

"Nothing worth repeating. At least in polite company." Samantha forced a chuckle. "Goodness, where she picks up such language is beyond me."

Bathsheba took a bite from a biscuit covered in thick, white icing. "Probably from your manservant," she said around a mouthful. "I like Donny. He's very colorful."

"Almost as colorful as you."

"May I point out that I have much better fashion sense than your manservant?"

Samantha let out a genuine laugh. "You're ridiculous."

"I know." Bathsheba put down her plate. "But it's good to

see you laugh. You seem out of sorts, lately. John and I have been worried about you."

"So worried that you had to show up on my doorstep first thing in the morning?"

Bathsheba opened her eyes wide. "Can I not pop in and make a casual call on my dearest friend?"

"Not at this hour of the morning, at least not from anyone claiming to be fashionable."

"Claiming to be fashionable? Darling, have you any idea how much this outfit cost?"

Samantha eyed Bathsheba's stylish green walking gown, with its large gigot sleeves and silk pelerine that covered her shoulders. While her friend was the most down-to-earth woman she'd ever met, she was also the most stylish woman in Edinburgh and the envy of many a young matron.

"More than I can afford, I suspect," she replied.

Bathsheba wrinkled her nose in apology. "Is Lord Beath still keeping you on a tight leash?"

"We're fine, really. Roger made sure I would be suffi-ciently provided for in the event—"

She had to pause to clear her throat before she could con-tinue. "But Roger could not have anticipated that his grand-father would refuse to provide for Felicity, at least not while she remains with me. As you know, Beath doesn't approve of me, or of my *coddling* of the girl, as he calls it."

Bathsheba made a disgusted noise. "I would like to slap that man. He's the most mean-spirited poop I've ever met."

"True, but if I raise any sort of ruckus, he'll drag Felicity off to his country estate and lock her up. The only reason he hasn't done so is that it's easier for him to forget about her while she's in Edinburgh."

Just saying the words brought a hot flush of anger to Samantha's face. In her mind, Beath was little better than a monster when it came to his granddaughter.

"What a monster," Bathsheba said, echoing her thoughts. "He's the one who should be locked away, not that dear girl."

"Fortunately, he prefers to remain on his estate, so he generally leaves us alone."

"As long as you don't raise a fuss or make demands."

"Exactly. Thankfully, Felicity no longer needs special tutors, and her health has been good."

When Felicity was still a little girl, Roger had moved her to Edinburgh, where she could receive training from the best teachers at the school for the deaf. Lord Beath had bellowed and blustered, but Roger had refused to back down. As Beath's heir, he'd had a fair degree of influence on the old man. Roger had always done the right thing for Felicity, with a quiet but firm determination.

Samantha had never met a man with more integrity and courage than her late husband.

"I'm simply being cautious," she added. "Any extravagance on my part would be bound to attract Beath's attention, and lead to consequences for Felicity."

"Hmm. Perhaps Lord Beath could have an unfortunate accident whilst riding about that disgustingly large estate of his. That would certainly solve more than a few of your problems." Bathsheba snapped her fingers. "I know. Donny could sneak into his lordship's stables and tamper with his saddle. God knows I'd do it if I had half the chance."

Samantha almost choked on her tea. "Bathsheba Blackmore, you are an exceedingly bad influence on me."

"Someone has to be. It's been two years, pet. Don't you think it's time to cast off your widow's weeds and have a bit of fun? You certainly deserve it."

Samantha winced, feeling oddly defensive. "I gave up my widow's weeds months ago, but you know I'm not much for socializing."

Bathsheba eyed Samantha's simple lavender gown, her silence offset by her sardonic expression.

"All right, it's half-mourning," admitted Samantha. "Look, I'm already courting trouble by retaining a seat on the foundation board. Playing the part of the grieving widow does garner me a degree of sympathy and acceptance."

"Except you're not playing the part," Bathsheba gently admonished. "I understand how difficult it is to move beyond such a deep loss, but it cannot be healthy for you to dwell on it. John agrees with me, I might add."

"I don't dwell on it."

That had to be the biggest, bounding lie she'd ever told.

"It's *your* foundation, Samantha. Do whatever you want with it, and the men be damned. And stop hiding away. If it wasn't for the foundation, I don't think you would ever leave this blasted house."

"But it's a very nice house, you must admit."

And she got out a great deal more than her friends ever suspected.

When Bathsheba cocked her head, the dyed green feathers on her high poke bonnet gently shimmered in the firelight. "Have you ever thought about moving back to the Highlands, to be with your family?"

Samantha shook her head. "After Papa died, my mother moved to Inverness to live with her sister. My cousin and his family now live on the estate. Besides, I don't think Beath would allow me to take Felicity away from his sphere of influence."

In any case, she still had business to attend to in Edinburgh. Samantha would never leave until she saw it completed.

"So, Beath doesn't want the poor girl, but you're not allowed to take her away, either."

"Sadly true. But enough about my boring troubles. Now, what's bothering you that you're rousting me out of bed at the crack of dawn?"

Bathsheba snorted. "I've always said you're the smartest woman I know."

"Thank you. Out with it, please."

When her friend looked suddenly hesitant—and Bathsheba was *never* hesitant—Samantha mentally braced herself. Whatever it was, it must be bad. Felicity had obviously sensed it, too.

"John heard a very strange tale yesterday," Bathsheba finally said. "He thought you might be able to shed some light on it."

Samantha forced a smile. "Go on."

"A friend of John's had an alarming encounter in Old Town the other night. While returning home from a late-night call, he was set upon by two ruffians."

Hell and damnation.

"Goodness, I do hope he wasn't injured."

"It was a near thing," Bathsheba replied.

Samantha adopted a concerned expression. "We both know how dangerous Old Town can be, even for a physician who is helping the locals."

When her friend's eyebrows ticked up, Samantha mentally cursed.

Stupid, stupid, stupid.

"Who said he was a doctor?" Bathsheba asked.

She managed a casual shrug. "Since he's a friend of John's, I simply assumed he was. And you did say he was making a late-night call. In any case, why else would a gentleman be in Old Town after dark? Unless he was . . ."

She trailed off, letting the unspoken assumption resonate.

Bathsheba scoffed. "Braden Kendrick is the last person to visit a brothel. Have you ever met him?"

"I don't believe so."

Samantha had seen him, though, at one of John's lectures on childhood illnesses last month. Her attention had been instantly captured by the tall, broad-shouldered man leaning against the wall next to the stage, with a casual stance that belied the intensity of his focus. She'd also noticed that he was *quite* handsome, with thick chestnut hair, strong features, and eyes the most riveting color of jade. That her gaze had often strayed back to him throughout the lecture had been more than a little annoying.

"You should meet Braden," Bathsheba said. "Since he and John are such good friends, I'm sure there will be an opportunity for an introduction." Her lips parted in a sly smile. "I think I should arrange a meeting as soon as possible. The two of you would get along splendidly."

Samantha tried to ignore the anxious twitch in her stomach. Meeting Braden Kendrick was not something she wanted to chance.

"Entirely unnecessary, I assure you," she replied. "And now, if we're quite finished with talking about Dr. Kendrick—"

"Don't you want to find out what happened to Braden after he was attacked?"

"Er, of course. It's just that since he lived to tell John the tale, I assume he escaped. Thank goodness."

"Ah, but it's how he escaped that's so interesting."

Bathsheba paused dramatically, obviously waiting for her to respond.

After an awkward silence, Samantha raised her hands. "Are you going to tell me, or leave me hanging?"

Bathsheba's gaze remained uncomfortably penetrating. "A man and a woman appeared out of thin air, apparently, and they rescued him."

"Well, that was certainly fortunate. I presume the man was armed, and was thus able to chase off the ruffians?"

"Yes, as was the woman—but not with a pistol."

"Ladies generally don't carry pistols, do they?" Samantha warily replied.

Bathsheba's perfect eyebrows went up in exaggerated surprise. "I didn't say she was a lady."

"It was a figure of speech," Samantha said, trying not to clench her teeth. "This is all very interesting, and of course

I'm happy that your friend was rescued, but what has this to do with me?"

"John thought you might be able to identify the couple."

Samantha did her best to look perplexed rather than panicked. "Really? I don't see how."

"Because the man and woman communicated using sign language," Bathsheba calmly replied. "And they were adept at it."

Samantha's wits rarely failed her, but this nightmare of a conversation was making her brain freeze like a Highland pond in the dead of winter.

"And Dr. Kendrick knows sign language, does he?" she managed.

Bathsheba leaned forward, her gaze all but pinning Samantha to her chair. "Will you please stop pretending that you don't know what I'm talking about? It was obviously you and Donny who rescued Braden. It was you bolting around the stews in disguise! Samantha, what in God's name are you doing?"

Her heartbeat accelerated, making her chest go tight. "Why in God's name would I do something so utterly foolhardy?"

"Something to do with Roger, I imagine. Which would be the *height* of insanity."

When Samantha flinched, Bathsheba put out a quick hand. "I didn't mean it like that, my dear. It's just that John and I are terribly worried about you. This coincidence is too strange and too close to home to ignore."

An alarming thought penetrated Samantha's frazzled brain. "Did you say something to Felicity?"

"Of course not. I simply asked her how you were feeling. But if you've been doing something as reckless as trying to hunt—"

Samantha chopped down a hand. "No. I do nothing but

take care of Felicity and work at the foundation. Good God, Bathsheba. You know my situation. Do you really think I would risk scandal by running around Old Town like a common footpad?"

Bathsheba's mouth twisted sideways for a moment. "I think you wish to avenge your husband's death."

"I certainly wish to see Roger's killers brought to justice, but I would never do anything to risk Felicity's situation."

Except you already do.

That was a horrifying thought that she needed to continue to ignore, at least for now. And she needed to get out of this perilous conversation.

Thankfully, the mantel clock chimed, providing her with an escape.

She rose. "You must excuse me, Bathsheba. I have a meeting at the orphanage, and I cannot be late."

Her friend exhaled a frustrated sigh as she stood. "I'll let you put me off for now, but only because I've made my point. But Samantha, whatever it is you're doing, please take care. Do not jeopardize your safety or your reputation. That warning comes not only from me, but from John."

"It is not necessary, I assure you." Samantha tried for a wry smile. "I'm not exactly an Amazon, or a heroine who faces down thugs. A year ago, I was barely out of my sickbed."

"You are stronger than you look," Bathsheba said as she collected her gloves and her reticule, "and you know it."

"Tell that to my aching head," Samantha muttered under her breath.

Bathsheba paused. "What?"

"Nothing. By the way, I do hope John didn't discuss these imaginings with Dr. Kendrick. How embarrassing that would be."

"My husband is not an idiot, Samantha."

"No, but he's a worrier, as are you."

Bathsheba wrapped her in a softly scented hug. "Just be careful, my dear friend. All right?"

"I'm always careful."

Except when you're not.

CHAPTER 5

Braden jogged up the front steps of Heriot Row, home in time for dinner for once. He'd been in surgery since lunchtime. Come to think of it, he'd not actually *had* lunch—so he was ready for an evening off.

He pulled out his key and let himself into the spacious entrance hall. Then he stopped dead because there was a stupendous pile of luggage stacked in the middle of the marble floor.

The junior footman, struggling with three carpetbags to the foot of the staircase, glanced over his shoulder. "Good evenin', sir. Sorry I canna collect yer hat and coat."

"So I see. Sam, who is—"

A high-pitched yap interrupted him. A gray mophead emerged from the back hall, trundling forward on stiff little legs.

Braden sighed. "When did he get here?"

Sam cracked a smile. "Yer grandfather and Mr. Kade arrived a half hour ago. We're still gettin' them settled."

Braden eyed the ancient terrier doing its best to gambol about his feet. "And the dogs, too, of course. How jolly."

"Just Daisy and old Teddy, here."

"Thank God for small mercies."

When the entire pack was in residence, mayhem and a variety of unfortunate accidents were usually—

Braden hastily scooped up the dog, since Teddy had been getting ready to lift his leg on his boots. He was back out the door in a flash.

"Sorry, Dr. Kendrick," Sam called after him.

He pelted down the front steps and over to a strip of grass before gently plopping Teddy down. Thankfully, the old fellow had managed to hold on, and was now panting happily as he did his business.

Will appeared in the doorway, his expression one of pained resignation. "I apologize, sir. Teddy managed to slip by me."

Braden smiled. "I am deeply shocked to hear that you could not control the most poorly trained dog in Scotland."

Angus MacDonald elbowed Will out of the way. "Ho, I'll not have ye insultin' the wee fella. He was just that happy to see ye, lad. And when Teddy gets excited . . . well, he forgets himself."

"A perfectly sensible explanation," Braden wryly replied.

If there was ever a man who resembled his dogs, it was Braden's elderly grandfather. Like them, Grandda usually appeared endearingly disreputable. His white hair was like an exploding puffball, and his thin frame was generally attired in an old kilt, a moth-eaten tam, and tatty vest. Logan had once said that Angus was the Highland version of an Old Testament patriarch, albeit one with a fondness for good Scottish whisky.

Tonight, though, Grandda looked mostly respectable, having already changed for dinner.

Angus pointed at his dog. "I think the laddie is done. Best bring him in before he catches a chill."

When Braden clicked his tongue to get Teddy moving, his grandfather waved a hand. "Ye'll have to pick him up. His wee back legs are botherin' him, so he dinna like stairs these days. I'll be askin' ye to take a look at the puir laddie."

Resigned to his fate, Braden scooped the dog up. Teddy, of course, had managed to find the one patch of damp dirt, now already transferred to Braden's coat, along with a generous slobber of drool.

As he lugged Teddy up the stairs, he made a mental note to slip the laundry maid an extra bob. The lass had yet to recover from the time he'd been dissecting a brain and had failed to notice that he'd transferred a portion of gray matter onto his sleeve.

"I'll take him, if you like, sir," Will offered.

Angus beamed. "Aye, ye'll want to be visitin' with Teddy. I have nae doubt ye've missed my lads and lassies."

To his credit, Will preserved a straight face. "Indeed I have, sir."

Braden handed the drooling pooch to their butler. "Did you forget to tell me about this impending invasion, Macklin?"

"Nae, it was a surprise," Angus proudly said. "Kade worried a bit about givin' old Will the jump, but I said the servants would be that glad to see us, too."

"It's a splendid treat for us, sir," Will said with diplomatic aplomb as the dog snuffled his neckcloth. "If you'll excuse me, I'd best take Teddy down to the kitchen."

Angus turned to Braden. "Now, give yer grandda a proper hug. Ye'd think ye weren't happy to see me."

Braden carefully pulled his grandfather into his arms, mindful of his aged, thin physique. "Och, I'm always happy to see you, Grandda."

Angus had seemed forever indomitable to Braden, but he was now in his eighties, and although robust for his years, he was starting to look a bit frail. Long trips could not be good for him.

Obviously reading his thoughts, Angus gave him a little shove. "I'm fine, lad. Strong as an ox, ye ken."

"You could use a little meat on your bones, though. We'll have to fatten you up while you're here."

"Fah, save yer doctorin' for Teddy. He kept us busy on the trip. We had to stop every few miles to let the puir lad do his business."

"Grandda, why didn't you leave him at home?"

"Because I want ye to treat him. Yer a doctor, are ye not?"

Clearly, he would indeed be treating his grandfather's decrepit terrier.

"Ho, Braden. There you are." Kade came trotting down the central staircase. A wide smile split his little brother's handsome features.

Of course, referring to Kade as *little* had become ridiculous, given that he now stood over six feet tall. Frail and sickly as a child, it had taken him years to recover his health. Braden knew better than anyone how hard the lad had fought for his life, since he'd been with him every step of the way. It was because of Kade that Braden had long ago decided to become a physician. He'd vowed that if he accomplished only one thing in life, it would be to cure his little brother.

Thankfully, his brother had eventually recovered from the fevers that had plagued him, in part due to Victoria, Nick's wife. Initially joining the Kendrick household as Kade's governess, she'd loved and nurtured the lad as if he were her own child. Now, ten years on, Kade was the picture of health and as brawny as the rest of the Kendrick men.

"You cheeky bastard." Braden gave him a fierce hug. "I thought you were still in London, finishing up your tour."

Kade thumped his back. "I've missed you, brother. It's *so* bloody good to see you."

A surge of emotion tugged at Braden's throat. Of all of his close-knit family, he was closest to Kade. They'd spent so much time together as children, weathering many trials. Sadly, given Braden's work and Kade's flourishing career, they now rarely saw each other.

"Did London finally get tired of the prodigy and send you on your way?" he asked.

"As if those bloody *Sassenachs* would even ken good music," scoffed Angus. "Kade was doin' them a favor."

"Yes, I distinctly remember the king making just that point at my final concert." When his grandfather's eyes widened, Kade grinned. "I'm joking, although I agree that I *am* a prodigy."

He'd been one from a young age. Now, at twenty-five, Kade was a renowned pianist as well as an accomplished violinist and composer. He'd already performed in some of the finest concert halls in Europe, and spent a good part of the year in London. It was splendid to see him doing so well. But his growing popularity meant that his visits to Scotland were becoming increasingly limited.

Braden glanced at the pile of luggage. "You two look like you're planning to stay for a month."

"We are stayin' for a month," Angus said. "We've come for the holidays."

Braden frowned. "But you always spend the holidays at Kinglas with the rest of the family, as does Kade, if he's about. I can't imagine Nick will be happy about the change." He lightly punched his brother's shoulder. "And Vicky will be missing her favorite lad, will she not?"

It was a running joke that Kade was Vicky's favorite. Their sister-in-law often teased that the rest of the Kendricks were Highland barbarians compared to the urbane, polished young man that Kade had become.

"Vicky is currently busy with a wee man named Kyle Aden Kendrick," Kade replied. "He's a fussy little fellow. He drools quite a bit and keeps her up late at night."

Kyle, Nick and Vicky's third child, was now almost four months old. Braden had made a point of traveling to Glasgow for the delivery, determined to see that Vicky and her child got the best care.

"Sounds just like one of Grandda's terriers," Braden said.

"Fah, he's a grand little lad," Angus proudly said. "In the pink of health, or I wouldna have left him."

Their grandfather was mad about babies, especially Kendrick babies. He fussed over them to the point of driving the family nursemaids insane.

"Glad to hear it," Braden said, "but that still doesn't explain your decision to decamp to Edinburgh, when you always spend the holidays at Kinglas. Without fail, I might add."

Angus scratched his chin, suddenly looking furtive. "We dinna want ye to feel neglected, particularly at such a special time of year."

Braden narrowed his gaze. "That sounds a bit fishy, Grandda."

"Why don't we join the others in the drawing room," Kade smoothly interjected. "Braden, I'm sure you must be wanting a drink before dinner, yes?"

Braden nodded. "I should change, first."

Donella emerged from the back hall. "No need to rush. You can change when I send Pippa upstairs. She's much less likely to fuss if you take her up to the nursery."

Pippa, a sweet-tempered four-year-old, was the least fussy child Braden knew.

Over the years, he'd developed excellent instincts when it came to his family. At the moment, his instincts were giving him a good thump between the shoulder blades.

"Why are you all trying to manage me?" he asked.

Donella simply gave him an innocent smile. No one did innocent better than his sister-in-law, but he wasn't fooled.

Angus heaved a dramatic sigh. "Och, laddie, yer growin' paranoid. That's what comes from workin' so hard. Yer picklin' yer brain, which canna be—"

"Why don't we pickle our brains with a nice whisky," Kade said as he steered Angus toward the staircase. "I hear you just got a new batch from our Graeme's distillery."

"Yes, Logan says it's quite excellent," Donella brightly replied.

Braden followed the others up the stairs, listening to their cheerful—and disingenuous—conversation about Graeme's thriving distillery business. The more he listened, the more he became convinced that some plan was afoot. This visit was not a spur of the moment decision by any means.

Logan was ensconced in a leather club chair by the drawing room's fireplace, reading his paper. "Ah, finally. I thought I'd have to drink all this splendid whisky myself."

Pippa, who'd wedged herself into the chair beside her father, shook her head. "That would be bad, Papa. Mamma would have to scold you for being a scaly hog grubber."

Donella scowled at Angus. "You've been here less than an hour, and you're already teaching Pippa cant?"

"Me? I never teach the bairns rough words."

"Grandda, you do it all the time," Kade said.

Joseph walked into the room, catching the tail end of the conversation. "Grandda knows all the best swear words."

Logan snorted. "Aye, he always had a talent."

Angus pointed a finger at his great-grandson. "Laddie boy, yer not to be sharin' any of our secrets. It's breakin' the code."

"There is no such code, and you've never been able to keep a secret in your life," Braden dryly noted.

Donella eyed each of the males. "I would still like to know who is teaching my daughter inappropriate language."

"Papa," Pippa replied with lethal candor. "But he told me not to tell you."

Logan winced. "Oh, bloody—"

Donella whipped up a hand. "Do. Not. Goodness, husband, I expect better of you."

Braden snorted. "Mistake number one."

"Of course I didn't actually teach her," Logan explained. "She just overheard me talking to one of the grooms." He did his best to look contrite. "Sorry, love. I promise it won't happen again."

She scoffed. "It will absolutely happen again. You are a very bad man, Logan Kendrick."

"I'll show you just how bad I can be the next time we're alone," he said with a grin.

Joseph grimaced. "Ugh. Papa is trying to be romantic again."

"Are you in trouble, Papa? I'm sorry if I got you in trouble," Pippa said, placing her little hand on his arm.

He winked at her. "Papa is usually in some sort of trouble. Grandda might have to take me out behind the mews for a paddling."

Pippa giggled. "Now you're just being silly."

"A natural state of affairs," Donella said. "Now, we have time for one drink before dinner. Cook has gone to a great deal of trouble to make a special dinner for Grandda and Kade, and we mustn't spoil it."

"Oh? I thought their arrival was a surprise?" Braden casually asked. "When did Mrs. Brady have time to pull together a special dinner?"

If he hadn't been watching her closely, he would have missed his sister-in-law's slight wince.

"That's why we had to set dinner back. Mrs. Brady had to reorganize the menu a bit," she said.

"Then we'd best get to it," Angus said. "I'm that eager to try the new brew."

While Logan poured the drinks, the rest of them chatted about the new batch from their brother's distillery, and the general state of affairs in Clan Kendrick. It was as pleasant a family scene as one could imagine. While it might be a cold and gusty evening in late November, in the house all was warm and inviting.

Too bad his blasted family was up to something. Now he

had to figure out what it was before they embarked on one of their typically deranged—if well meaning—plans.

When a glass appeared under his nose, Braden glanced up to see Logan regarding him with a quizzical expression.

"You look rather lost in thought," his brother said.

"Oh, thanks." He took the glass. "Just thinking about the family."

Angus heaved a dramatic sigh. "It's not much time ye have for us. We never see ye, what with yer doctorin' work and them bodies ye like to cut up for fun. Ye'd think ye love those cadavers more than ye love us."

"What's a cadaver?" Pippa asked.

Braden shot his grandfather an irritated look. "I do not cut up dead bodies for fun. Besides, Kade's away far more than I am. We barely know where he is from one day to the next. Which is perfectly reasonable," he hastily added. "He's building his career as a pianist, just as I'm building my medical practice."

"Aye, but ye—"

"Braden's right," Kade said. "If you're going to bite off anyone's nose for flying the coop, it should be mine."

"Aye, but yer in London or on the Continent. Our laddie here is only a few hours away from Glasgow, yet he canna find the time to visit his own family. And the laird himself—that would be yer brother, Nick," Angus pointedly said to Braden, "is worried about ye."

"I know who the laird is," Braden dryly replied.

"Everything is fine, Grandda," Kade said. "Stop fussing." Angus subsided with a mutter.

"By the way," Braden said, "where's the rest of the family spending Christmas this year?"

"Oh, at Kinglas, I suppose," Kade vaguely replied.

"You suppose?"

Angus frowned. "Of course they'll be at Kinglas. Where else would they be?"

"All of them, including Graeme and Sabrina?"

"Aye, unlike some people we willna mention."

Donella jumped up. "More whisky, anyone? I can fetch it."

Joseph frowned. "But Mamma, you said there was only time for one glass, remember?"

When Donella sighed, Braden was tempted to laugh. His family's clumsy charade was falling apart before his eyes.

"We're not sure about Graeme and Sabrina," Logan hastily put in. "Awfully long trip from Lochnagar to Kinglas at this time of year."

"Of course they're goin' to Kinglas, ye ninny," Angus said. "I told ye that."

Logan shook his head in disbelief.

"Do ye really think our Braden doesn't ken what we're doin'?" Angus demanded. "He's got more brains than the rest of ye put together."

"True," Kade said. "But we were trying to be slightly more subtle about it."

"This family doesn't know the meaning of the term," Braden said. "You're here because of me, although I'm not entirely sure why. It's not like I'll be alone for the holidays. I've already got a house full of Kendricks, in case you failed to notice."

"Hardly a houseful, my dear," Donella said.

"And you and Logan are in on this scheme to save me from whatever it is, correct?" Braden asked.

She looked slightly guilty. "It seemed a good idea at the time."

"Fine, but what exactly are you all so worried about?"

"They're worried that you're suffering from melancholy," Joseph said.

Braden didn't know whether to laugh or pour another glass of whisky down his throat. "Melancholy, really?"

"I overheard Papa and Mamma discussing it."

Logan, who'd been looking sheepish, frowned at his son. "You overheard, or you eavesdropped?"

"You were quite loud, Papa. I didn't have to eavesdrop."

"Your papa speaking loudly? Hard to imagine." Braden eyed his brother. "So you decided to write to Nick, did you?"

"You do realize that I write to Nick on a regular basis."

"True, but this time you apparently got him worked up about me."

"The laird worries about all of us," Angus said. "It's his job."

"He doesn't have to worry about me. For the hundredth time, I'm fine," Braden said, exasperated.

Angus scoffed. "Yer not. Practically wastin' away, ye are. And what's this we hear about ye larkin' about in Old Town, almost gettin' yerself—"

"A-hem," Logan said in warning, nodding in Pippa's direction.

"Why in blazes did you tell them about *that*?" Braden asked his brother.

Now they would *all* be dogging his steps like faithful, fretful hounds.

"I told them," Donella calmly said. "They needed to know."

Angus nodded. "Aye, so Nick asked us to come check on ye. To settle his mind, ye ken. And to help ye take a rest and spend time with yer family over the holidays."

Braden had to unclench his teeth to get out the words. "What I need is peace and quiet, not a houseful of nervous ninnies fussing over me."

Kade tilted his head, studying him. "Braden, aren't you happy to see us? It's been ages, after all."

His brother's calm question caught him up short.

"Yes, of course I'm happy to see you. It's the fussing I can't stand. It doesn't mean I don't love you. It just means . . ."

"That you're a man who likes his solitude?" Logan wryly said. "Yes, we are very aware of that. That doesn't mean you can't spend a wee bit of time with your loved ones over the holidays."

"Thanks for twisting the knife, old man," Braden said with a sigh. "All right, I see your point."

And he did, which was the hell of it. He'd been acting like a complete prat.

Angus lifted a trembling hand to his brow, doing his best to look on death's doorstep. "We dinna want to fash ye, laddie, but I'm an old man. Can ye blame me for wantin' to spend time with my grandson before the guid Lord calls me to join my ancestors?"

Logan covered his mouth, but Pippa turned a surprisingly stern expression on Braden.

"I think you're being mean, Uncle Braden," she said in her sweet little voice. "Grandda and Uncle Kade came all this way to see you. *And* Teddy, even though he's old, too."

The one-two punch—true affection combined with finely honed guilt—was a Kendrick specialty passed down through generations.

"Really, even the children?" Braden said to Logan.

"My little lassie is a chip off the old block," he replied with a grin.

Braden held up his hands. "All right, I surrender. We'll have a true family holiday, but no fussing. I still have to work."

Kade nodded. "Absolutely no fussing."

"And I can help ye with yer emergency visits, so ye have more time for relaxin'," Angus said in an encouraging tone. "I was a dab hand at doctorin' when ye were little bairns.

I took care of all yer hurts, and better than some bloody sawbones."

Braden's mind staggered over the appalling image of his grandfather trying to assist him.

"Another drink, dear?" Donella asked in a sympathetic tone.

"One for me, too." Angus briskly rubbed his hands together. "Aye, it'll be grand, us working together, lad. Just ye wait and see."

"Good God." Braden handed Donella his glass.

CHAPTER 6

"Thank you for meeting me here," John said as he locked his office door. "If Donny had been able to escort you, I would not have worried for your safety."

Donny was Samantha's usual escort when she ventured into Old Town, but his hulking physique made him unforgettable. She couldn't take the risk that Braden Kendrick might recognize him.

"He took Felicity to visit the orphanage school today. You know how she enjoys spending time with the teachers."

And while that was true, it was also a convenient excuse for keeping her manservant away from this ill-advised excursion.

"Ah, of course Donny would go with her, if you were not able to take her."

There was no mistaking the skepticism in John's voice. He knew how unusual it was for Felicity to go anywhere without Samantha, even under Donny's protection.

And blast John for putting her in such a dodgy position. His suspicions about her secret mission were dead accurate, of course. But if he decided to challenge her directly, Samantha would go on denying that she was the unknown woman who was ghosting about the slums.

It was her only choice, especially now that she was searching for more than Roger's killers. She and Donny simply *had* to find the children that had mysteriously disappeared from the orphanage. Most of the board thought they were common runaways, but Samantha didn't believe it. Every instinct told her those children were in danger.

"Shall we walk to Braden's clinic?" John asked. "The weather is quite mild."

Samantha relaxed a degree, grateful that he'd let the matter of Donny drop. "Yes, please. The exercise will do me good."

"Splendid."

They made their way out of the college toward the densest section of Old Town. High tenements, winding staircases, and old mansions that had formerly housed the aristocracy meandered down the slopes in this most ancient quarter of the city. With their irregular rooflines and multiple chimneys, the buildings looked picturesque, even quaint. But the tenements cast deep shadows onto the alleys and winding passageways, shadows that turned into inkblots at night.

There was something romantic about Old Town. At sunset on a clear evening, the old stone buildings glowed with a soft patina and looked like the tall towers of a mythical kingdom. The first time Samantha had glimpsed the city from a distance, she'd found it magical—until she'd gotten her first whiff of Old Town streets.

They entered a narrow lane that cut directly from the college yard through to Cowgate. At this time of day, it was busy with open shops and college staff hurrying to and fro.

"I'm eager for you to see the clinic," John said. "Braden's done a splendid job with it. He's got a knack for winning the trust of the locals, and God knows we need more physicians of his caliber *and* courage."

"He sounds like an excellent physician and a kind man," she cautiously replied.

"Which is exactly why we need him on the board of the Penwith Foundation."

She sighed. "Very neat, John. I didn't even see the blade until it slipped between my ribs."

"It's not a nefarious plot, Samantha. We clearly need someone who isn't a spy for Lord Beath."

"Right now at least half the board are his spies," she admitted. "I understand better than anyone how much Beath hates the foundation and would do anything to shut it down—through his toadies on the board, if possible."

"Braden is impervious to that sort of negative influence."

So far, she'd been resisting the notion of Kendrick joining the board. The more time he spent in her presence, the greater the chance that he would recognize her as the woman who'd rescued him. Still, John was right—they desperately needed help.

"I really wish you would consider bringing Bathsheba on the board," she said. "She'll stand up to anyone."

"We had enough trouble getting *you* on the board. Arthur Baines and I practically had to beat the other members into submission before they agreed to give you Roger's seat."

Arthur Baines was an influential barrister who had been a good friend of Samantha's husband. He was one of their only other supporters on the board.

"I do remember. It was gruesome."

"Besides, Bathsheba would probably murder half of them at her first meeting. It would be the equivalent of shooting off a cannon in a very small room."

Samantha laughed. "It would almost be worth it for that alone."

"Thank you, but I prefer to keep my wife *out* of trouble, not have her cause it."

She sobered. "Sometimes it's necessary to cause trouble."

"Agreed. Braden will do that nicely, and without fireworks. He's strong but very even-tempered."

"You paint a fine portrait, but rumor has it that Kendrick does ruffle feathers at the medical college. He's unconventional."

From what she knew, that word fairly well described the entire Kendrick family.

John glanced down at her. "Braden only ruffles feathers when necessary, and they're almost always the right feathers. I lose my temper with the board now and again, as you may have noticed, but Braden is unflappable."

Rationally, there was no reason she should keep objecting to Kendrick, and John knew it. She could only hope and pray that the blasted man didn't recognize her.

"Then if not Bathsheba, I suppose we must make do with Dr. Kendrick."

John flashed a smile. "Truly, Samantha, I'm sure you'll be pleased with him."

She doubted it.

They turned into Old Peter's Close, a narrow street gated at both ends and lined with high tenement buildings. Like many of the closes that threaded through Old Town like a maze, it seemed respectable enough during the daylight hours. Shops filled the lower floors, while apartments and flats on the higher floors provided homes for the people that owned or worked in those small businesses.

But at night, as she knew from experience, passages like Old Peter's Close could turn deadly.

They stopped in front of a storefront that was better maintained than its neighbors. A physician's sign hung over the black-trimmed green door, and crisp white curtains hung in the windows. The stoop was well swept. Compared to its surroundings, the establishment radiated an air of quiet order.

"Shall we?" John asked.

She braced herself. "Of course."

He opened the door, and she stepped down into a good-sized room with a surprisingly high ceiling. A faint waft of pine oil mixed with lemon teased her nose. The knotted boards under her feet were worn but scrupulously clean. The walls were whitewashed and lined with waist-high cupboards stacked with towels, sheets, and medical supplies. Three wooden bedsteads, separated by blue curtains hung from the ceiling, were made up with military precision.

A middle-aged woman in a black stuff gown and striped blue apron rose from behind a desk. "Good afternoon, Dr. Blackmore. Dr. Kendrick is with a patient in the back room. Is he expecting you?"

"Mrs. Culp, it's a pleasure to see you. Dr. Kendrick is not expecting us, and we'll be happy to wait."

"Staging an ambush, are we?" Samantha murmured to her friend.

John ignored her. "Mrs. Culp, this is Lady Samantha Penwith. She's been pestering me for a tour of the clinic, so we thought to pop in and impose upon you."

Samantha threw him an ironic glance but went along with the fiction. "How do you do, Mrs. Culp? I hope we're not inconveniencing you."

The woman bobbed a curtsy. "Not at all, your ladyship. Just one patient in the back, and Dr. Kendrick should be finishing up with him soon."

"An overnight patient?" John asked.

"Aye. The lad's father is a drover, from north of Perth. They were delivering a herd to the cattle markets when the lad fell from their cart. Broke his ankle, the poor wee thing."

John frowned. "Not a compound fracture, I hope."

A deep voice, colored with the hint of a Highland brogue, came from the rear. "No, clean break, fortunately."

Dr. Kendrick emerged from the back room, dressed casually in breeches, boots, and a white linen shirt topped by a green vest. He paused to jot something down in a small notebook.

"We just need to avoid a fever," he murmured to himself. "He's a bit weedy for my liking."

"Poor lad," John said. "Want me to have a look?"

The doctor glanced at John over the top of his silver-rimmed spectacles, as if finally registering his presence.

"Blackmore, you have plenty of patients. No need to steal mine."

John put up his hands. "Just trying to be helpful, old boy."

"No, you'll peruse my notes, check my work twice, and then after a period of hemming and hawing, pronounce yourself *mostly* satisfied."

John snorted. "I must be a complete prat."

When Braden Kendrick laughed, Samantha's nerves actually fluttered. Her nerves hadn't fluttered in quite a long time.

It wasn't just his laugh that was disconcerting. Up close and in good light, the man was ridiculously attractive, with broad shoulders and a lean, rangy physique. She'd already noted his strong features and thick auburn hair, and now it was the eyes that riveted her. Even the silver-rimmed spectacles couldn't detract from those eyes, but rather drew attention to the spectacular green of his gaze.

That gaze now shifted to her, narrowing with focused intensity. Samantha felt her face begin to flush, and she wondered if his stare had something to do with a sense that he'd met her before.

Damn and double damn.

Quickly enough, he switched his attention back to John, much to Samantha's relief.

"My regrets that you've caught me off guard. Otherwise I certainly wouldn't have come out in my shirtsleeves." Again, he looked over the top of his spectacles at John. "But I suspect you wanted to catch me off guard."

When he rolled down his sleeves over his muscled forearms, Samantha couldn't help thinking it rather a shame.

Ninny.

"Spur of the moment decision," John replied. "Lady Samantha was visiting the college, so it seemed the perfect opportunity to introduce you."

Kendrick raised his eyebrows. "Really?"

Although Samantha winced at the doctor's tone, John blithely carried on.

"Dr. Kendrick, allow me to introduce you to Lady Samantha Penwith, head of the Penwith Charitable Foundation. You've heard of it, of course."

"Yes, from you, the president of that foundation board," Kendrick sardonically replied.

Samantha had to resist the urge to shuffle her feet. She also had to stifle the impulse to whack John with her reticule for putting her in such an embarrassing position.

Kendrick turned to her again, but this time with a genuine and thoroughly devastating smile.

"Lady Samantha, you are most welcome here. I only wish my colleague had given me notice, so we could have prepared for your visit."

"Oh, I . . . I'm sorry we interrupted you while you're working," she stammered.

"No, it's perfectly fine. But if you'll allow me a moment, I will then be able to give you my full attention."

Concisely, he provided Mrs. Culp with instructions for the boy's care. "If we can avoid a fever, he'll be ready for travel within the week," he finished up.

Mrs. Culp grimaced. "The lad's father says he must be off tomorrow."

Kendrick shook his head. "Absolutely not. He will not be fit for travel."

"But the father was clear, sir. He can stay in town but one more night."

"I'll speak to him in the morning and tell him that we can send the lad home in my family's traveling coach."

The matron nodded before disappearing into the back room.

"And how much will you be charging for this patient's care and transportation?" John asked in a humorous tone.

Kendrick slipped his spectacles into his vest pocket and shrugged into the frock coat that had been hanging on a hook by the shelves. "Nothing at all."

"Do you ever charge your patients?" Samantha asked.

He waggled a hand. "Only if they insist on it. Since very few can afford coin, I am often paid with food or home-brewed ale. I rarely have to worry about feeding my patients."

"How do you fund the clinic?"

"Some comes out of my own pocket, but I have a few generous donors."

"All going by the name of Kendrick," John noted.

"No, there's a donor named Blackmore in there, too."

John shook his head. "A minor one, I'm afraid. I wish I could do more."

"Your volunteer work here is infinitely more valuable than money," Kendrick replied.

"You still need a full-time physician to assist you. With all your other duties, you're burning the candle at both ends, Braden."

"I manage perfectly well." Then Kendrick inclined his head to Samantha. "But I am forgetting my manners. Would you care to sit, my lady? I believe we can rustle up some tea and biscuits for you."

She smiled. "I'm fine, thank you."

"Then how can I help you?"

She looked at John, who gave her a nod as if to say, *well, go ahead*.

"I'm going to regret this, aren't I?" said Kendrick, observing their silent exchange.

"I should hope you wouldn't regret helping orphans," she felt compelled to reply. "Dr. Blackmore assured me that you were the perfect man for the position we have in mind for you."

As soon as her statement was out, Samantha felt herself

color up to the roots of her hair. She glared at John, who suddenly became very interested in inspecting the contents of the clinic shelves.

After a short silence, she met Kendrick's gaze. He seemed entirely unperturbed by her tart response.

"You're talking about a position on your foundation's board?" he asked.

"Yes."

"Well, I am flattered by John's confidence in me, but I'm afraid I'm not much for administrative positions. Or board meetings."

She frowned. "Why not?"

"They're boring, for one thing."

"That is a rather unreasonable assumption to make, since you've never been to one of ours."

When his expressive eyebrows ticked up, she mentally grimaced. She was acting like a dimwit. Then again, he was blunt to the point of rudeness.

John came to her rescue. "There's nothing boring about those meetings, old man, though I wish there was."

Kendrick sat on the edge of the table and crossed his arms. For such a lanky man, he had quite a broad chest. Of course, that was entirely beside the point.

"John, I already told you how I felt about this. There was no need to drag her ladyship down here for nothing."

"He didn't drag me," Samantha countered. "I was quite eager to come and speak with you. *Quite* eager."

It was a miracle that John didn't burst into laughter on the spot. Fortunately, he had excellent self-control, although his eyes gleamed with unholy amusement.

"I'm honored, ma'am," Kendrick said. "But I think that John has given you the wrong impression about me. My talents hardly lie in administrative work."

She pointedly looked around the neatly ordered clinic. "Such would not seem to be the case."

"I have Mrs. Culp to thank for organizing this place."

"Bollocks," John said. "This place runs like a top because of *you*."

Kendrick held up a hand. "John, I—"

"Braden, I wouldn't be asking if we didn't truly need you," John cut in. "Nor would Lady Samantha. In fact, she initially tried to talk me out of it."

"Not really," Samantha hastily said.

"Yes, really," John replied. "It took a great deal of work on my part to convince her, Braden. So I would prefer not to expend energy having to convince you, too."

Kendrick studied her for a moment. "May I ask why you initially didn't want me on your board, Lady Samantha?"

She blushed again, which was *very* annoying. "Er . . ."

"Because she knows how busy you are," John said. "She worried you wouldn't be able to devote the necessary time to us."

"She's right," Kendrick replied.

"Actually, no. It's only a few hours a month, along with the occasional social function."

"Still—"

"Braden," John impatiently interrupted. "We're rather hanging on by a thread at the foundation, and we need your support."

Kendrick's attention flicked back to Samantha.

She took a deep mental breath and faced facts. John was right. They desperately needed someone like Kendrick on the board, despite the risk that he might recognize her as the woman who'd rescued him.

At the moment, the foundation and its work had to take priority over that concern.

"John is correct," she admitted. "We really do need your help."

"Could you be more specific?"

"Certainly. We need a strong ally who can help us manage the old twiddlepoops on our board."

Kendrick choked out a laugh.

"I'm sorry if my language shocks you, sir," she said, trying not to sound defensive.

"You didn't shock me. Please continue, my lady."

She took a moment to formulate an answer that did *not* make her sound like a ninny.

"Our goal is to keep the school and the orphanage operating at humane and appropriate standards. That goal is often challenged by a board that is, with a few exceptions, very old-fashioned. The notion of a school that aims to properly educate young females, especially ones from impoverished backgrounds, strikes them as ridiculous. They also think that we *spoil* the orphanage boys by providing a home-like establishment. It's immensely frustrating, but there you have it. John, however, assures me that you would share our beliefs. To have another professional man on the board, especially a noted physician from one of the best families in Scotland, could make a great difference for us."

"Plain and simple, we need another reformer," John added. "We're outnumbered."

"About the girls' school," Kendrick said. "If money is an issue, I can always get you more."

Samantha shook her head. "We have adequate funds. It's how we wish to spend them. Most of the board members have no interest in providing a real education for the girls. According to them, teaching math or how to properly read is simply encouraging them to get above their proper station."

Kendrick looked annoyed. "That's backward and ridiculous."

"I make that point on a regular basis."

"They must love that," he said with a slight smile.

"Which is why we need you. You're a professional man, so they're much more likely to listen to you than to me." Samantha tried not to sound bitter about that.

"Not that they always listen to me, either," John added.

Kendrick grimaced with sympathy. "I'm sorry, Lady Samantha. They *should* listen to you. It's your foundation."

"Which is exactly why we need another voice and another vote," John said. "You also know how things work here in Old Town, which makes you an even greater asset."

Kendrick rubbed his chin. "Not everyone would see having a Kendrick on the board as an asset. We're not exactly known for our tact."

John waved a hand. "Oh, I'm much worse than you when it comes to that."

"True enough." Kendrick stared down at the floor, obviously thinking. "The clinic is my first priority, though. That has to come first."

"Then perhaps hire another doctor?" John said in a long-suffering voice.

"What I really need is another Mrs. Culp, but women like her aren't easy to find. She's an excellent manager *and* my patients trust her. That's important in Old Town."

Samantha blinked. For several minutes, a wisp of an idea had been drifting at the edges of her brain, one so formless she'd scarcely been aware of it. Now, it coalesced into sharp definition.

"I'm a good manager," she said, "and people in Old Town know my work. They know they can trust me. I'd be happy to volunteer at your clinic, if you would agree to take up a position on our board."

Kendrick straightened up, obviously startled. "Are you serious?"

"Certainly. I can help with your management problem," she said with an encouraging smile.

John frowned. "Samantha—"

She shot up a hand. "It's the perfect solution."

Kendrick regarded her with a perplexed expression. "My patients aren't exactly from the aristocracy, or even the merchant class," he finally said. "Some are . . . let's just call them people from the rougher edges of Old Town."

He meant criminal types, or those associated with them. People who knew the criminal underworld of Edinburgh because they lived in it.

Even better.

"Dr. Kendrick, I am not unfamiliar with the rougher edges of Edinburgh, either in my work or . . ." She paused for effect. "Or in my personal life."

"You mean your husband's murder," he said after a few moments of surprised silence.

She was impressed by his willingness to state the matter so clearly. Most people shied away from even mentioning it.

"Yes."

"Samantha, this is not appropriate," John said in a warning tone.

"Charitable work is always appropriate, John. And might I point out that your wife works with women engaged in prostitution."

John scowled. "That's entirely different. She's a married woman."

"And I'm a widow. You don't get more respectable than that."

"But I'm always with her," John protested.

"And I'm sure Dr. Kendrick or one of his other staff would always be here with me." She flashed him a smile. "Isn't that so?"

"Oh, am I part of this conversation?" Kendrick asked.

She ignored his sarcastic tone. "Also, I can bring my housekeeper along with me. She's an absolute demon of efficiency."

John adopted a stern expression. The dratted man obviously suspected what she was up to, but she didn't care.

"Samantha, I really don't think—"

"John, do we want Dr. Kendrick to join our board, or not?"

"Hang on," Kendrick said. "I haven't actually—"

"Of course we do," John tersely replied.

"Then Dr. Kendrick needs help, and I am willing to provide it."

"You really wish to work in a clinic in Old Town?" Kendrick asked, still skeptical.

"I am no dainty town miss, Doctor," she said, doing her best to look down her nose at his six-foot-something physique. "And I am not afraid of hard work. Besides, the timing is perfect. We have a board meeting later this week, and then I'll be free to start volunteering at your clinic the following week."

"Holy hell," John muttered.

Samantha ignored him. "The day is getting on, so I must be off, Dr. Kendrick. But I will send my maid over with a packet of information about the foundation first thing tomorrow morning."

Kendrick was now staring at her like she was a medical experiment gone horribly wrong. She ignored that, too. "Well, sir?"

He glanced at John, who was fuming but appeared to have conceded the battle.

"Do I even have a choice?" Kendrick asked.

"Apparently not," John groused.

Samantha grabbed her friend by the elbow, all but pushing him toward the door.

"We'll see you soon, Dr. Kendrick," she tossed over her shoulder.

"Lady Samantha—" he said, starting toward her.

"It was lovely to meet you," she cheerily replied before slamming the door in his face.

CHAPTER 7

The porter ushered Braden into the entrance hall of the Penwith Charitable Foundation, a distinguished old building that once served as the residence of a Scottish nobleman. Though sparsely decorated, the hall retained an air of grandeur, with its impressively high ceiling and a magnificently carved oak staircase that decades of polishing had mellowed to a smooth patina.

Braden handed over his coat, hat, and blasted new walking stick. Logan, the old fusspot, had insisted he begin carrying the thing.

"A sturdy cane can be very handy if you don't have your pistol," Logan had said to him the other morning at breakfast. "Especially if it's got a good knob on it."

Little Pippa had scrunched up her nose. "But, Papa, you don't carry a walking stick."

"Papa just uses his fists, darling," Logan had replied. "That usually does the trick."

"I'd like to note that I'm quite handy with my fists," Braden had then pointed out. "I was on the boxing team at university."

Logan had flashed him a smile. "Were you? Well, that's splendid."

Needless to say, Braden now carried an ebony walking stick with a heavy silver knob.

"That's a dandy stick," the porter said in an admiring voice. "Ye could give someone a right good clobber with that one."

"I don't suppose you've been speaking with my brother, have you?"

The man frowned. "Er, what, sir?"

"Pay me no mind. Where's the boardroom?"

"I will take you up, Dr. Kendrick," came a voice from behind him.

Braden turned to see a woman approaching across the hall. She stopped a few feet away and dipped into a graceful curtsy.

"Good afternoon," she said in a low, well-modulated voice. "I am Mrs. Girvin, the housekeeper for the foundation."

She was a remarkably attractive woman, probably in her early forties. Her wheat-gold hair was neatly braided, and her features were lovely enough to grace a lady's magazine. She also possessed a lush figure that didn't square with Braden's image of a housekeeper—at least the housekeepers he'd known over the years.

"It's a pleasure to meet you, Mrs. Girvin."

She gestured toward the staircase. "Lady Samantha and the board are waiting for you."

A medical emergency had delayed him. He almost wished his late showing would get him kicked off the board, but he doubted John—or Lady Samantha—would tolerate that.

For such a dainty lass, Lady Samantha certainly was masterful. While he'd initially thought her a bit awkward, the lovely widow had soon rolled him up. When she'd hustled John out of the clinic, it left Braden gaping after them like a booby.

"As you might already know," Mrs. Girvin said as she led him up the stairs, "this building serves as the girls school."

"Yes, and the orphanage is next door."

"The boys are both housed and taught next door. As you

would understand, it makes sense to keep our facilities separate. Most of the rooms on this floor are given over to classrooms," Mrs. Girvin explained when they reached the first floor. "Kitchen and service rooms are on the ground floor, and offices and a dormitory for some of the girls are on the upper floors."

"Do you also serve as housekeeper for the orphanage?"

"I manage both institutions," she replied in a rather clipped tone.

For a moment, Braden thought he'd offended her. Then he realized that her speech carried a very precise inflection, as if every word had been weighed and measured before it emerged from her lips.

"How many boys live at the orphanage?"

"There are fifty-one in residence now. The numbers vary from time to time."

"You certainly have your work cut out for you," he said with a smile.

"I am well able to handle it," she stiffly replied.

Apparently he *had* offended her.

"I'm sure you can. From everything Dr. Blackmore has told me, both institutions are very well run."

"We are indeed fortunate to have Dr. Blackmore on the board."

Since her chilly tone conveyed the opposite sentiment, Braden decided to leave off with the questions. Perhaps Mrs. Girvin was not someone John or Lady Samantha considered an ally. Still, her unfriendly attitude struck him as odd, since he was now on the board that she must answer to.

After knocking on a door at the end of the corridor, Mrs. Girvin ushered him into a long, narrow room with a marble fireplace at the far end. The oak-paneled walls were hung with portraits of what were presumably benefactors or previous board members. A polished mahogany table and matching chairs took up most of the available space. Both a coffee and tea service were laid out on a sideboard, along with plates of pastries. The fact that a substantial number of those pastries had apparently been consumed suggested the board had been kicking their heels waiting for him.

"Dr. Kendrick," Mrs. Girvin intoned.

Lady Samantha, seated near John at the head of the table, looked up from a pile of documents stacked before her. A warm smile lit up her pretty features, and her velvety-brown eyes glowed with relief.

"Dr. Kendrick, you made it," she exclaimed, jumping up. "We were beginning to worry that something had happened. I do hope all is well."

Then she made a funny little grimace, as if she'd just committed a faux pas.

From some of the disapproving looks around the table, it appeared that she had. Braden, however, thought her utterly charming.

Of course, that had nothing to do with anything.

An older man with enormous gray whiskers huffed with apparent indignation. He put Braden in mind of a walrus.

"Lady Samantha," said the walrus, "such dramatic exclamations are unnecessary. And I do hope Dr. Kendrick has a reasonable explanation for his late arrival. To keep the board waiting in such a manner is unacceptable."

Dignified nods of agreement, along with equally dignified huffing, followed that salvo.

Braden bowed. "Lady Samantha, please accept my apologies. I was detained by a medical emergency and could not get away."

"Gentlemen," he added, scanning the room, "I beg your pardon for keeping you waiting."

A spectacularly ancient fellow at the end of the table snapped out of a half-doze. He peered at Braden through a pair of pince-nez spectacles, as if trying to focus.

"What's that? Speak up," he querulously said. "Can't hear a blasted thing at this end of the room."

"Dr. Kendrick has arrived, my lord," Lady Samantha said in a raised voice.

The old man adjusted his spectacles so he could scowl more effectively. "Just like a Kendrick, always causing trouble. And half the day gone already. At my age, that's nothing to sneeze at."

Lady Samantha crossed to the sideboard. "Let me pour you another cup of tea, Lord Robertson. That will be just the thing."

"You're already making quite an impression," John murmured as he shook Braden's hand.

"I'm only fifteen minutes late," he murmured back.

"And yet a capital crime with this group."

"I'm guessing my goose is already cooked, then?"

John chuckled. "You're not slipping away that easily."

"Bad luck, that."

John pointed to the empty chair next to Lady Samantha, who was busily refilling cups around the table. Braden found that odd, since Mrs. Girvin remained by the door, not making the slightest attempt to help her employer.

Lady Samantha, meanwhile, chatted to the gentlemen in a cheerful voice as she waited on them. Why in God's name did the blasted fellows treat her like a serving girl?

"Can I get you some tea or coffee, Dr. Kendrick?" she asked as she came back around the table.

"That won't be necessary," he said, more brusquely than he intended.

When she colored up, he wanted to kick himself.

"But thank you all the same," he added. "Most kind."

She cast him a wary glance, before sliding into the chair that he held out for her. When Braden took his seat, he felt like ten times an idiot.

"I believe we're ready to start," John said.

"Finally," muttered the walrus.

John glanced over his shoulder at the housekeeper, still observing the room.

"That will be all, Mrs. Girvin," he pointedly said.

She nodded. "Please ring if you need anything else."

When she'd closed the door, John called the meeting to order. The first item was to introduce Braden.

Braden recognized the names of the mix of businessmen, bankers, and barristers, with a clergyman and two aristocrats for good measure. The bristling walrus was Sir Gregory Arthur, and the venerable ancient, Lord Robertson. It didn't take a genius to realize that they were members of the old guard on the board.

In fact, most of the men seemed to be old guard, with the exception of Arthur Baines, a noted barrister who was one of the younger board members. He actually acknowledged Braden's introduction with a smile and a friendly word.

Clearly, John and Lady Samantha had their work cut out for them against this lot.

"As you know, this is mostly a formality," John said, "but I need a motion to accept Dr. Kendrick to fill the current vacancy on the board."

"So moved, and delighted to do so," said Arthur Baines. "Dr. Kendrick will make a fine addition."

Sir Gregory loudly sniffed.

"Perhaps someone can second the motion," John dryly noted.

"Seconded," Lady Samantha said.

"Thank you. Dr. Kendrick, would you mind giving the board a brief overview of your experience and training?"

John had already given him a few suggestions, so Braden made a point of emphasizing his extensive education in Edinburgh, as well as his additional training in Hanover.

"Very impressive credentials," Baines said with approval.

"I'm grateful that I was able to train in Edinburgh," Braden replied. "The medical college is certainly on par with any university in Europe. And our hospitals are, naturally, second to none."

Murmurs of approval rose from around the table. As John had predicted, a little national pride went a long way with this group of staunch, old-fashioned Scots.

"Yes, that's all very well," said Sir Gregory, "but we already have one physician on the board. Why do we need another?"

Arthur Baines leaned slightly forward. "We have two aristocrats and two businessmen, so why not two physicians? They would certainly seem to be more useful than the rest of us." He chuckled. "And we certainly don't need more barristers."

Mr. Paisley, a textile magnate, scowled at Baines. "The foundation certainly seems to need our money, or am I mistaken in that?"

"Your generosity is greatly appreciated," Lady Samantha said with a winning smile. "I cannot imagine how we would get along without you, or without any of our board members. You are all quite invaluable."

"Well, I should think so," Paisley replied. "Eh, Haxton? We'd be in a fat lot of trouble without your money, too."

Mr. Haxton, the head of the accounting committee, blinked several times, as if startled. He had a retiring demeanor that seemed at odds with his position as one of the most powerful bankers in the city.

"Oh, ah . . . I say," he stammered. "More than happy to make my contribution, you know."

"Of course you are, my good man," said Baines in a jolly voice. "Now, perhaps we could get back to the business at hand."

"Dr. Kendrick?" John prompted. "Care to elaborate on your work experience?"

Again following John's suggestion, Braden took his time,

outlining in detail both his teaching and surgical experience. Most of the men around the table seemed at least reluctantly impressed. He finished up by emphasizing his work at the free clinic, which would be of the most relevant experience for them.

"Outstanding," Baines enthused. "Aside from Blackmore, I can't imagine anyone more suited to the work we do here at the Penwith Foundation."

The man's enthusiasm seemed a bit over the top. Perhaps he was trying to forestall more objections from the old guard.

"Do quite a lot of work at the clinic of yours, eh?" said Paisley. "I suppose you see all sorts of Old Town riffraff, including the usual collection of street urchins."

Braden was ready for this, too. "I have indeed encountered all sorts at my clinic, and I generally find them to be good people. As for the rougher sorts, I'm well able to handle them."

Lord Robertson, who'd dozed off during Braden's recital, jerked awake and re-entered the conversation.

"Can't say as I like all this clinic business. Or Kendricks." He scowled at Braden. "Are you as wild as the rest of your kin, like those blasted twins?"

While Braden loved his brothers, sometimes he wondered if he would ever live them down. "I am the boring Kendrick, my lord. Dr. Blackmore will be happy to confirm that."

"Yes, Dr. Kendrick is *quite* boring," said John with a barely repressed smirk.

Lady Samantha smiled at Lord Robertson. "Dr. Kendrick has also informed me that his brother, the Earl of Arnprior, is eager to make a substantial contribution to the foundation."

That had *definitely* not been part of their discussions.

"*Very* substantial," John swiftly added.

"That is indeed splendid," said Baines. "Quite a coup to

get the support of the Kendrick family. Well done, Lady Samantha."

She gave the barrister a sweet smile. "Thank you, my dear sir."

When Baines flashed her a quick wink, Braden had the impulse to drag the man across the table and give him a sturdy belt to the jaw.

Don't be a moron.

If there was something between Baines and Lady Samantha, it was certainly no business of his.

"Then if there is no further discussion, I propose we install Dr. Kendrick," John said. "Especially in light of the very generous support we will be receiving from the Kendrick family."

Not surprisingly, most of the board members voiced their approval. Sir Gregory glared but held his peace, and Lord Robertson once again dozed off.

Without further ado, Braden found himself officially dragooned into the sort of job he most disliked.

When he felt a small hand on his arm, he glanced over to meet Lady Samantha's mischievous gaze. He was beginning to realize that the lass hid her light under a bushel, restraining a personality that was both naturally charming and determined.

"Congratulations, Dr. Kendrick, and thank you." Her expression suddenly turned serious. "Truly."

"You are most welcome, my lady."

To his surprise, he meant it.

"Are we done, then?" asked Paisley, half-rising from his chair.

"There is one more pressing issue that we must address," said John.

Paisley settled back, breathing an aggrieved sigh.

"Oh, uh, but I must be getting back to the bank," Haxton said. "I am already quite late."

John shook his head. "It won't take long, but it's important enough to command our immediate attention."

"Let me guess," Sir Gregory said in a sarcastic tone. "You wish to talk about the retention issue at the orphanage or bring up more foolish ideas about female education. I shouldn't be surprised if you now wish to add Latin to the curriculum."

Paisley guffawed. "That's a good one, old fellow. Next, Blackmore and Lady Samantha will be telling us that women should attend university."

Most of the men, including Baines, chuckled. As for Lady Samantha, Braden could practically hear the poor lass grinding her molars into dust.

He adopted a mildly puzzled frown. "Why shouldn't women attend university?"

Under the table, Lady Samantha gave him a hard jab to the thigh.

Don't cause trouble was the clear message.

At least not yet, he assumed.

"We do need to discuss the problems at the orphanage," she said in a firm voice. "Boys are going missing, and that surely is something that should greatly concern us."

Braden threw John a startled glance.

His friend responded with a grim nod. "To bring Dr. Kendrick up to speed, several boys have disappeared from the orphanage over the last year or so. There one day, gone the next."

"Without any indication of unhappiness on their part?" Braden asked.

"None," Lady Samantha said in a worried voice. "In some cases, all their belongings were left behind."

"That's very odd."

No child of Old Town would willingly leave his belongings behind. If any possession wasn't falling to pieces, it could be sold for a few shillings at a local pawnshop.

"There's nothing odd about it," Sir Gregory said. "They've simply run away. Can't take discipline or structure, so they return to their old ways."

Haxton nodded. "I'm afraid Sir Gregory is correct. These boys generally come from dodgy backgrounds, to put it mildly. They've got criminality bred in the bones."

Braden scoffed. "No child is born a criminal. It is not a biologically determinative factor."

While Haxton look confused, Sir Gregory made a point of sneering across the table at him. "Impressive words from a new fellow who knows nothing about our establishments."

"I don't need to know how your orphanage is run to distinguish truth from falsehood," Braden replied.

Lord Robertson jerked awake with a snort. "What's the to-do? Isn't this blasted meeting over yet?"

"We are now listening to a lecture from Dr. Kendrick about the sterling character of slum children," Sir Gregory said with contempt. "Apparently, they are not to be blamed for their actions."

"Guttersnipes, the lot of them," huffed Lord Robertson. "Can't imagine why we bother with them in the first place."

"Our boys are not guttersnipes," Lady Samantha hotly replied. "They are good children, and they all wish to be here. And if you find our work so distasteful, Lord Robertson, you may wish to tender your resignation from the board. Naturally, I will be very disappointed, but will respect your decision."

Braden smothered a grin. Apparently, Lady Samantha had fire in her character, as well as charm and determination. With her eyes glittering like jewels and her cheeks flushing pink, the fire sat well on her, too.

"I suspect Lord Robertson will not be resigning from the board any time soon," John said in a cool tone. "His friend, Lord Beath, would not approve."

The old blighter fumed but didn't challenge the assertion.

Braden glanced around the table, taking in the various expressions. Most of the men seemed annoyed, although Haxton looked strangely nervous as he mopped his brow with a large kerchief. Baines, however, seemed not one whit perturbed. If anything, the barrister seemed amused.

Apparently, one needed a nautical chart to figure out the undercurrents on this blasted board.

"I will continue to discharge my duties, just like the rest of you," said Robertson with a rheumy glare.

"Then I suggest we return to the issue," Lady Samantha firmly said. "I have thoroughly questioned the orphanage staff, and they are mystified by the disappearances."

"How old were the boys?" Braden asked.

"All under the age of eight." She grimaced. "Two of them were only six, and that truly concerns me. That's much too young for them to be out on their own."

"And no family to run to for any of them, I suppose?"

She shook her head.

Braden could understand older boys running away. They sometimes chafed under rigid rules and structures. But children that young? In his experience, if they were given good food, a little comfort, and a safe place to stay, they would mightily resist any effort to return to the streets.

"But what can be done?" asked Mr. Wallace, the clergyman, who'd finally decided to join the discussion. "We give them so much, and yet they still run away. I hate to contradict Lady Samantha or the good doctor, but perhaps these particular lads were simply not able to resist the sinful temptations of the stews."

"Temptations like starving to death?" Braden sardonically responded.

The clergyman bristled. "I simply meant—"

John held up a hand. "Lady Samantha and I have a proposal. We feel it makes sense to hire extra security for the orphanage, especially during the evenings when only one assistant matron and a porter are on duty. With fifty boys, those two are stretched thin."

Sir Gregory let out a derisive snort. "Out of the question. We can't afford more staff, thanks to Lady Samantha's insistence that we hire a new cook *and* a composition teacher for the girls' school."

"The board agreed to those hires, sir," Samantha said in a clipped voice. "They were necessary."

As close as she was, Braden could practically feel her quivering with fury.

"Agreed over my objections," Sir Gregory retorted. "In any case, those hirings mean we have no additional funds. Besides, if we want to hire security, it should be just to keep them from stealing from the larder."

Lady Samantha's slender hand, resting on the table, curled into a quite respectable fist. "But it is—"

Sir Gregory faced Haxton with a glare. "You're the head of the accounts committee, Haxton. Do we have the money to hire more staff?"

"Er, no, not given our other expenses," Haxton stammered.

"Then that settles it," Sir Gregory triumphantly said. "Really, those boys are running back to their old lives, and that's it."

"That's the most logical explanation," said Paisley. "No point in wasting time *or* money."

"Gentlemen, please," John started.

"I move that we end this meeting," Sir Gregory loudly barked.

"I second the motion," Paisley quickly added.

John's gaze narrowed to slits as cold as the North Sea. "Since a motion to adjourn is now on the table, I will of course hold a vote. But I would ask you all to consider both the gravity of the situation and our request."

"Get on with the blasted vote," snipped Lord Robertson.

The vote brought the meeting to a swift end. Since the

president was required to abstain, Braden and Arthur Baines were the only two members to support Lady Samantha.

With a weary sigh, the lass rested her forehead on her palm.

"I'm sorry," Braden said to her in a low voice. "I wish I could have been of more help."

She looked sideways at him, forcing a small smile. Her gaze looked infinitely sad, and Braden had to resist the impulse to cuddle her.

This was *not* a woman who needed rescuing, and he would do well to remember that.

"I appreciate your support, Dr. Kendrick." Then her smile curled up into something a little more real. "And don't think for a moment that I'm giving up."

He smiled back. "I'm glad to hear it."

Baines, who'd come around to their side of the table, rested a hand on her shoulder. "Bad luck, old girl."

She patted his hand, which continued to rest, almost caressingly, on her shoulder. Braden had to restrain himself from knocking the man's bloody hand back to where it belonged.

"Thank you, Arthur," she said. "Though I was expecting it, it's immensely frustrating."

Braden rose and wandered away from the table, yet kept an eye on Lady Samantha and Baines as they carried on their quiet conversation. Baines was probably a good twenty years older than she, but he was a fit man with an affable manner and a face that most women would probably deem handsome. The lass obviously considered him a friend, if her easy manner with him was any indication.

He glanced over to meet John's sardonic gaze.

Bloody hell.

His friend had clearly deduced his train of thought.

"So, how bad is this situation at the orphanage?" Braden abruptly asked.

John's amusement vanished. "Bad enough. And as you

saw, we can't get the board to acknowledge that a problem even exists."

At that moment, Sir Gregory stomped past them, with Lord Robertson leaning heavily on his arm.

John gave them a polite nod. "Good day to you, gentlemen."

They ignored him and left the room.

"Good God," Braden said. "You've certainly got your hands full with those two."

"Now you know why we needed you."

Braden glanced back to see Baines still standing over Lady Samantha. Thankfully, his hand was now off her shoulder, although they continued in their earnest conversation.

He resolutely turned back to John. "Yes, but I won't thank you for pitching me into a right, good mess."

And if he allowed his thoughts about Lady Samantha to enter the mix, it would be a right, good mess in more ways than one.

CHAPTER 8

Samantha hurried up the stairs from the kitchen to the main floor. Her legs felt like lead, and exhaustion dragged at her body. It had been more than a full day since she'd slept.

Mrs. Johnson waited for her in the entrance hall. "Dr. Kendrick has arrived, my lady. I put him in the drawing room." The housekeeper gave her an anxious perusal. "Yer lookin' plum wore out. Ye should go rest. I can manage this."

Samantha wavered, sorely tempted by visions of her soft mattress. But giving in would be foolish. They were taking a huge risk sending for Kendrick. If the good doctor became even slightly suspicious, it would be up to her to divert him.

Besides, it was her fault that Donny had been injured. She had no intention of leaving his side.

"Donny is not thinking clearly. I need to do the talking for him."

"Aye, half a bottle of whisky for the pain will do that to a man." Mrs. Johnson grimaced. "It's a bloody shame that Dr. Blackmore is away."

As it was, they'd waited until a marginally respectable hour to send for John, only to discover that he was out of town. That had left them with no choice but to send for Kendrick.

Bathsheba's note had insisted that Samantha should not hesitate to do so and that she could trust him, no matter the circumstances.

She really had no choice. If Donny had broken his ankle, it would need to be set by a professional.

After tugging her cuffs into place, she smoothed a few errant curls behind her ears. "Do I look respectable?"

"Neat as a pin. The guid doctor will never suspect ye were sneakin' about Old Town only a few hours ago, up to yer ankles in muck and corruption."

"Let's hope not. Please bring some fresh hot water and towels to Donny's room. Oh, and where is Felicity?"

The last thing they needed was her sister-in-law stumbling into the middle of this.

"Upstairs. Hercules somehow cut his wee paw, so I told the lass to keep him in bed with her. I'll bring her some breakfast as soon as I fetch the water and towels."

Samantha pressed fingers to the lurking headache behind her right temple. "An injured cat. Just what we need at the moment."

"At least it'll keep the lass up in her room."

"All right, I'll fetch Dr. Kendrick and join you."

With a brisk nod, the housekeeper disappeared down the stairs.

Samantha suddenly became aware of her thudding heartbeat. She was about to put herself and the entire safety of their household in the hands of a man she barely knew. The fact that something inside her instinctively trusted Kendrick didn't make her feel any better. She couldn't afford to trust *anyone*, not even handsome doctors whose jade-green eyes seemed to see right through to the heart of who she was.

Romantic nonsense, old girl.

Kendrick was just an ordinary man, and couldn't see through to anything. It was one thing to be careful, it was another to be paranoid.

She opened the door and calmly walked into the room. Kendrick, dressed for riding, stood in the window. The clear morning light flowed around him and did a splendid job of showcasing his broad shoulders and his long, muscular legs, garbed in breeches and tall boots.

As he turned around, a smile lit up his features.

And very handsome features they are, too.

Ignoring the part of her brain addled by fatigue, Samantha came forward with an outstretched hand.

"Good morning, Dr. Kendrick. Please accept my apology for calling you out so early."

He bowed over her hand. "Actually, your timing was perfect, since I was about to set out for an early morning ride. I usually take one first thing before the traffic builds."

"And I pulled you away from that. I'm so sorry."

He kept hold of her hand, his sharp gaze darting over her. "No need to apologize. And how are *you* feeling this morning, my lady?"

Drat.

She mustered up a smile, hoping it didn't look as ghastly as she felt. From the uptick of his eyebrows, she'd obviously failed to impress.

"I'm perfectly fine." She gently tugged her hand away. "As I mentioned in my note, one of my servants suffered an injury. I'm terribly afraid that he's broken his ankle."

Anxiety shook her like a rattle. When she was a young girl, one of their neighbors had taken a tumble from his horse and broken his ankle. It had healed badly, and the poor man had forever been crippled by the injury.

If that were to happen to Donny, she would never forgive herself.

"And when did this happen?" Kendrick asked.

"Sometime in the early hours of the morning." She adopted an exasperated expression. "The foolish man didn't wish to bother anyone, so he waited until the kitchen maid was up before calling for help."

"Then let's get to it. If it is broken, then the sooner it's set, the better."

"If you'll follow me."

Kendrick retrieved his satchel, which he'd set by the door, and followed her out. "What is your servant's name?"

"Donny Broch. He's been with my husband's family for decades and has continued in my service. Donny accompanied my husband when he toured the Continent before our marriage, in fact. He's like family, and I doubt we could manage without him."

Now she was babbling, from nerves regarding the man pacing behind her or the fraught situation or both. Samantha felt entirely frazzled, which was not a helpful sensation when trying to keep her secret life from blowing up in her face.

Kendrick followed her down into the kitchen. "We also have staff that we regard as family," he said. "They've brought us through many a scrape, especially when my brothers and I were just rambunctious lads." He chuckled. "It's a miracle they've put up with us all these years."

"That is the Highland way, after all. On my father's estate, we were related by clan ties in some way or another to almost everyone who worked for us."

"I fancied I heard a brogue in your voice. You're a true Highlander, I ken."

"You ken correctly, Dr. Kendrick. My family is from Inverness-shire."

She led him through the long, narrow kitchen and past the bustling Mrs. Johnson to Donny's room, which was next to the stairs that led up to their garden. The location of the room allowed them to easily slip in and out of the house at night. That was imperative, both for avoiding notice from the neighbors and for keeping Felicity in the dark, as well.

Although the girl had some idea that efforts were afoot to track down Roger's killer—thus, her warning to be careful with Bathsheba—she had no idea that Samantha and Donny were the ones doing the searching.

She intended to keep it that way, too. As much as possible, she wanted Felicity to have a normal life, free from the burdens Samantha carried herself.

Now the searches would have to be curtailed. With Donny at her back, Samantha had never worried that she'd come to harm. They'd obviously grown overconfident, as last night had disastrously shown.

She opened the door and stuck in her head. "May we come in?"

Propped up on several pillows, Donny looked whey-faced and grim. He gave a terse nod.

Samantha's heart contracted with worry and guilt. He'd not uttered a word of complaint but was clearly in monumental pain.

She stepped aside to let Kendrick into the tidy room, where a large bed took up most of the space. Donny was a big, brawny man—a hulking oaf, he joked about himself. But he wasn't as young as he used to be, as the light filtering through the high window over the bed revealed. His red hair was shot through with gray, and deep wrinkles were carved across his broad forehead and around his mouth.

Her faithful companion was getting older, and she'd been too blasted selfish to notice before. Not that he would ever admit to what he would see as weakness. Donny was just as determined to find Roger's killers as she was.

Samantha squeezed past Kendrick to stand at the head of the bed.

The doctor glanced at her. "You needn't stay. I will give you a report when I'm finished."

"I'd like to stay, if you don't mind."

"Ye dinna have to, my lady," Donny said through clenched teeth. "I'll be foine."

She patted his shoulder. "Of course I'm staying."

That pat was as much a warning as a reassurance. Donny hadn't really had a half a bottle of whisky, but he had definitely imbibed a good amount. Between that and his exhausted state, he might stumble over his explanation. She intended to do as much of the talking as possible.

Kendrick's eyebrows had briefly ticked up at her declaration. It wasn't the done thing for ladies to sit in on examinations of male servants, so she knew how odd her insistence must seem.

"I'm not squeamish, if that's what worries you," she said.

His mouth twitched. "Good to know. Very well, then, Donny, I'm Dr. Kendrick."

"A pleasure to meet ye, sir."

Kendrick flashed a wry smile. "Probably not, under the circumstances, but I'll do my very best to make you comfortable. I understand that Lady Samantha fears you've broken your ankle?"

"Och, my lady worries too much. It's just a stupid sprain."

"Donny, you can barely walk. Getting you back from—" Samantha bit her lip. And she was the one worried about Donny blurting out the truth?

"Getting my stupid self back from the jakes," Donny quickly corrected. "Sorry, my lady."

She gave a weak smile. His intervention made sense, since proper ladies also weren't supposed to speak of such things as outhouses and necessaries.

Kendrick frowned. "You injured your ankle in the necessary?"

Of course, when he put it like that, it did sound ridiculous.

"Nae, on the way back. I was half asleep and stumbled on a flagstone. Went down hard on my ankle, clumsy oaf that I am."

"Very hard, if you broke it," Kendrick said. "But let's have a look."

As he folded back the covers at the foot of the bed, Mrs. Johnson appeared with a basin of steaming water and cloths.

"Just put them on the table, please," Samantha said.

The housekeeper placed them on the small side table, and then backed out. "I'll be in the kitchen, my lady."

Samantha gave her a distracted nod, too horrified by the sight of Donny's ankle to respond.

When she and Mrs. Johnson had gotten him into bed, they'd propped up his foot on pillows and wrapped his ankle in cloths wrung out in cold water and vinegar. Mrs. Johnson or Lucy, their kitchen maid who was Donny's niece, had been diligently changing them every thirty minutes since. But his ankle looked even more ghastly now than when they'd cut off his boot. The swelling was worse, and the gruesomely purple bruising had spread across the top of his foot.

Of course, she shouldn't be surprised, given how badly Donny had fallen while fighting off that nasty pair of foot-pads. The poltroons had surprised them, which was her fault. She'd been talking to Donny about a possible lead instead of paying close attention to her surroundings. When one of them had leapt out of a pitch-black alleyway and yanked her almost straight off her feet, Donny had turned to defend her. He'd clubbed her attacker with the butt of his pistol, but then stumbled on a broken cobblestone and gone down sideways, brutally turning over his ankle.

Fortunately, Samantha had quickly recovered her footing and slashed their other attacker with her blade, sending the pair scrambling away. Then she and brave Donny had to traverse a steep set of stairs and make their way to Grassmarket before they could find a hackney. God only knew how much damage had been inflicted on Donny's foot by having to walk that far on it.

Kendrick glanced over at her, frowning. "All right, Lady Samantha?"

"Yes. Perfectly fine."

"Tell me if you're not. I don't need you fainting on me."

As Samantha bristled, Kendrick ignored her as he washed his hands and turned back to Donny.

Bossy man.

However, he was obviously a competent one as he gently and skillfully examined Donny. When he probed the arch of the foot, Donny sucked in a harsh breath.

"I'm sorry—that's obviously very painful." Kendrick handed Donny a cloth to wipe his perspiring face.

"Obviously," Samantha responded. Then she winced. "Sorry."

Kendrick smiled at her. "Pain is actually a good sign. If his ankle was broken, Donny would more likely experience numbness and tingling rather than this degree of pain."

Donny emerged from behind the cloth, looking hopeful. "Oh, aye?"

"Aye. But I need to be sure, so that means I'm going to have to move your foot. It'll hurt like the devil, so feel free to yell."

Donny scoffed. "As if I would ever yell in front of my lady."

Samantha patted his shoulder again. "You go right ahead, dear."

Kendrick shot her another quick glance before returning his focus to his patient.

His hands probed the entire ankle and then the heel. "Does it hurt when I press on the bone?"

Donny shook his head.

"How about here?"

"Aye," Donny gasped.

"Can you wiggle your foot? Ah, excellent, thank you, Donny. Now, when you went down, did you hear a pop?"

Donny peered at him, apparently confused.

"What do you mean?" Samantha asked.

Kendrick straightened up. "With a ligament tear, there is often a popping sound. When one breaks a bone, it's more like a crack."

"Didn't hear nothin' at all," Donny said.

Since they'd been busy fighting for their lives, a cannon probably could have gone off and they wouldn't have noticed.

Kendrick stared down at the ankle, stroking his chin.

He has a very strong jawline.

Samantha closed her eyes. What in God's name was wrong with her?

"At what time did you fall?" Kendrick asked.

Donny frowned, as if thinking. "Before dawn. It was still full dark, ye ken."

"As I said, we didn't realize he'd hurt himself until our kitchen maid came to light the fire." Samantha wagged a finger at Donny. "You should have called for help immediately. I'm quite annoyed with you."

"Yes, my lady," he meekly replied.

Kendrick reached into his bag for a neatly coiled bandage and a small green bottle. "I suppose that explains it. If I didn't know better, I'd have thought you'd walked some distance with the injury."

Drat. Dr. Kendrick was clearly too clever by half.

"In case ye failed to notice, sir, I'm something of a lummox. I came down full weight on it."

Kendrick began to rub the contents of the bottle on Donny's ankle. "Yes, you're as big as some of my brothers."

"Ye'll be talkin' about Mr. Graeme and Mr. Grant, I reckon."

Kendrick looked surprised. "You know the twins?"

"Aye, sir. They were at university with the master. Good friends they became. My master was that sad when they, er, had to return home to Glasgow."

"You mean when they were kicked out for acting like idiots," Kendrick said in an amused tone.

"Roger was friendly with the Kendrick twins?" Samantha asked, astounded. "My Roger?"

"Aye. He thought they were a grand pair of fellows." Donny huffed out a chuckle. "Always cuttin' up larks, them two. But I never had to worry about the master when he was with Mr. Graeme and Mr. Grant. Even when they took him to the taverns in Old Town, I knew he'd be safe."

Samantha could feel her eyes bugging out. "Roger went to taverns in Old Town back then?"

"First time he could have a bit of real fun in his life, what with Lord Beath always fussin' over him. But Kendricks always look after their own, was what Mr. Graeme used to say, and I reckon they saw the master as one of their own. He never came to harm."

The idea of Samantha's gentle and eminently sensible husband cutting up larks with two of the biggest hellions to ever hit Edinburgh was mind-boggling.

Kendrick started wrapping Donny's ankle. "If my brothers considered your husband as one of their own, that practically makes us family, Lady Samantha."

For some unaccountable reason, his remark brought a flush to her cheeks.

"I don't think yer much like yer brothers, sir," Donny said.

"No, I was never the troublemaking sort," Kendrick replied with an easy smile.

Samantha couldn't help returning his smile. "You didn't cut up larks, or brawl your way across Edinburgh?"

"I had a difficult enough time just trying to live down my brothers' reputations," he wryly said. "Donny, hang on while I finish wrapping. This will hurt, I'm afraid."

The wrap didn't take long, but Donny looked on the verge of fainting by the end of it. Samantha felt another jab of guilt, straight to the heart. The poor fellow wasn't as young as he used to be. Wasn't it selfish of her to keep putting him in the line of fire?

"All finished," Kendrick said as he tied off the wrapping. "I'll cease torturing you now and let you get some sleep."

"Thank ye, sir," Donny faintly replied.

"Can you please let me know how to care for the injury?" Samantha asked.

Kendrick packed up his satchel. "I'll write up instructions and send them around with some additional liniment. Donny needs to stay off his feet, of course. If the pain is too bad, I can give you some laudanum drops—"

"No laudanum," she and Donny simultaneously exclaimed.

Kendrick looked startled. "I certainly won't force it on you."

Samantha had to repress the urge to blurt out an explanation.

"The bloody stuff curdles my stomach, Dr. Kendrick," Donny said. "I'll nae be wantin' to shoot the cat, ye understand."

"Yes, it can do that sometimes. Not everyone can tolerate the drug."

And some tolerate it all too well.

Samantha gestured to the door. "I'll show you out, sir."

If Kendrick was offended by her terse suggestion, his manners were too good to show it.

He smiled at Donny. "Stay off your feet, all right? I'll check in on you in a few days."

"Och, I'll be right as rain by then. Thank ye, and give my best wishes to yer brothers."

Kendrick allowed Samantha to show him out. It appeared she and Donny had managed to pull it off, with the good doctor none the wiser.

"Thank you so much, sir," she said, mustering a smile. "I'm sure you have a thousand things to do, and we mustn't keep you any longer."

He remained where he was, calmly studying her. "Actually, Lady Samantha, I would like to speak with you before I leave."

Samantha glanced around the kitchen, where Lucy kneaded bread and Mrs. Johnson lurked by the stove. Both were unsuccessfully pretending not to listen.

"Oh? About what?" Samantha faintly asked.

"It might be best if we speak in private."

CHAPTER 9

Samantha stared at Kendrick as her fatigue-fogged brain tried to formulate a rational refusal. Sadly, nothing came to mind.

"I simply wish to ask you a few questions about the orphanage," he said after a few moments. "I'd also like you to sit and rest while I take your pulse. I'm concerned about you, my lady."

"I'm in the pink of health," she finally managed, flapping a hand. "No need to—"

He snagged her wrist. "Fine, I can take it while you're standing."

"What? No," she squawked, sounding like an outraged chicken. "There is no need—"

"Hush, please." He deftly turned her wrist up and pressed the tips of his fingers onto her pulse.

Samantha cast a desperate gaze toward Mrs. Johnson. For once, though, her housekeeper failed to take the hint, as she made a show of setting up a tea tray and arranging the cups. As for Lucy, she ducked her head as she tried to hide a smirk.

"Bloody traitors," Samantha muttered.

"Just a few moments longer," Kendrick quietly said.

Fuming, she held still, deciding she might as well let him get on with it.

But as she stood there, his long fingers gently holding her wrist, and his head bowed as he silently counted, she felt her heart and her irritation begin to settle. The warmth of the kitchen, the smell of baking bread, and Kendrick's calm presence gentled her nerves. For a few moments, all seemed . . . peaceful.

"That's better," he said as he released her. "Your pulse was too rapid for a few moments."

"I'm sure it was just because I'm worried about Donny."

"Donny will be fine. You, however, could use a good cup of tea and a wee sit-down."

"I will be sure to—"

He turned to the housekeeper. "Mrs. Johnson, is that tea for Lady Samantha?"

"Aye, and for ye as well, if ye'd like a cup."

Behind his back Samantha frantically signaled *no*, but Mrs. Johnson steadfastly ignored her.

"I would love a cup," Kendrick replied. "Thank you."

By the time he turned back to her, Samantha had whipped her hands down to her sides, trying to appear as if she hadn't just been flapping her arms like a goose about to take flight.

"My lady, shall I bring the tea tray up to the main drawing room?" prompted Mrs. Johnson.

Samantha concluded that it was best to act normally and have a blasted cup of tea with the blasted doctor. Putting him off would send the message that she was trying to dodge the conversation.

"Yes, that will be fine." She nodded at Kendrick. "If you'll follow me."

"Thank you."

She couldn't fail to notice the glint of amusement in his deep, green gaze.

Stalking up the kitchen stairs, she didn't hear him follow, so she glanced over her shoulder. And stumbled on the step, because he was only inches behind her.

Lightning quick, he grabbed her waist. "Careful, lass. Don't want you breaking your noggin."

Suddenly, he lifted her straight up and over the top step before settling her back down on the hallway carpet. Not only was he uncannily quiet, but strong, too. If her pulse had been rapid before, now it was racing like deerhound.

"Ahem," she said, clearing her throat as she gathered her wits. "Is noggin the technical term, Dr. Kendrick?"

"Only in the Highlands," he replied with a roguish smile.

For a man who was nothing like his scapegrace older brothers, the good doctor had apparently inherited his share of the notorious Kendrick charm.

Ignoring a prickle of heat under her stays, Samantha marched into the drawing room and waved him to one of the wingchairs. She took a seat on the chaise as Mrs. Johnson bustled in, setting the tea tray on the table between them. The housekeeper set out the cups, gave Samantha a surreptitious wink, and then swiftly retreated.

Clearly, Dr. Kendrick had won the female staff's approval, which Samantha supposed wasn't surprising. She, however, was entirely immune to his handsome features and charming smiles.

There was certainly no reason to be nervous, she told herself as she prepared his tea. In the last year, she had faced down more tricky situations than she could count. If she couldn't manage a mild-mannered doctor, then surely it was time to hang up her disguise and her blade and go back to a life of quiet widowhood.

That clarity lasted until she glanced up to meet his gaze and very nearly lost her grip on the cup. Kendrick studied her with an almost unnerving intensity, his gaze seeming to strip away any pretense, as if he could burrow deep inside and find all her secrets. Even more disturbing, his perusal made her intensely aware of herself as a woman, most particularly as one sitting alone in a room with a very attractive man.

For several long moments, all she could do was stare back as the prickle under her stays turned into a full body flush of heat.

He frowned. "Lady Samantha, you're beginning to worry me. Are you sure you're feeling perfectly well?"

She forced herself to rally. "Goodness, yes, I'm fine. Please don't worry."

"That's what doctors are paid to do. Worry about our patients."

"I'm not one of your patients," she corrected.

"No, but you're John's patient, and I cover for him when he's away. He'd take me out behind the woodshed if I failed to take care of one of his favorite patients. Ergo, you are my worry."

She had to smile at the ridiculous image. "You are an incredibly stubborn man, sir. Has anyone ever told you that?"

"Frequently."

"Well, there's no need to be stubborn on my account," she said, handing him a cup. "I will admit to feeling pulled about the edges these days, but it's nothing that a good night's sleep won't fix."

"John has mentioned that you carry a great deal of responsibility at the foundation."

"I do, but the work is important. It's also what my husband would have wished me to do," she quietly added.

Kendrick's gaze warmed with understanding and sympathy. At least she hoped it was sympathy and not pity. She'd had more than enough pity to last a lifetime.

"I'm sure your husband would be very proud of you."

Her throat went tight. "I hope so."

"From what I've heard, I suspect your husband would not wish you to wear yourself to the bone, either."

Roger certainly wouldn't want me hunting killers in Old Town.

Samantha ignored that massively inconvenient thought. Too bad she couldn't ignore nosy Dr. Kendrick.

Do you really want to ignore him?

Another massively inconvenient thought.

"What my husband would wish is my determination to make," she brusquely said. "Now, how can I be of service to you?"

He smiled, clearly impervious to snubs. "The opposite, actually. I was wondering how I might be of assistance to *you*."

She frowned. "I don't understand."

"John mentioned before he left town yesterday that another boy has disappeared from the orphanage. He was dismayed that his trip would leave you without any support in that matter and wished me to follow up with you. I had planned on sending round a note to you later today."

Yes, another boy had gone missing, and it was incredibly distressing.

Also distressing was the fact that John remained convinced that she was searching for the missing children, and that she would step up those efforts in light of this new disappearance. He was right on both counts, of course. Why else would he put Kendrick on her trail?

Her heart suddenly seized at the thought that John might have revealed his suspicions about her to Kendrick. Would John truly betray her in that way?

She carefully chose her words. "Yes, the situation is most upsetting. What else did John tell you?"

He leaned forward, resting his forearms on his thighs. "According to John, none of the disappearances make sense. They were all biddable lads who seemed happy."

She breathed out a shaky sigh of relief that John had not betrayed her. "He's correct. I know those boys, and they were perfectly content. It beggars belief that they would wish to return to their former lives."

"How long has this been going on?"

"It's hard to give a specific date. There were a few who disappeared in the months before my husband died. He was beginning to feel concerned but only mentioned it to me a few times. That was before I sat on the board, so I wasn't privy to many details."

Kendrick looked startled. "It was that far back, and yet no one on the board besides you and John is concerned about it?"

She wrinkled her nose. "Hard to believe, isn't it? With the exception of Arthur Baines, they're as hardheaded and old-fashioned as one can imagine. They are very much of the spare the rod and spoil the child mentality."

"Yes, they seem a dreary lot. I can't imagine how you manage them."

She glanced down at her teacup. "It's been an uphill battle since Roger died. There was quite a lot of slippage right after his death. Unfortunately, I was not in a . . . a proper state of mind to deal with the foundation until several months later."

Those bleak, blank months had felt like she was standing on the edge of a precipice, facing nothing but an empty, howling wind. Most days, she'd been too weak to even get out of bed.

He leaned forward, forcing her to meet his gaze. "Grief is a tremendous challenge, both physically and mentally. You cannot blame yourself, my lady."

For just a brief moment, she found herself back on the edge of that precipice. "It's hard not to," she whispered.

He reached over and took her teacup, placing it on the table. Then he took her hand in a firm, warm grip. Samantha couldn't help but notice that he had fine hands. Long-fingered, strong, and slightly calloused, they were hands of a man who worked hard and knew what he was about. His very touch seemed to pull her back to herself.

"As your doctor, I forbid it," he said. "No blaming allowed."

Samantha let out a watery laugh. "Are you going to write a prescription to that effect?"

"If I must."

He held her gaze for a moment longer before releasing her

fingers. She felt strangely off-kilter, as if she'd lose her balance without his steadying grip.

"So, it sounds like boys have been going missing for at least two years," he said.

She nodded, grateful for a return to the business at hand. "Once I took up my position on the board, I checked the records."

"How many?"

"Twelve, in all."

"All about the same age?"

"The first three boys were older, thirteen and over." She opened her hands. "Old enough to begin champing at the bit. At that age, running with a gang might seem more exciting than apprenticing or going into service."

"But the others were younger."

"All under the age of eight." It made her ill just thinking about it.

"And there have been no formal attempts to investigate?"

"John and Arthur thoroughly questioned the staff. Arthur even talked to his contacts among the police to see if they had any information about new gangs recruiting children, that sort of thing. Unfortunately, nothing turned up."

"That Baines supports you was very evident at the board meeting," he said in an oddly flat tone.

"Arthur was my husband's dear friend, as well as his barrister. He helped Roger set up the foundation. And . . . and he was very good to me after Roger died."

"I'm glad to hear you had such steadfast support."

For some reason, she felt compelled to explain. "Roger's grandfather, Lord Beath, wished to shut down the foundation. He also insisted that Roger's sister, who lived with us, return with him to his country estate. Felicity and her grandfather do not get on, so Arthur convinced Lord Beath to leave the foundation untouched and to return Felicity to my care."

He frowned. "Why would Lord Beath wish to shut down the foundation?"

"Because he's a nasty old . . ."

"Twiddlepoop?" he supplied.

"I was about to say bastard," she confessed.

When he laughed, she suddenly felt quite a bit better. Talking about those months after Roger's death was always difficult. But Kendrick seemed to take the conversation—and her—in stride, with an easy empathy that was enormously appealing. That also meant that she needed to have a care. She couldn't afford to trust him, no matter how kind and sympathetic he might be.

Not to mention handsome, competent, and strong.

She mentally scowled at her stupid self before carrying on. "But Lord Beath has nothing to do with this particular issue. The board is the roadblock in this case."

"Have you ever thought about hiring an inquiry agent to investigate?"

The question caught her off-guard. The reality was, she and Donny were acting in that capacity. Samantha knew beyond doubt that they would do a better job of searching for the missing children *and* hunting for Roger's killers.

"Lady Samantha?" Kendrick prompted.

"Oh, sorry. Arthur has also used his connections in the legal community to make enquiries. Unfortunately, they've not born fruit. Of course, we hear rumors about gangs who recruit children, but nothing has come of them, I'm afraid."

Kendrick looked thoughtful. "Several years back, one of my brothers rescued a pair of children from a gang."

That piqued her curiosity. "Really? How did he manage it?"

He waggled a hand. "Very carefully. Lady Samantha, with your permission, I'd like to write my brother for his opinion." He flashed a brief smile. "Graeme was an inquiry agent for some years, and a very good one."

Oh, blast.

The last thing she needed was a professional man poking about. Still, to refuse would likely sound downright suspicious.

"Of course, doctor. I would be most grateful." She made a point of glancing at the ormolu clock on the mantel. "Now, if you will ex—"

When the door opened and Felicity hurried into the room, Samantha all but bit her tongue. Could this morning get worse?

Mrs. Johnson followed hard on the girl's heels, looking grim. "I'm sorry, my lady, but Miss Felicity heard that the doctor was here, and she wondered if he could look at Hercules."

In other words, Felicity had slipped past Mrs. Johnson's guard.

Felicity lugged her big gray cat over to Kendrick. Hercules was probably the most ill-tempered feline in Edinburgh, but he'd been a present from Roger, and Felicity adored the old grump. For her sake, the entire household ignored scratched furniture, ripped upholstery, and the occasional dead bird Hercules proudly brought into the house.

Normally, Samantha would do anything to soothe Felicity's worries, but this situation had the makings of an epic disaster.

When Kendrick stood and gave Felicity a warm smile, the girl gave him a quick, head-to-toe perusal before carefully depositing the cat at his feet. Looking at Samantha, she tapped her right fist on her left palm, and then pointed at Kendrick.

Can he help?

The doctor's gaze flickered over to Samantha and then back to Felicity.

A fraught silence settled over the room. Felicity tapped her foot, impatient for an answer, while Kendrick waited patiently for someone to do something.

Meanwhile, Samantha once again found herself trying to think through a panicky, exhausted haze.

Felicity tapped two fingers to her lips and then mouthed a word. *Please?*

Samantha mentally shook herself. There was nothing to do but play it out, and hope Kendrick didn't make the connection.

She dredged up a smile. "Dr. Kendrick, this is my sister-in-law, Miss Felicity Penwith."

Felicity mustered an awkward curtsy, while Kendrick executed a faultless bow.

"It is a pleasure to meet you," he said, speaking clearly to Felicity.

The girl shyly smiled and waved hello.

Kendrick returned the smile and touched a finger to the side of his mouth. "Do you read lips?"

Felicity nodded.

Hell and damnation.

Of *course* he would know to ask that question. As a friend of the Blackmores, he would know Bathsheba's sister, Rachel, who was also deaf.

Samantha's stomach pitched like a boat in a storm. The blasted man would obviously be familiar with sign language and might very well have seen her signing with Donny that night in the slums. At this point, she could only hope that it had been too dark for Kendrick to notice.

Play the hand you're dealt.

"As you can see," Samantha said with an apologetic smile, "Hercules has injured himself, and Felicity is quite worried about him. She wonders if you might look at his paw. I know it's a lot to ask, but—"

He held up a hand to interrupt, smiling. "My grandfather

regularly employs me to care for his extremely decrepit terrier. I'm sure this old fellow can't be any worse."

"You don't know Hercules," Samantha said with a sigh.

"Let's have a look, shall we?"

He crouched down in front of the cat. Hercules stared at him, his expression especially annoyed, his tail twitching ominously.

"Och, laddie," Kendrick murmured in a warm brogue as he gently scratched the cat's head. "Ye hurt yer wee paw, did ye?"

Samantha held her breath. Hercules had been known to bite when annoyed, and today he was very annoyed.

Astonishingly, his tail stopped twitching and he actually started to purr.

"Good Lord," she said.

Felicity lowered herself onto the floor next to her pet. She pointed to his right paw, and then waved her hand over it.

Kendrick nodded. "How did he cut it?"

Felicity lifted her hands as if opening a window, and then wiggled two of her fingers.

Samantha sighed. "Apparently, Hercules made an outside foray and came back injured." She leaned down to meet her sister's gaze. "He is a house cat, not a street cat."

Felicity shrugged.

"Cats don't like to be confined, especially not the male of the species," Kendrick said as he ducked his head to inspect the paw.

"Aye, just like a man," Mrs. Johnson said in a snort. "Always gettin' up to trouble."

Samantha shot her housekeeper a disbelieving look. The situation was now officially beyond ridiculous.

Felicity held out her left arm and then rolled her other hand over it. Kendrick looked at Samantha.

"She wants to know if you can bandage it," she explained.

"Most certainly. Mrs. Johnson, would you fetch my satchel?"

"Aye, Dr. Kendrick."

Samantha held her breath when he lifted the injured paw to examine it. When Hercules simply kept purring, she couldn't believe it. Only a few weeks ago, the blasted cat had bit her when she'd tried to remove a thistle from his fur.

"Would ye look at that," Mrs. Johnson murmured as she shot Samantha a little grin. "Yer a miracle worker, sir."

Clearly, all the females in the house had lost their minds over the handsome doctor Kendrick.

"More a scrape than a cut." Kendrick smiled at Felicity. "Someone did an excellent job of cleaning his paw."

When the girl beamed and tapped her chest, he grinned and gave her a thumb's up. Clearly, they had no trouble communicating. That was quite . . . wonderful.

He's wonderful.

Samantha simply had to stop thinking like an idiot when it came to the good doctor.

He applied some tincture to the wound, with Felicity keeping a firm hold on the cat just in case, and then deftly wrapped a small bandage around the paw, tying it off. He gave Hercules another pat on the head before uncoiling himself and rising with easy, masculine grace.

"Well done, Miss Felicity," he said as he helped the girl to her feet. "You make an excellent assistant."

She touched her fingers to her lips and mouthed *thank you.*

"You're welcome."

Samantha touched her sister's arm and looked toward the door. Felicity grimaced, circling her fist in front of her chest. *Sorry.*

"It's fine," Samantha replied. "Take Hercules upstairs. I'll be up soon."

The girl hoisted the cat in her arms and shyly smiled at the doctor.

"It was a pleasure to meet you," he said.

She dipped an endearingly lopsided curtsy and carried her beastly beast from the room.

Kendrick stared thoughtfully after her, waiting for Mrs. Johnson to close the door. Then he looked at Samantha.

"I'm assuming your sister's condition is the reason for Lord Beath's poor behavior to her?"

When she blinked, he turned up his hands.

"Sorry," he said. "I am sometimes much too blunt."

Samantha waved a hand. "It's actually rather nice, not having to pretend. And you assume correctly. Lord Beath finds my sister-in-law's condition distasteful."

"That is entirely moronic."

She choked out a surprised laugh. "I certainly wouldn't disagree."

"Was Miss Felicity born deaf?"

"She contracted a raging fever when she was three and lost her hearing. Her parents, who were alive at the time, kept her confined to the country. They were ashamed of her, you see." Then she paused, embarrassed to have blurted out such private details. "I'm sorry. I don't know why I'm telling you all this."

He shrugged. "It's because I'm a doctor. People tend to tell us everything."

"That sounds rather awful."

"We do learn to keep secrets."

"Oh, uh, that's good."

Ninny.

"So, Lord Beath would rather she remain in the country," he said as he finished packing up his satchel. "That's why he took her with him after your husband's death."

She grimaced. Despite his matter-of-fact attitude, it was still embarrassing to reveal the family's dirty laundry.

"I'm sorry," he quietly said. "That must have been very difficult."

For a long moment, they stared at each other. Samantha found herself again transfixed by his gaze. Time seemed to slow, and a sensation she'd not felt in a long time stole over her.

Peace.

Then his gaze flickered, as if an unwelcome thought had intruded. He turned back to his satchel, fastening the buckle before hoisting the bag to his shoulder.

"But your sister is back with you, and is clearly flourishing," he said in his professional man's voice. "You are to be commended, my lady. Well done."

The rapid change in his manner was disorienting—and annoying. The dratted man had succeeded in throwing her off balance again.

"Goodness, look how late it's become," she said. "Dr. Kendrick, we've certainly taken up more than enough of your precious time. Do be sure to include any costs for Hercules when you send me your bill."

He returned a polite smile. "Not to worry, my lady. Pets come free."

As he opened the door to the hall, he glanced over his shoulder. "If Donny has any problems before John gets back into town, please send for me. I am at your service, Lady Samantha."

"Oh, I'm quite sure that won't be necessary. But thank you."

He gave her a friendly nod and took his leave.

Samantha collapsed onto the chaise. Now that the crisis had passed, she could acknowledge the beginnings of the very nasty headache that was going to soon take hold like a crown of iron thorns. This had been a morning from hell, one she would very happily forget.

Not forget him, though.

And wasn't that a problem she didn't need? Liking Kendrick meant she was letting him get too close. And if he got too close, then he could burrow his way into her secrets, endangering everything.

Including your heart.

She would never take that risk again.

CHAPTER 10

"Mrs. Blackmore is expecting ye, sir," said the housemaid before she took Braden's coat and hat. "She thought ye'd be callin' on yer way home from work."

So, Bathsheba and John must harbor the very same suspicions about the fair Lady Samantha that Braden had been mulling over all day. He'd be willing to wager his best scalpel that he'd been the one to twig John to the situation in the first place, albeit unwittingly. That morning after his attack in Old Town, when Braden had described the mysterious couple and their use of sign language to John, it was no wonder his friend had acted so oddly. John had obviously deduced that Samantha and Donny perfectly fit the profiles.

That also explained John's alarmed reaction to Samantha's offer to volunteer at Braden's free clinic. Clearly, her ladyship was up to something, and it was something that John didn't approve of.

Well, Braden didn't approve of the way he'd been moved about like a pawn on a chessboard, both by his old friends and Lady Samantha. It was time for answers, and he knew Bathsheba would be more forthcoming than her irritatingly close-mouthed husband. After all, she'd been the one to send

Braden to the Penwith household this morning, knowing he would put the pieces together.

Braden followed the maid up the narrow staircase to the first floor. Although not large, the Blackmores' townhouse was elegantly appointed and in the best neighborhood in New Town. It was directly across from the Queen Street Gardens and was only a short carriage ride to the medical college.

The maid gave a quick tap on the drawing room door before opening it. "Dr. Kendrick is here, ma'am."

Bathsheba, seated in an overstuffed armchair by the fireplace, looked up from her book with a smile. "Finally. I was about to give up on you."

She rose and put the book aside, greeting Braden with an extended hand.

"And if I hadn't shown up on your doorstep?" he asked.

"I would have tracked you down at Heriot Row. I've been in a fever of impatience all day."

Not only was she suspicious, but worried, too. Braden had to admit he was as well.

Bathsheba dismissed the maid and then crossed to a brass drinks trolley tucked between a set of bow windows. "What can I get you, dear boy? I know it's been a long day."

"Since John keeps a supply of Graeme's excellent whisky on hand, I'll have a glass of that."

Bathsheba splashed a dram into a crystal tumbler and poured herself a sherry.

"I must admit that I've finally acquired a taste for the stuff," she said, carrying the drinks over to the cozy seating arrangement in front of the fireplace. "But too much and I'm snoring away like an old granny."

"No one could mistake you for a granny, even if you were snoring."

"Too kind," she said in a wry tone. "Now, sit. You must be exhausted."

"No, although I did have an early start to the day, thanks to you," he said with a smile.

Bathsheba wrinkled her nose. "Sorry, but I knew John would have wished for you to take the call."

"You too, I suspect."

"*Moi?*" she replied with exaggerated surprise as she handed him the whisky.

He settled into the other armchair. "Yer a cheeky lass, ye ken."

Bathsheba daintily scoffed as she resumed her seat, her wide skirts belling around her. As always, the lovely Mrs. Blackmore was dressed bang-up to the mark. But even more than her appearance, it was her incisive mind and sharp wit that made her so attractive. If not for the fact that he was perfectly happy with his bachelor status, Braden might even be jealous of John's domestic bliss. As it was, he considered himself fortunate to have the Blackmores as good and true friends.

"How is little Mary? Will I be seeing her today?"

"My daughter is spending the afternoon with friends. I wanted to make sure we had the chance for a full discussion of the problem without being interrupted."

Braden shook his head. "I was hoping my suspicions were far-fetched, but I suppose that was too much to ask for."

"Sadly, yes. That's why I asked you to attend the call. I knew you would keep your counsel and not pester Samantha with questions. But, first, tell me how Donny fares. Is he much injured?"

"A badly sprained ankle and possibly a small tear in the ligament, but nothing that won't mend. He'll have to stay off the foot at least for a few weeks, if not longer."

Bathsheba grimaced. "Hmm. That's likely to be a problem."

"And why is that?"

"Because Donny goes everywhere with Samantha. He watches over her."

"You mean like a bodyguard?"

"Exactly like that."

Bathsheba absently tapped the stem of her wineglass, deep in thought. Braden guessed that she was trying to decide which details to share with him. After all, a woman's reputation was at stake, as well as the loyalty one friend owed to another. Braden had little doubt that Lady Samantha would be appalled to know that he and Bathsheba were about to discuss what could laughably be described as a very delicate matter.

"What do you know about Roger Penwith's death?" she asked.

"Very little, but for the fact that he was killed during a robbery attempt."

Bathsheba shook her head. "It wasn't a robbery attempt."

He frowned. "That's the common understanding, though. And how would one know? I don't believe there were any witnesses."

"No, unfortunately. The murder occurred in one of those dreary little alleys off Westbow. So it was quite deserted."

The wynds and laneways of Old Town could be like the depths of Hell after nightfall, with only the dim lights from tenement windows to break up the gloom. Taking the alleys or the staircases after dark was a risky venture at best.

"What was Penwith doing in that part of town at night by himself and unarmed?"

She arched an ironic brow. "Oh, like some doctors we know?"

"Trust me, lesson learned."

"I'm relieved to hear it. Unfortunately, poor Roger was not given the opportunity to learn that lesson. He'd been working late at the orphanage and for some reason decided to walk home instead of taking a hackney. He was shot not far from the orphanage, but his body was not found until a few hours later."

Braden surveyed his mental map of Old Town.

"I suppose he could have been taking a shortcut up the hill. Seems rather foolish, though."

Bathsheba nodded. "And Roger was not a foolish man. Samantha has always maintained that he would never take such a risk."

"Perhaps he encountered his assailants closer to the orphanage, and they forced him up into the wynd."

"That's what the authorities claimed—that he was dragged up into the wynd, robbed, and then murdered."

"It's a reasonable explanation."

Bathsheba chopped down an impatient hand. "If it was only a robbery, why would only a small change purse—which contained but a few guineas—have been taken? He was wearing an heirloom signet ring and carried a very fine gold watch, but they were untouched. Surely you know how unusual it would be to leave those, especially the watch."

Thieves were drawn to watches, particularly gold ones. They could fetch a substantial sum at pawnbrokers or resellers.

"Why then was it labeled a robbery in the first place?" he asked.

"Probably because it was the easiest explanation," Bathsheba sardonically said. "And because Lord Beath, although truly grief stricken, hates scandal. Roger's murder caused a great deal of gossip, some of it rather salacious since it happened in Old Town. When no suspects were found after a few weeks, Beath used his influence to have the case closed. Arthur Baines argued for a more thorough investigation, but he was overruled."

Braden again felt a stab of jealousy that Baines was so intimately connected to Lady Samantha's life. Irritated with himself, he took a healthy swallow of whisky before continuing.

"So, Beath squashed any investigations into what was

clearly a suspicious death. Surely Lady Samantha must have objected."

Bathsheba breathed out a weary sigh. "Roger's death had a dire effect on her. She was ill for quite some time."

"She did make a vague reference to that but gave no details."

"Samantha was with child, about five months into her pregnancy. The shock caused her to have a miscarriage."

God.

To lose both her husband *and* her baby would be gutting. Braden's family had weathered similar tragedies, sometimes just barely. They generated emotional riptides that could sweep through a life, leaving devastating consequences in their wake.

He shook his head. "No wonder she didn't wish to speak of it."

"People knew she was pregnant, of course, so I'm not truly revealing any confidences. Samantha doesn't speak of it now, but it took her months to recover."

"I am indeed sorry for her loss," Braden quietly replied.

"So you see that she was in no condition to do anything after the murder. It was touch and go, according to John. He is of the opinion that Samantha was not well cared for in the aftermath."

Braden frowned. "He wasn't her doctor?"

"Not at first. John had only met Roger a few months before his death. Beath's physician, Dr. Lane, attended Samantha."

"That quack? He probably used leeches on her." The notion of his poor, wee lass under the care of such a fool made his gut twist with anger.

"I can't really say," she vaguely replied.

Her odd response suggested that Bathsheba was holding something back. "She seems healthy now, though," Braden said.

After all, she was running about the stews at night, slicing up villains with her blade.

"Thanks to John—and to Arthur Baines. Given his friendship with Roger, Arthur felt responsible for Samantha. When he learned of her poor condition, he overruled Lord Beath and immediately sent for John." She gave a quick smile. "Arthur can be quite forceful, despite his rather jaded persona."

Braden had thought the man an arrogant prat, one not inclined to exert much energy on anyone but himself. Apparently, it was not so.

"Well done for him. Lady Samantha is fortunate to have such a loyal friend."

A sudden twinkle lurked in Bathsheba's gaze. "Not to worry. She has no interest in Arthur Baines, and he apparently has no interest in her other than as a friend. He's probably been a bachelor for too long, like some other people I know."

Braden ignored her teasing jab. "Lady Samantha's safety is what I'm concerned with, at the moment."

Her amusement vanished. "You're correct, of course. And I don't mean to make light of a very serious situation. John and I are worried about Samantha. He believes she's become obsessed with avenging Roger's death, and that this obsession will lead her into a dangerous place."

"Like a deserted alley in Old Town, on a dark night?" he grimly replied.

"Exactly. And now there's the added complication of the disappearing children. Clearly, she and Donny are looking for them as well." She held up a hand. "By the way, what story did they concoct to explain his injury?"

"He tripped on the way back from the necessary," he dryly replied.

"How nonsensical."

"Bathsheba, how long have they been engaged in this quest for justice?"

"The searching? John thinks for at least a year, after Samantha was unable to convince anyone that Roger's death was not a random happening."

"Does she have any idea why someone would want to murder Penwith?"

"Only in a very general sense. Samantha told John that her husband was concerned about something in the last few weeks before his death. Apparently, Roger was vague whenever she asked him about it. She thinks he didn't wish to upset her."

"Because she was pregnant."

Bathsheba nodded. "Yes. However, Samantha has now come to believe that the issue was somehow related to the foundation. But John can find nothing wrong, and he has looked through all the accounts and the foundation's paperwork. If it's there, he's not seeing it."

"But there is a problem. Boys are disappearing."

She grimaced. "Well, yes. But that doesn't seem to be connected to Roger's murder. How could it?"

Braden had no idea, and he wouldn't until he did some digging.

Bathsheba waved a hand in front of his face. "Are you still with me?"

"Sorry, I was just thinking."

"About what?"

"A number of things, including the fact that Lady Samantha and Donny have been exposing themselves to danger. Obviously, something went seriously wrong last night, and it cannot be allowed to continue."

"Yes, it's incredibly . . ."

"Reckless," he finished.

"Agreed. By the way, how did you figure out that Samantha was your mysterious lady? I certainly didn't give you any indication."

"Felicity came into the drawing room." Braden flashed a brief smile. "Her cat had injured his paw, and she wished me to fix it."

"Ah. And how did Samantha respond?"

"She was not best pleased."

"I imagine not," Bathsheba wryly replied. "What did you do?"

"I pretended that I was too stupid to make the obvious connections and went about my business treating the cat."

"And Samantha believed you?" Bathsheba skeptically asked.

"I think so. It was very dark in the alley that night, when she and Donny rescued me. She probably thought I didn't notice them signing."

"I almost wish you'd confronted her on the spot. It's all become much too dangerous."

"She would have surely denied it. And making those sorts of accusations would certainly not prompt her to trust me."

She wrinkled her nose. "I'm afraid she doesn't trust anyone outside of her own household. Well, Felicity doesn't know, of course, but I'm sure the rest of her household are loyal accomplices."

"Good God. Why the hell doesn't she just hire an inquiry agent?"

"John suggested just that, but she refused. She's afraid of Lord Beath, you see. If he found out, he would take Felicity away again."

"If Beath finds out she's roaming the stews exacting vigilante justice, he'll probably try to lock her up," Braden tartly replied.

"But you know what happens when one is seeking justice on behalf of a loved one. It's hard to leave the matter to someone else—especially when everyone has failed you."

"I cannot believe she doesn't trust you and John."

"Not enough to share her secrets. Besides, do you really think John wouldn't try to stop her if he could? The stubborn girl simply ignores him."

"But I take it *I'm* expected to stop her," Braden sardonically replied.

Bathsheba held both hands up, as if to say, *of course.*

"And how am I supposed to do this?"

"You're a Kendrick. You'll figure it out."

"Naturally, I'm flattered by your confidence in me," he retorted.

Frustrated, he stood and began to pace. Why the *hell* were women so damn stubborn when it came to their own safety?

"Braden, she needs help," Bathsheba quietly said after a minute or so.

"I'm aware."

"So, what do you plan to do?"

"Frankly, I haven't a bloody clue."

He'd figure it out, though. The lass had saved his life, and now it looked like he might have to be the saving of hers.

CHAPTER 11

Mrs. Culp leaned into Braden's cramped little office. "I'll just finish cleaning up for the day, sir. Unless ye have something else needs doing?"

Braden glanced at the clock, surprised to see how late it was.

It had been an extremely busy few days with his patients, both at the clinic and at the Royal Infirmary. He'd also spent a chunk of the last two nights lurking like a footpad outside Samantha's townhouse. Though she was an intelligent woman and he didn't think she'd venture into Old Town without Donny, he'd decided not to take the risk. Grief coupled with a desire for justice could often turn to vengeance. And a need for vengeance could override any sense of caution.

So far, Samantha's caution had won the day.

"Whatever you have left," Braden said, "you can leave it for tomorrow. You've had a long enough day as it is, Mrs. Culp."

"It'll take just a wee minute. And yer day's been longer, I reckon."

He flashed her a wry smile. "I don't know what I would do without you. You are a treasure."

She snorted. "You'll nae be getting around me with yer pretty words, because I'll be giving ye a lecture. Ye've been working too late these last few weeks, and I'll not have it. Yer wearing yerself to the bone, Dr. Kendrick. It canna go on like this."

Braden took off his spectacles and rubbed his eyes, then stretched his arms out to the side. His cubbyhole office was so tight that his fingers brushed the bookshelf shoved up against his desk. He desperately needed a larger space for his growing roster of patients.

It would soon be time to hit up his brothers for additional funding, a chore he dreaded. Not because they begrudged him the money. Nick and Logan would build him a hospital, if he wanted it. But they'd already supported him in so many ways, Nick especially. He'd always given Braden everything he needed to achieve his dream even in those dark days when the family had staggered from one crisis to the next. More than anything, Braden wanted to give back to his family, to make them as proud of him as he was of them.

They would all protest at that, of course, and insist they couldn't be prouder of him. But his brothers were all larger than life—successful in their work and with happy marriages and thriving families. While Kade wasn't married, he was fast becoming the toast of the musical world, his light shining ever brighter in that sphere.

Braden's professional life was a worthy one, and he was proud of it. But there was so much misery and want surrounding him, and he barely made a dent in it. He needed to do much more, so he'd again ask Nick and Logan for help because he couldn't let his stupid pride get in the way of the work that had to be done.

"Dr. Kendrick, are ye listening?" Mrs. Culp asked with some asperity.

He slipped his spectacles into his pocket and stood. "I always listen to you. I'm afraid you'll box my ears if I don't."

"As if I would ever do such a thing," she huffed. "But I *will* send a note around to yer sister-in-law, telling her that yer working too hard."

He smiled. "Not to worry. I already received a scolding on the very same subject from my grandfather."

Over breakfast, Angus had delivered a lecture about choosing work over family and neglecting *the kith and kin of his bosom, the nearest and dearest to his heart.* Braden had thought it more than slightly redundant and had made the mistake of saying so. An Angus eruption had resulted, one that required Kade's intervention to calm the old fellow down. Braden had finally managed to make his escape, but not before Kade had stopped him on the way out and made him promise to spend some time with their grandfather.

"He's not getting any younger," his brother had said. "Grandda won't be with us forever, you know. And he does miss us."

Braden had then spent the rest of the day feeling guilty about his family, piling yet another problem on his plate.

"Good for yer grandda," Mrs. Culp said. "Ye have circles under yer eyes as big as coins. Not enough sleep, for certain."

Well, holding surveillance on a woman's house did cut into one's sleeping time. Braden was now convinced, though, that Lady Samantha had the good sense not to venture out without Donny. So tonight he would finally get some much-needed rest.

"I'll be on my way home soon," he said with a reassuring smile, "and you should be off, too. I'll lock up."

Mrs. Culp snapped her fingers. "I'm that woolly in the head that I almost forgot. This note came earlier, while ye were with that last patient."

When she pulled a cream-colored envelope from the pocket of her apron, Braden recognized the elegant scrawl as belonging to Bathsheba. He tore it open and scanned the note.

"Dammit to hell," he muttered.

Mrs. Culp sighed. "I'm thinking ye'll nae be getting that extra sleep now, after all."

Braden slipped the note into his pocket. "Probably not."

"Anything I can help with, sir?"

Why not tell her? After all, born and bred in Old Town, few knew it better than Mrs. Culp.

"It's from Mrs. Blackmore. One of the girls who attends school at the Penwith Charitable Foundation has disappeared. When the staff followed up with her relatives, they claimed they hadn't seen her in a week. Needless to say, Mrs. Blackmore is quite concerned, and since her husband is still out of town, she wants me to follow up."

What she really wanted him to do was keep an eye on Samantha. With another disappearance, this time a girl, Bathsheba was no doubt afraid Samantha would take matters into her own hands. Without Donny to serve as guard, that could be disastrous.

"That would be Betsy McNair," Mrs. Culp said.

Braden frowned. "Yes. How did you know?"

"One of my neighbors is friendly with Betsy's aunt. She thinks her niece grew tired of classes and all that learning. Betsy was sweet on a local fella who was moving to Glasgow to find work, so Mrs. McNair thinks the lass up and went with him."

"She thinks?" Braden skeptically replied. "Wouldn't the girl tell her relatives?"

"Maybe not. Last year, Betsy's folks sent her over from Ireland to stay with her aunt and uncle. They weren't best pleased about the situation. They already have five of their own little ones to feed, after all. Mrs. McNair was more relieved than not to have the lass out of her hair."

"How old is Betsy?"

"Fifteen, maybe sixteen."

Braden stared at Mrs. Culp in disbelief. "Good God, she's

barely more than a child. And her family isn't concerned about her running off with a man?"

Mrs. Culp grimaced. "It's not so unusual in Old Town, sad to say. And the lass would ken that she was a burden to her kin. It wouldn't be a wonder if she thought going to Glasgow with her fella would be better for everyone."

"That's an ugly choice for a such a young girl to have to make, and according to Mrs. Blackmore, not one that entirely makes sense. Betsy was an excellent pupil with good prospects. It seems much riskier to go off to Glasgow."

"People will do all sorts of fool things for love, especially the young ones."

He couldn't dispute that. God knows he'd been a complete fool when it came to love.

Mrs. Culp tapped her chin. "Still, Betsy is such a good girl."

Braden waited for a few moments then reached over and gently nudged her shoulder. "And?"

"It's these bairns that keep disappearing. From the orphanage, and now the school."

"You know about them?" Braden asked, surprised.

She rolled her eyes. "We all do, here in Old Town. Word travels, ye ken."

The foundation board had tried to keep the news of the disappearances under wraps, since it didn't reflect well on the charity. They'd been successful when it came to the upper echelons of society, but clearly not so in Old Town.

"And what does the word say?"

"Nothing good. Everyone knows that the lads are well treated at the orphanage. There'd be nae reason for them to be joining up with bully boys or the gangs."

Braden frowned. "People think the boys have been recruited into criminal gangs?"

"None of us ken what to think. But the folks of Old Town

are keeping a close eye on their little ones, I can tell ye that. No one's taking any chances."

"Understandable. Anything else you can tell me about Betsy, or what the residents of Old Town think about all this?"

She rolled her lips inward, as if reluctant to share her thoughts.

"What?" he gently prompted.

"Ye'll think it plain odd, sir."

He flashed her an easy smile. "I'm a Kendrick. We specialize in odd."

She snorted. "That ye do. Well, there be rumors about a couple ghosting about Old Town, all dressed in black and never saying a word. No one knows what they're up to. The more ignorant-like think they're faceless ghoulies that take the children. Nonsense, of course, but the fear is real."

Hell and damnation.

Braden waved a dismissive hand. "They're probably just a team of thieves. As you know, it's not unusual for women to be part of these criminal gangs, either."

"I suppose," she replied, sounding doubtful.

And wasn't this a splendid development? Those rumors could swell to the point where they attracted the attention of the local police. Even worse, if the residents of Old Town grew frightened enough they might band together to take action to protect their children. With just a little bad luck, Samantha could find herself in the middle of a mob looking for vengeance.

"If you could find out the name of Betsy's fellow, I'll write to my brothers in Glasgow. They might be able to turn up information on them."

His instincts, however, told him that the girl had not left Edinburgh. Bathsheba obviously thought so, too, or else she wouldn't have sent him the note expressing her concerns.

Mrs. Culp nodded. "I'll get back to ye with that name."

"Now, be off with you, Mrs. Culp. I've kept you late enough."

"Thank ye, sir."

Braden checked the time. Already going on six o'clock. He'd have to go home first to change, since a frock coat and shoes was hardly appropriate attire for spying—or for searching through Old Town, if it came to that. And since he suspected it *would* come to that, he'd better arm himself, too.

So much for a quiet evening at home.

Thanks to the crusading Lady Samantha, a quiet night would obviously have to wait.

Samantha crept along the kitchen passageway to the back door. Tonight's mission wasn't especially risky, but her staff would vociferously object to her venturing out by herself. So, instead of facing a phalanx of over-protective servants, she'd claimed after dinner that a headache was coming on and retired early. Then she'd waited until the house had settled for the night before venturing forth for her rendezvous.

Lifting the skirts of her black wool gown, she hurried up the back stairs and through the kitchen garden, exiting through the gate to the laneway. Since the gate was well oiled, the only sound was the snick of the latch. Her security depended on the ability to come and go in secrecy, and every detail of her life now revolved around that.

At the moment, there were only a few people who could pose a threat to that security. John and Bathsheba would never betray her, but Braden Kendrick was another matter. Fortunately, by neither word nor deed had the doctor given any indication that he suspected Samantha's role in his rescue, even after meeting Felicity. She could only conclude that the stygian darkness of Old Town had provided enough cover that night to hide the fact that she and Donny had communicated by signing.

She adjusted her short veil and shifted her walking stick to her right hand. Then she set off, heading down the silent laneway to the street on the typically damp and chilly November night. The weather meant that few residents of New Town would be out on foot, so she would be able to make it down to Old Town without—

"Out for a late-night stroll, my lady?" came a deep, brogue-laced voice from behind her.

Samantha whirled, instinctively pulling her blade even as she registered the identity of the man in the shadows.

Kendrick put up his hands. "No need to gut me, lass."

She slammed her blade back into its sleeve. "If you don't wish to be gutted, don't sneak up on people."

"I don't think I was the one sneaking, actually."

"No, you were lurking here like a footpad," she snapped, more rattled than she cared to admit. "And you look like one, too, I might add."

He stood in the shadow of a high brick wall, dressed in a black greatcoat and boots, a slouchy hat pulled low over his forehead. Blending into the darkness, he was a shadow within shadows.

Even though she couldn't see his face, she felt the incredulity. It was coming off him in waves.

"Pot, meet kettle," he said, gesturing to her coal-black garb.

Samantha repressed the desire to whack him with her walking stick. Instead, she took a deep breath to settle her racing heart before opening her mouth again. If there was ever a time she needed to keep her wits, it was now.

"Dr. Kendrick, what are you doing here?"

He propped a shoulder against the wall, as if settling in for a nice, long discussion. The thought flickered through her brain that the dratted man looked very attractive and more than a little intimidating dressed as a footpad.

Ninny.

She didn't have time for this. She needed to get down to the Grassmarket before her source closed up for the night.

"I should think it obvious," he said. "I was waiting for you."

"Do you generally make it a habit to lie in wait for unsuspecting women, nearly giving them heart attacks?"

He let out a sardonic snort. "No, only for you. Most women I know have the sense not to sneak off to Old Town in the middle of the night."

Absurdly, she felt defensive. What business was it of his? "It's barely past ten. Hardly the middle of the night."

"Really? That's the tack you're going with?"

"Look, why would you assume I'm sneaking off to Old Town? Perhaps I'm just out for a pleasant stroll before bedtime."

"Because it's bloody freezing out," he said. "And it'll be a miracle if we don't get rained on, by the looks of the sky."

She waved an airy hand. "Oh, I hadn't noticed."

"Good God," he muttered.

The quarter hour chimed from the bell tower of a nearby church. She *needed* to be gone.

"This has been a most enlightening chat, but I must be on my way. Good night."

"So, where are you going?" he asked, as if she just hadn't rudely dismissed him. "To meet a secret lover, perhaps?"

Samantha's jaw sagged for a moment.

Of all the nerve.

"Of course I'm not, you idiot. I have a meeting in Old Town—"

She clamped her lips shut. Blast the man for tripping her up so easily.

He watched her fume for a few seconds, but then slowly took a few steps closer, as if she were a skittish foal about to bolt.

"Lady Samantha, there is no need to engage in this charade," he quietly said. "I mean you no harm, but I cannot allow you to put yourself in the way of danger."

"Oh, that's rich," she retorted. "If not for me, you'd be lying dead in a back lane of Old Town right now. Or, you would have been. Lying dead, I mean. In Old Town."

Oh, my God. The man was truly scrambling her brain.

She flapped a hand. "You know what I mean."

"Yes, I do. And I am both grateful and in admiration of your skills. Then again, you were not alone that night. Does Donny know that you've snuck out?"

"I don't sneak," she replied, avoiding the question.

"Certainly looks like you were sneaking."

"Not very effectively," she grumbled. "Although you, sir, are a bloody ghost. I didn't even notice you standing there."

Annoyed with the ridiculous conversation and worried that she might miss her meeting, she spun on her heel and stalked off down the street. As she fully expected, Kendrick quickly fell into step beside her.

"So, Old Town it is?"

"Yes."

"No chance I can talk you out of it?"

"No, and I must say that your company is not needed, Dr. Kendrick. I am well able to take care of myself."

"As I am acutely aware. Bathsheba, however, would have my head if I allowed you to go into the stews without an escort."

Samantha blew out a disgusted breath. "I knew it. How much did she tell you?"

"Enough to know that you likely would be out tonight, even without Donny to serve as your watchdog."

She threw him a glancing scowl. "He's much more than that."

"Yes, I know. He's your friend."

His tone was so kind, so . . . understanding, that it made her throat unaccountably tight. She needed half a block to regroup and organize the questions rattling around in her skull.

"How long have you been watching my house?" she asked as they turned into Princes Street.

"For the last three nights. And don't worry. Only Bath-sheba knows."

Something inside her staggered with relief. Still, the danger to herself and to Felicity was acute, especially if Lord Beath ever got wind of her activities. As tempting as it might be, she couldn't allow herself to trust Kendrick.

Not yet, anyway.

"All night?" she asked.

"Only until I was sure you wouldn't try sneaking out the back laneway."

She ignored his wry tone.

"And what does your family think about all these late nights, Dr. Kendrick?"

"That I have an uncanny number of pregnant patients, who have all decided to give birth in the same week."

She couldn't hold back a snicker. "Surely you could have come up with a better excuse."

"It must be the lack of sleep. It's impeding my ability to tell convincing whoppers."

"It's not my fault that you're losing sleep," she said, again feeling defensive and more than a wee bit guilty. After all, he worked harder than almost anyone she'd ever met.

"And isn't that a pity?" he said.

She threw him a startled glance. "Um, what?"

Since they happened to be passing under a streetlamp, she finally got a good look at his face. He flashed her what could only be described as a roguish grin. Was he actually enjoying this benighted outing? What in heaven's name was wrong with the man?

"Was that a question, Lady Samantha?"

"Yes. No. Oh, bother. I haven't a clue what you're talking about."

She picked up the pace, all but jogging across the street as they headed into the park.

Kendrick easily kept stride, as if he hadn't already spent a long day teaching and tending patients. There was nothing showy about Braden Kendrick. There were no overt displays of physical prowess, just a steady, quiet strength and a toughness of mind and character that was more valuable than brute muscularity. She'd witnessed those qualities when he'd faced down two murderous thugs with a chilly calm.

And that calm had also, she now understood, allowed him to exercise his obviously keen powers of observation, which was dismaying under the present circumstances.

"It wasn't just what Bathsheba told you, was it?" she asked. "You guessed it was me after you met Felicity."

"Yes."

Oh, he was a marvel, all right—brilliant, observant, and quietly relentless. They were all admirable qualities but ones that could prove massively inconvenient if he decided to get in her way.

Halfway down the deserted path, she stopped under the shelter of an oak. He overshot her but then turned, observing her for a few moments before crossing his arms over his chest.

"Is there something you wish to say, my lady?"

His enquiry was so polite that she was tempted to laugh.

"Dr. Kendrick, while I appreciate your concern—and your stamina, since you have clearly expended a great deal of energy on my situation—"

"Oh, not yet I haven't."

His voice had suddenly gone deeper, colored by more than a hint of the Highlands, and it sent shivers dancing across her nerves.

She pushed back against the unaccountable reaction. "What does that mean, Dr. Kendrick?"

He took a step closer, looming over her. She tilted her head back to look at his face. Even under the shadow cast by the brim of his hat, she swore she saw a devilish gleam in his eyes.

"Nothing that I'm willing to share, at the moment," he replied.

"And when will you share it with me?"

He tilted his head. "When you're ready to hear it."

And . . . yes, he was laughing at her.

"Oh, do get out of my way." She elbowed past him and stalked off.

He caught up with her almost instantly. "Samantha, I am not some annoying pest for you to shoo away."

"At the moment, I do find you very annoying. And who gave you permission to use my given name, Dr. Kendrick?"

"I just did. And I suggest you also stop calling me Dr. Kendrick in that snippy tone. *That* is very annoying."

"Well, *doctor*, what should I call you?"

"You might try Braden."

"Really? Might I point out that we hardly know each other? Certainly not enough to be on a first-name basis."

"Lass, we're about to head into the most dangerous part of town on an equally dangerous mission to find a missing girl. If that doesn't put us on a first-name basis, I cannot fathom what would."

She sighed. "Ah, so you do know about Betsy. Bathsheba, again?"

"Partly. The rest I gleaned from Mrs. Culp. She's a wealth of information when it comes to Old Town. The consensus seems to be that Betsy ran off with her man."

"That is absolutely *not* true. Betsy has become an accomplished seamstress, and we've found an excellent placement for her with a dressmaker. I spoke to her only last week. She was very excited about it."

He seemed to ponder all that as they exited the park. Ahead of them was one of the narrow streets—part laneway and part staircase—that would take them down the hill into Old Town. It was one of Samantha and Donny's preferred routes, since it was usually deserted at this time of night.

She'd been a bit worried about traversing it alone and couldn't deny relief that Braden was now serving as escort.

So he's Braden now, is he?

"Do you suspect she's been kidnapped?" he finally asked.

She stopped him at the top of the wooden set of steps.

"What is it?" he asked.

"How much do you really know about . . . all this?" she asked, gesturing toward the decrepit old buildings that flowed down the hill in a jumble.

"Quite a bit, actually," he said in a carefully neutral tone.

Samantha muttered a curse. "I take it that Bathsheba told you most everything, including about my . . . my illness."

God, after all this time, she still had trouble saying the word.

"Yes, and I cannot tell you how incredibly sorry I am, for all of it."

She swallowed hard against the lump at the back of her throat. "Thank you. But what is most important now is finding out what happened to the children. Donny will be out of commission for some weeks yet, and I cannot afford to wait that long. Not while these disappearances keep occurring."

"You believe the children have been coerced into joining one of Edinburgh's criminal gangs."

She heard the skeptical note in his voice. There was no point in pretending she didn't understand his doubts. "I think they've been kidnapped."

"How is that even possible? Betsy, perhaps, since she didn't live at the school. But the boys, right out from under your noses?"

"I haven't figured that out yet," she confessed. "But it's the explanation that makes the most sense—if one is willing to look the facts straight in the face."

So far, the only one on the board so willing was John. She held her breath, praying that Braden would believe her, too.

"Children can be valuable assets to an arch rogue," he said. "They are often highly prized in criminal operations."

It took her a moment to recover from the shock that he seemed to agree with her. "Arch rogue?"

"The leader of a thieving gang or a flash house. The problem is that many of these children willingly join the gangs. If that's the case with your students, then it's going to be bloody difficult to get them away without a fight."

So he probably didn't agree with her, which was more depressing than it should have been. What did she care what he thought, as long as he kept her secrets.

"My children did not willingly join any gang."

"You're certain of that?"

Samantha was about to flash out a retort when he put up both his hands.

"I'm just trying to get as much information as I can," he said. "After all, this is the first time we've actually been honest with each other. And that is as much my fault as yours."

"Sorry." Samantha tried to give the question its fair due. "It's possible one of the older boys might have been persuaded, but not the little ones. They were terrified of being left on their own in Old Town."

So terrified that it made her heart cramp with anxiety whenever she thought of what might have happened to those sweet little boys.

"And I understand you never took the matter to the police."

"Arthur said they wouldn't believe me, because we didn't have proof of any crime."

"Ah, the excellent Mr. Baines. Do you agree that they wouldn't believe you?"

She wondered at his sardonic tone but mentally shrugged it away. "No, but I do agree with his assessment that the police won't do anything about it." She paused. "I'm the only one who will."

When she started down the steps of the wynd, he followed closely behind.

"My presence would suggest otherwise," he said, "although I certainly don't intend to let you bash headfirst into a dangerous situation."

"I don't bash into anything, sir. I do what I must. Please do not get in my way."

She swept down the last few stairs and into the laneway at the bottom of the wynd. He caught up with her in two long strides.

"I'm not trying to stop you," Braden said, becoming exasperated. "I'm trying to help you."

"So far, all you've done is hold me up."

"Not my intention."

She scoffed. "So kind of you."

They moved quickly and quietly, with their way only illuminated occasionally by flickers of light from candles in the windows of the tenements crowding over them. Samantha couldn't help noticing that Braden navigated the broken cobblestones and blind turns as easily as she did.

"So, you wish to volunteer at my clinic," he said as they entered one of the closes leading to Lawn Market Street.

She frowned at the change in subject. "I said I did."

"Because you're looking for information sources, I'm assuming. Many of the residents of Old Town pass through my doors, and they do like to gossip."

Too clever by half, he is.

"Sorry. I know it's rather horrible of me to use you like that."

"Och, lass, you can use me whenever you want, as much as you want."

She scowled up at him. "It's not a joke, you know. And I wish you would stop laughing at me."

"My apologies. And the only thing horrible about it is that you didn't tell me what you needed."

"Well, I didn't know if I could trust you."

He placed a hand between her shoulder blades, gently steering her past a jumble of broken cobblestones that she'd failed to notice.

"It's hard for you to trust people, isn't it?" he asked.

The question carved out a hole in the middle of her chest. "Can you blame me?" she tightly replied.

"I cannot. Samantha, I want you to believe me when I say I will help you in any way I can."

She halted, peering up at him. Thanks to her veil and the blasted dark alley, she couldn't read his expression.

"Really?" she whispered.

"Aye, lass. I will. Word of a Kendrick."

Samantha had to blink back a sudden rush of tears. To have a man like him make such a promise was utterly . . . wonderful.

"But no bolting off to the stews by yourself," he added. "That's loony and dangerous."

His comment killed any impulse to cry.

"It's not loony." She jabbed him in the chest. "Nor am I putting myself in danger."

He snorted.

"Dr. Kendrick," she frostily said, "I'm simply meeting a friend tonight. That is all."

"What kind of a friend?"

"A very reliable source of information who runs a coffee house near Grassmarket. Perfectly respectable and perfectly safe."

"Oh, how boring," he said.

"I thought you would approve, since you *are* the boring Kendrick."

She regretted her words immediately. Unfortunately, they hung in the air like a dirty rag flapping in the wind.

"If by boring, you mean I don't care for the high drama and hair-brained adventures my brothers used to engage in, you would be correct. I am, however, capable of taking the appropriate action when necessary."

Now she felt like an utter worm. "I didn't mean to offend you, sir."

"I'm a doctor, Samantha. There is very little that can offend me."

And with those trenchant words, he took her arm and marched her along the street.

CHAPTER 12

Braden glanced over his shoulder. He had a nagging feeling that someone had been following them. The hairs on the back of his neck had been bristling for the last ten minutes—not for his sake, but for Samantha's. Old Town had never frightened him, since he knew it so well. But with her by his side and danger lurking in every shadow, it scared the hell out of him.

Because of that fear, Samantha Penwith was now officially under Kendrick protection, and he didn't give a damn if she liked it or not.

They entered the Grassmarket, a large, cobblestoned square that stretched all the way to Victoria Street. Lined with pubs, shops, and blocks of flats, it was fairly active even at this time of night and was also decently lit. Another glance over his shoulder confirmed again that no one was following them.

Samantha glanced up, her pretty features obscured by the light veil over her face. "You may ease your vigilance, Dr. Kendrick. No murderers, footpads, or even a ghost or ghoulie to bedevil us, so I believe we're now safe."

"There's nothing remotely safe about this, Samantha. And I don't believe in ghoulies."

"In any case, I never take unnecessary risks, sir. Besides, what kind of Highlander doesn't believe ghoulies?"

"The kind that went to medical school. And as to your assertion about risk, let me just say that we will have to agree to disagree."

They'd argued enough for one night. All he wanted was to keep them both alive and unharmed. That meant keeping his full focus on their surroundings rather than verbally sparring with the alluring but frustrating Lady Samantha.

"Oh, look," she said, "there's a hackney stand. Feel free to make use of it, sir. I am perfectly fine on my own from here."

Swallowing a tart reply, he took her elbow and hurried her past the front door of the White Hart Inn, dodging a pair of medical students who'd stumbled out. The two were clearly surprised to see one of their professors in the company of a veiled woman.

"Oh, I say, is that Dr. Kendrick?" one of them said, slightly slurring his words.

Braden stalked on, hauling Samantha with him.

"That was rather a bit of bad luck," she puffed.

"Indeed."

"I'm sorry for that, but you needn't race me down the street. You'll give me a stitch."

He slowed his pace. "My apologies."

"Those young men obviously know you."

"Obviously."

"There's no need to be rude, sir. And it's not as if they can recognize *me*."

"For which I am profoundly grateful."

"Then what is the matter?"

He threw her an incredulous look. "You mean besides strolling around Old Town with a mysterious veiled woman? What could possibly be taken amiss in that scenario?"

She yanked her arm free. "I repeat that I do not require your escort. My meeting place is only a few minutes from here, and I'm sure I'll be quite safe without you."

He throttled back his irritation. If he wanted Samantha to trust him, he needed to stop acting like a jumped-up rooster.

"It's just that I would prefer, for both our sakes, not to be the object of salacious gossip."

"Oh, drat, I'm an idiot," she instantly said. "Of course you have your reputation as a physician to consider."

"I'm not overly concerned about my reputation, but I want to avoid questions or gossip. Kendricks have a tendency to generate quite a lot of both, as I suspect you know."

"I'm sorry if I put you in a difficult spot. Were they friends or colleagues of yours?"

"Students, actually, and half-shot from the looks of it. If they have the brass to say even a word, I'll deny the whole thing and *then* tear a strip off them. I don't want students of mine drinking their heads off in the first place, or anywhere near my patients while suffering hangovers."

She chuckled. "That is admirably ruthless of you."

"If I'm going to embark on a career of sneaking about Old Town, I'd better learn to be ruthless."

"Once again, we are *not* sneaking. We are walking down a street like two sensible people, and at a perfectly respectable time of night."

He snorted. "We look like highwaymen, Samantha. It's bloody ridiculous."

She pulled him to a stop at the entrance to a small laneway. "Then it's fortunate we have arrived at our destination."

A short, dank passageway lined with decrepit old buildings loomed before them.

"There's an inviting prospect," Braden said. "I can already feel the shiv between my shoulder blades."

"It's perfectly safe. I've been here at least half a dozen times."

"After dark?"

"Well, no. But it's not that sort of place."

"Looks like that sort of place."

She blew out an exasperated breath and started in. "Try for a degree of optimism, sir. We've not encountered a whit of trouble as yet."

"The night's still young, my lady."

There's trouble, and then there's female trouble.

It was the sort of trouble that involved pulling a pretty widow into the shadow of a doorway and kissing her silly. His brain—obviously disordered by the idiocy of this expedition— insisted on kicking up images of sweeping Samantha off her feet and having his way with her.

You're a moron.

"It's just at the other end of the laneway," she said, oblivious to his deranged thought processes. "I thought it best to come around the back way. Less likely to run into anyone."

"Except the poor souls who live in the tenements."

"Most of them have the good sense to remain inside after dark."

Samantha lifted her skirts to avoid a pile of garbage before stopping in front of a three-story building. At least this one looked slightly less grim than its neighbors.

"And we're here," she said, pointing to a cellar entrance.

A short staircase led to a door several feet below street level. A lamp in a half-window to the left of the door sent feeble rays into the stairwell. A faded sign swung from the bracket over the door. Braden was just able to make out the words *Wee* and *Dog*.

"I know this place," he said.

Samantha cast him a surprised glance. "You've been here?"

"No, but my twin brothers know the proprietor. Emmy Fraser, correct?"

"Yes. How do they know her?"

He took her arm to escort her down the steps. "Long story. I'll tell you sometime."

She smiled. "From what I've heard of the twins, I imagine it's an exciting one."

"So exciting that I hope Miss Fraser doesn't strangle me when she finds out I'm a Kendrick."

"Don't worry, I'll protect you," Samantha replied as she opened the door.

"I'm counting on it, because right now I'm quaking in my boots."

When she giggled at his lame joke, a warmth invaded Braden's heart that he'd not felt in a very long time. It was a clarion call to warn that *he* was bashing headfirst into trouble—not the villain-with-a-club sort but the female sort, which was infinitely more dangerous.

They stepped into a narrow room with a low, timbered ceiling. A counter ran along one side of the room, and from behind it wafted the enticing scents of coffee, cinnamon, and fresh-baked bread. The furniture was plain—roughly hewn tables and benches—but the floor was swept and the service counter orderly. The Wee Black Dog was far from fashionable, but it was a respectable coffee house that served the locals who worked in the nearby markets.

A young woman with a kind face and a wealth of red hair barely crammed under a mobcap was stacking plates behind the counter. The only other occupant was a man sitting in the corner reading a tattered book. The broad-shouldered fellow had a nose that had obviously met more than a few fists. When he glanced up from his reading, he subjected them to a gimlet-eyed stare. After Braden gave him a friendly nod, the fellow let his gaze linger for a few beats before returning to his book.

"Dinna mind Joe," said the woman. "He's just here to keep an eye on things."

"I'm here to keep an eye on *ye*, Emmy," Joe said in a gruff voice.

Emmy rolled her eyes as she reached below the counter

and brought out two glasses and a corked bottle. "As if I need a man to protect me."

Joe calmly turned a page. "Ye'll nae be walkin' these streets at night without me."

"You listen to Joe," Samantha said as she lifted her veil. "I'm terribly late, and I hate to think of you walking home by yourself."

"I was about to give up on ye, truth be told," Emmy replied as she poured out two neat whiskies.

"I apologize. I was unavoidably detained."

"Aye, Kendricks do tend to complicate things. Yer the doctor one?"

"I am." Braden extended his hand and received a brisk shake in return. "How did you know I'm a Kendrick?"

"Yer not much like the twins, but ye have the look of the other one—that Royal." She winked at Braden. "Now he's a good-looking fella and he's got such lovely manners. Best of the bunch, I reckon."

When a grumble that sounded more like a growl came from behind Joe's book, Braden bit back a smile.

"Dr. Kendrick is very kind," Samantha said. "And I'm sure he's just as nice as his brother."

"If not as handsome," Braden joked.

"You're perfectly handsome." Then Samantha winced. "Er, what I mean, is—"

"We ken what ye mean," Emmy said with a grin.

"The doctor offered to escort me here tonight," Samantha said in a firm tone. "To play bodyguard, as it were. That is all."

Still, the lass had fired up with a rosy glow that had a re-markable effect on Braden's mood. For the first time all night, he was beginning to enjoy himself.

"Just a bodyguard?" he said. "You wound me, Lady Samantha."

"I ken the feeling," muttered Joe.

Samantha gave Braden a frosty glare. "Are you quite finished?"

He adopted a frown. "Hmm. I'll have to think about that."

Emmy let out a snort. "Aye, Kendricks are trouble. But as long as ye don't break any furniture, ye can stay."

"Destruction of furniture is not my particular specialty."

He picked up his glass and took a cautious sip. Watering holes in Old Town rarely served the good stuff.

Yet apparently this one did. "This tastes like the last batch of whisky from Lochnagar, my brother's distillery."

"Aye. Sir Graeme keeps me well supplied." Emmy smirked. "To make up for breakin' the furniture, ye ken."

Braden toasted her with his glass. "As well he should."

"Why *do* your brothers keep breaking furniture?" Samantha asked.

"It seems to be an inborn tendency. I'm a scientist, Kade is a musician, and the twins break furniture."

When the small casement clock behind the bar chimed out the hour, they all glanced at each other.

"I suppose we should get on with it," Braden said.

Samantha rounded her eyes at him. "Yes, I'm sure it's well past your bedtime, Dr. Kendrick."

Cheeky lass. She'd obviously been waiting for the proper moment to exact her revenge for his teasing.

He followed Emmy and Samantha to an alcove in the back of the room. Emmy sat across from them, while Braden and Samantha shared a narrow bench. When Samantha brushed against him, he caught a hint of orange blossom drifting up from her glossy dark curls. The candlelight played over her delicate features, her smooth skin looking as soft as velvet.

Braden curled his hand into a fist to resist the almost overwhelming urge to stroke her cheek.

Get ahold of yourself, man.

Samantha's gloved hand tapped the tabletop. "Emmy, you have information to share?"

"Aye, about Betsy. Not good, I'm afraid."

Samantha grimaced. "So, she didn't run away with the beau."

"Not according to her uncle. He was in here yesterday. Says his missus is convinced the girl bolted, but he thinks not. Said Betsy is a good Christian girl and would never shame her family like that."

Samantha nodded. "That was always my impression of her."

"Then what does her uncle think happened?" Braden asked.

"He doesna ken—or doesna *want* to ken. Some of my other customers, though . . ." Emmy shook her head. "It's more rumors than not, but they're worried about the bairns. And not just the ones from the orphanage. A few others from the stews have disappeared in past months—little ones set to beggin' on the streets by their good-for-nothin' parents who only care about their drink."

Samantha massaged her forehead, as if trying to rub away the horrific image. "I hadn't realized that other children were disappearing."

"Ye have to keep yer ear to the ground, or else ye'd miss it. Most folks ignore the wee bairns, especially the law and the nobs up in New Town."

"But you notice them, Emmy," Braden said. "My brothers told me that you keep an eye on the children of Old Town."

"I do my best. I'm always hopin' they'll come to me if they're in trouble."

Samantha tapped her fingertip on the table again. "Then you must know most of the children in Old Town who run in the gangs."

"Mostly, or I ken those who do. Old Town's small enough to keep track of them."

"But the children who've gone missing lately are not part of existing gangs, are they?"

Emmy grimaced. "That's what got me in such a puzzle. I canna figure out where they're goin'."

"Is there any evidence that a new gang may be forming?" Braden asked. "One that might be lying low at this point?"

Samantha tilted her head to look at him. "Why would they do that?"

He frowned, thinking it through. "They might be preparing to move in on another gang's territory, so they're building up their network."

"With children?"

"Children are useful to gangs in many ways, as we've already noted."

"Ye may be right, sir," Joe said, putting down his book. "There's some fierce battles over turf whenever someone new moves into town."

"Or they might be setting up for something that requires more planning," Braden added.

Emmy snapped her fingers. "Like robbin' a warehouse. There was a theft at one of the warehouses in Leith just a few months ago. Made off with a good haul, I hear."

Braden had heard about that crime from Logan. Though, fortunately it hadn't been a Kendrick warehouse, that particular company had lost a significant haul of alcohol, silk, and other goods.

"That makes sense," he said.

Samantha looked startled. "But why use children for something so difficult and complicated? Why not adults?"

"They use the bairns to crawl up the drainpipes or the sides of the buildings, and get into the windows," explained Emmy. "Then they let in the adults. The kiddies also keep lookout or help cart the goods."

"I would like to kill people who use children like that," Samantha said in a voice taut with repressed fury.

Braden briefly covered her clenched fist with his hand. "We'll find them, lass. Never fear."

But soon, he hoped. Something bad was happening here, something that put the bairns in mortal danger.

"For the time being," he added, "let's assume it's a new gang that's formed. That means, like other gangs, they must have a bolthole or hideout. If nothing else, they'd need a place to stow the children."

Samantha turned up her hand. "But where? None of us have heard anything, and it's been months. What are they doing with them?"

"Probably using them right now for smaller jobs, ones that wouldn't raise much suspicion. Look, I know you don't want to hear this, but I think we're going to have to enlist more help in searching the stews."

She grimaced. "Perhaps, but it's an awful risk."

Emmy muttered something under her breath as she rubbed at a tiny spot on the tabletop.

"What is it, Emmy?" Braden quietly asked.

Startled, she looked up. "Uh, sir?"

"You know something."

For a few moments, she seemed to debate with herself before answering. "It's just a rumor, sir. It's probably not true, but if it wasn't, I wouldna go near the bloody place. And not much scares me in Old Town, ye ken."

Joe got up and stalked over to join them. "Ye'll nae be goin' there, Emmy. I dinna care how worrit ye are for the kiddies."

She flapped a hand. "Och, dinna be a fool. 'Course I'm not goin' there." She fixed her earnest blue gaze on Samantha. "And ye'll nae be goin' there, either, if ye know what's good for ye."

Samantha reached across the table and took Emmy's

fluttering hand. "I know you're worried for me, but those children are in danger. Even if it's a rumor, you must tell me."

"Emmy," said Joe in a warning voice.

"It's all right," Braden said to the young woman. "I'll keep Lady Samantha safe."

"Ye promise?" she asked.

"Word of a Kendrick."

Samantha shot him an irritated glance but held her peace. She was a woman who didn't like ceding control over anything, including her own safety. But she was also an intelligent woman who knew she needed help.

"It's a tavern off Niddry," Emmy reluctantly said. "It's called the Hangin' Judge."

Dammit to hell.

Braden shook his head. "That's nae good."

Samantha frowned. "You've been there?"

"I wouldn't set foot in the damn place unless someone held a gun to my head—something which no doubt occurs there on a regular basis."

Joe nodded. "Like rats in a nest they are in that place. Worst den of cutthroats and thieves in Old Town."

"Not your average cutthroats, either," Braden added. "Some of the most violent thugs in Edinburgh frequent the Hanging Judge. Even the police avoid it."

He'd heard tell of it at the clinic. All sorts of ugly rumors hung over the place like a foul smoke, including those involving body snatchers and killers for hire.

Samantha nodded. "It sounds like the perfect hiding place for a new gang of criminals and for hiding the children, too. Especially if the police avoid it."

When she made to stand, Braden wrapped a hand around her wrist and gently pulled her back down. "We are not running off half-cocked to the most dangerous spot in Old Town."

She turned to him, her eyes glittering with a dangerous combination of anger and determination. "I never run off half-cocked, sir. But I will have a look at this tavern from a sensible distance. There is much that can be learned by watching the comings and goings of such an establishment."

"There's nae safe place when it comes to the Hangin' Judge, my lady," Joe warned.

"I promise to keep a respectable distance and remain well out of sight."

Her narrowed gaze challenged Braden to disagree. Since he couldn't watch the bloody woman twenty-four hours a day, he at least needed to control the situation as best he could.

"All right, but we need a plan," he said.

Samantha stood and picked up her walking stick. "In order to develop a credible plan, one needs accurate information. Which means a reconnaissance."

She headed for the door.

Cursing, Braden rose and strode after her. "Samantha, we need a plan for *tonight*."

She wheeled and jabbed a finger at his chest. "The plan is to find the place, stay a safe distance away, and see what we can see. Those children are in trouble, Braden. We *need* to do this."

He stared down into her stormy gaze, every instinct telling him to hustle her back home where she would be safe. But she was right, blast it. The longer they waited, the more danger the children would continue to be in.

"You will recall that I am not without skills," she added. "I've been doing this for quite some time."

Now there was something else in her gaze besides a storm of anger. There was a question, one that pleaded with him to listen to her, to trust her when perhaps no one else had.

Ye canna say no.

"Are you armed with anything more than your blade?" he tersely asked.

"I have a pistol. Do you?"

He patted the inside pocket of his greatcoat.

She rewarded him with a dazzling smile that mingled surprise and relief. Clearly, she had expected him to say no.

"Then I think we are ready. Shall we, Dr. Kendrick?"

Braden snorted. "It's not like I have a choice, do I?"

"One always has a choice, sir. This time, you are choosing me."

CHAPTER 13

Samantha could feel the masculine ire flowing in her direction like waves beating against the shoreline. Dr. Braden Kendrick was *tremendously* annoyed with her.

Despite his disapproval, he remained by her side, a silent guardian. And for that she was so grateful. Regardless of what he might think of tonight's venture or her conduct in general, Braden would not abandon her.

She pointed to an arch in the line of buildings up ahead. "The fastest way is through Fishmarket to Barrie's Close."

"A verra bad idea." His unhelpful reply was growled out in a deep Highland brogue.

Normally, Braden was very much a man of the city. Tonight, however, she'd caught more than a few glimpses of the Highlander. To her dismay, she found that version of the man just as attractive as the other one. Still, one needed to be firm, so she took his sleeve and towed him through the entrance to the narrow laneway.

He let out a derisive snort. "Och, lass."

"I know you think I am both managing and impulsive, but we are both very familiar with Old Town and are both armed. Besides, we're simply going to take a quick look at the Hanging Judge from a safe distance."

"And then what? What if we do actually see something?

What is the next step in the grand plan, if I may be so bold as to ask?"

His snarly attitude might be a wee bit irritating, but she knew it stemmed from genuine worry for her safety.

"The entire point of this reconnaissance is to come up with the plan, remember?" she patiently replied. "And at some point, we'll have to gather hard evidence to bring to the police."

"Would that require a visit *inside* the Hanging Judge? If ye have that notion, I would suggest ye forget it. Yer not setting a bloody foot inside that bloody tavern."

When Samantha stopped dead in her tracks, Braden almost ran into her but quickly sidestepped. The lower half of his face was visible in the flickering lamplight from the houses that ringed the close. His mouth was set in a grim, flat line.

"Dr. Kendrick, while I am aware of the risks, I will not sit idly by while children are in danger. This is the best lead I've had in months, and I will follow it."

He crossed his arms over his chest. "I don't disagree with the need for some scouting. I disagree with *you* doing it."

"Who else should do it?"

"I can do it. You should return home."

"No. You need someone to watch your back."

"Then I can fetch one of my brothers. They are—"

She chopped down a hand. "No. Just us."

Braden pulled off his hat, rubbing a quick hand through his hair before he slapped the hat back on. "I understand your concern about trusting strangers. But I assure you that my brothers *are* trustworthy."

She couldn't help feeling slightly guilty, as if she'd insulted both him and his family. "I realize that my lack of trust might seem excessive. Just know that I have my reasons."

"I'm sure they're good ones, and yet you can't do this alone, lass. *We* can't do this alone."

The tender way he said *lass* muddled her insides, but then she firmed her resolve. "I don't agree. Donny and I have been doing this on our own for months."

"And just where is Donny right now? How is that working out?"

Well, no tenderness there.

When a nearby kirk chimed out the hour, impatience nipped at her heels. Every moment they wasted was a moment children remained in danger.

"Dr. Kendrick, you are free to return home. I will not hold it against you."

When she turned and marched off, he quickly matched her stride. She glanced over, pretending surprise. "Oh, decided to come along, did you?"

"Don't think for one moment that I'm happy about this, Samantha. And we *will* be discussing it later."

She ignored the little kick of her heart at his reassuringly possessive attitude. "Duly noted, sir."

"So, what actions do you propose if we happen to see something?" he asked a few moments later. "That question has yet to be sorted."

"I'm wondering if it would be best to go to Arthur first. As an influential barrister, he might be best placed to help us."

"Ah, yes. The inestimable Mr. Baines," he sardonically replied.

She frowned. "Is there some reason you—"

Braden grabbed her arm and pulled her back.

"Now what?" she groaned.

"That," he replied.

Two men were advancing toward them out of the darkness at the other end of the close. Since both carried large clubs, they clearly had less than friendly intentions.

Braden swiftly extracted his pistol.

"That's far enough," he said, raising his voice. "If robbery is your intention, be on your way. You'll get nothing from us."

Samantha quickly transferred her walking stick to her left hand, trying to calm her suddenly racing heart. This was an echo of the incident that happened last week, when Donny was injured. Was it a simple robbery or something else?

She slipped her hand into her skirt pocket, one specifically sewn to hold her pistol.

"Och, listen to Dr. Fancy, with them breakteeth words," sneered one of the men.

Hell and damnation.

She recognized that voice from the night she and Donny were attacked.

"These are the men who injured Donny," she whispered to Braden.

"Oh, splendid."

He took a step forward, his pistol up and cocked. "So, not a simple robbery, after all. To what do we owe the honor of this encounter?"

The larger of the two, a burly fellow garbed in the rough clothes of the docks, lifted his club in a menacing gesture. "For starters, ye'll keep yer bloody voice down, or I'll bash yer bloody brains out."

Braden scoffed. "I see clubs have become the weapon of choice for morons. I'm sure they're very effective against unarmed victims, but you might have noticed that I'm aiming a pistol right at your heart. And since I am an excellent shot, I suggest you step back. Because I will take you down, I promise."

Instead, the idiot took an angry step forward. "See 'ere, ye piece of—"

His companion jerked him back. "Yer a moron, all right. He's trying to get a rise out of ye."

"Looks like it worked," Braden replied. "In any case, I will shoot you if necessary. So I suggest you be off."

"We'll no be takin' orders from ye, doc," said the second man, apparently not the least bit perturbed.

He reached inside his greatcoat and pulled out a pistol. He pointed it at Braden while still keeping a firm grip on the club in his other hand.

"That evens the odds a bit, don't it, doc?"

Samantha extracted her pistol before he finished talking. "Not precisely."

The man laughed. "Yer gonna shoot me with that little popper? That's a joke and a half."

He sounded both genuinely amused and entirely in control. Clothed in a heavy wool coat that hung open to reveal breeches and riding boots, he was clearly a cut above his companion, as well as the average criminal that roamed Old Town.

Samantha flashed him a toothy smile. "This is the new Deringer pistol, which I recently acquired. It's extremely accurate at close quarters. And, like the doctor, I am a very good shot."

He snorted. "Go ahead and try it, m' lady. We'll see how far ye get before I blow yer pretty little skull to pieces."

When he shifted slightly, as if to point his weapon at her, Braden growled deep in his throat. "Try it, ye bastard, and I'll shoot yer fecking head off and kill yer fecking mate, too."

Samantha mentally blinked. The man standing by her side suddenly sounded more like a Highland berserker than a physician. He was intimidating enough that their would-be attackers did indeed take a step back.

"That's better," Braden said, reverting to his usual cool control. "Now, since this is obviously not a robbery, get on with whatever message you've come to deliver, and make it quick."

The moron with the club growled. "Or what, ye'll shoot us?"

"Since I am pointing a gun at you," Braden said, "why the hell would you think I wouldn't shoot you?"

"Because yer a feckin' doctor, that's why. Ye dinna kill people."

"Oh, Lord," Samantha said. "You truly are an idiot."

"Why ye—"

The man in the greatcoat rammed an elbow into his companion's side, effectively silencing him.

"Yer right, m' lady," Greatcoat said in a genial voice. "But dinna be fooled that a shootin' match will go yer way. Or that it's just the four of us here in Barrie's Close. Ye'd be surprised what's hidin' in them dark little corners."

Samantha had to clamp down on a sudden shiver, one not caused by the cold, damp air. The ancient buildings looming over them cast obsidian shadows into every corner and doorway. Old Town suddenly seemed to stir from an uneasy slumber, like a great beast waiting to devour them.

"Point taken," Braden dryly responded. "Now since you obviously know who I am, I assume you also know who my family is."

"Aye, yer Kendrick," Greatcoat replied. "So, who gives a shite?"

"My brother, the Earl of Arnprior, would give a shite. He'd hunt you down, along with your dimwitted companion and everyone who works for you. And then he'd exterminate you, like the lice-ridden vermin that you are."

Greatcoat calmly observed them, holding his pistol steady. His companion, though, was still agitated and too stupid to hold his tongue.

"Bollocks. We're nae afraid of yer poncy earl of a brother."

"No? Then perhaps you've heard of my brother Logan," Braden replied.

"Oh, aye," said Greatcoat. "Great lummox, that one."

"He is indeed a big man, but did you know he once wrestled a bear in Canada? Throttled it dead, in fact. So, you lot would be child's play to him. And then there's Graeme, the former inquiry agent for the Crown, not to mention my other brothers. You'd be insane *not* to be afraid of us, because Clan Kendrick stands as one and kills as one. My enemy is their enemy. Therefore, I strongly suggest you not make me your enemy."

"Point taken," Greatcoat sardonically said, echoing Braden's words from a moment ago. He stashed his pistol back inside his coat.

Samantha had to admit the man was remarkably cool headed, given that he had two pistols aimed at him.

"I've truly no quarrel with ye, doc," the man added. "It's the lass who needs to be careful, if she knows what's good for her."

"Be very clear," Braden said, the snarl returning to his voice. "The *lass* is one of ours, and Clan Kendrick protects its own."

"Nor does the lass take kindly to threats," Samantha added. "So deliver your message and be on your way."

"Then here it is," Greatcoat said. "Yer to stop meddlin' in Old Town, lookin' for things ye have no business lookin' for. It'll not end well if ye keep on the way ye are. Stay home like a good girl, and all will be well."

Samantha barely managed to rein in her impulse to snap at the deliberate insult. "How I spend my time in Old Town is no business of yours. Nor will I be frightened off. I will do what I must."

Still, it was hard not to be disconcerted and dismayed. These men knew who she was and what she'd been doing. She and Donny had been very careful, but clearly not careful enough.

"If ye want to keep them kiddies safe," Greatcoat said, "stop lookin' for them."

Anger burst through her, like fireworks exploding in the night sky. She extended her arm to the limit and pointed her pistol at his skull. "If you've hurt them, I'll kill every last one of you. And I won't need any Kendricks to do it."

Greatcoat waved a dismissive hand. "They're fine. No need to get in a twist."

"Fine? You're forcing them to be criminals," she exclaimed.

"No one's forcin' them to do anything," he shot back. "They're where they belong."

"They belong with me, and I *will* find them."

Greatcoat bared his teeth in a snarl. "Now, see here, ye silly bitch—"

A door was flung open in one of the houses behind them, throwing a wide shaft of light into the close. Greatcoat retreated, pulling his companion along with him.

"This is yer last warnin'," he said. "Keep out of Old Town, or the deaf girl will be next."

With that, they vanished into the night.

When Samantha tried to bolt after the pair, Braden managed to catch her arm and clamp her against his side.

"Let me go," she yelped. "I have to—"

"What's goin' on out there?" barked a voice in the doorway behind them.

"Stop struggling, sweetheart," Braden murmured to Samantha. "They're gone, and if we're not careful, we'll have the Watch down on us."

Although she subsided against him, he could feel the tension vibrating through her slender form. Braden half-turned to see an older man standing in a doorway behind them. He was holding a lantern and peering at them.

"My wife and I were returning home when those two villains tried to rob us," Braden called back. "Fortunately, your appearance gave them fright and they ran."

"Missus, are ye all right?" asked the man, obviously suspicious.

"Y . . . yes," Samantha said in a quavering tone. "I'm fine. It . . . it was frightening. I thought my husband and I might be killed."

Although she was doing a bang-up job of playing the terrified wife, Braden knew part of that terror was genuine—for her sister, not for herself.

"Do ye want me to fetch the Watch?" called the man.

"No need." Braden gently began to tug Samantha back the way they came. "We made the mistake of taking a shortcut, that's all. We'll head back to the street and find a hackney."

"These closes are no place for folks like ye after dark," the fellow said. "Yer a damn fool fer takin' yer wife through here."

"I couldn't agree more," Braden dryly replied.

The man slammed the door, plunging the close back into gloom. Braden glanced over his shoulder as he hurried Samantha to the street. Though he needed to wear spectacles to read, he had excellent night vision. Thankfully, he could see no one was following them.

"Please stop rushing me," Samantha said in a cross voice. "You'll give me a stitch. Besides, those poltroons are obviously long gone, and you know it."

"Then thank God for small mercies."

They exited the narrow lane into Cowgate. Although quiet this late at night, the streetlamps pushed back the darkness and they could see a Watch box just up ahead. Even better, a hackney approached from a few blocks away.

Braden stopped them under a lamp. "Samantha, I know you're upset, and you have every right to be. But it would have been deranged to follow those men."

She voiced a frustrated little growl. "I need to know where their bolthole is."

"I think we can safely assume it's the Hanging Judge. It's likely they have men guarding the perimeter. Maybe they were even looking for us."

"Yes, and that's incredibly disturbing."

Braden had to agree. He could understand that the bastards would have gotten wind of Samantha's activities, since she'd been roaming the stews for months. But they'd immediately recognized him as well, and it almost seemed that they'd expected him to be in Samantha's company.

She removed her arm from his grasp and began absently rubbing her elbow.

"Lass, did I hurt you?" he quietly asked.

She shook her head. "No. And I think it was me they were looking for."

"Very possibly, which means you are not to go out by yourself at night. In fact, we won't go out at all until we come up with a better plan. Either that, or we'll both end up like Donny."

Or worse.

When she snorted in derision, Braden bent down so he could look her straight in the eye. Even obscured by her veil, her expression mingled fear and defiance.

"I repeat that you are not to go out at all. Understand?"

She rapped her walking stick against the cobblestones in frustration. "We *need* to find them, now more than ever."

"I know. But if anything were to happen to you, who would take care of Felicity?"

Her quick grimace told him that he'd made a home hit.

"All right," she reluctantly said. "But we can't sit around doing nothing. Those men made it very clear that they're not stopping, so we need to stop *them*."

Braden waved down the hackney. "Agreed. We have to come up with a better plan than wandering about Old Town looking for clues, or trying to sneak up on the Hanging Judge. Your cover is blown, Samantha, so it's time to regroup."

When she mumbled a salty oath under her breath, Braden had to smother a grin. His lass might look dainty and unassuming, but she had the heart of a lion.

Your lass?

"So, what do we do?" she asked.

He shook off the sense that he'd somehow just made a momentous decision.

"First, we'll get off the street. Then you're going to tell me everything you know. No more half-truths or evasions."

"For a supposedly mild-mannered physician, you're very bossy," she said sardonically.

"Surely you've heard the old adage that physicians view themselves as God-like?"

When she scoffed, some of the tension eased out of his shoulders. Samantha now had her fear under control, which meant they could think and plan from a rational standpoint. Unfortunately, he wasn't quite sure how to begin navigating through such an epic mess.

That's why he needed information. He also needed her complete trust.

The hackney pulled to a halt. Braden helped Samantha up to the seat, gave the driver the address, and climbed in beside her. He had to crowd her in the small carriage, thigh to thigh, which his stupid brain didn't mind one bit.

They jolted off, the horse clopping slowly along the street. Samantha went quiet as she stared down at her gloved hands, curled around the top of her walking stick.

"All right there?" he asked.

"Didn't you find the conversation with those two thugs rather bizarre?"

"This entire night has been rather bizarre, but I take your point. The one fellow was studying us. The other was simply muscle, most of which was between his ears."

"He certainly didn't take kindly to you calling him a moron. Why did you keep insulting them?"

"I was doing a little studying of my own. I wanted to see how they would react to being pushed."

"Seemed rather risky to me."

He gave her an incredulous glance. "Really? You're calling my behavior risky?"

She flapped a hand. "You know what I mean. Under those specific circumstances."

"I'll remind you of that the next time we find someone pointing a pistol at us."

"Now you're just being annoying."

"It's been an annoying evening. I can think of better ways to spend my time."

Like wooing and kissing the pretty lass by my side.

Surprisingly, rather than snapping at him, she let out a weary sigh. "So can I."

And didn't that sad little response break his heart right in two?

For how many months had Samantha carried this lonely burden, one freighted with so much weight and sorrow? She'd come from the Highlands a sweet, innocent girl, and then life had dealt her one cruel blow after another. Yet, from the depths of despair, she'd pulled herself up, determined to seek justice and to help those who couldn't help themselves, no matter the personal cost.

And it had cost her indeed. That he knew, because he'd suffered the same sort of loss himself. Right then and there, Braden vowed that he would do *whatever* was necessary to restore Samantha to the life she deserved—one filled with happiness, peace, and love.

Oblivious to the silent revolution reordering his life, she tapped a thoughtful finger on her chin. "Why did they need to study our reactions?"

Braden forced himself to focus on her question. "Study *your* reaction I'm sure, not mine. It must be because you're getting close. They now see you as a threat."

"But how did they discover who I was? Donny and I are always incredibly careful." She balled her hand into a fist and knocked it against her forehead. "And they know about Felicity, too. I led them right to her, fool that I am."

Braden took her hand and pulled it into his lap. "You are

most certainly not a fool, Samantha. Unfortunately, even though you and Donny have been extraordinarily careful, you've been doing this for months now, and Old Town is full of eyes and ears. It's not surprising that the villains would eventually get wind that someone was looking for them. And since they now know who we are, our first order of business is to ascertain who *they* are."

She fell silent as the carriage turned a corner and started up to New Town. Braden held his peace, keeping her hand in his lap. He was rather amazed that she allowed him to do so.

A few minutes later, she twisted a bit and peered up at him. He could now see her mouth under the edge of her veil—a full and tempting mouth, pink as a rose and just as soft and inviting.

"Did your brother really throttle a bear?"

"Ah, what?" he said, distracted by her loveliness.

"A bear, in Canada. Did he throttle one with his bare hands?"

"Oh, of course not. It's an old family joke. Logan looks like he could, though. And he did throw a few men off a bridge once."

"Good heavens."

"In all fairness, they were attempting to kidnap his future wife at the time."

She chuckled. "Your brothers seem to be very exciting, by all accounts."

Unlike him, seemed to be the implication.

"They're also very capable. That's why we should ask for their help, especially Logan's. He's good at solving problems *and* tossing poltroons off bridges."

"No," came the instant, emphatic reply.

Braden swallowed his frustration. He understood her fear, but she needed his help and likely that of his family's, as well. Tonight had proved conclusively that Samantha wasn't wrong to believe there was a larger conspiracy afoot.

She was now in danger, too, whether she cared to admit it or not. The men they'd encountered tonight would kill her without a second thought if she got in their way. And if her husband's killers had yet to be found, there was no reason to think *her* killers would be brought to justice, either.

He frowned at the thought. "Why haven't his killers been found?" he murmured to himself.

Samantha threw him a startled glance. "What?"

The carriage drew to a halt, slightly jostling them.

"In a minute," he said.

He handed her out and then paid the driver.

"Thank goodness you had him drop us at the end of the street," Samantha said, shaking out her skirts. "I didn't relish the notion of sneaking in through the front door. My housekeeper is a very light sleeper, and she would no doubt hear me."

"So you're going to sneak in through the back door?"

"Exactly. I'll just nip down the lane and through my garden. It's just there, so you needn't worry about escorting me. Thank you—"

She gasped when he took her arm and propelled her into the laneway.

"You're not getting rid of me that easily, Samantha. Not without a full explanation of tonight's events. Plus you're going to tell me what you truly think happened to your husband."

She huffed with indignation. "I believe I already have explained. And although I am exceedingly grateful for your assistance tonight—"

"You should be, since I saved your pretty arse."

She yanked her arm away. "Dr. Kendrick, that sort of language is entirely inappropriate."

"It's entirely appropriate, as long as you insist on shutting me out."

By now, they'd reached the back gate. He put his hand on

the latch, preventing her from going in. Samantha faced him, one hand slapped on her hip and the other gripping her walking stick. Even though the blasted laneway was as black as pitch, he had no doubt she was steaming like a teakettle.

"Dr. Kendrick—"

"Braden. I think after tonight's adventures we're on a first-name basis."

"You certainly seem to think so. Now, if you get out of my way, I will open the gate."

He kept his hand on the latch. "Are you going to talk to me?"

"Yes, but only because you otherwise will keep us standing here all night. That would mean you'd get no sleep before seeing your patients tomorrow, and I will not be held responsible if you slice off the wrong body part because of fatigue."

"I hold to a firm rule of never slicing off the wrong body part. It's hell on one's reputation."

"You are ridiculous. Now, there's a bench over there by the kitchen garden. We'll have to keep our voices down, though. I do not need my neighbors imagining all sorts of wrong-headed things if they were to see us out here."

Braden could imagine all sorts of delightful things with her—before a warm, cozy fire, clothing optional.

Stop it.

Samantha led him to a wrought-iron bench. Beside it was a raised vegetable bed that held the last straggling herbs of the season. After she rested her walking stick against the edge of the bench, they sat side by side for a minute or so, staring up at her townhouse. The windows were dark and all was quiet but for the wind rattling through the leafless branches of the trees.

"I'm convinced my husband was murdered because he found something amiss at our charitable foundation, most likely what he learned about the orphanage finances," she finally said in a hushed tone. "It must have been something so significant that someone needed to kill him to cover it up. As you know, they tried to make it look like a robbery, and I couldn't convince the police that it was not the case. So Donny and I have been trying as best we can to find evidence to support our belief—and find the killers, too."

Braden briefly squeezed her hands, which were clenched in her lap. "I'm sorry, lass. That's bloody awful."

Her shoulders lifted in a tiny shrug. "I have grown accustomed to the awfulness of it, if that makes sense."

It did, because he'd grown accustomed to something similar. Although the pain never truly went away, the shock of it subsided over time. If lucky enough, one found a reason to go on. For him, it was his work. For Samantha, it was seeking justice for her husband and finding the children.

"Bathsheba mentioned that valuables were left on your husband's body. I take it you pointed that out to the police."

"I did, but it didn't matter to them. And I became unwell shortly after, so I was in no condition to press the point."

She meant her miscarriage. It was obviously still too painful to discuss, especially with a man who was little better than a casual acquaintance. He intended to change that, though.

"How do you know your husband found something amiss at the orphanage?"

"Because he told me."

Not the answer he'd been expecting. "Really?"

She canted her head sideways. Even behind her filmy veil, he could see her disapproving expression.

"Roger shared most everything with me. Some husbands do, you know. They actually trust their wives and treat them like rational creatures instead of overgrown children."

Braden held up a placating hand. "I wouldn't expect you to marry a man who didn't treat you that way."

"Then why did you seem surprised by my answer?"

"If your husband flat-out told you of his concerns, why have you hit so many brick walls in your investigations? And why the difficulty in convincing others?"

"You can partly thank Roger's grandfather," she bitterly replied. "He thought me hysterical and discounted everything I told him. Lord Beath thought I was kicking up a fuss for no good purpose and besmirching Roger's good name in the process. As if I would ever do anything of the sort."

"He sounds like an idiot and a cold-hearted prat. How could you besmirch your husband's name by wishing to see his killers brought to justice?"

"To be fair to Beath, he was genuinely devastated by Roger's death. But he was also angry with Roger for always exposing himself to what he deemed *unsavory elements*. A proper gentleman didn't muck about with thieves and gutter-snipes or go about unescorted in the stews. He acted as if Roger brought his death upon himself."

A familiar anger burned in Braden's gut. He'd heard that sort of accusation before, and it made him want to throttle any fool who could say something so ugly.

"That is an incredibly callous view of the situation, and it grieves me that you were forced to listen to such nonsense."

She let out a weary sigh, as if her little burst of fury had exhausted her. "Lord Beath never approved of Roger's progressive ideas. And in some ways, I think it's easier for him to simply blame his grandson. Roger did something foolish against his grandfather's wishes and counsel and unfortunately paid the price for doing so."

"I encounter some of those backward attitudes in my work, too."

"It's immensely frustrating, isn't it? Some days I don't know why I bother with the foundation."

He gently bumped his shoulder into hers. "Och, lass, none of that nonsense. You do an immense amount of good. Everyone knows that."

She rubbed the bridge of her nose through her veil. "Thank you, but it doesn't feel like it lately."

"Then we'll simply have to get to the bottom of this mystery, so you can get back to your work."

There was a fraught pause.

"We?" she cautiously said.

"Yes. You're stuck with me, at least until we find those children and make sure the threat against you and Felicity is eliminated."

Braden sensed her weighing his words, trying to decide if she could truly trust him with everything.

Finally, she inclined her head in a nod. "Then how do you propose *we* go about that?"

Yes!

He felt a tremendous surge of relief that she'd finally accepted him. But since that response felt out of proportion to the moment, he just flashed her a brief smile.

"First, I have a question. While I understand Lord Beath's motivations, why wouldn't anyone else believe you, especially since you had proof?"

She shook her head. "But that's just it. I don't have proof. All I have are the suspicions Roger shared with me. He'd only just started to audit the foundation's books. He was doing it himself, because he wouldn't trust anyone else, at least initially."

"Not even the other members of the board?"

Samantha waggled a hand. "Generally speaking, he trusted them. Under the circumstances, though, it made sense not to involve them. After all, someone managed to gain access to either the accounts or to the orphanage itself, which would suggest an insider. So he intended to keep digging till he found something and then go to the board."

"And he was murdered before he had a chance to find anything."

"Yes."

"Was the board made aware of any of this after your husband's death?"

"They all thought it was humbug, except for Arthur Baines. He and Roger were very close, so Arthur was quite distraught about the situation. The rest of them . . ." She let out a bitter snort. "I was just a hysterical woman, not to be taken seriously. Weak in the mind from grief."

His heart ached for her, and for the wounds she'd been forced to carry.

"If any of them thought you weak in the mind," he replied, "then they are a fat lot of nincompoops and chuckleheads, as my grandfather would say."

She let out a ghost of a laugh. "He'd be right about that. Of course, it didn't help that I then fell ill, because it seemed to confirm their theory. The weaker sex and all that nonsense."

"Let me just say that my sisters-in-law would be delighted to give that pack of idiots a resounding thump on their tiny skulls—with the full support of my brothers, I might add."

"It must be quite wonderful to have a family like that," she said in a wistful tone.

Braden fought the urge to pull her into his arms. Only the knowledge that he would be taking advantage of her stopped him from doing so.

"Yes, it's grand," he replied.

He realized again just how lucky he was to have his family, no matter how irritating they might occasionally be.

They sat quietly, listening to the whispering wind in the night-shrouded garden. Braden got the impression that she was wrestling with herself—or, perhaps in some way with him. After a while, she lifted her veil, folded it neatly over her hat, and turned on the bench to face him.

"I was pregnant when Roger was killed, and the shock caused me to miscarry. That's why I was so ill. That's why Lord Beath—and the others—treated me the way they did." She ducked her chin. "And perhaps in one way they were right. If I'd have been stronger, I might not have lost my child."

This time, he didn't hesitate. He took her hand, uncurling her clenched fist and lacing their fingers together. She twitched a bit before clutching his hand with a surprisingly strong grip.

"Samantha, that's sheer nonsense. You'd suffered a life-altering shock, and shock affects the body in many different ways. Most times, we don't even know why a woman miscarries. I've known perfectly healthy women who've lost their babies for no reason that medicine can explain. What I do know, however, is that you were not at fault. Your body was not at fault. Anyone who blames you or thinks you were weak should be hanged, drawn, and quartered."

"Thank you," she said in a gruff little voice, staring down at their hands.

She was trying to hide her emotion, and hide from him.

Oh so gently, he tilted up her chin so he could look into her eyes.

"I *am* a doctor, lass," he said. "Running down villains might be your area of expertise, but this is mine. I know what I'm talking about."

She stared at him, wide-eyed, and for a moment he was lost in the shadowed beauty of her delicate features. Then her gaze suddenly narrowed, and she pulled her hand from his.

"Bathsheba already told you, didn't she?"

When he shrugged, she muttered under her breath.

"Your friends worry about you because they love you," he explained.

"They're busybodies. And you're a busybody, too."

He held up his hands. "Guilty as charged. But you can trust me, just like you can trust John and Bathsheba."

"We'll see. So, what's next, Dr. Kendrick?"

He'd lost a wee bit of ground, if she was back to calling him Dr. Kendrick.

You'll make it up.

"One more question. Did Baines do anything when you shared your suspicions with him?"

She bristled. "Of course he did. Arthur believed me, so he went through the books very thoroughly but could find nothing suspicious. As did John later on, you will recall."

"I don't mean to denigrate their efforts, but neither is a financial expert."

"Well, no," she confessed.

"Then that's our next step, I think. Someone needs to dig deeper into the books and find what your husband found."

"Perhaps," she cautiously replied. "But I'm afraid someone on the board would surely inform Lord Beath. He'd pitch a fit. Besides, I don't wish to cast an ill light on the foundation unless absolutely necessary."

"That's why my brother Logan should do it. He's a financial genius and verra canny, ye ken."

She gave him an apologetic smile. "I don't mean to cause offense, but . . ."

"Can he be trusted to keep his mouth shut? Yes, absolutely. Only the three of us would know."

She pondered for a few moments before nodding. "All right, then. But you cannot tell him about my other investigations . . . what I'm doing in Old Town. No one can know that, not even your brother."

"Agreed, on one condition."

She let out a dramatic sigh. "Which is?"

"Until Donny's ankle is healed, you're not to go out at night without me."

"Does that include social occasions?" she sarcastically replied.

"Since you apparently never go out to parties and such, that won't be a hardship. You're a recluse, lass, and that's a fact."

"Nonsense," she said, rising to her feet. "I am not a recluse. Well, not really."

He stood. "I'm one myself, you know. My family thinks

I'm a mad scientist, locked away in my lab performing bizarre experiments."

She chuckled as they walked toward the house. "And are you?"

"No, I'm just hopeless when it comes to social functions. Never can think of what to talk about besides what I do. You'd be amazed how many people remain unmoved by the workings of one's digestive system."

"Except for people with digestive problems, I imagine."

When he laughed, she shushed him.

"Sorry," he softly replied.

She descended the steps to the kitchen entrance, fishing a key out of her pocket. When he followed her down into the shallow stairwell, she threw him a startled glance.

"Was there something else?" she whispered.

A wee kiss would be grand.

"You still haven't promised not to venture out at night without me. I must insist on that, Samantha."

She stared up at him. Her eyes, huge and dark, held an expression that seemed wistful and almost shy. "I promise. And, thank you for tonight. I . . . I was just teasing, you know. I'm really very grateful for your help."

Braden felt a pull he'd not felt for a very long time, an invisible magnetic force. His gaze drifted to her full lips, which suddenly parted on a wavering inhalation. He could feel his head dip down, as if under the control of that force. Her hand stole up to rest on the lapel of his coat, just as her eyelids fluttered shut. Her sweet breath was on his mouth, and—

The door behind her flew open, and light flooded the stairwell. Samantha jerked back, smacking her walking stick against his knee.

Hard.

"Ouch," he muttered.

"Oh, sorry, sorry," Samantha gasped. "Are you all right?"

"I'm fine."

Braden narrowed his eyes on the big man standing in the doorway. Donny glowered back, clearly ready to rip off his head and toss it into the garden.

Samantha turned to her manservant. "Er, Donny, I didn't realize you were awake."

"Ye snuck out," he tersely said, switching his ire to his mistress.

"Yes, well, I can explain."

"Donny, you really shouldn't be up on that ankle," Braden said.

"And what are ye doin' out with my lady?" Donny asked in a rather menacing voice.

"Making sure she doesn't get killed."

Samantha whipped her head around to glare at him. "That's not helpful, Dr. Kendrick."

"Sorry," he said, not feeling the slightest bit sorry.

After all, he'd been about to kiss the lass and instead got a right good knock to the knee.

Samantha's housekeeper, dressed in a wrapper and night-cap, appeared at Donny's shoulder. "Goodness, my lady! What were ye doin' out at this time of night?"

"That's what I'd like to ken," Donny said.

"Hush, you'll wake the neighbors," Samantha hissed. Then she flashed a quick look at Braden. "Good night, sir. And thank you."

She hustled her staff inside and slammed the door in his face.

CHAPTER 14

Braden stuck his head into the study where his brother was working at his desk.

"Got a few minutes to talk?" he asked Logan.

"For you? Always. Besides, I need a bit of a break."

"It might not be much of one," Braden replied, hoisting up the box in his hands.

Logan eyed him over the top of his spectacles. "What the hell is that?"

"Ledgers." Braden lugged his burden over to the mahogany desk and placed it on the one corner not covered with papers.

His brother pushed his spectacles up onto his head before reaching into the box and pulling out the top volume.

Braden frowned. "Since when did you start wearing spectacles?"

"Since about a year ago." Logan flipped open the ledger. "I need them when I'm doing close work, which you apparently failed to notice."

"Apparently. Also, I am a terrible brother," Braden said.

He sank into the buttery-soft leather club chair in front of the desk. The well-padded upholstery cushioned his weary body, tempting him to close his eyes and have a snooze. After his adventures with Samantha, slumber had eluded him last night. Too much to think about, including Samantha's various revelations *and* the fact that he'd almost kissed her.

Logan scoffed. "Braden, you're the best of us, but you work too hard. Speaking of which, you look like hell. How much sleep did you get last night?"

"I'm perfectly fine." He ruined that assertion by having to smother a cracking yawn.

Logan eyed him with brotherly disapproval. "Another late night with a patient?"

"Hmm."

"What does that mean?"

"Nothing. Just work, is all."

"You've had a run of late nights. I'll say it again—you'll wear yourself out if you're not careful."

"There's no need to glower at me like a disapproving nanny. You're as bad as Nick."

"That is literally impossible. Nobody nags and fusses as much as Nick."

"You're a close second," Braden dryly said.

"A fairly recent development, as you know. And we've all deserved a clout in the head and a nagging from our big brother and clan chief on more than one occasion." Logan waggled a hand. "Well, you and Kade never did."

"Kade has always been kind and thoughtful, down to the bone. I was simply the boring one."

"No, you were always the serious one, even as a boy," Logan corrected. "So now it might not be such a bad thing to kick over the traces, lad. Spend some time with your family. Have a little fun. You might like it."

"I'm hardly likely to kick over the traces with my family. Well, except with Grandda. He'd no doubt manage something that would land us behind bars."

Logan grinned. "True enough. Then go to a party or spend a night out with your friends. You do have friends, right?"

"I'll have you know that I have at least one friend, possibly two. And speaking of Angus, I assume he's been complaining about me again."

"They've been here for over a week, Braden," his brother gently replied. "And they've hardly seen you."

Braden winced at the dead hit. "I'm sorry about that. I promise I'll spend more time with them over the holidays."

"I'll hold you to that promise, if for no other reason than to get Angus off my back. The old fellow's bored, I reckon. Joseph is hard at work at his studies, and even Pippa can't keep him amused all day. You have to do your bit, old son, before he drives us all demented."

"Perhaps I can take him to a nice dissection."

His brother laughed. "He'd probably enjoy it."

"That's what I'm afraid of. So I'll take him for a tour of the college library. There are some fairly gruesome medical exhibits there that should satisfy his bloodthirsty tendencies."

"We would all be in your debt." Logan started to flip through the ledger. "Now, what have we here?"

"Financial records for the Penwith Charitable Foundation."

Logan brought his spectacles down to his nose. "And why am I looking at them?"

"Because there's something wrong in there."

"Can you elaborate?"

Braden rubbed his jaw. "Actually, I haven't a clue."

Logan shut the ledger. "I think you'd better start at the beginning. Why do you have these in the first place?"

Braden had prepared for this question, of course. "Lady Samantha Penwith fears that someone, either a staff person or a board member, has been less than honest when it comes to foundation business."

"That's helpful," Logan sardonically replied. "Since you just joined the bloody Penwith Foundation, why the hell are *you* doing this?" He took off his spectacles. "Braden, what aren't you telling me?"

Naturally, he'd been prepared for that question, too.

"If it seems like I'm withholding information—"

"You clearly are."

"It's because I promised Lady Samantha that I would be discreet."

"Are you seriously saying that you don't trust me?" his brother demanded.

"Dolt, of course I'm not. But much of this involves Samantha's—"

Logan's eyebrows shot up.

"Lady Samantha's personal life," Braden corrected. "Despite my absolute trust in you, I'm not at liberty to divulge as much as I would obviously prefer."

His brother had a remarkable gaze—a clear, penetrating blue that Braden swore could almost drill a hole in a man's brain. Logan had reduced any number of blustering, arrogant fellows to babbling incoherence with that gaze alone. It was an ability he shared with Nick, and they'd used it to extract legions of embarrassing admissions from their younger brothers over the years.

Now that lethally sharp gaze was trained on Braden. Keeping secrets was practically a mortal sin in the Kendrick family, because long-buried secrets had inflicted a great deal of damage on all of them over the years. As a result, family members now did their best to be honest with each other, sometimes ruthlessly or even comically so.

Still, there were secrets that he wasn't ready to share, including Samantha's.

"You can leave off at any time," Braden said. "Unlike most of the blockheads you deal with, I'm immune to your attempts at intimidation."

Logan snorted. "Either that or I'm losing my touch. In any case, you're certainly no blockhead."

"I'm sure that if I didn't know you, I'd be utterly terrified."

"In truth, I recall *you* intimidating the rest of us into good behavior on more than one occasion. You were excellent at delivering scathing lectures, even as a boy."

"You provided me with a great deal of useful material."

"Sad but true. Very well, I shall cease trying to intimidate you. I just want to make sure that you're not being drawn into anything dodgy or beyond your ken."

Braden lifted a hand. "That's why I'm coming to you. I know when I'm in danger of dodgy. Or, at least, not working within my area of expertise."

"Ah, are we still talking about the books, or about Lady Samantha? You seem to be spending quite a bit of time with her."

While Logan couldn't intimidate him, he could certainly be annoying. Shrewd, but annoying.

"The books, idiot. And of course I wish to assist Lady Samantha. Her foundation does excellent work. If someone is taking advantage of her or the foundation, I want to put a stop to it."

"Entirely reasonable and altruistic. Well done, you."

"Thank you, but are you going to help me or not?" Braden asked with some asperity.

Logan flashed him a crooked smile. "Just teasing. You're a little too serious for your own good, lad."

"This is very serious business, Logan."

After another shrewd look, his brother nodded. "Tell me what you can, and I'll do my best to figure out what's going on."

As Braden outlined the situation, starting with the disappearing children, Logan's expression turned grim. He asked a few questions, and then began flipping through the pages again.

"Most of the board members are convinced that the children ran away," Braden said. "So they're dead-set against police involvement."

"Don't want the scandal," Logan commented.

"Exactly."

Logan glanced up with a sympathetic grimace. "Sorry, lad. It's an awful business, and I'll do what I can to help. Right now, though, I don't see the connection between the missing children and issues with the books."

Braden sighed. "There might not even be a connection, which I know isn't very helpful."

"I'll manage. Is Lady Samantha the only person concerned about this?"

"Blackmore supports her, although, again, it is not his area of expertise. Arthur Baines apparently gave the books a thorough working over at one point but came up empty. While sympathetic, his conclusion was that there's nothing amiss."

"Ah, Baines the barrister, correct?"

Braden caught the hint of disapproval in Logan's voice. "What have you got against Baines?"

"Probably the same thing you've got against him."

"I was trying not to be obvious."

"Braden, I might not be able to intimidate you, but I *can* read you."

"Then, oh mighty seer, perhaps you can further elucidate your dislike of Baines?"

"He's slithered up to me at a number of social events, trying to get my business. Bastard even cozied up to Donella. He no doubt hoped that if he flirted with her, she'd fall for his charm and persuade me to engage him as my lawyer."

"Good God. I'm surprised you didn't throttle him or toss him out the nearest window. You *are* losing your touch."

"Oh, I was going to throttle him, all right. But Donella managed to persuade me that the man was simply an idiot and not worth my time."

"Donella can be very persuasive." Braden said.

Logan waggled his brows. "*Very* persuasive, if you get my drift."

"I do, and if I wasn't a physician I would be properly revolted. Now, let's get back to the issue at hand."

"I have one more question," Logan said. "Why is Lady Samantha asking you? More specifically, why does she trust you over everyone else?"

Braden shrugged. "Because I'm so trustworthy?"

"Och, have it your way, then."

"Splendid."

His brother studied him for several long moments and then shook his head. "Lad, this makes no damn sense, and I don't like it when things lack sense. If you're in trouble, you need to tell me. I mean it."

Braden heard the worry in his brother's voice. In light of that unpleasant confrontation with two armed thugs, Logan's worry was reasonable. And, truthfully, if he couldn't trust his big brother . . .

"Lady Samantha is convinced that her husband was murdered because he discovered something amiss at the foundation," he said. "Something obviously serious enough to get him killed."

For almost a minute, Logan didn't say a word. Braden could practically hear him rifling through the information in his head.

"How did Lady Samantha arrive at that conclusion?" Logan finally asked.

Braden gave a brief explanation that left out the dodgy bits.

Logan shook his head. "I've met Lord Beath a few times. Man's a right, old bastard, and doubly so if he shut down the investigation into Penwith's murder."

"Beath's another reason Lady Samantha came to me," Braden said. "She's afraid that if he twigs to her digging around, he'll remove her sister-in-law from her care."

"Yes, Felicity Penwith. Donella's told me about her."

"Then you know the situation. If Beath gets any hint of scandal, he'll punish the both of them."

"Then perhaps Lady Samantha and her henchman might wish to leave off skulking about the stews at night. That strikes me as fairly scandalous behavior."

Braden almost toppled out of his chair but managed to keep a straight face. "Not a clue what you're talking about, old fellow."

"I know I look like a big lummox, Braden, but I'm quite good at connecting seemingly unconnected bits of information."

Braden eyed him. "You're also very good at collecting information."

"Yes." Logan jabbed a finger at him. "And I do not want you stumbling into that sort of nonsense. Is that clear?"

"Absolutely. You have my word."

Logan sighed. "Oh, God. You're already in neck deep, aren't you?"

Brandon tapped his chest. "More like this deep?"

"You're obviously quite taken with the lass."

His heart rate kicked up a notch, but he kept his tone bland. "No, though I respect her a great deal."

"Well, that's a load of bollocks."

"Logan, she's a widow," Braden said, starting to feel exasperated. "Her husband was murdered, for God's sake. She's not in any mood for courting. Nor am I, for that matter."

"Sure about that, are you?"

Braden narrowed his gaze. "Are we done now?"

His brother crossed his arms and studied him. "Lad, what happened to you?"

He frowned, surprised by the question. "What are you talking about?"

"Something happened to you in the last few years, and it

wasn't good," Logan said. "Was it during one of your visits to Hanover? Did something go wrong over there?"

For the first time in ages, Braden felt himself standing at the edge of that awful, gaping abyss. He instinctively rebelled against it. Unfortunately, his throat was now so tight that all he could do was shake his head in denial.

"You know you can tell me anything, Braden. I would never judge you," Logan quietly said. "If not me, then tell Nick. We all love you and would walk over hot coals to help you."

Braden now felt like a mountain-sized boulder was lodged in his throat.

"I know that," he gruffly managed. "But the one who needs help is Lady Samantha. And I need your help in order to help her."

Logan's smile was wry. "Stubborn, that's what you are."

"I'm a Kendrick. We're born stubborn."

"True, that. All right, leave these blasted ledgers with me. I'll see what I can find."

Braden expelled a relieved breath. "Thanks, old man. I'm in your debt."

"Speaking of being in debt, I believe I hear Grandda heading our way. Get ready for that lecture, laddie boy. You've earned it."

Unmistakable footsteps sounded from the hallway outside the study. The door flew open and Angus stomped into the room, heading over to the desk. He propped his hands on his hips and glowered down at Braden.

"Ye'll be makin' yer excuses to flee, I suppose, now that I'm here." He waved his hands in the air. "The great doctor savin' all them lives. Why, ye'd rather be muckin' about with blood and guts than spendin' time with your nearest and dearest."

Braden pointed at his grandfather's head. "What in God's name *is* that?"

Angus was garbed in his preferred attire, a linen shirt

topped by a ratty leather vest, an old kilt, and boots that had seen better days even twenty years ago. But all that paled in comparison to his bizarre headgear.

The old fellow drew himself up with offended dignity. "What does it look like, ye ninny?"

"A moldy bush," Logan said, trying not to laugh.

Braden eyed the gigantic wreath of wilting branches and leaves that all but swallowed up his grandfather's head. "Not moldy, but certainly dusty." He glanced at his brother. "Can a bush even get moldy?"

"If you don't know, then I certainly don't," Logan said as he stood and came from around his desk. "I've actually seen that before. It's some sort of Christmas decoration, isn't it? But, Grandda, why is it on your head?"

Angus jabbed Logan in the shoulder. "I'm supposed to be Father Christmas, ye jinglebrains. I wore it one year at Kinglas, when yer da and yer stepmother—my dear daughter—were still alive. Surely ye remember. It was the grandest celebration in the entire county."

Braden smothered a laugh. "Actually, it was a Twelfth Night celebration and you were the Lord of Misrule. Wasn't that the year Logan tipped over the flaming punch bowl and set Mamma's best carpet on fire?"

"That was the twins," his brother dryly replied. "I took the blame because I'd grown too big for Da to thump me."

"Och, he kenned who it was," Angus said. "But I managed to talk the old bugger out of punishing the lads. It was just an accident, ye ken."

"An accident that could have burned down half the castle," Logan tartly responded.

"Fah, ye exaggerate."

Braden snapped his fingers. "Now I remember. Grandda, you also wanted to decorate Da's mounted stag head in the library. You climbed up on one of the bookcases and tried to wrap ivy and mistletoe around its antlers, but you ended up pulling the whole thing off the wall."

"Pulled half the wood paneling down with it." Logan grinned at Angus. "Our father was *right* fashed about that."

Angus waved a dismissive hand. "The twins were causin' trouble over somethin' or other. Everyone was gettin' fashed, so I came up with that little prank as a discretionary tactic to get yer da's mind off the twins."

"Grandda, that is not what that word means," Braden said.

His grandfather rounded on him. "I'll be havin' no sass from ye, laddie boy. Just because yer a high and mighty doctor doesna mean yer too big for me to paddle yer bum."

"How did you get that god-awful head thing down from Kinglas?" Logan said, clearly trying to *divert* their grandfather's wrath. "Isn't there an equally appalling outfit to go along with it?"

"I had Taffy send down the whole kit and caboodle, along with some of the other decorations." The old man beamed. "She knew we'd want to be havin' a right and proper holiday, even if we're not at Kinglas."

Taffy was the castle's redoubtable housekeeper and one of the few people capable of controlling Angus. The two of them seemed to have a mysterious understanding that the family had by common accord thought best not to question.

"You'll be missing Taffy and everyone else at Kinglas, Grandda," Braden said. "But I know Pippa and Joseph are thrilled that you're here for the holidays."

Angus waved his arms, sending the mess on his head sliding backwards. He managed to catch it and jammed it down until it tangled with his bushy white eyebrows.

"I'm here for ye, too, lad. If ye'd stop runnin' off all the time, ye'd figure that out. Ye'd think ye didn't want to spend time with me and Kade."

Braden mentally winced. "I promise I'll make it up to you.

I'm just finishing up some work at the clinic, and then I'll have more free time."

Angus perked up. "Mayhap I could come down and help ye. I'm a wonder with diagnosin' the ailments, ye ken." He tapped the side of his nose. "It's the old knowledge that's best."

For a moment, Braden's mind reeled at the image of his grandfather let loose on his patients.

"That's not such a bad idea," Logan said, trying to stifle another laugh.

Braden threw him a dirty look before dredging up a smile for his grandfather. "I'm sure that can be arranged at some point."

Angus rubbed his hands together. "Grand. I'm free this afternoon."

"Oh, God," Braden muttered.

Fortunately, Logan took pity on him.

"Grandda, why don't you take Joseph and Pippa Christmas shopping today?" he said as he returned to his seat behind the desk. "I know they want to pick out gifts for Donella and their uncles, and I'm too blasted busy to take them. I'd consider it a great favor if you could help them find gifts."

"Oh, aye." Angus craned over the desk, trying to read the open ledger in front of Logan. "What are ye workin' on? Those be not Kendrick books, I'm thinkin'."

"They're from the Penwith Foundation," Braden said. "I asked Logan to take a quick look at them."

Angus yanked off his headgear and tossed it onto a nearby chair, where it sent up a cloud of dust. "Sounds like trouble. Let me have a look, laddie boy. I have the best head for keepin' the books in the family, as ye ken."

In fact, he had the worst head for it—not that it mattered.

Braden wouldn't let Angus anywhere near so tricky and dangerous a situation. Mayhem would surely ensue.

"There's nothing wrong. Logan is simply giving them a quick check."

"But—"

Braden interrupted by placing a firm hand on his grandfather's shoulder then started moving him toward the door. "You have to take the children shopping, remember? I'll go with you in the carriage, and you can drop me off at the college."

His grandfather's wrinkled features turned suspicious and watchful. "What aren't ye tellin' me, son?"

"Nothing, Grandda. Now, let's get to it, shall we? The day's not getting any younger."

He gently propelled his grandfather down the hall, doing his best to ignore his protests and maintain the fiction that all was business as usual.

CHAPTER 15

Samantha absently rubbed her temple, trying to ignore the headache threatening like a summer storm in the distance. No matter how long she stared at the column of figures, they still didn't add up. The number neatly penned at the bottom of the page should be larger.

"Where have you gone to?" she muttered.

"What's that, my lady?"

Samantha glanced up, startled to see her housekeeper. "Oh, Mrs. Johnson. I didn't hear you come in."

The housekeeper deftly balanced a tea tray in one hand as she moved aside a pile of correspondence on Samantha's desk to make room. "Ye'll give yerself a headache staring at those numbers. And all this paper, my lady . . . I'll never know how you find what you need."

The study was Samantha's favorite room, and she preferred it cozy and quiet, with books, journals, and papers stacked on every shelf and tabletop. For both Felicity and Samantha, the study, although a trifle messy, served as a welcoming place to work, or simply curl up in front of the fireplace with a good book.

Samantha put down her pen. "I'm fine, but these numbers certainly are not. They simply refuse to make sense."

The foundation was losing money, to the point where some operations were now truly at risk.

Mrs. Johnson fixed her a cup of tea. "The books won't be growing legs and running away. Ye can work on them later."

"I wish they would run away. Then I wouldn't have to look at them."

The housekeeper clucked her tongue as she crossed over to the fireplace. She reached down to shovel some coal into the grate and then stirred up the embers.

"Ye let the fire go down again, my lady. Ye'll catch yer death, sitting all hunched up and no heat."

"Hardly. I'm wearing a thick tartan shawl, as you can see. Besides, I grew up in the Highlands. November in Edinburgh is balmy compared to that."

The real explanation was that coal was expensive, and she needed to keep an eye on costs. Her widow's portion was as generous as Roger had been able to negotiate on her behalf, but most of the Beath estate was entailed. If she wanted to maintain the townhouse in Edinburgh—and keep Felicity with her—Samantha couldn't afford to waste a shilling.

Mrs. Johnson returned to the desk. "Money worries at the foundation, too?"

"Yes. The blasted numbers don't appear to add up."

"Would ye like me to take a crack at them?"

The housekeeper did an excellent job managing their household finances, and she also often helped Samantha with the daily accounts from the orphanage. But this was something different.

"It's not the numbers, precisely. While they're adding up in the conventional sense, something's not right. We're short of revenues because we've lost a few donors, but not enough to show such an imbalance on the final accounting. We're shorter in funds than we should be."

She'd handed over the endowment and investment accounts to Braden and his brother for exactly this reason. The recorded numbers were technically correct but no longer made sense in the larger scheme of things.

"Mayhap a supplier is trying to pad their charges or cut back on supplies," Mrs. Johnson said.

"Mrs. Girvin would have caught it. She's scrupulous in her dealings with our suppliers."

Mrs. Johnson made a not unexpected scoffing noise at the mention of Girvin. For some reason, Mrs. Johnson disliked the foundation's housekeeper, without ever explaining why. Samantha had finally put it down to professional rivalry or even a wee bit of jealousy.

Mrs. Johnson topped up her teacup. "Losing those two donors was a bad bit of luck, too."

Samantha grimaced. "Yes. Mr. Dorrence was one of Roger's most steadfast supporters. It was rather a shock that he declined to make a donation this year. Even worse, he convinced his cousin to do likewise. Mr. Baines and I tried to convince them both to stay, but to no avail."

"And we can guess who put them up to it," Mrs. Johnson gloomily replied.

Better than guess. Lord Beath must have talked Dorrence into pulling his funds. Beath would do whatever he could to damage the Penwith Foundation, or even bring it down altogether. After all, he blamed it for his grandson's demise, and no argument Samantha made could dent that view.

"Now some of the board members want to close the girls' school to save costs," Samantha said. "Fortunately, Mr. Baines and Dr. Blackmore were able to talk sense into enough of them."

It would be over Samantha's dead body that the group of old blowhards would close her school—a true haven for the girls and a way to escape life on the streets.

"Maybe Dr. Kendrick can help ye. Talk to those rich brothers of his," the housekeeper suggested.

Samantha hesitated. "I'd rather not go there just yet."

"The Kendricks are always willing to open their wallets for a good cause, I hear." A crafty smile formed on the housekeeper's face. "And from the way the good doctor looks at ye, I'm thinking he won't mind doing what he can to help."

That was exactly why Samantha was reluctant to ask him. After that fraught, exciting moment when he'd almost kissed her, her emotions had been in a tumult. For her to ask for financial support, especially when he was already doing so much, struck her as manipulative.

She loathed the idea that Braden would think she was using him.

"The doctor and his family are doing quite enough. I don't want to go begging for money unless I have no alternative."

"He was happy to save yer life the other night. I imagine he'd be happy to help ye out with this, too."

Samantha blew out an annoyed breath. "I was perfectly safe at all times."

Mrs. Johnson started making her way around the room, plumping pillows and straightening stacks of books. "Because Dr. Kendrick caught up with ye before ye got to Old Town. I shudder to think what would have happened if he'd not been there."

"Then I would have delayed visiting the Hanging Judge until daytime. I'm not a complete nitwit."

"I never said ye were. But Donny and me can see how this chafes on ye. Ye can't go out on yer searches with him laid up, and that has ye in a right good fret."

"Time is not on our side. If another child goes missing . . ."

"Yer doing everything ye can, so there's no good working yerself into a stew." She glanced at Samantha. "Mayhap the doctor can go out with ye tonight? Even Donny trusts him, now that ye've explained the situation."

Samantha picked up her teacup. "I hope he can. He's been busy with patients the last few nights, and I've been stuck at home, feeling utterly useless."

Mrs. Johnson went back to her tidying. "He'll help, and Mr. Logan will no doubt get to the bottom of yer money troubles. Clan Kendrick is a force of nature, and all of them verra handsome, too. Ye could do much worse than Dr. Kendrick, my lady."

Thankfully, Samantha had already swallowed her tea or she would have spit it out all over the ledger. "And what is that supposed to mean?"

"Yer still looking peaked," said her housekeeper, ignoring the question. "Mayhap ye should talk to Dr. Kendrick about those headaches."

"You may have noticed that I already have a doctor, and he's a very good one."

Besides, Braden was the last person she wanted to know about her headaches.

"Aye, Dr. Blackmore is a grand physician, but he's married."

"Which has nothing to do with anything," Samantha tartly replied.

The doorknocker sounded from below, interrupting Mrs. Johnson's embarrassing observations. Samantha's feelings for Braden Kendrick, or his feelings for her, were not something she wished to think about.

"Are ye expecting anyone, my lady?" Mrs. Johnson asked.

"Not today. Is it Dr. Kendrick?" she couldn't help asking as the housekeeper peered out the window.

Mrs. Johnson let out an aggrieved sigh. "We should be so lucky."

Samantha rose. "Who is it?"

"Lord Beath. That's his carriage."

"That cannot be right. He never comes to town at this time of year."

Samantha hurried over to the window. Sure enough, Beath's old-fashioned town coach was parked below, liveried grooms at the ready. Her stomach pitched.

Hell and damnation.

Muted voices told her that the maid had answered the door. Beath's sharp tones overrode the girl's soft voice, with a harsh demand to see the mistress of the house, *immediately*.

"Riled up old bugger," Mrs. Johnson grumbled as she hurried to the door. "Ripping up at poor Sally."

"When isn't he riled up?" Samantha smoothed down her dress, annoyed by the trembling in her hands. "Put his lordship in the main drawing room and serve up tea. And please try to keep Felicity away. If Lord Beath asks for her, then she can come down. If not, best to keep her out of the line of fire."

"Aye, my lady."

Samantha crossed to the mirror over the sideboard by the door. Her whey-faced complexion, combined with shadowed eyes, was not an inspiring sight. She smoothed down an errant curl and tugged her collar and sleeves into starched alignment. Thankfully, her dress was beyond reproach—a lavender gown with few embellishments. The old poop would probably still wish her to go about in full widow's weeds, but even the highest stickler couldn't expect her to wear black crepe two years after Roger's death.

After waiting a few moments to make sure her grandfather-in-law was properly settled, Samantha made her way downstairs. She paused outside the drawing room, pinned a smile on her face, and then opened the door and went in.

"Lord Beath, you've caught us a bit by surprise. If I'd known you were coming, I would have met you at the door."

The baron, standing by the fireplace with his back to her, glanced over his shoulder. As she expected, a frown dominated his jowly, aging features.

"That is why one has servants, Samantha, although I see you still have only a maid to answer the door instead of a proper footman. And as for catching you by surprise, I certainly do not need your permission to stop by and see my granddaughter, however unexpected."

Samantha mentally sighed. Barely in the room and she'd already offended him. Of course, her very existence had offended him from the moment they'd met.

"We are always happy to see you, sir. Won't you have a seat? Mrs. Johnson will bring up tea directly, unless you would prefer a sherry or a port."

He waved an impatient hand. "Refreshment is unnecessary. I don't intend to stay any longer than I have to."

That pronouncement, which should have been welcome, instead set off shivers of foreboding. The old man was fashed about something, and more so than the usual.

Lord Beath was tall and portly, with a touch of gout that usually had him walking with a cane. Despite his size, he carried himself with innate dignity, his posture ramrod straight despite his advanced years. Although at first glance his broad and jowly features suggested amiability, his cold blue gaze was sharp and disapproving. That gaze now swept over her with ruthless assessment.

As he took a seat in front of the low sofa table, Samantha cracked open the door to tell the worried maid in the hall to cancel the tea service. Then she settled into the wingback chair opposite him and arranged her skirts, taking a moment to prepare for the coming discussion.

"Do you wish me to fetch Felicity, sir?"

The old man glowered. "Women in your position do not fetch anyone, Samantha. Again, that is a task for servants—proper servants, not a girl who can barely gabble out two coherent words."

It would never occur to Beath that his unpleasant behavior might be the reason that Sally was nervous. To him, servants were a lower order of species, only worth noticing when they offended him.

"A liveried footman is an expense I cannot afford," she calmly replied.

"If you and Felicity would move to the estate and take up

residence at the dower house, I would provide you with staff.
You would be well cared for, and in proper style."

They'd be all but invisible, is what they would be. Tucked
away in the old dower house in the back garden, their daily
movements closely monitored by a man who actively disliked
them. For Felicity, especially, it would be a prison.

And Samantha would rather die than live under Beath's
thumb.

"Thank you, sir, but Felicity benefits greatly from Dr.
Blackmore's care. As well, I must be present to oversee the
foundation, which would be difficult to do from your estate."

He made a disgusted noise. "That demmed foundation.
Never understood why Roger wanted the blasted thing in the
first place."

"Which is why Roger made arrangements for me to manage
it should anything happen," she replied, keeping her voice
level. "He did not wish to burden you."

"No person of taste should *burden* himself with such an
enterprise," he snapped. "For the heir to one of the most distinguished baronies in the country to waste his precious time
on vagrants and brats was beyond understanding. If only
Roger had done what I told him, he'd still be—"

He pressed his lips together as he struggled to master his
emotions. Samantha knew that Beath genuinely grieved. At
the same time, he also harbored an unreasoning anger, with
part of him blaming poor Roger for his own death.

"That blasted place got him killed," he finally said.

Roger's work *had* gotten him killed, though not for the reasons his grandfather imagined. When she'd tried to present him
with those reasons after the murder, the old man had refused to
listen.

"I assume you did not visit today to speak about the foundation," she said.

"You assume correctly."

She forced a smile. "Then to what do we owe the pleasure of your visit, sir?"

"There is nothing pleasurable about this visit. Quite the opposite, in fact."

Daggers drawn, then.

When he continued to simply glare at her, she was tempted to roll her eyes.

"Perhaps you could elucidate, sir?" she prompted.

"There are rumors circulating about you, Samantha. Ones so unfortunate, that I was forced to make this trip into the city to apprise you of them."

For a moment, her mind went blank. Then panic threatened to storm through her body. Samantha forced herself to ignore it, willing herself to respond with polite dismay.

"I cannot imagine what anyone could find to gossip about, much less start rumors. Felicity and I lead exceedingly quiet lives. We barely socialize, and when we do it's only with friends you approve."

When his gaze turned flinty as granite, her heart sank. Still, the rumors must have nothing to do with her nocturnal searches through Old Town. If that were the case, he'd have stormed upstairs and immediately dragged Felicity out of the house.

"My source is unimpeachable and quite specific about what she saw."

She couldn't hold back a sigh. Beath had many friends and acquaintances in Edinburgh, especially among the old guard of the aristocracy. It was one of the reasons she had to be so careful. One misstep in public and many of those people would be happy to report her misdeeds to the old prat.

"Might I ask the nature of these rumors?" she said.

"Scandalous ones—you, sneaking back from an assignation with a man." He gave an angry snort. "I could not believe it at first, but my correspondent was quite specific in detailing what she saw."

Samantha gaped at him. Of all the accusations she'd expected, this wasn't one of them.

"Ah, I beg your pardon?"

"You heard me, and I demand an explanation. Why were you sneaking into your own back garden the other night with some fellow dressed like a footpad?"

A burst of anger shot through her dismay. "Are you truly suggesting that my neighbors are spying on me and then writing to you with inaccurate—not to mention outrageous—gossip?"

Beath leaned forward in a clear attempt to intimidate her. "Answer the question, young woman."

"I will not. Instead I will ask one of my own. Have you set one of my neighbors to spying on me?"

He snorted. "I have no need to stoop to such behavior. *Your* behavior, however, is apparently scandalous enough to prompt concern among our mutual acquaintances."

Samantha wrestled her tumultuous emotions into some semblance of order. She needed to be careful, because the old man would happily punish her if he could.

"Lord Beath, I am certainly not engaging in assignations with any man. Do I occasionally go out at night on foundation business? Yes, and when I do, I take my manservant with me. For protection," she emphatically added. "If I choose to enter my house through the back garden, I fail to see why that is anyone's business."

"Ha, so you were sneaking into your house. I thought as much."

Samantha mentally cursed the slipup. "Again, I always take my manservant with me when I must go out at night. I would never travel through the city after dark without him."

Beath smiled with triumphant malice. "I know for a fact that your manservant has suffered a serious injury. Was he hobbling about with you the other night? I think not. You were gallivanting about with another man, and returning from God knows what."

A spurt of disbelieving laughter almost escaped her. Gallivanting? She and Braden had been trying not to get killed.

"I most assuredly was not *gallivanting* anywhere. I must add that I find it extremely distressing to learn that my neighbors are spying on me and reporting back to you. Truly, Lord Beath, you cannot think that sort of behavior is either necessary or appropriate."

The sneer marking his heavy features told her that she was fighting a losing battle.

"I suppose you would accuse me of spying, too," he said with contempt. "Such imaginings are no doubt the result of your unstable character. I had assumed you had recovered from your unfortunate illness, but I was mistaken, I see. I would not have allowed Felicity to remain here had I known you were not capable of exercising good judgment."

Everything in Samantha went as still as if she were cornered prey. For him to throw her illness back in her face, to remind her of that terrible time . . .

You can't let him rattle you.

She folded her hands, assuming a calm expression. "Very well, sir. With whom was I supposedly gallivanting?"

"Kendrick. The doctor. You were seen with him down in Old Town, near the taverns—as well as sneaking back to your house. Disgusting behavior, and worthy of a doxy, not a lady."

His words felt like a nail driven into the back of her skull. Pain shot out in barbed tendrils, making it hard to think.

"Dr. Kendrick is a member of the foundation's board," she managed. "In the last few weeks, he's been kind enough to escort me to the occasional evening meeting. If I was seen with him, it must have been on one of those occasions."

It was a desperate attempt, a lie that could be easily dismantled. But what choice did she have?

"That explanation is hardly better for your character than the rumors," he replied. "No respectable woman would go about town at night with a man unescorted."

"Sir, I am hardly a child, and I am also a widow. There is nothing scandalous in allowing Dr. Kendrick, who is an eminently respectable man from an eminently respectable family, to escort me anywhere. You certainly have no objection to Arthur Baines doing so."

"Baines is a distinguished barrister from a good family. The Kendricks are practically hooligans," he huffed. "And Highlanders, to boot."

"As am I," she gritted out.

"I am painfully aware of that fact."

Suddenly, the door flew open. Unfortunately, the interruption was Felicity, who stalked into the room. Mrs. Johnson appeared a moment later, looking harried as she grimaced an apology.

Felicity paused only long enough to throw a searing glance at Beath before coming to stand in front of Samantha, turning her back to her grandfather.

"*Why is he here?*" she signed.

Samantha forced herself to clearly enunciate, so Felicity could easily read her lips and Beath could hear.

"Your grandfather has come to pay us a nice visit. Now, please give him a proper greeting."

Felicity's eyes narrowed to suspicious slits. Samantha held her gaze, willing her not to kick up a fuss. Thankfully, the girl finally turned and dipped a quite respectable curtsy to her grandfather.

Beath's mouth twitched with disapproval. He ignored Felicity and addressed Samantha.

"Is this how you let my granddaughter come in to company? She's as disheveled as one of your orphanage brats."

Samantha was tempted to retort that her *brats* were always neatly dressed—more neatly than Felicity was at the moment. Her sister-in-law had obviously been helping out in the kitchen on baking day. Sadly, she'd failed to remove her apron, which was liberally dusted with flour, and her long hair was pulled back in a single messy braid instead of being tidily coiffed.

"Shall I bring up tea, my lady?" Mrs. Johnson said, attempting a diversion.

"Get out and close the door behind you," Beath ordered.

Samantha bristled. "Sir, there is no need to bark at my staff."

"Since they are incapable of keeping my granddaughter in some semblance of respectability, they are in need of correction. I am most displeased, Samantha." Beath waved a finger at his granddaughter. "And why is she dressed like a servant?"

Felicity signed him a sharp retort, one Samantha would definitely *not* translate.

"I don't understand all that hand waving," Beath irritably replied. "What is she saying?"

"It's baking day, and Felicity was down baking pies. We will take some of them to the orphanage tomorrow."

Now the old man looked genuinely aghast. "You take my granddaughter down to that benighted place? Have you lost all your wits, Samantha?"

She tried not to wince at the dig. "Only occasionally, and just to get out of the house. She is in my sight at all times, or she is with Donny. We would never allow any harm to come to her."

"It is distressing enough that you go there, Samantha, but to take my granddaughter? I absolutely forbid it."

Felicity, who had been reading her grandfather's lips, blew

out an angry sound. Palms out, she thrust her hands straight out from her chest and then sharply pulled them apart.

No.

Samantha stood to get the girl's attention. "Felicity, it's fine."

Scowling, her sister-in-law brought her hands up, and then thrust them forward, palms facing down. Then she pointed at Beath.

Hate him.

"What is she saying?" Beath asked in a suspicious tone.

"Felicity is disturbed that we seem to be arguing," Samantha replied. "I'll explain your wishes to her later, but perhaps it might be best if she went upstairs now to change."

She placed her hands on her sister-in-law's shoulders. The girl's body quivered with repressed fury.

"She should certainly go change," Beath said. "I will visit another day, when she—and you—are in a proper condition to receive me."

"An excellent idea," Samantha replied as she steered Felicity toward the door. She all but shoved the poor girl out of the room and then returned to the fray.

Naturally, Beath resumed firing first. "I will no longer tolerate this situation, Samantha. Changes have to be made."

"What situation are you referring to, sir? We go on here as we always have."

"And I have tolerated that long enough. You are keeping company with inappropriate men and allowing my granddaughter to run about town like a hooligan."

By now, pain clanged in her skull as if a blacksmith's hammer was pounding there.

"I repeat, sir, I am doing nothing of the sort. Felicity is a lovely, intelligent girl, well liked wherever she goes."

"Felicity should not be going out at all. The girl will never be normal, and yet you embarrass her and yourself by parading her in public. Out of respect for Roger's wishes, I have allowed the girl to stay with you. However, it has now become clear that you are an unfit guardian." He leaned forward, his face ugly with contempt. "Once and for all, it is time for you to recognize that you are mentally incapable of caring for my granddaughter."

Samantha's lungs seized, stunned both by his declaration and his threat. It was beyond belief that he would throw her illness back in her face—an illness made infinitely worse by his unfeeling treatment of her.

Beath sat like a canny old wolf, waiting for her to make a mistake.

She wouldn't give the bastard the satisfaction.

"I reject your assessment of the situation, Lord Beath. I am perfectly well and entirely capable of taking care of your granddaughter, and that is what Roger certainly wished. Since you have never desired Felicity to live with you, I am mystified as to what you truly want."

He leaned forward, spearing her with his gaze. "What I want is a life free of scandal and fuss. What I want is my grandson *alive*."

Since there was nothing she could say to that, she didn't try.

Beath heaved his bulk up from his chair. "I will be staying at my mansion in the—"

He stopped when the door opened again. Bathsheba sailed into the room, a brilliant smile on her beautiful features. Samantha mentally cursed. Of all the bad timing . . .

"What are you doing here?" she blurted.

Bathsheba rounded her eyes. "Why, I saw Lord Beath's carriage, and I simply *had* to stop in and say hello."

She swanned up to the old man, who was looking bemused by her dramatic entrance, and dropped into a deep, graceful curtsy.

"Such a pleasure to see you, my lord," Bathsheba enthused

as she came up. "Goodness, it's been ages since you've visited the city. You've been most remiss in depriving us of your company."

"Er, well, yes," Beath replied. "And how do you do, Mrs. Blackmore?"

"I am simply splendid, now that I know you're in town. I do hope it will be for a long stay."

When Bathsheba actually batted her eyelashes at him, Samantha could only stare in disbelief. Beath, in turn, looked more than slightly flummoxed.

"Well, I don't know what my plans are at this point," he said.

"I do hope you'll join us for dinner one evening," Bathsheba replied. "My husband will insist on it."

That was a bridge too far, since Beath and John cordially disliked each other. A scowl returned to his face, and he gave Bathsheba a stiff bow.

"Give my regards to your husband, ma'am." Then he flicked a cool glance in Samantha's direction. "I will be staying in town for several days, Samantha. Before I leave Edinburgh, I will make whatever decisions I feel are necessary."

Samantha managed a shallow curtsy. "Please know that I am at your disposal, sir."

He gave a brusque nod before stomping out of the room.

"Pleasant as always, I see," Bathsheba sardonically commented.

With a groan, Samantha plopped down onto the sofa, rubbing the back of her skull. Her friend settled next to her.

"I suppose I overdid it by telling him that John would wish to see him." Bathsheba wrinkled her nose. "Sorry, pet."

Samantha tried to think past the furious headache. "It wasn't you. The old bastard wants to take Felicity away from me. He says I'm an unfit guardian."

"That's *ridiculous*," Bathsheba said, outraged. "And John will certainly have a few words to say about that. We'll think of something, I promise. John and I will fix everything. We won't let Beath take Felicity away from you."

"I'm not sure anyone can fix it," Samantha wearily replied. "Not this time."

Because this time, she'd made a cock-up of everything, and she had only herself to blame.

CHAPTER 16

Bathsheba, dressed in a frilly wrapper while she lounged on the silk chaise in her dressing room, scooped up a coconut pastry from the tea tray.

"Samantha, you *must* try one of these. They'll be smashing for your fundraiser."

Samantha looked up from yet another checklist in her notebook and cast Bathsheba a distracted glance. "If I sample anything else, I'll not be able to fit into this silly dress."

Donella Kendrick was seated on a padded stool at a dressing table that was piled high with bandeaus, turbans, and other expensive headgear, gingerly inspecting a gigantic, feathered headband.

"That dress is far from silly," she said, glancing up. "And it's the perfect color for you, Samantha."

"It should be," Bathsheba said. "I picked it out for her."

"Unfortunately," Samantha muttered as she inspected her reflection in the standing mirror.

Miss Boland, Bathsheba's dresser, critically eyed her before pulling another pin out of the pincushion strapped to her wrist. "You could use a little more weight on you, my lady. I'll have to take in three inches of fabric at the waist."

Boland was a truly estimable woman who had served her mistress with unswerving loyalty for years. Although a bit stern and always dressed like a widow in perpetual mourning, she had impeccable taste and an unerring eye for the latest fashions. Unfortunately, Bathsheba had decided to unleash her on Samantha. The last thing she wished was to parade about in a stupidly stylish gown designed to attract attention—particularly male attention.

She juggled her notebook and pencil as she tugged at the alarmingly low neckline. "Boland, I'm practically falling out Surely it's not supposed to be this revealing."

The dresser gave her a gentle slap on the hand. "It's just sagging because I haven't made the adjustments yet. And it's not too low. It's just right for the line of the gown."

"Lord Beath will have an absolute conniption when he sees this. Besides, I'll probably catch pneumonia from exposure."

Bathsheba chuckled. "I know a certain man who *won't* have a conniption. Then again, you might give him heart palpitations when he sees that you actually do have a bosom."

Samantha waggled her notebook, dropping her pencil in the process. "Stop. You're being absolutely ridiculous again."

Her dratted friend had been teasing her about Braden Kendrick all morning. It was driving her batty, all the more so since it would appear that she'd developed an unfortunate schoolgirl crush on the annoying man.

Bathsheba widened her eyes. "I only ever speak the truth."

"That's true, although you are occasionally ridiculous, too," Donella teased. "Which is why you're so much fun to be with."

"I'm glad someone appreciates me," Bathsheba replied with a dramatic sigh.

"I'm sure your husband does, too, especially when you're wearing that dressing gown," Samantha sarcastically commented.

"Outfits like this are rather wasted on John, since they tend not to stay on for very long."

Samantha bent to pick up her pencil. "Now you're just bragging."

Boland yanked her back up. "My lady, if you don't stop wiggling about, I'll never get this gown finished."

"Best do what she says, old girl," Bathsheba said. "With the gala fundraiser tomorrow night, Boland doesn't have much time left."

"Why can't I just wear one of my regular ball gowns? They're perfectly fine."

"Actually, they're boring and three years out of date," her friend ruthlessly replied. "If you show up to your own fundraising gala looking like a church mouse, you'll present a bad impression—like you're desperate. That sort of thing tends to frighten off donors."

Samantha shook her head. "That makes no sense."

"Sadly, it makes perfect sense," Donella said, "at least in the minds of people with money and influence. They would see it as throwing good money after bad. That attitude is certainly not the essence of charity, but it is the way of the world."

"The world is stupid," Samantha groused.

She knew she was acting like a ninny and a grump, but these last few days had shredded her nerves, thanks to Lord Beath and his threats. On top of those were the threats made by the mysterious villains in the slums, whose voices lurked constantly at the back of her mind.

"I need my pencil," she said. "I've got to finish my list."

Donella retrieved the pencil, and then plucked the notebook from Samantha's hand. "Let me finish. I'm quite good at organizing holiday parties, especially large ones."

"Thank you," Samantha replied with a grateful smile. "I'd be lost without your help."

She'd met Logan's wife a few days ago, when Bathsheba had brought her for a visit. Although feeling shy about meeting one of Braden's near relations, Samantha had found herself instantly comfortable in Donella's company. The lovely young matron radiated a quiet self-assurance and a genuine kindness that made her easy to be with. And she'd been brilliant with Felicity, taking the time to have a genuine conversation with her.

Still, the more Samantha got involved with the Kendricks, the more she got tangled up with Braden. Given Lord Beath's feelings about the Kendricks in general and Braden in particular, that was a problem. It was a problem for Samantha's heart, as well, which stupidly insisted that getting involved with Braden Kendrick might be the solution to several of her problems.

"You worry too much, darling," Bathsheba said. "The gala will be a huge success, and you'll raise gobs of money."

"Thanks to you two."

After that dreadful encounter with Lord Beath where he had threatened to remove Felicity, Samantha had skated on the edge of a full-blown panic, unable to come up with a plan to appease the old scoundrel. Bathsheba, though, had seen right to the heart of the matter. Appeasing Beath meant catering to his pride. Since his true bone of contention was the foundation, they could spike his guns by showing him that the charity was held in high esteem by Edinburgh's elite. Nothing, Bathsheba had claimed, could illustrate that more effectively than a grand charity gala attended by the best families in the city.

"But how do we get them to attend?" Samantha had exclaimed. "I'm not exactly the most popular woman in Edinburgh."

"We give them something they can't resist," Bathsheba had mysteriously replied before whisking off.

She had then reappeared on Samantha's doorstep the next morning, Donella in tow, to deliver the news that the Penwith Foundation would throw a grand holiday party in five days' time. It was to be sponsored by the Kendricks and would feature an exclusive piano recital by Kade Kendrick, the toast of the Continent.

"The ladies of Edinburgh are madly in love with Kade and would kill to attend one of his concerts," Bathsheba had said. "You'll raise money *and* prove to nasty Lord Beath that the Edinburgh establishment is firmly behind you and the Penwith Foundation."

Donella had agreed. "My husband is already telling his business associates that attendance is obligatory."

Overwhelmed, Samantha had pointed out that five days was barely enough time to plan a dinner party. Donella had countered that the Kendricks would provide the staff and the resources, under her supervision. All Samantha had to do was draw up a guest list and instruct the foundation's staff to assist as required.

Samantha had been stunned. Aside from Braden, she'd never met any of the Kendricks, and yet they were willing to go to a great deal of trouble and expense for a perfect stranger.

"It's . . . it's incredibly generous of you," she'd stammered to Donella. "But I couldn't possibly put your family to such trouble. You don't even know me."

"True, but you're Braden's friend. Which means you're our friend, too."

Need outweighed her objections, so Samantha had given in.

Now, Bathsheba inspected the tea tray. "Donella is a wonder, but you've worked very hard as well, Samantha."

Boland pointed at her mistress. "Not another one of them tarts, or you'll be popping out of your new dress."

Bathsheba winked as she selected a petit four. "I doubt most of the men at the party will mind."

"Yes, but the wives will," Donella said as she crossed off a line on the list. "Since they often control the charitable purse strings, we don't want the husbands staring at your décolletage all night and then finding their wives lacking in that category."

Samantha laughed, but Bathsheba simply popped the tiny cake into her mouth. "I'm quite shocked to hear a former nun make such a risqué comment."

Donella snorted. "Only mildly risqué. Besides, living with a houseful of Kendrick men has forced me to adjust my standards."

"You were a nun?" Samantha asked, surprised.

"Until Logan Kendrick got a good look at her," Bathsheba said.

Donella flashed Samantha a wry smile. "It's not quite as outrageous as it might sound. I never took my final vows, and I left the convent before I met Logan."

Bathsheba snorted. "You met him the very *day* you were kicked out."

"You were kicked out?" Samantha asked, trying not to laugh.

"I was dreadfully inept at being a nun. The sisters put up with me for much longer than they should have."

"And then Logan came along, and the rest is history," Bathsheba said.

"He didn't give me much of a choice," Donella confessed with a little grin.

"A trait afflicting other Kendrick men," Samantha muttered to herself.

Bathsheba put a hand to her ear. "What was that, dear?"

"Nothing at all. Donella, is there anything I can do to help with that list?"

"No, I've got all the details regarding the staff thoroughly organized. It will be tight, given that *everyone* has accepted the invitation, but that will also make the party a success."

"Let's hope Lord Beath thinks the same," Samantha replied.

"There, you're done," said Boland after making a final adjustment on the neckline.

Bathsheba got up to inspect the burgundy-colored silk dress with its extravagant lace trimming. "Oh, Braden is going to love you in this. You look absolutely scrumptious."

"Lord Beath, however, will be appalled." Samantha pointed to her bare shoulders. "I'm half-naked."

Donella shook her head. "That gown is perfectly appropriate, and it isn't nearly as revealing as what most of the other women will be wearing."

"Do you really think so?"

The young woman pointed to herself. "Former nun, remember? I've got a nose for these sorts of things. And Braden *will* love it. I cannot wait till he sees you."

"Yes, well done, Boland," Bathsheba said. "The poor lad will fall head over heels, if he hasn't already done so."

Samantha felt her cheeks flame with heat.

"This affair or the dress has *nothing* to do with Dr. Kendrick," she said as Boland swiftly undid the buttons on the back of the gown. "And I'm sure you're both quite wrong about him, anyway."

"Not true." Donella handed Samantha her regular dress. "Braden has been an absolute bear these last few days. Logan says he's grumpy because you've been too busy to see him."

Samantha struggled with her sleeves and then yanked the dress down over her head. "That's nonsense. Besides, *he's* been the one who's been too busy to see me."

As soon as the words were out of her mouth, she winced. "What I mean, is—"

"What you mean is that he's been too busy to go out slinking about Old Town with you in the dead of night, looking for trouble," said Bathsheba. "One cannot blame the poor man for not wanting to work all day and then spend half the night acting like a blasted footpad. Not to mention the danger you put yourself in."

Donella dropped her pencil. "Er, what?"

"I haven't the faintest idea what you're talking about," Samantha said, twitching a hand in Boland's direction.

"Don't worry about Boland," Bathsheba replied. "She knows all about your adventures with Braden. She'd never say a word, either, even if Lord Beath or some other ninny tortured her with hot irons."

Boland, who had carefully draped Samantha's silk gown over her arm, scoffed. "I'd give them a good box on the ears if they tried. And we'd see who'd be getting hot irons."

"That's the spirit," Bathsheba said with a grin.

Donella twirled a hand. "Might we get back to the part where Samantha and Braden slink about like footpads?"

"We don't slink about like footpads," Samantha exclaimed.

Bathsheba waggled a hand. "Maybe you do a bit."

"How would you know? You never even saw us."

Then she froze, aghast.

"Ah, finally admitting it, are we?" Bathsheba softly said.

Samantha pressed her lips shut, regretting that she hadn't pressed them shut as soon as her friend initiated this deranged conversation. Instead, she'd just blurted out the truth—in front of Braden's sister-in-law, no less. He would be far from thrilled about that little slipup. She must truly be losing her mind.

Just like Beath said you were.

Suddenly, she felt like someone had just stuck her with a pin. A sigh softly slid out of her, like air from a tired old balloon.

Bathsheba tilted her head. "You're looking green all of a sudden."

"That's because you've been jabbering at her," Boland said, steering Samantha to the chaise. "Her ladyship needs a cup of tea."

"I think she needs something stronger," Bathsheba said.

"Well, then fetch her a sherry while I get on with this dress." Boland pointed a finger at her mistress. "And don't you be teasing her, anymore. She's got enough on her mind without your stuff and nonsense."

Bathsheba gave her dresser a flourishing bow, her frilly lace cuffs brushing the plush carpet. "Yes, oh mighty one. To hear is to obey."

With a derisive snort, Boland exited the room.

"She's so dreadfully bossy," Bathsheba said.

Samantha slumped onto the smooth silk cushions of the chaise. "Like her mistress, perhaps?"

Bathsheba wrinkled her nose, then fetched a tray with a crystal decanter and small wineglasses from a dresser tucked behind an ornate Chinoiserie screen. She poured out drinks and handed them around.

Samantha took a generous sip and was grateful for the soothing heat that made its way down her throat.

"I don't mean to be a bother," Donella apologetically said, "but can you please explain why you and Braden are going about the stews? I am certainly aware that Braden has feelings for you, but that seems a very odd thing to do, even for a Kendrick."

Samantha's heart stuttered. "Braden has feelings for me?" Then she flapped a hand. "Never mind. It doesn't matter."

"Of course it matters," Bathsheba said.

"It certainly does. Now, though, I would still like an explanation of this mystery before we engage in that discussion," Donella replied.

"It's rather complicated," Samantha said, hedging. "And I'm not sure Braden . . . Dr. Kendrick would appreciate me telling you."

"I strongly suspect he's already told my husband," Donella dryly noted. "Logan has been spending quite a bit of time on your foundation's books. Whenever I ask him why, he tries to put me off or distract me, which is *quite* annoying."

Bathsheba flashed a sly smile. "I suppose it depends on the distraction."

"Oh, he's tried *that*, believe me," Donella said. "And don't think I won't be having a little chat with him *and* Braden when I get home."

Samantha grimaced. "Splendid. Now I've gotten them both in trouble."

Donella put down her glass and took Samantha's hand. "No one's in trouble, my dear girl. I simply wish to know how we can help you."

"It's rather a long, complicated story."

"There's no rush," Bathsheba said. "Anything you wish to tell us will be fine."

Samantha sighed. It was pointless to pretend any longer that she and Braden weren't doing exactly what they were doing.

Haltingly, she began to tell the story. Except for a few questions, the two women listened with quiet sympathy.

When she finally came to the end of the sad and sordid tale, Samantha felt lighter, as if she'd given up part of her burden. She also realized that in the confines of this cozy dressing room, in the company of the generous women who'd become her friends, she felt safe. She'd only felt that way a few other times in these last, lonely years.

Mostly when she was with Braden.

Donella took her hands and squeezed them. "Oh, Samantha, I am so sorry for all that you've endured. What a terrible cross to bear."

"It's simply wretched," said Bathsheba in an outraged tone. "I knew it was bad, but all this? I would love nothing better than to murder that disgusting Lord Beath. What a monster."

"He's certainly not my favorite," Samantha admitted. "But he didn't kill Roger, and he's not responsible for the disappearances at the orphanage."

"Are you sure about that?" Bathsheba asked. "He'd love to bring down the foundation."

Samantha blinked, surprised by the question. "That never occurred to me, but . . ." Then she shook her head. "Beath would never soil his family name by associating with the criminal classes. He'll just try to get all his friends to pull their support, because that would effectively shut us down."

Donella held her glass out to Bathsheba for a refill. "I believe my nerves stand in need of bracing, especially after hearing how those awful men accosted you and Braden, Samantha."

"You must think me demented to engage in such a quest." Samantha rubbed her brow. "Sometimes I wonder if Lord Beath isn't right, after all. Perhaps my illness did make me unstable or . . ."

She couldn't bear to finish the thought.

Bathsheba scoffed. "Nonsense. Anyone who says otherwise needs a kick to his tallywags, not to mention his diddler."

When Donella choked on her sherry, Bathsheba thumped her on the back. "Sorry, old girl. Still, you really should be used to that sort of language, living with Kendricks."

"It's just that I've not heard those particular expressions before," Donella hoarsely replied.

"You can share them with Angus." Bathsheba then pointed a finger at Samantha. "But the sentiment is correct. You may be reckless, but you are not dicked in the nob."

Samantha tried to make a joke of it. "You have to say that because you're my friend."

In truth, though, she was beginning to worry that she had become obsessed with Roger's death to the point where she was putting others in danger.

As Donella studied her, Samantha twined her fingers together, feeling a bit nervous under the young woman's calm scrutiny.

"What?" she finally blurted out.

"I'm very familiar with mental afflictions," Donella said,

"and how they affect one's behavior. You strike me as an eminently sane person."

"Listen to her, pet," Bathsheba said. "Donella's mother *was* actually dicked in the nob, so she knows the signs."

Samantha's jaw almost hit the floor. "Your mother was . . ."

"Yes." Donella lifted her eyebrows at Bathsheba. "Although we generally preferred to use less colorful terms."

Bathsheba wrinkled her nose. "I thought our lass needed a bit of a jolt to pull her back from the edge."

"I'm so sorry about your mother," Samantha said to Donella.

"The poor old gal tried to kill Donella's cousin," Bathsheba said with her usual bluntness. "Luckily, the shot went wide and hit Donella instead."

Samantha goggled at her. "That doesn't sound very lucky to me."

"It was just a graze," Donella explained before leveling a stern look at Bathsheba. "And hardly the point."

Bathsheba waved a hand. "Then you'd best explain the point, so she truly gets it."

"The point is, dear Samantha, that you are not mentally unstable," Donella said. "I realize that, at times, you may worry that you could be unwell. I used to think the same about myself when I was feeling melancholic or lonely."

"Surely not," Samantha protested. "You're so utterly sane."

"As are you. But there will always be mean-spirited people who gossip or accuse, and those voices can be hard to ignore."

Samantha thought about that. "How did you learn to ignore them?"

"I listened to the people who loved me." She grinned. "One person, in particular, told me I was daft to believe such nonsense."

Bathsheba laughed. "That would be Logan, of course. Quite an interesting way of making his point."

"It was, but it was convincing precisely because he

mocked both the accusation and the accusers. Which brings me to my next point," Donella said, raising her eyebrows at Samantha. "Did Braden in any way suggest that your actions indicate hysteria or an unhealthy obsession?"

Samantha shook her head. "No. And he believed me from the start, too. Although I will admit that he was quite fashed that I was going to Old Town by myself."

"Typical," Donella said. "Kendrick men are very protective of their women. Even now, Braden is doing everything he can to keep you safe from both physical harm and gossip."

"But . . . but I'm not his woman," Samantha managed to sputter.

Donella frowned. "Are you sure, dear? Because he's been very blunt that we're to do everything we can for you. When Kade made an exceedingly mild objection that perhaps five days was not enough time for him to prepare for a concert, Braden actually yelled at him. He said—and I'm quoting here—to *bloody well start practicing*. Since Braden never raises his voice, we were all quite astonished."

"That sounds very promising," Bathsheba said with approval.

Samantha could feel the blush go right up to her hairline. "Oh, dear. It's actually very . . ."

She was about to say embarrassing before realizing that it was thrilling that he felt so strongly.

But then grim reality reared its head, and she remembered what she owed to Roger. What she owed to Braden, too, because whatever he might feel, or whatever she might feel, anything beyond friendship was impossible. She was too damaged, and a man like Braden Kendrick deserved so much more than she could ever give him.

She dredged up a smile. "You're both so kind. I'm afraid, though, that what you're suggesting is out of the question."

"Oh, why is that?" Donella calmly asked.

"I'm not fit—" She stopped to correct herself. "I'm not

looking to get married again. I loved my husband, and he was more than I could ever deserve."

"Samantha, no one's life is ever beyond redemption," Donella said. "Or restoration, for that matter. Joy is entirely possible."

Those gently uttered words sliced through her heart like a stiletto blade. It took her a moment to recover. "I don't know if I believe that."

Bathsheba leaned forward, her expression earnest. "Darling, you didn't know me as I was years ago. I was *unredeemable*, and I don't use that word lightly. I didn't start out that way, but time and circumstance made me so. I became a bad person, and I hurt people—good people. Compared to me, you're an absolute saint."

She stared at her friend, astonished. "You're one of the kindest people I know."

"You can thank my husband for that." Bathsheba's quick smile flashed like sunlight after a storm. "John saw what I couldn't see. He saw the person that I could become, and the life that we could have together. Not that it was easy, mind you. I resisted mightily. But John kept chipping away until he got past the stupid, hard shell I'd put round my heart. You're not like I was at all. Your heart isn't the least bit hard. In fact, you're an absolute peach, old girl. We know it, and Braden knows it."

Samantha had thought she'd safely walled off her heart, but right now it ached with a terrible longing she couldn't even express. "I . . . I don't know what to say to any of this."

Donella also leaned forward, tapping Samantha on the knee. "My dear girl, regardless of what happened in your past, you *can* move beyond it. You've already proven you have the strength to do so. Not only did you survive a terrible tragedy, you fought back. So, don't limit yourself or your future. Both can be so much more than you think you deserve right now."

"You *can* be happy again, dearest," Bathsheba softly added. "But first, you must truly want it."

Samantha wanted to believe that. She wanted to believe she could have a future, one full of laughter and joy. A future that might even include Braden Kendrick.

But again she heard the whisper in her head. It was the voice she'd been living with for the last two years—the one that told her that Roger must be avenged. She still had to put to rest the great injustice and sorrow of the past that she'd shared with her husband.

For now, any other future would simply have to wait.

CHAPTER 17

As he and Logan surveyed the entrance hall of the Penwith Foundation, Braden noted with satisfaction that the atmosphere of faded grandeur had been transformed into one of holiday splendor. Swags of greenery with tartan bows bedecked the halls, and evergreen wreaths hung in the high windows. The bannisters of the grand staircase were wrapped in lengths of red and green velvet, and the overhead chandelier, polished to a high gleam, was festooned with mistletoe boughs.

They'd planned and organized the entire affair in only five days. Most of the Kendrick house staff had been involved, as had Logan, Kade, and himself. They'd spent the last two days carting furniture and climbing ladders. It had been a pain in the arse, but it would be worth it if it helped Samantha and the orphanage.

"The old pile is looking grand," Braden said to Will, who was passing their coats and hats to a waiting footman. "We couldn't have done it without you and the Heriot Row staff. Well done."

Their butler, having overseen the lion's share of the preparations, allowed himself a smile. "Thank you, sir. I believe it's turned out rather well."

Logan shrugged out of his topcoat and handed it over.

"It's a bloody miracle. I had my doubts, especially when I was teetering at the top of that bloody ladder, hanging those bloody wreaths. I thought I'd never make it down alive."

"Och, ye wee ninny," Angus said as he unwound his wool muffler and dumped it over Will's shoulder. "I could have run up that ladder in a trice *and* done a better job of decoratin'."

Logan, a veritable giant compared to Angus, snorted. "A wee ninny? No doubt that's why Donella almost had a heart attack when she saw me on top of that decrepit thing."

"Which is why ye should have let me go up. I'm as fleet-footed as a mountain goat, ye ken."

"No more climbing ladders, Grandda," Logan firmly said. "You're too—"

Angus jabbed a finger toward his grandson. "Watch yerself, laddie boy."

"Grandda, you helped a great deal, from what I heard," Braden hastily interjected. "Donella said they couldn't have pulled this off without your decorating ideas."

Partially mollified, Angus left off jabbing his gnarled finger into Logan's cravat. "Kind of ye to say so, lad. Takes a real organizer. Young Will does his best, but I've got the brains for plannin' things out."

Logan swallowed a muffled laugh. Their grandfather's utter lack of organizing skills was legendary.

Angus glared at Logan. "Got somethin' to say, lad?"

"Sorry, just a frog in my throat," Logan replied, faking a cough.

"So, when are the other guests arriving?" Braden put in. "And where is Lady Samantha?"

Properly diverted, Angus gave him a sly grin. "Ye'll be wantin' to see her ladyship as soon as ye can, I reckon. Ye've been mopin' all week because ye've barely seen her."

Good God.

"She's our hostess, Grandda. I was simply enquiring as to her whereabouts."

"Really? Because I suspect you'd like to have a wee, private chat with her," Logan said with a wink. "*Verra* private."

Braden eyed his brother. "And I suspect you're a moron. No, I'm *sure* you're a moron."

Will tactfully intervened. "Her ladyship is upstairs with Mrs. Kendrick, seeing to the last-minute details regarding Mr. Kade's concert. There are some concerns about the placement of the piano."

Angus clucked his tongue. "Och, I told them footmen that they were placin' it wrong. I'd best get up there. Ye ken how nervous Kade gets when he performs, especially if I'm nae there to help him."

Contrary to that assertion, Kade had iron nerves and rarely got fashed about anything.

Braden patted the old fellow's shoulder. "Excellent idea, Grandda. I'm sure Kade is already wondering where you are."

As Angus beetled off, Logan sighed. "This evening is going to be a nightmare. Besides keeping Grandda under control, Donella has ordered me to rustle up large donations from the guests. I cannot tell you how much I'll enjoy trying to convince a fat lot of ninnies to open their purses."

"Just threaten them. That usually works."

"Oh, very helpful. It's not as if we don't have other things to worry about, either."

Braden and Logan planned to keep a close eye on the foundation's board members, noting whom they talked to and how they behaved. Logan believed that something dodgy *was* at play with the finances—possibly money laundering, although the precise means were not yet clear. The logical conclusion was that someone connected with the foundation had to be involved. But since they had little evidence to point them in the right direction, Braden feared that tonight would be a futile exercise in that regard.

Still, if they could manage to raise a goodly amount of

funds *and* convince Lord Beath that Samantha's work was entirely respectable, the evening would count as a win.

"Do we know when Lord Beath is arriving?" he asked Will.

"No, but the guests should start arriving momentarily," the butler replied. "Mrs. Blackmore has agreed to remain in the hall to greet them, since Lady Samantha is organizing the children's choir for their performance with Mr. Kade."

Logan nodded toward the staircase. "And speaking of Mrs. Blackmore."

Dressed in a resplendent green velvet gown that showcased her generous curves, Bathsheba arrived at the foot of the staircase, accompanied by Mrs. Girvin. They made a handsome pair, although Mrs. Girvin was dressed in a severely cut, black gown devoid of trimmings. Still, the woman's blond beauty was startling, as was the haughty demeanor that seemed oddly out of place.

"Hallo, and who is that with Bathsheba?" Logan murmured.

"The foundation's housekeeper," Braden replied.

His brother cast him a startled glance. "She doesn't look like the housekeeping sort."

"Indeed, no," commented Will in a clearly disapproving tone.

"Good evening, gentlemen," Bathsheba gaily said. "You both look splendid, although I'm disappointed that you decided to forgo the kilt. I do so love a man in a kilt."

According to Samantha, Lord Beath was allergic to most anything to do with the Highlands, so they'd decided on traditional evening wear. Unfortunately, Angus had clattered downstairs at the last minute wearing full dress kilt. Because it had been too late for him to change—and since he was, for once, looking respectable—Braden had not pushed the issue. He could only hope the rest of them would pass Beath's muster.

Logan bowed over Bathsheba's hand. "You, dear lady, are

beyond splendid. You'll have the poor fellows slavering in your wake all night."

She wrinkled her nose. "That sounds rather disgusting, nor do I think my husband will approve."

"Speaking of John, where is he?" Braden asked.

"He had a tricky case to finish up this evening but should be along before Kade's recital begins."

Braden smiled at the housekeeper, who stood quietly at Bathsheba's shoulder. "How do you do, Mrs. Girvin?"

"Very well, Dr. Kendrick." She glanced at Will. "Mr. Macklin, I believe you should make a final check on the waiters before the guests arrive. If you will accompany me to the kitchen?"

"Of course, Mrs. Girvin."

Will sketched a bow before departing with the housekeeper, his stiff posture radiating his disapproval of her.

"Well, that's bollocks," Logan commented. "As if Will needs to be told how to do his job."

"Yes, I'm afraid he's not very keen on Mrs. Girvin," Braden said.

Bathsheba shook her head. "That woman is even more arrogant than me. But she *is* terrifyingly efficient, and she seems to deal with the children quite well. Samantha speaks very highly of her."

"Speaking of her ladyship, I suppose we'd best go up and find her," Logan said, throwing Braden a smirk.

"She's in the recital room," Bathsheba said. "I'll hold the fort down here and greet the guests."

"Would you like me to stay with you?" Braden asked.

She scoffed. "Don't be silly. I can tell you're champing at the bit to see Samantha."

"I'm simply trying to be polite," Braden said, annoyed that he was so obvious. "Besides, I thought you might like reinforcements when it comes to managing Lord Beath."

"Since Beath is not well disposed toward you at the

moment," she said, "he'll probably bolt if you're the first person he sees."

"I can stay, if you'd like," Logan offered.

She shook her head. "He'd definitely bolt with you. In his eyes, you're barely civilized."

"That's true enough," Braden said, turning the teasing back on his brother. "Donella is still trying to teach him how to use a fork."

Logan poked him in the shoulder. "It's the knife that's the problem. I find I keep wanting to stab my annoying little brother."

"Thank God I'm a doctor, so I can stitch myself up."

"Hilarious," Bathsheba sardonically commented. "Now, please be off. The other guests are beginning to arrive, and I cannot be distracted by Kendrick blather."

"As her majesty commands," Logan said with a formal bow.

Huffing out a laugh, she turned her back to greet three arriving couples.

"If Beath thinks I'm bad," Logan said as they mounted the staircase, "just wait until he meets Angus."

"I'm going to do everything I can to prevent that. Since the man is exactly the sort Angus can't abide, the outcome would likely be disastrous."

"Let me manage the old boy. You just worry about Lady Samantha, eh? See what you can do to relieve her mind." Logan winked at him. "After all, you're a doctor. I'm sure you could come up with some sort of tension-relieving activity."

Braden sighed. "It never stops, does it?"

His brother laughed. "All right, I promise to behave, if you just try to relax for once. And you should spend some time with Lady Samantha. God knows you've both earned it."

"I intend to, but we also need to keep an eye on the board

members, while simultaneously making sure this evening doesn't blow up in poor Lady Samantha's face."

"You and Lady Samantha already have quite a bit of experience when it comes to sleuthing. Just carry on as you were, with the occasional break to have fun. You do remember how to have fun, don't you?"

"Logan, I frequently have fun," Braden said as they reached the top of the stairs and headed toward the largest classroom, which had been converted into a recital hall for Kade.

"Oh, and when was the last time you did so?"

When I came so close to kissing Samantha.

"I took part in a cracking good dissection the other day. Can't get more fun than that."

"Good Lord," Logan muttered, following him into the room.

Donella, a picture of quiet elegance in her gold-colored gown, came to greet them. "There you are. I was afraid you were going to stand us up."

Logan wrapped an arm around his wife's trim waist and pulled her close. "No, but you look so delicious I might have to whisk you away, party be damned."

"Before you even hear me play?" said Kade, strolling up. "That cuts me to the quick, old man."

"I get to hear you play every day," Logan sardonically replied. "For *hours*."

Donella patted her husband's cheek. "Poor you, having to live with one of the finest concert pianists in Europe."

"Maybe we could ask Angus to play his bagpipes instead," Braden said. "That should be a nice change."

Logan grimaced. "Lad, don't even suggest it. He'll have Taffy send him the bloody things from Kinglas, and then we'll all have to shoot ourselves—or him."

"He's already written to her," Kade dryly replied. "Grandda

suggested that he and I give a Christmas recital at the family holiday party."

"That's it," Logan said, "I'm loading my pistols as soon as I get home."

Angus was undoubtedly the worst piper in the Highlands, but loved the damn things and played them whenever he got the chance.

"No need for bloodshed. Just shoot the bagpipes," Braden suggested. "By the way, where is Grandda?"

"He and Samantha are checking on the seating arrangements in one of the supper rooms," Donella said. "Ah, here they are now."

Braden turned to see Samantha and Angus come into the room and promptly felt his jaw drop to the floorboards. While she was always bonny, Samantha's style was generally subdued, even stark. Tonight, though, she was an absolute stunner in a gown that made her look like a fairy princess.

An exceedingly lush fairy princess.

Her wine-colored dress shimmered in the candlelight, providing a perfect template for her creamy-white skin. And there was *quite* a bit of skin on display. Her neck and shoulders were exposed by the low neckline of her form-fitting bodice, and a hint of bosom peeked over the curved top. Her sleeves, lacy little contraptions that defied gravity, prompted a desire in him to conduct an intimate investigation of their workings, all in the interest of science, of course. From the narrow waist, the gown belled out in a graceful sweep of satin that was lavishly trimmed with lace.

Even more appealing was the shy smile that parted her pink lips when she spotted him. And for once, that smile reached her beautiful dark eyes. Samantha was so lovely that it made Braden's heart ache with a longing he'd not felt in a very long time.

And if ye keep starin' like that, somethin' else will start to achin,' too.

He ordered his body to calm the hell down and mustered a smile that he hoped wasn't that of a lust-smitten idiot.

"Och, the slackers are finally here," Angus said. "The puir lassie and I have been doin' all the work."

Samantha patted his arm. "It's been a team effort. We never would have managed this event without your family's help. I'm so grateful."

"It was our pleasure," Braden said, smiling down at her.

She dimpled back at him. He'd never noticed the dimples, likely because she hadn't had many opportunities to smile.

"Even when you were dragooned into carrying classroom desks to the third floor?" she asked. "Or sent up rickety ladders?"

"Hang on," protested Logan. "I was the one risking life and limb on that blasted ladder."

"And we were most impressed, my love," said Donella, with a twinkle. "But you've not yet been properly introduced. Lady Samantha wasn't here yesterday, when you were risking life and limb."

Samantha extended her hand. "Indeed, sir, I cannot thank you enough for *all* your help. I owe you a great debt."

Logan bowed. "For such a good cause, I'm happy to be a beast of burden."

"And then there's them ledgers," Angus said. "Bit of a mystery, that."

Braden mentally sighed. When it came to mysteries, his grandfather was a dog with a bone.

"Nothing mysterious at all, Grandda," Logan said. "I was just helping Lady Samantha figure out the best way to recoup some of the losses from the past year."

Angus snorted. "That's a load of—"

"Your grandfather was just saying that he remembers

meeting me when I was a little girl," Samantha brightly cut in. "Isn't that amazing?"

Donella smoothly picked up the diversion. "What an extraordinary coincidence. Was it a clan gathering? I wonder if my family was there."

If there was one topic Angus could never resist, it was clan business.

"Nae, it was a lass from one of the MacDonald families marrying one of the Campbells. A grand affair it was, but not a true gatherin.' The Kendricks attended, as did Lady Samantha's family. But mostly it was Campbells and MacDonalds."

"Sir, your memory is amazing," Samantha enthused. "You even remembered what I was wearing."

"That's because you were the prettiest of all the little lassies, all decked out in your wee plaid dress and matching tam."

"Was I there, Grandda?" Braden asked. "I don't remember it at all."

Angus snorted. "That's because ye spent the entire time off in a corner, yer head in a book."

Ouch.

Samantha gave Braden a sympathetic grimace. "I didn't remember either until your grandfather jogged my memory. But then it all came rushing back." She nodded at Logan. "I especially remember you."

Logan's eyebrows ticked up. "And why is that?"

"Because you were rather . . . exuberant."

"You mean loud," Donella said.

Samantha tried to bite back a smile and failed.

"As for me, I'm sure I was the soul of courtesy," Kade said with a grin. "But what about the twins?"

"Even louder," Samantha replied.

While the others laughed, Logan snapped his fingers. "I remember now. Good Lord, I'd forgotten all about it."

"You were representing your clan as head of family, I

think," said Samantha. "I don't recall Lord Arnprior being there."

Logan hesitated before answering. "Yes. Nick couldn't make it."

Kade frowned. "Oh, right. That was . . ."

"Now I remember that year," Braden interjected. "Nick had duties at home."

Samantha glanced at him and then at Logan, clearly puzzled by the sudden and odd undertone to their conversation.

Donella glanced toward the door. "I see the first guests are arriving. Ready to play hostess?" she said to Samantha.

"Oh, yes, I suppose so," she said, sounding uncertain.

Donella smiled. "I'll come with you, shall I?"

"Thank you. It's been so long since I've been at a proper party. I think I've forgotten how to behave."

Donella pointed to herself. "Former nun, remember? My social skills cannot be any worse than yours."

As the ladies moved off, Braden gave Logan a sympathetic grimace. "All right, old man?"

His brother nodded. "It's just odd when your past jumps up and smacks you in the face."

The tragic death of Nick's first wife was the reason he'd missed the event. It had been a difficult time for all of them and one that would only get worse in the years to follow, especially for both Logan and Nick.

Angus sighed. "Sorry, lad. Lady Samantha was right skittish about that scabby Lord Beath, so I was tryin' to distract her. I didna think what it meant for ye."

"I'm fine, Grandda. Not to worry."

"It was a kind thing you did for Lady Samantha," Kade said to Angus. "And your memory *is* truly amazing, Grandda."

Angus struck one of his heroic poses. "Someone has to remember our glorious history. Ye'd all forget everythin' if I didna remind ye."

"It was a family wedding, not the Battle of Bannockburn," Braden dryly said.

His grandfather rounded on him. "And shame on ye for not rememberin' that sweet lassie. A ray of sunshine she was, always with a laugh. Hard to forget so grand a little miss."

"In my defense, she didn't remember me until you reminded her, either."

"Like I said, it was because ye had yer head stuck in a stupid book." Angus glowered at him. "With all them brains of yers, I hope yer doin' a better job of courtin' the lassie now."

"Grandda, I was only ten," Braden exclaimed in disbelief.

Fortunately, Logan intervened to end the absurd discussion. "Angus, I hear there's a stash of Graeme's finest about. Care to show me where?"

"Best hold off," Kade warned. "I see trouble heading our way."

The room had slowly been filling with Edinburgh's finest, dressed in their finest. Several of the ladies had already started to hover in Kade's vicinity, albeit discretely. Most of the guests, however, had headed for the refreshment tables or were strolling about, chatting and admiring the festive décor.

"I canna see a bloody thing," Angus complained. "All these ladies twittering around our Kade—it's annoying."

"Even more so for Kade, I imagine," Logan said.

"I will not have you offending my most dedicated fans," Kade responded in a droll tone.

Braden ignored them, his gaze fastened on Samantha. With Donella and Bathsheba, she was making her way back to them, and stomping beside her, his cane practically digging holes into the floor, was Lord Beath. He was decidedly unhappy, from his expression.

"Och, now I see the old poop," Angus said. "He looks like someone rammed a pole up his—"

"Grandda, no," Braden interjected. "For Lady Samantha's sake, you need to behave yourself."

Angus waved a dismissive hand. "I'll be the soul of courtesy. The old bastard won't know what hit him."

"That's what I'm afraid of."

"Not to worry," Logan said. "I'll cart the old fellow off if I have to."

"Ye'll be doin' no such thing," Angus indignantly replied.

"Grandda, I was talking about Lord Beath, not you."

"Would you all shut it?" Braden hissed.

Then he mustered a welcoming expression as the small party joined them.

"Gentlemen," Samantha said in an artificially cheerful voice. "May I introduce you to Lord Beath? Sir, these are—"

"I know who they are. You're the doctor, I take it," Beath said to Braden.

"I am indeed, sir." He gave a slight bow. "It's a pleasure to meet you."

Beath's eyes narrowed to cold slits. "Unfortunately, I cannot say the same."

CHAPTER 18

Samantha repressed the impulse to whack Lord Beath with her fan. The dratted man had only just arrived and he was already insulting Braden.

Thankfully, Braden remained unperturbed. "I sincerely regret that, my lord. But allow me to at least introduce my family."

"This evening is *most* irregular," Beath complained, dodging the request. "I expected Samantha to greet me at the door. Now I've found she has not seen fit to hold a proper receiving line."

In unison, the Kendrick brothers ticked up their eyebrows to register polite incredulity. Angus, on the other hand, let out a frankly derisive snort. Disaster loomed and the party had barely started.

"That's because I insisted on playing hostess tonight," Bathsheba said, smoothly stepping in. "Samantha was going to be so busy, since we're expecting such a splendid turnout." She gave the old goat a winsome smile. "And I was especially happy to have you as my escort upstairs. You did me a great honor, sir."

Beath tried to hold on to his irritation, but even he couldn't resist Bathsheba's charm. "It's always a pleasure to see you,

Mrs. Blackmore, although I cannot say the same for your husband."

Bathsheba didn't blink an eye. "Then let's just ignore him, shall we? John will no doubt wish to talk about his work, which is utterly dreary at a party. I'd much rather chat with you."

That her outrageous flattery worked wasn't truly a surprise. Beath was arrogant enough to believe that any person of taste would prefer his company.

"We shall see, Mrs. Blackmore," he replied, unbending a bit. "I must say I was relieved to see that Samantha has employed appropriate staff for the evening, including properly attired footmen and a quite respectable butler."

"Aye, our Will is a prime one," said Angus. "A nice, modest fellow, too, unlike some I could mention."

Braden discreetly elbowed his grandfather.

"The Kendricks very kindly loaned us their staff for the evening," Samantha hastily interjected. "They have been extremely generous. And Mr. Kade Kendrick will be performing a special recital for us, which is really splendid."

Beath harrumphed, seeming, if not impressed, at least slightly mollified. "I suppose you'd best introduce me, Samantha."

She quickly made the introductions. Braden and his brothers were the soul of courtesy, although Angus remained brusque. Clearly, separating the old men for the rest of the evening was an imperative.

A silence then ensued, its awkwardness amplified by the cheerful bustle around them.

Donella finally broke the ice. "Lord Beath, I do hope you're enjoying your stay in town. The weather, fortunately, has not been overly cold."

"I find Edinburgh exceedingly damp and unpleasant in the winter months," he replied in a blighting tone. "Family matters," he added, glaring at Braden, "required that I make this visit."

Samantha found herself wishing for an earthquake that would crack open the floor and send Beath straight down to the netherworld. She was, however, impressed with Braden's calm under such withering fire. His entire manner suggested nothing but polite interest.

"I entirely sympathize, my lord," said Logan in a hearty tone. "I have a touch of rheumatics, myself. A good flannel waistcoat is just the thing, I find."

That did get an amused rise out of Braden. "You should have told me, Logan. I've got an excellent liniment for that."

"Och, Logan's never worn a flannel waistcoat in his entire bloody life," Angus said. "He's just—"

"My lord, what do you think of the decorations?" Samantha desperately cut in. "The building is quite transformed, don't you think?"

Beath looked even more annoyed now, which was quite a feat. "I have never approved of this building as suitable for a foundation associated with my family. Dressing it up with silly decorations does not detract from its location in a highly undesirable part of town."

Hopeless.

"I know, sir. But I'm most grateful that you made the trip, regardless."

Of course, that trip involved a carriage ride of only ten minutes.

"You can be sure that my grooms are well armed. Very unsavory characters frequent this area, Samantha. I do not approve."

Since he never approved of anything she did, she simply nodded.

"It's true that Old Town isn't what it used to be," said Logan, gamely trying to carry on. "That's why we built our house up in New Town. Safe and very modern, you understand. Very elegant, too."

Beath sniffed, as if scenting a noxious odor. "The most distinguished families in Scotland have always lived near Holyrood Palace. Whilst in the city, the Penwith family resides in our mansion in Canongate, not in a newfangled neighborhood full of upstarts and merchants."

Angus bristled like an offended hedgehog. "Now, see here, ye jumped up—"

Braden's hand landed on his grandfather's shoulder. "I think you'd best go with Kade and help him set up. He needs to get his music organized."

"Good idea." Kade hastily sketched a bow. "Lord Beath, ladies, I'll see you after the recital."

He bustled his protesting grandfather off to the piano, a trail of twittering ladies forming in their wake.

"Samantha, I do not approve of Mr. MacDonald," Beath said in a severe tone. "He is obviously a Highlander."

This time, even Braden sighed.

"Well, I don't approve of that fact that I don't have a beverage," Bathsheba cheerily commented. "Lord Beath, may I ask for your escort to the refreshment table? I find myself quite parched by all this excitement."

Samantha flashed her a grateful smile. "Excellent idea. I'll join you shortly and show you to your seats. I've set aside the best for you and Lord Beath."

Grumbling, his lordship allowed Bathsheba to lead him away.

Logan shook his head. "I just met the old fellow, and somehow I managed to annoy him. My apologies, Lady Samantha."

"Sir, your efforts were heroic," she wryly said. "It's almost impossible *not* to offend him."

Donella patted her husband's arm. "You were splendid, dearest. Although I think the flannel waistcoat was a bit much."

"I was trying to empathize with the old goat . . . er, the old fellow."

Samantha wrinkled her nose. "That's what I call him—the old goat."

"And I *am* going to make a liniment for you," Braden sardonically said. "One that is highly odiferous."

Logan snorted. "I suppose I deserve it after that performance. Why they let us loose in polite company is beyond me."

"Nonsense, as Donella said, you were quite splendid," Samantha said. "But in all fairness, Lord Beath's unfortunate behavior is somewhat understandable. He finds it difficult to come down here. It reminds him too much of . . ."

Emotion gripped her throat.

"It reminds him of his grandson," Braden gently finished for her. "Perfectly understandable, as you say. No one need apologize for that."

"Indeed, no," Logan gruffly responded. "We're a bunch of untutored Highlanders, so pay us no mind at all."

"Well, this untutored Highlander is quite thirsty," said Donella. "Perhaps, husband, you could escort *me* to the refreshment table. Then you could try chatting with Lord Beath again about your rheumatics."

"Only if you promise to give me a nice, relaxing massage with that ointment Braden's going to make up for me."

Braden shook his head. "I guarantee you'll regret it."

Donella laughed, gave Samantha a quick hug, and then went off with Logan. Their departure left Samantha and Braden standing in the middle of a crowded room, staring at each other.

"Alone at last," he said with a glimmer of a smile.

"I really should attend to Lord Beath," she regretfully said. "He'll start fussing if I don't."

When she started to follow the others, Braden took her wrist and reeled her back in.

"Sorry, lass. You need a break from the old goat, or he'll give you a headache."

He didn't know how true that was.

"Doctor's orders," he added.

"I hope you don't intend to make up odiferous potions for me," she joked.

"No, just a stroll to one of the supper rooms. This room is getting too bloody crowded, and I could use a drink."

She pointed. "There's a refreshment table right over there."

"And so is Lord Beath."

He tucked her hand through his arm and started for the door.

Against her better judgment, Samantha allowed him to lead her away. For some deranged reason, she couldn't seem to resist Braden Kendrick, especially when he was looking so handsome in his formal attire.

"You look lovely, Samantha," he said.

When she let out a slight huff of derision, he glanced down at her.

"I mean it. You're utterly delectable in that dress."

His rather intimate compliment sent a flush of heat throughout her body. "Oh, uh, thank you."

Then she mentally winced. The dratted man was scrambling her brain.

As they proceeded into the hall, they passed some late-arriving guests. They were only vaguely familiar to her, so she simply nodded her head and smiled. Most returned it, but one elderly gentleman gave her a disapproving sniff instead.

"A friend of Lord Beath's, no doubt?" Braden asked.

"Probably, although I don't recognize him. I don't know many of the guests, to be honest. Most seem to be friends of your brother and his wife."

"That's because Logan ordered every deep-pocketed person he knows to attend."

"I feel rather guilty about all the work your family has done on my behalf. You've all been so kind."

"We're happy to help, especially Angus. Let me add that you've earned our undying gratitude in that respect. Planning this party has kept the old gaffer busy, so he hasn't had time to drive the rest of us crazy."

Samantha laughed. "I like your grandfather. He's rather hilarious."

"Feel free to employ him on as many projects as come to mind, as long as it doesn't involve the need for discretion or greeting guests. As you can probably tell, he's a disaster in that respect."

"Fortunately, Arthur Baines and Mrs. Girvin are holding down the front door for any late arrivals. Arthur is much better at that sort of thing than I am."

"Ah, the estimable Mr. Baines. It appears there's nothing he cannot do well."

Samantha would be lying if she denied enjoying the note of irritation in his voice. Braden seemed jealous of Arthur, although surely he must realize that her friendship with Arthur was platonic.

Still, she couldn't help teasing him. "Arthur is a man of many talents."

Braden halted them outside the supper room. "Samantha, are you deliberately trying to irritate me?"

She widened her eyes. "Why ever would I do something like that, Dr. Kendrick?"

"Och, yer a cheeky lass," he said, adopting a heavy brogue.

"Don't let my grandfather-in-law hear you talking like that. He'll have an apoplectic fit."

"Then I would promptly treat him, thus earning his approval." He led her into the room.

"I cannot imagine why his approval would be important to you. He's a dreadful piece of work."

"Yes, but it would relieve a degree of pressure on you if he discovered that Kendricks are neither unrepentant rogues or blustering Highlanders."

"Even non-blustering Highlanders would annoy him, I'm afraid."

He flashed a wry smile as he pulled out a chair for her and then settled into the one beside it. "Well done on this room, by the way. It's quite the transformation."

"Thank you."

The large room where the girls generally worked on their sewing projects had been converted into a credibly elegant supper room. The long worktables were covered in white linen tablecloths topped with tartan runners that were trimmed with gold tassels. The foundation's mismatched collection of chairs was now draped in white cotton secured with red velvet ribbons. Brass candelabras marched down the middle of each table, interspersed with bowls of red apples nested in sprigs of holly. Swags of greenery decorated the windows and doors, and tartan bows festooned the wall sconces.

At the moment, only a few small groups of older ladies were seated, enjoying a quiet cup of tea as they waited for Kade's recital to begin.

"I hope we have enough food and seating to go around," she said. "I truly didn't expect that all the invitations would be accepted."

"I have it on good authority that there's more than enough champagne and whisky to keep all in an excellent mood."

She smiled. "Your brother has been more than generous in supplying the refreshments. Nevertheless, I'm annoyed that he won't allow us to pay for any of it."

Braden shook his head. "Logan has more money than he knows what to do with. Since you won't allow us to make a direct donation to the foundation, this is our way of making up for it."

"You've all helped so much, though."

"It's what Kendricks do, Samantha. We look out for the people we care about."

The words were casually spoken, but the intensity of his forest-green gaze made her nerves flutter like hummingbirds. He wasn't flirting with her, or at least she didn't think so. It felt more serious than that.

Then again, she could be reading him wrong. Perhaps he *was* just engaging in a light flirtation, the kind that sophisticated people did on occasions like this. After all, he was a man of the world, and she was a widow, and hardly naïve. By society's standards, it was a perfect alignment for a charming interlude.

Yet with him, she did feel almost naïve again—and certainly out of her element.

"What's bothering you, sweetheart?" he quietly asked. "Tell me, so I can help."

So, definitely *not* flirting. That conclusion was even more unsettling.

I'm not ready for this.

She retreated to a safer topic. "Logan seemed perturbed when I asked him why Lord Arnprior hadn't attended the wedding that your grandfather was reminiscing about. In fact, you all seemed somewhat discomforted."

He grimaced. "It was a difficult time for my family. Nick's first wife had died only a few months before. He was still in mourning and preferred to stay at Castle Kinglas with his son."

"I'm so sorry. I didn't mean to upset anyone."

He briefly pressed her hand. "Not to worry. No one was offended."

"Are you sure? Because—"

She mentally cursed her stupidity. How *could* she have forgotten?

"Sir, I must apologize again. I remember my parents talking

about the loss of Lord Arnprior's little boy some months later. What an utter tragedy. And there I went, blundering right into it. No wonder you all looked so uncomfortable."

When Braden took her hand, she almost startled. It was highly improper of him, but it was also . . . lovely.

"Lass, you didn't blunder into anything. Yes, it was a terrible time for all of us. But despite those devastating events, Nick found love again. My sister-in-law is a splendid woman, and she has given my brother three splendid children. He is a happy man and grateful for the second chance and all his blessings. The whole family shares his gratitude."

His gentle response brought a prickle of tears to her eyes. She thought of all she'd lost . . . her husband, her baby . . . and the prickle threatened to turn into a flood.

He tipped up her chin, making her realize that she'd been staring down at her lap, lost in a welter of ugly memories.

"No tears, sweetheart, or that gaggle of old gals across the room will wonder what I said to make you cry. Since I'm a Kendrick, they'll assume I'm being either rude, salacious, or both. Fortunately, Logan isn't here, or he'd tell them to mind their own bloody business, thus confirming their worst suspicions."

Samantha smiled and released his hand. "I'd rather enjoy seeing that."

"Stick with my family and you certainly will. Logan is particularly well known for scaring the locals, especially those inclined to gossip. That, of course, generates even more gossip, which tends to annoy his poor wife."

She couldn't help but chuckle. "It appears Donella manages him quite well, however."

"Kendrick women have a talent for managing Kendrick men."

"And exactly how do they manage that?"

He adopted a thoughtful frown. "More a carrot and stick method, from what I can observe."

"I imagine it would need to be a very large stick. You're all quite brawny."

Braden waggled his eyebrows. "Or a very large carrot."

"Dear me, and there we have the salacious remark."

"Samantha, I haven't even started on the salacious remarks," he said in a voice suddenly gone smoky and deep.

Her brain—and emotions—stuttered. "Er . . ."

"So, tell me if you actually do remember meeting me at that long-ago wedding," he continued, reverting to his normal tone. "Or were you just being polite?"

Samantha forced herself to regroup. "Once your grandfather reminded me, I remembered. Although the entire event was quite a ruckus, as you might recall. It was a very grand wedding."

"I have vague memories of cheerful chaos, which is the norm at clan events. Can't stand the bloody things, if you must know, although I realize that makes me a stick in the mud."

"I do remember you reading that time I saw you in the castle's library, tucked away in one of the nooks."

"Purely a defensive tactic, I assure you. The twins were always trying to recruit me for one of their schemes, or Royal, one of my other brothers, would be attempting to drag me into a sword dancing competition. I'm a respectable fencer, but when I have to leap over the blasted things, I'm more inclined to fall on my arse."

She laughed. "That would have been fun to see, especially since you would have been in a kilt."

Then she realized what she'd said and clapped a hand over her mouth.

"Sorry," she mumbled.

He studied her with a faint smile. "Not at all. Tell me about yourself, though. You grew up in the Highlands . . ."

"*Deep* in the Highlands. Small clan, small estate, small family."

"No siblings?"

"No, there was just me. Still, I had a wonderful childhood, riding about the countryside with my father and visiting with our tenants. I learned so much from Papa." She smiled. "He used to call me his little shadow, although he also gave me a great deal of freedom."

"There are many advantages to growing up in the country. It must have been a bit of a shock when you moved to the city."

"A complete shock." She mentally grimaced at the memory of being labeled a bumpkin. She was the butt of more than a few jokes in those first wretched weeks.

"Why did you leave the Highlands, anyway?"

"My father insisted on it. The estate and title were going to pass to a cousin on Papa's death, and he wanted me to make the best marriage possible. So he sent me and Mamma to Edinburgh for a season." She gave a mock shudder. "I felt like Daniel thrown into the lion's den."

"I sympathize with your pain. The marriage mart is gruesome at the best of times. In London, one can get lost in the crowd, but in Edinburgh . . ."

"You can't hide from anyone," she said, smiling at his comical grimace. "My mother did her best, tricking me out in the latest styles. Still, everyone knew I was from the middle of nowhere in the Highlands."

"Och, it's the brogue," he teased. "It'll catch ye up every time."

"No brogue for me." She wrinkled her nose. "Well, not much of one, anyway. My parents provided me with an excellent governess, and she worked very hard to rid me of my untutored ways."

Still, it had been a secret source of shame that she didn't

possess the cultured accents of the Edinburgh and English elites.

"Samantha, anyone who treated you poorly because of a brogue was a snob and a prat," Braden firmly said. "From one Highlander to another, you have nothing to be ashamed of."

"Yes, but you don't often speak with a brogue, nor do your brothers."

He inclined his head. "True. Although Nick is a clan chief and truly devoted to our traditions, he was determined that we receive a good education and learn to get along comfortably wherever we found ourselves. He didn't want our brogue holding us back. Still, it comes out now and again."

"I've noticed that it's generally when you're fashed about something."

"Like facing down armed villains?" he dryly replied.

She waggled a hand. "Still, you're very cultured. One might almost take you for a *Sassenach*."

"Lady Samantha, are you trying to insult me?"

She widened her eyes in mock innocence. "My dear sir, never."

"Cheeky lass. Well, you might not sound like a *Sassenach*, but you clearly didn't allow the nobs and snobs to get the best of you. Here you are, and we're indeed lucky to have you."

She gave him a rueful smile. "You're very kind. However, it had nothing to do with me. It was all Roger. I was floundering, you see. After only a month here, I was so unhappy that I was ready to walk back to the Highlands. But then I met Roger, and everything changed. He . . . he rescued me."

Braden's expression turned serious. "I'm dead certain that Roger Penwith counted himself a very lucky man to gain your hand. And I suspect he felt you rescued him, too."

"Roger could have picked any girl from here to Inverness. He had legions pursuing him, you know. I always found it rather astonishing that he set his sights on me." She let out a ghost of a laugh. "Practically from the moment we met."

His gaze turned thoughtful as he studied her. As the silence stretched between them, Samantha suddenly became aware of how odd—and oddly intimate—their conversation had become. She rarely talked about Roger to anyone, and certainly not to a man she'd been flirting with only a few minutes ago. It was terribly confusing, and she hated feeling confused.

"Dr. Kendrick, I really should return—"

"I know exactly why he married you," Braden interjected.

"Well, yes. It was because he fell in love with me."

"But you're not sure *why* he fell in love, are you?"

She shrugged, feeling even more awkward. "Not really. It was enough to know that he did love me. I never needed effusive compliments."

Braden took her hand again. "Roger Penwith married you because you're a kind, intelligent, courageous woman who outshines almost every other woman in this bloody city. Of *course* he married you. As for how *you* rescued *him*, that's perfectly obvious."

Oh, Lord, he was going to make her cry again. "It is?"

"Absolutely. You rescued him from his nightmare of a grandfather."

She choked out a laugh that was part sob.

Braden let out a dramatic sigh. "I don't mean to criticize your nearest and dearest, Samantha, but Beath is possibly the most rotten person I've ever met—alive or dead. And I have encountered some truly rotten dead people, as you can imagine."

She practically choked. "Sir, that is just *dreadfully* inappropriate. And I am a dreadful person for laughing."

He smiled. "Good. We were both growing much too serious, given our surroundings. Shall I fetch you something to drink?

You could no doubt use a moment to compose yourself before we return to the horrifying Lord Beath."

Samantha stood. "I think I'll visit the retiring room if you don't mind. I have a feeling my nose has turned quite red."

"Yes, but it's a delightful shade of red."

"And you really are *quite* outrageous," she said with mock severity.

"No one's ever told me that I'm outrageous. I like it," he said as he escorted her out to the hall. "Shall I wait for you?"

"You'd best go in. I'd rather Lord Beath not see us enter together."

His smile was wry, but he simply nodded. "I'll have a glass of champagne waiting for you when you return."

"Thank you."

She hurried off to the ladies' retiring room, which was a parlour at the far end of the hall. This early in the evening, it was empty, with only one maid in attendance. The girl kindly fussed over Samantha's dress for a few minutes, retying the bow at the back. After she'd finished, Samantha firmly blew and powdered her nose.

Emotions now firmly in place, she headed out to the corridor.

She was about to turn toward the recital hall when she heard voices behind her. It was a conversation between a man and a woman, which while quiet, was intense enough to suggest an argument.

One of those voices belonged to Mrs. Girvin. The other one . . .

Samantha trod softly down the back hall. When she came to the cross-corridor that led to the service rooms, she hesitated and then peeked around the corner. Several feet away, Girvin and Samuel Haxton, a foundation board member and its banker, were engaged in an obviously unpleasant discussion.

About what? And why was a board member arguing with one of the staff in the first place?

Even more curious and slightly alarmed by the nasty undertone in their voices, Samantha stepped forward, trying to catch their words. Unfortunately, when a board creaked under her foot, the conversation abruptly ceased.

She flattened herself against the wall, cursing her bad luck. What in blazes should she do now?

CHAPTER 19

This is your foundation, old girl. You're in charge.

Samantha squared her shoulders before briskly rounding the corner. She stopped short, affecting surprise at the sight of Haxton grasping Mrs. Girvin's wrist. The housekeeper, cheeks flushed and eyes snapping, radiated fury.

Haxton hastily released her. "Er, Lady S . . . Samantha. What in blazes are you doing here?"

"I might very well ask the same question," Samantha exclaimed. "Mrs. Girvin, are you all right?"

The housekeeper flicked a hand down her skirts before crossing her hands at her waist. She adopted a cool expression, although her color remained high.

"I'm perfectly well, my lady. Is anything amiss? I did not expect to see you in the service rooms after the party started."

Samantha heard the note of skepticism in her voice, and Haxton now looked suspicious. Best to immediately go on the offensive.

"I was looking for you, Mrs. Girvin," she replied. "But I certainly did *not* expect to find you and Mr. Haxton engaged in what appears to be an intimate conversation."

Haxton turned a bright red. The man had always been the nervous sort and something of a bumbler, though he hadn't seemed like a bumbler when he'd held Girvin in a firm grip.

"Oh, I thought I'd take the opportunity to ask Mrs. Girvin a question about a . . . a financial matter," he said, clearly grasping at straws. "Just a passing thing, really. Hardly worth mentioning, my lady."

Samantha raised her eyebrows. "So, you decided to accost her in the service corridor, in the middle of a party?"

The banker pulled a large kerchief from an inner pocket and dabbed his brow. "Yes, rather silly of me, wasn't it? Apologies to you both. I'll just return to the party now, shall I?"

When he hurried past, Samantha didn't try to stop him. At the moment, she was more interested in the distinct wariness behind Girvin's calm demeanor.

"Mrs. Girvin, what is this about?"

"Nothing important, my lady."

Samantha frowned. "I generally don't like to pry—"

"Then don't."

She blinked, astonished by the acid response. Girvin could be a touch arrogant, but she'd never addressed Samantha with anything less than respect. "I beg your pardon?"

Girvin rolled her lips inward before dipping a contrite head. "I apologize, Lady Samantha. I am a trifle flustered by my conversation with Mr. Haxton."

"Your private conversation, it would seem."

"Yes," Girvin reluctantly said.

For a moment, Samantha was flummoxed. Then she gasped. "Good Lord, Mrs. Girvin, never say that dreadful man was importuning you?"

The housekeeper quickly put up her hands. "Oh, no, nothing like that. At least, not in the way you mean."

"But he was importuning you about something?"

Girvin lapsed into silence, clearly thinking. Samantha got the distinct impression that her housekeeper might be cocking up a lie.

"Mrs. Girvin?" she finally prompted.

"Mr. Haxton was, in fact, questioning me about my work," Girvin admitted.

"In a negative sense?"

"Yes."

"But your work is impeccable. What could have troubled him?"

"We didn't get very far in the discussion before you came upon us."

There was the lie. Samantha would have bet a bob that the discussion had been going on for several minutes.

"Mrs. Girvin, if any board member has a complaint about your work, they are to bring it to me. They are not to harass you."

"I was attempting to explain that to Mr. Haxton when you arrived." The housekeeper paused. "Thankfully."

Samantha studied the woman, noting her still closed-up attitude. She concluded that it might be better to have a go at squeezing Haxton for information.

"Very well, Mrs. Girvin. You may return to your duties."

"My lady." The housekeeper dipped a quick curtsy before heading toward the front rooms.

Only after Girvin had disappeared around the corner did it occur to Samantha that the housekeeper had failed to ask why she'd been looking for her in the first place. That, too, was most un-Girvin like. The woman never forgot a thing and was always attentive to Samantha's wishes.

Turning on her heel, Samantha followed her. Since there were only a few other people in the corridor, she easily spotted Girvin at the end of the hall. But instead of turning right into the supper rooms, the housekeeper turned left and started up the staircase.

Why would she go upstairs? There were only offices and a few smaller classrooms on the second floor, and all were locked for the evening. Nothing about the woman's behavior made any sense.

She hurried along the hall, sending a quick glance into the supper rooms. The fact that they were empty and that Braden was not in sight meant that Kade's performance was about to begin.

Drat.

John, as chair of the Penwith Foundation, had agreed to introduce Kade on behalf of the board. While Samantha had no official duties to perform in that respect, she should be present. Everyone, including Lord Beath, would expect it.

She hovered outside the door of the recital room, mulling her choices. Her instincts, honed after months of investigating Roger's death, urged her to follow Girvin. Something was wrong here, and that something had to do with foundation business. She'd stake her reputation on it.

Macklin, the Kendricks' butler, appeared in the doorway. "May I be of assistance, my lady?"

Samantha craned a bit, so she could peek into the room. "Everyone seems to be seated."

"Yes, my lady. Dr. Blackmore is about to introduce Mr. Kade, but we were waiting for you."

"Where is Lord Beath?"

"In the first row, with Mrs. Blackmore and Mr. Baines."

She nodded. "That's good. Then they won't expect me to make a grand entrance and disrupt things."

Macklin frowned. "My lady?"

"Please tell Dr. Blackmore that there is a slight problem in the kitchen, and that I'm attending to it. He should therefore begin without me."

His surprised frown turned into one of concern. "Perhaps I should fetch—"

"You needn't say anything to anyone. I won't be long, and I'll just slip into the back of the room when I return."

Before he could raise further objections, she hurried to the staircase. Obviously, the butler knew where the kitchens were, so he would realize that she was not dealing with a problem there. But Macklin was an excellent butler and, hopefully, discreet. If he told Bathsheba or one of the Kendricks where she'd gone, it didn't really matter. And as long as Beath was kept in the dark, all should be well.

At the top of the staircase, she glanced both ways along the corridor. To the left, where the classrooms were situated, all was dark. To the right, light filtered out from under one of the office doors—out of her office, in fact.

She soft-footed it down the hall and quietly opened the door. Mrs. Girvin was seated behind Samantha's desk. With her head bent over an open ledger, she was intently studying the contents by the light of an Argand lamp.

"Mrs. Girvin, what are you doing?" Samantha sharply asked.

While she was expecting at least a bit of a guilty start, the housekeeper simply froze for a moment before shutting the ledger and coming to her feet. Her expression was calm and frustratingly inscrutable.

"Well?" Samantha impatiently pressed.

"I beg your pardon, my lady. I wasn't expecting you."

She stepped up to her desk. "I would think not, since I asked you to return to your duties. Why are you in my office?"

Under normal circumstances, there would be nothing odd about Girvin's presence. The housekeeper had keys to every room in the building, as well as access to Samantha's desk and work cabinets. Since much of the foundation's paper-work was kept in this office, and since Girvin worked with Samantha on the daily accounts, the housekeeper was in the room on a regular basis.

But tonight, Girvin's actions were decidedly suspicious.

The housekeeper stood and turned to one of the glass-fronted cabinets behind her, depositing the ledger back onto a shelf.

"My apologies, Lady Samantha," she said as she closed and locked the cabinet. "I will attend to the supper rooms immediately."

As she came around the desk, Samantha held up her hand. "Just a moment, please. Why are you checking the ledgers in a manner I can only describe as furtive?"

The housekeeper took a step back, looking—for once—genuinely unsettled. "I . . . I simply wished to check on something before I forgot."

Samantha crossed her arms. "Mrs. Girvin, you never forget anything."

The housekeeper dredged up a weak smile. "It's kind of you to say so, ma'am, but I do forget a detail, now and again."

Samantha shook her head. "Cut line, Mrs. Girvin. You need to tell me what is so important that you had to look at it tonight, in the middle of the party, no less."

When the woman hesitated, Samantha shot out a flat hand. "I want the truth. Now, please."

She'd always trusted Girvin, even defending her to board members who found her cold, even arrogant. Yes, Girvin was private and reserved, but so was Samantha. The woman was also incredibly competent and an excellent role model for the girls.

This behavior was decidedly out of character.

Girvin breathed out a sigh, losing some of her starch. "I . . . I needed to check on a detail that I think I might have overlooked regarding a supplier."

Samantha frowned. "That was the ledger you had out, wasn't it? It's tallied by Mr. Haxton at the end of the quarter, like the others."

The housekeeper grimaced, which in itself was an unusual

occurrence. The woman normally had iron control over her emotions. "Yes, my lady."

"Did you make a mistake with one of the supplier contracts?"

Girvin stared down at the floor for a few moments. Then she straightened up, meeting Samantha's gaze. "I think it quite possible mistakes have been made, but not by me."

"So, Haxton then?"

The woman nodded. "I believe he's grown careless in some of his quarterly audits. Particularly regarding foodstuffs we bring in for the orphanage."

"Negligent, you mean," Samantha grimly replied.

Girvin shrugged. "I cannot say, my lady."

"You might as well say it, because that's what it certainly sounds like."

Could Haxton's mismanagement be the source of their financial problems? That seemed too mundane a solution to the problem she'd been chasing for months.

"I take it that's what you were arguing about," she added.

"Yes, he accosted me. I believe he realized I was growing suspicious and wished to address my suspicions."

Samantha struggled to repress her growing anger. "It seemed, rather, that he was trying to intimidate you."

A fatalistic shrug was Girvin's answer.

Along with anger came a growing sense of impatience. Samantha needed answers, and she also needed to get back to the party. "Tell me right now, Mrs. Girvin. What, specifically, do you believe is the problem?"

"It's possible we've been overcharged by some of our suppliers."

Samantha shook her head. "How? You check all the invoicing and all the supplies that come to us."

Girvin spread her hands wide, apparently waiting for Samantha to arrive at the right conclusion.

She sighed. "Of course. You were growing suspicious because you *do* check everything."

"Yes, my lady."

"Then why in blazes didn't you come to me?"

"I did not wish to impugn a board member. Especially not one who serves as the foundation's banker."

"Girvin—"

The housekeeper's gaze suddenly flared with resentment. "He's a nob and a man. Who would ye believe? Him or me?"

Samantha mentally blinked. Girvin never used cant, nor ever sounded like she'd just stepped out of a tavern in Old Town. And she'd never seen the woman so fashed. In fact, she'd never seen Girvin fashed at all.

"I'd be more likely to believe you than Haxton," she replied. "I've never been unduly impressed by that man's skills."

For a moment, Girvin seemed genuinely nonplussed. Then she collected herself and gave a dignified nod.

"Thank you, my lady," she said in her usual, well-modulated tones.

But since that slip into cant, Samantha now realized there was something artificial about Girvin's speech. Every word seemed carefully parsed, as if trying to hide something. Her origins, perhaps? But she didn't give a fig where Girvin came from, as long as she did the job.

When the small casement clock on the mantel chimed out the hour, Samantha grimaced. She needed to get back to the party right now.

"We'll have to finish this later, Mrs. Girvin. We've been gone much—"

She turned at the sound of a firm tread out in the hall. Braden appeared in the doorway, a frown marking his brow.

"There you are," he said. "I was beginning to worry. Is everything all right?"

"Yes, of course," Samantha replied.

"I'll return downstairs, my lady," Girvin said, and hurried to the door.

Braden studied her for a moment before stepping out of the way to let her pass. He watched her retreat down the hall, then turned back to Samantha.

"What was that all about?"

She blew out a sigh. "I caught Haxton and Girvin in the back hall, where he was clearly trying to intimidate her."

Braden's eyebrows shot up. "Haxton? That's hard to believe. The man practically jumps at his own shadow."

Samantha scowled at him. "I didn't imagine it."

He joined her by the desk. "Lass, of course not. I'm just surprised, since Haxton's more mouse than man. As for Girvin, let's just say I wouldn't want to get on the wrong side of her. The woman's bloody terrifying. In any case, why did you feel the need to investigate their dispute right now?"

"Because Mrs. Girvin was behaving very oddly. Instead of attending to her duties, she snuck up here to inspect one of the ledgers."

Braden frowned. "Why?"

"She suspects Haxton of financial mismanagement. Or perhaps something worse."

"Did she explain?"

Samantha shook her head. "There wasn't time. We were getting ready to return to the party when you appeared."

Braden cast a quick glance over his shoulder. "Yes, the party. Your presence has been missed by more than a few, I'm afraid."

"I'm assuming Macklin sent you up here."

"He did. And as tempted as I am to take a look at that ledger right now, we'd best return." He held out a hand. "Come along, bonny lass."

His compliment made her blush with pleasure, but then a sobering thought darted into her head. "If there is incriminating evidence, I don't want to leave it in my cabinet. Haxton knows that Mrs. Girvin is suspicious."

"Samantha, you can come back up when everyone goes in to supper. I'll keep an eye on Haxton until then."

"It'll just take a minute."

She picked up a book from the top of the cabinet behind her. Although it looked like a perfectly normal volume, it was hollowed out. It was where she stored keys for the desk, as well as for the cabinets and the small lockbox in the bottom drawer of her desk.

Braden came right up behind her. "Lass, we don't have time—"

She turned to see him looming over her, radiating impatience. She put a hand flat on his chest. "Braden, please. It will only take another moment, and I—"

"What the devil is going on in here?" thundered a voice from the doorway.

Samantha froze, her hand still flat on Braden's waistcoat. Surprise, followed by panic, seized her brain.

Braden gave her hand a brief squeeze before calmly removing it from his chest and turning around.

"Lady Samantha and I were just returning to the party, Lord Beath," he said. "She came upstairs with Mrs. Girvin to fetch some information for a guest who enquired about the foundation. I was simply escorting her back downstairs."

Though it wasn't a bad excuse, Samantha could tell from the cold fury in Beath's gaze that he didn't believe it. Or simply didn't *care* to believe it.

"And where *is* Mrs. Girvin?" he demanded. "I see only you and my granddaughter-in-law, in a clearly compromising position." He glared at Samantha. "I suppose I shouldn't be surprised that you could behave with such a lack of conduct. But at your own party, with dozens of people downstairs? It truly defies belief."

Stung by the accusation, Samantha glared back at him.

"That's a nonsensical accusation, sir. I've done nothing wrong."

"You are far off the mark, Lord Beath," Braden replied in a clipped tone. "There is no need to insult her ladyship."

The old man snorted, rather like a bull. "I will say whatever I wish. And your presence is not needed or wanted, Kendrick. You will leave now."

Braden had already moved to place himself squarely between Samantha and Beath. His broad shoulders were bunching under his coat, as if he were preparing for a fight.

A fight was exactly what she didn't need.

She squeezed between him and the desk. "It's all right, Braden. You go downstairs, and I'll—"

"Braden, is it? So, you *are* on intimate terms with the man," Beath rapped out.

Samantha mentally kicked herself. "Sir, I—"

Beath, his jowly features practically glowing red, cut her off. "So this is how you honor Roger's memory? By sneaking off like a common lightskirt for an intimate rendezvous at my grandson's own foundation. I am almost glad that he's dead, so he cannot see your disgrace."

For a moment, she was too shocked to respond. Then fury swept through her, freeing her tongue. "That is an incredibly ugly thing to say, even for you. I would *never* dishonor Roger's memory, and you know it."

Braden stepped up beside her. "And I suggest ye watch yer blasted—"

Samantha jerked up a restraining hand. "Thank you, sir. But I will manage this."

"I'll not have him insultin' ye," Braden growled. "Ye've done nothin' wrong."

"I will be the judge of that," Beath replied in a haughty tone. "Not some bumpkin from the Highlands."

"Dr. Kendrick is not a bumpkin," Samantha said, adopting

an equally haughty tone. "And this entire conversation has become ridiculous. If you will simply give me a chance to explain—"

"Ho, Braden? Are you in there?" called a cheery voice from out in the hall.

Logan appeared in the doorway. The genial smile on his face was at odds with his sharp gaze that swept the room, taking a swift assessment.

"I beg your pardon," he said to Lord Beath. "My wife sent me to fetch Lady Samantha." Then he turned and smiled at her. "Donella says you must put work aside and come enjoy yourself."

"Yes, I was saying the same thing," Braden said, his voice returning to its normal tone. He glanced down at her with a slight smile. "Are you ready to return to the party, my lady?"

"She's not going anywhere," Beath snapped. "And I'll thank the both of you Kendricks to mind your own business and be on your way."

"Sorry to disoblige, but Lady Samantha is coming with me," Braden replied.

Both his voice and his stance conveyed cool implacability. Unfortunately, although Samantha appreciated his protective instincts, she knew it was the worst tactic to employ with Beath.

Samantha touched Braden's arm. "It's quite all right, sir. I'll come down after I speak with Lord Beath."

He stared down at her, his gaze a turbulent storm of emotion that no doubt mirrored her own. That emotion was also dangerous, because right now she had to calm Beath down and needed everyone out of her way to do it.

"I need to speak with my grandfather-in-law," she said, deliberately reminding him that Beath was, for better or worse, part of her family. "In private."

He gave a slight grimace. "Are you sure?"

"*Quite* sure," she replied.

In fact, she was now in a fever of impatience, because Beath looked ready to go off like a bottle rocket.

"All right, Logan and I will—"

"Ho, laddie boy, where are ye?" called yet *another* voice from the hall. It was one that likely spelled their doom.

Angus appeared in the doorway, looking like he'd stepped straight from the pages of Rob Roy. For some reason, he was now sporting an ancient Highland bonnet on his snowy-white head.

"Oh, God," Braden sighed.

Logan shot out an arm to keep his grandfather from entering the room. "Hold on, Grandda. Why are you here?"

"When half the family disappears, I tend to get a wee bit concerned." Angus glanced at Beath. "Ho, what's amiss? His lordship is lookin' mighty fashed."

"It's nothing for you to be concerned about," Logan said. "Why don't you go back downstairs? We'll join you in a minute."

The old fellow frowned. "It dinna look like nothin.' In fact, his lordship looks like he swallowed a manky oyster. That's nae good."

Samantha squeezed her eyes shut, certain she'd tumbled straight into a nightmare. Although Angus was clearly concerned and meant no harm, his very presence would likely send Beath into full-blown fury.

She opened them to find her grandfather-in-law evidently speechless with outrage. Naturally, the haughty baron would find it offensive to be addressed by someone he would deem thoroughly unacceptable.

"Can I fetch ye a whisky, Beath?" Angus asked with evident concern. "A wee nip will settle yer grumbly guts in no time."

"Not true," Braden tersely said. "And not a helpful intervention, Grandda."

Angus waved a hand. "Lad, I was just sayin' that—"

"You will cease saying anything," Beath thundered, apparently recovering from his shock. "Samantha, why would you invite such a person of low character to this sort of gathering? I insist that he leave immediately."

"For God's sake," Logan said, "can everyone please stop insulting each other?"

"I was nae insultin' anyone," Angus replied with wounded dignity. "His lordship here is the one takin' sad offense, ye ken."

"What is offensive is your family," Beath retorted. "I suppose one cannot expect anything better from a Kendrick."

Angus put up a finger. "There's where yer wrong, Beath. I'm a MacDonald."

"You're a fool is what you are," Beath shot back.

Logan made an impatient sound. "Now see here, you old—"

"Just stop," Braden cut in, shooting his brother a warning look. "Lady Samantha has made it clear that she wishes to speak with Lord Beath alone. We will honor her wishes." He glanced at Samantha. "My lady, I will wait for you out in the hall. Once you're finished your discussion, I'll escort you back to the party."

Beath thumped the tip of his cane on the floor. "You'll do no such thing, you pompous ass."

"Now there's the pot callin' the kettle black," Angus muttered.

Braden kept his gaze steadfast on Beath. "My brother and grandfather will go downstairs, but I will wait for Lady Samantha out in the hall."

Now Beath looked ready to whack Braden with his cane. "Now, you see here, you—"

"That will be fine," Samantha hastily interjected, giving Braden a little shove toward the door. "I'm sure Lord Beath and I will only be a few minutes longer."

"It is *not* fine, Samantha," Beath said in a lethally cold tone, "and I see now that it's a waste of my time to speak with you. You are associating with people outside the bounds of polite society—some entirely mad—"

"Ho, now," interrupted Angus.

"Which simply confirms your utter lack of judgment, Samantha," Beath continued, rolling over him. "I will call on you tomorrow, and we will discuss arrangements for Felicity to return to the country."

The breath stalled in Samantha's lungs.

"No!" she managed to gasp, stumbling forward.

Braden caught her arm to steady her. "Hold on, lass," he whispered.

Beath regarded her with something close to hatred. "Both your conduct and your choice of company indicate a lack of stability that I can no longer tolerate. Your time has run out, my girl. Felicity will return home with me."

Those devastating words froze her to the soul. Samantha couldn't think, much less move.

Beath turned and, without a backward glance, stomped to the door. Logan stood in his way for a moment, his gaze ice-cold, but then stepped aside to let the old man pass. They all stood in silence, listening to the thump of Beath's cane fading down the hall.

Braden ducked his head to be eye level with her. "Samantha, it's all right. We'll fix it."

Misery almost choked her. "You can't. He hates me."

He stood up straight and jerked his head at his brother.

Logan nodded and took his grandfather's arm. "Come on, Grandda. Lady Samantha needs a minute alone."

Angus grimaced at her. "I'm that sorry, lassie. I didna mean nae harm."

She managed a nod before Logan steered him out the door, closing it behind them.

"Come, sweetheart," Braden said, resting gentle hands on her shoulders, and urging her toward the desk chair. "Sit yourself down."

He crouched down in front of her. His big hands wrapped around hers, cupping them in welcome warmth. Her whole body felt chilled to the bone.

"I don't know what to do," she whispered. "I cannot let him take Felicity away from me."

He chaffed her hands, his gaze tender and full of concern. "I won't let him."

"But you can't stop him. He's Felicity's legal guardian." She closed her eyes against the sudden sting of tears.

"Samantha, look at me."

She opened her eyes and stared miserably into his fatally handsome features. *Why* had she been so stupid? *Why* had she let herself get trapped like this?

"We'll sort it out, I promise," he firmly said. "And as my grandfather would say, a Kendrick always keeps his promise. I will not let him take Felicity away from you."

"But—"

"I *promise*."

She stared at him for a moment, and then nodded. There was no point in trying to convince him otherwise.

Braden stood, pulling her up with him. His hands rested lightly at her waist until she was steady.

"Now, we've got to get back to the party, and you've got to pretend that nothing is wrong. Half of Edinburgh is here tonight watching us. Can you manage it?"

God.

He was right. No matter what happened with Beath tomorrow, she couldn't afford to let anyone see how distressed she was. As for the problem with Haxton and the finances, that would have to wait.

She nodded. "Yes."

He smiled and briefly cupped her cheek. "That's my brave lady. And, don't forget, we'll get it sorted."

As he led her out of the room, Samantha did her best to calm her roiling emotions and the terrible sense that she'd just blown up her life. Braden meant well, and he would do his best to protect her and Felicity from Beath's wrath. But she knew—because she *knew* Beath—that this was one promise a Kendrick would not be able to keep.

CHAPTER 20

"Thank God that blasted party is done with," Logan said as he fetched whisky and glasses from the sideboard. "It felt like we were dodging bullets all night."

Braden sank into a chair in front of his brother's desk. "Sadly, a few managed to hit their targets."

After they'd arrived home only a few minutes ago, Donella and Angus, who were both worn out by the ghastly evening, had gone up to bed. Logan had insisted that Braden and Kade join him in the study for a nightcap and a discussion of next steps.

After the blowup with Lord Beath, they'd all managed to put up a credible show of normalcy for the rest of the evening. The old goat had stormed out in a huff, but thankfully unobserved by the guests.

Also thankfully, Kade had launched into a round of Christmas carols and encouraged the guests to join in. That had provided enough cover for Braden and Samantha to slip back into the recital room undetected. And although Beath's absence was later noted, Bathsheba had done an excellent job of putting it about that his lordship had suffered a sudden attack of the gout that had forced him to return home.

So, they'd pulled it off, raising a large sum of money for the foundation and averting damaging gossip, at least for now.

But that Samantha was quietly distraught was evident to Braden, at least. While the lass had put up a brave front during the party, he'd seen the bleak expression that lurked at the back of her lovely dark gaze. Still, she'd conducted herself with a quiet dignity that underscored the strength of her character.

Unfortunately, she'd made a point of avoiding him for the rest of the evening. Since John and Bathsheba had previously arranged to take her home, Braden had regretfully accepted that he wouldn't have a chance to speak with her until tomorrow.

"Here, lad," Logan said, handing him a glass. "Just what the doctor ordered."

He eyed the hefty pour. "Are you trying to knock me out?"

Kade settled into the chair next to him. "I wish it would. You could use the sleep."

Even with a large belt of whisky, Braden knew he wouldn't sleep until he figured out a solution to Samantha's problems. He stared at the glass in his hand, fighting a frustrating sense of helplessness.

"Braden?" Logan quietly said.

Braden glanced up to meet his brother's concerned gaze. "I cannot let that old bastard take Felicity away from Samantha. It'll kill her."

"We won't let that happen."

"I don't see how we can stop it." Braden grimaced. "Samantha wouldn't even talk to me after that brutal scene. And it's my own damn fault that it happened in the first place."

Logan frowned. "How was any of that nonsense your fault?"

"I shouldn't have gone up after her. I should have sent somebody else. Donella, or you."

"We were sitting near the front of the room. If you'd come to get us, you would have caused a stir."

"You were worried for Lady Samantha and went to find her," Kade added. "That was a completely appropriate response."

"No, it was a mistake."

Logan made an impatient noise. "Were you intending to embark on a seduction?"

Braden rolled his eyes. "Don't be daft."

"Then stop beating yourself up. You did nothing wrong."

"Logan's right. The fault lies with Beath," Kade said. He reached over and tapped Braden's glass. "Now, drink up, stop blaming yourself, and start figuring things out. You've got the best brains in the family, so use them."

Braden eyed his younger brother. "So, I'm acting like a prat, is it?"

Kade held up his thumb and forefinger about an inch apart. "Wee bit."

Braden scoffed, then took a healthy sip from his glass.

"Better?" Logan asked with a slight smile.

"Splendid. Now that you've sorted me out, do you have any suggestions for solving Lady Samantha's problems?"

"Actually, we've barely begun to sort you out," Logan replied, "but we'll put that aside for now. As for her dilemma, I think we know the answer."

Braden sighed and rubbed a hand over his face. "You think I should marry her."

The idea had been lapping at the edges of his brain ever since Beath stormed out of Samantha's office. It was a way out of the scandal and the best way to protect Felicity, too. As much as Beath might loathe the Kendricks, the family was more powerful than he was. If Braden and Samantha were to marry, rumors would be stopped in their tracks, and Beath would be hard pressed to remove Felicity from their household. Any attempts to paint Samantha as mentally unstable would strike most rational people as utterly foolish, especially since she would be married to a physician.

Beath's pride was his weak spot, and the man would not relish looking like a fool.

While these thoughts had persisted, as the evening had dragged on and Samantha had done her utmost to avoid him, the idea of marriage seemed increasingly unrealistic. After all, they'd only known each other for a month or so, and he hadn't even kissed the lass. What the hell was he thinking?

"It's the most logical solution," Kade said. "You'd get Samantha out from under Beath's thumb, and he'd lose his excuse for taking Felicity."

"Plus, you'd get Samantha," Logan added. "It's obvious that you're mad for the lass."

Braden narrowed his eyes. "Sure of that, are you?"

"We *do* know you, Braden," Kade said.

"You can't hide from us, old son," Logan gently said. "Even though you've been trying your damnedest to do so these last few years."

"I'll ignore that assertion for now," Braden replied. "Look, I understand what you're saying, and I don't disagree. Logically speaking, marriage would be the best solution. There's just one problem."

"Which is?" Logan asked.

"I sincerely doubt that Samantha would marry me."

Logan frowned. "Why not?"

"Perhaps because she's still a grieving widow?" Braden sarcastically replied.

"I have it on good authority that Samantha is quite taken with you."

"I would suggest that Donella is overstating the case," Braden said. "Samantha wouldn't even look at me after that scene with Beath. Does that sound like she's taken with me?"

"I'm sure that was purely a defensive tactic," Kade said. "She was struggling to keep control, and talking to you would have been too emotional. Her flood gates would have opened."

Braden cut him a questioning frown. "Really?"

Kade held up a finger. "I'm the sensitive one in the family, remember? I know these things."

"Then I suppose I'm the emotional dolt in the family," Braden ruefully replied.

"No, you're the scientist," Logan said, "so you tend to go on observable facts. But you're also one of the most compassionate people I know. It's what makes you such a good doctor—you utilize both your brain *and* your heart."

Braden smiled at his brother. "I hope so, but my powers of observation tell me that Lady Samantha still loves her husband and still grieves him."

"Of course she still loves Penwith," Logan calmly said. "And that's not going to change."

"Then marriage would definitely seem out of the question."

His older brother tilted his head. "Braden, do you think I stopped loving Marie?"

Logan's first wife had died shortly after giving birth to Joseph, leaving Logan a grief-stricken widower.

Braden thought about it, and then shook his head. "No."

"Absolutely not. But that didn't make me incapable of giving my whole heart to Donella. In fact, doing so healed *my* heart. Lad, it's not about forgetting someone or betraying that person's love. It's about mending one's heart and taking the second chance that's been offered to you."

"And I am sincerely glad for you. I'm just not sure it's the same for me. I mean, Lady Samantha," Braden hastily added.

"Ah, now we finally get to the nub of it," Logan said. "It's about what happened with *your* first love, and why you're still so bloody torn up about it."

Braden mentally grimaced. He did *not* want to talk about

that part of his past. Besides, it had nothing to do with Samantha.

Kade suddenly sat upright. "It was in Gottingen, wasn't it? On one of your visits, while you were studying there."

"It doesn't matter," Braden tersely replied.

Kade ignored that signal. "I wasn't with you on that second visit, but I do remember a woman from our first time around, in 'twenty-four." He snapped his fingers. "Her name was Annalise, wasn't it? Annalise . . ."

"Ritter," Braden said, forcing the name out.

Kade's words opened the door to a flood of memories Braden had never wanted to share with anyone. He'd made a terrible mistake back then, one with tragic consequences.

"You can tell us anything," Logan said. "We would never judge you."

Braden stared down at the plaid pattern in the carpet, his mind a thousand miles away in Hanover. It was a place he'd never wanted to go again, not even in his imagination.

He glanced up to find his big brother regarding him with infinite kindness.

"You might want to think twice about that," Braden replied.

Logan's gaze narrowed to something flintier. "Angus is always talking about the family code, though we know it's mostly a load of bollocks. But there's one vow we've made that *is* the essence of the code. You know what it is."

Braden sighed. "No secrets."

"Exactly. But you've been holding out on us, old son. It's time to come clean."

"Truly, Braden, it'll do you good," Kade earnestly said. "Whatever it is, it's a burden that you've been carrying alone for too long. Put it down now, here with us."

Braden eyed his little brother. "You know, you can be very pushy when you put your mind to it."

Kade flashed him a smile. "That's part of the code, too."

Braden snorted but then fell silent, trying to organize the memories he'd spent a long time trying to forget.

"So, Annalise Ritter," Kade gently prompted. "I do remember that she was a lovely young woman."

"And very kind to us, as you'll also recall." Braden glanced at Logan. "We met Annalise during our first trip to Hanover, while you and Donella were in Canada. Kade went to study with a violin master, and I was taking additional courses at the university in Gottingen."

"Nick provided letters of introduction to various people," Kade said, "but neither of us fit in very well over there. Too Scottish, for one thing, and my German was rather dreadful."

"Mine wasn't much better," Braden said.

Kade scoffed. "Your German was very good, but it didn't make a difference. The Hanoverian aristocracy can be *very* high in the instep."

"Especially for a pair of untutored Highlanders," Braden added.

Logan smiled. "If you two are untutored, then I'm a complete barbarian. So, you were on your own in Hanover and running into a Teutonic wall of snobbery. Is that where Annalise Ritter came in?"

Braden nodded. "Yes. She was an accomplished pianist and a true music lover, so she took quite a shine to Kade."

"I'm not the one she took a shine to," Kade dryly noted.

"I'm not surprised," Logan said. "Braden can be quite charming when he isn't talking about disgusting diseases."

"How kind of you," Braden sarcastically replied. "In any event, Annalise took us under her wing. Because her family was distinguished and wealthy, her support made a difference. She introduced us around town and opened useful doors for us. In my case, it didn't really matter, since I was there to study. But for Kade, the connections were important." He flashed a brief smile at his brother. "I recall that you were asked to perform at a number of court functions as a result."

Kade nodded. "They were my first true recitals and were excellent experiences. Annalise made that possible."

"She sounds like a good, kind person." Logan raised an eyebrow at Braden. "So, what was the problem?"

"She was married."

Logan looked stunned. "You had an affair with a married woman?"

Braden felt the shame crawl up the back of his neck. "No. Well, yes, but not on that first visit. And please do not tell Nick. You know how he drummed it into our heads never to do such a thing. He'd probably throw me off the Kinglas battlements, and I'd deserve it."

Kade jabbed him in the shoulder. "You absolutely would not. You never treated Annalise with anything less than the kindness and respect that was sorely lacking in her personal life."

Braden dredged up a smile. "Thanks, lad."

"It's the truth," Kade insisted. "Her husband was a right bastard."

Braden knew that better than anyone.

"Sadly, many husbands are right bastards," Logan said. "But I'm still a bit . . ."

"Astonished that I had an affair with a married woman?" Braden finished for him. "I'm not a saint, Logan."

"I'm glad to hear it," he replied with a slight smile. "But it does seem rather out of character. But also knowing you as I do, I strongly suspect there's more to it."

Braden nodded. "Annalise's husband was more than a right bastard. He was abusive to her, both emotionally and physically."

Even now, just thinking about the monster and what he'd done to the sweet lass sent fury surging through his veins like a raging storm.

Kade grimaced. "I knew she was unhappy in her marriage, but I didn't realize she'd been abused."

"Annalise didn't want anyone to know, because she was ashamed of it. Tragically, that's not an uncommon reaction."

"I'm so sorry," said Logan, his tone warm with sympathy. "But her family was influential, correct? Weren't they able to protect her?"

"Ritter's family was even more influential, having strong ties to the Court. He was a general as well, and he wielded quite a lot of power in that capacity. Annalise was convinced that no one would believe her, and even if they did, it wouldn't matter. She was his wife, and it was a wife's duty to be faithful and obey her husband, no matter the cost."

"When did she tell you about the abuse?" Kade asked.

"Toward the end of our first visit, after she'd grown to trust me. One day, she sent a note asking me to come to her house in a medical capacity. Her husband had beaten her quite badly the night before, and she needed treatment."

"A man like that deserves a hanging," Logan growled.

Braden's throat had gone tight at the memory, and he had to push down the sorrow and anger before he could answer. "Ritter certainly did."

He'd never forget that moment when Annalise had allowed him to unbutton the back of her gown, and he'd seen the vicious marks of the beating on her skin. He remembered his hands shaking with repressed rage, and it had taken all his discipline to keep his touch and his voice soft. Annalise had needed gentleness, and he'd ached to give it to her—and not just as a physician. He'd wanted to sweep her up and take her as far away from her brute of a husband as they could get. He'd wanted to rescue her from certain destruction, the same way he'd wanted to save Kade when he was a sickly little boy on the verge of death.

And the way he wanted to rescue Samantha, now.

Kade gripped his arm. "I had no idea, dear brother. Why didn't you tell me?"

"Annalise begged me not to say a word. She was terrified

of what Ritter might do if he found out I'd treated her."
Braden grimaced. "I wanted to tell you, but it was her decision to make. In my capacity as a physician, I had to honor
her wishes."

"You were more than just a doctor to her," Kade protested.
"She obviously considered you a friend."

"That didn't change the circumstances. You saw how much
influence Ritter exercised at Court. We were leaving soon,
and I was afraid of making the situation worse for her."

"I bet you did something, though. You would never leave
someone in need without help."

Kade's tone of unshakeable confidence in him was a
beacon of light in the darkness. "Thanks, lad. And, yes, I did
approach old Countess Geisler and sounded her out. You remember her?"

"She was rather a dragon, as I recall."

"And very fond of Annalise. She'd already suspected
things weren't well in the marriage. The countess was furious
when I told her about the abuse and promised to do all she
could to keep the bastard at bay. Before we left, I also pleaded
with Annalise to write me if she ever needed my help."

"And did she keep in contact?" Logan asked.

Braden hesitated. "Well, yes. We struck up a fairly regular
correspondence. I would write to the countess, who would
then pass my letters along to Annalise."

Logan sighed. "Och, lad."

"I know. It was incredibly stupid of me."

"You cared for her," Kade said. "There's no sin in that."

No, but there'd been danger. It was through their correspondence that Braden had fallen in love. Annalise's mind
had been like quicksilver, as lovely and bright as her counte-
nance.

"Then two years later you returned for additional medical
training," Logan said, prompting him to continue.

Now that it was out in the open, Braden was going to be

honest with his brothers, no matter how rotten and humiliating it felt to admit what he'd done.

"That was the excuse. I did take up studies at the university, but why I really went back was to see Annalise." He steeled himself to say the words. "I began an affair with her. I knew it was wrong, but I did it anyway."

He glanced first at Kade, whose gaze was nothing but sympathetic, then at Logan. His older brother was regarding him with an expression that could best be described as wry.

"Of course you did," said Logan. "I expect by then you were madly in love with the lass."

"That didn't make it right," Braden insisted. "I knew that Kendricks do not get involved with married women. We never take advantage of women, period. That actually *is* part of the code."

"But did you take advantage of her?" Kade asked.

Braden cut him a frown. "Of course I did. She was in a terrible situation, and I should never have been intimate with her."

Logan absently tapped his finger on the edge of his glass. "Hmm. I'm curious as to who made the first move."

"Why does that matter?"

"I'll wager it was Annalise," Kade said. "Even on that first visit it was obvious to me that she liked you very much."

"That hardly grants me absolution."

Logan made an impatient sound. "Annalise was a grown woman and, from the sounds of it, was capable of making her own decisions. Yes, an affair was a mistake, but stop pretending that she wasn't able to decide for herself what she wanted. No matter what happened subsequently, don't take that away from her."

Braden opened his mouth to protest but then shut it. He'd never looked at the situation in quite that light.

"She loved you, Braden," Kade said, "and she needed

someone to love her in return—someone good and kind. That was you."

They *had* loved each other, and they'd tumbled into a brief, mad affair that had burned as torrid and bright as a bonfire on Midwinter's Eve. But like that fire, the affair had burned them up, leaving in its wake a legacy of sorrow, bitterness, and shame.

"And my love got her killed," he said.

There was a short, fraught silence while Braden stared down at his clenched hands, waiting for his brothers to react.

"Look at me, lad," Logan finally said.

When Braden glanced up to meet his brother's gaze, he saw only understanding mingled with affection.

"Kade and I love you, as does the entire family," said Logan. "We know what a good, good man you are. Nothing you say is going to change our feelings for you."

"Aye, that," Kade added in a gruff voice. "So stop being an idiot and tell us what happened. Let us help you."

Braden managed a smile. "Sorry."

He took a moment to put on the emotional armor that protected him from the horrific memories of those last few days.

"I begged Annalise to come with me to Scotland. I told her that she could probably get an annulment under the Scottish marriage laws. But if not, we—our family—could protect her. We would keep her safe. I would keep her safe, even if it meant giving up my career and place in society. I know that would have been difficult for all of you—"

Logan interrupted. "As if any of us would have cared about difficulties."

Of course they wouldn't have cared. They were loyal to the bone, his brothers. Somehow, in the sorrow and rage of that dreadful time, Braden had forgotten that.

"At first, Annalise refused," he said. "She worried that she'd never see her family again. But more than anything, she was terrified that Ritter would kill her if he found out. But I was afraid he was going to kill her unless she left him."

"What about Countess Geisler?" Kade asked.

"She'd managed to put a degree of fear into Ritter, so he'd backed off. But then the countess suffered a stroke and was unable to protect Annalise. The abuse got worse after that."

"That's the reason you went back, wasn't it?" Kade asked.

"Yes. Eventually, I managed to convince Annalise that she had no choice but to flee before Ritter found out we were having an affair. We planned our departure for two nights after she made the decision. Ritter had a military function then, so that was our window. I hired a private carriage and arranged for passage out of the country. But the morning of the day we were to leave . . ." He briefly closed his eyes, collecting himself. "That morning, I received word that Annalise had suffered an accident. She'd fallen down the stairs and broken her neck."

Logan breathed out a weary sigh. "Oh, God, laddie boy. I'm so bloody sorry. Sorry I wasn't there for you, and that I couldn't help you save the poor lass."

Kade simply reached over and gave him a brief, fierce hug. Braden returned it, but then pulled away, now desperately wanting to get on with it.

"I stormed over to their mansion. I was out of my head with grief and fury, and I demanded to see her body. I was sure I could determine that Ritter had killed her. If I couldn't save her, I could at least get justice for her."

"Ritter no doubt refused," Kade said.

"Bastard laughed in my face."

Logan muttered a spectacularly foul curse under his breath. "What happened next?"

"I accused him of murder in front of half of his household. He first threatened to shoot me, but then had three of his biggest footmen throw me out of the house. Like an idiot, I raced off to the nearest magistrate, demanding that he file murder charges against Ritter. I actually expected him to do it. I also expected Annalise's family to back me up." He shook his head. "I was wrong."

"They were afraid of the scandal," Kade said.

"And of Ritter. Because who would take the word of an upstart physician from Scotland against one of their own, especially one as powerful as him?"

Logan leaned forward. "None of that was your fault, Braden. You needed someone like Nick to help you, someone who also had power."

Braden shrugged. "There wasn't time to write any of you. The next day, the imperial police showed up on my doorstep and said that I would be placed under arrest for assault and various other crimes if I didn't leave Hanover immediately. They also made it quite clear that a stay in one of their prisons would have dire consequences."

Logan's gaze narrowed to ice-blue slits. "They'd have killed you, in other words."

"I could have another tragic accident was how they put it."

"Right. I'm sending an express to Nick first thing in the morning," Logan said. "This cannot be allowed to stand."

"Unfortunately, there's nothing he or anyone can do. I went to Paris before I returned to Scotland and consulted with a few legal experts I'd met at the Sorbonne. They were sympathetic but clear that nothing could be done." He breathed out a long, weary sigh. "So, after I spent a few days at the bottom of a whisky bottle, I pulled myself together and sailed home."

"Blaming yourself the entire time, no doubt, both for that poor girl's death and your inability to hold Ritter to account," Kade said.

Braden frowned at the edge to his brother's tone. "In some measure, I was responsible for her death."

"So you concluded that you were unworthy of ever finding love again, or even being truly happy again."

Logan nodded. "Buried himself in his work, instead."

Braden glanced between his brothers, scowling. "In case I did not make the point, I caused all of this by violating my own principles. Annalise was a married woman. Yes, I should have done everything I could to help her. But, no, I should not have had an affair with her. That's what set Ritter off. That's why he killed her."

Logan ticked up an eyebrow. "I thought you said he would have killed her at some point, regardless. Or did I misunderstand?"

Braden found himself having to unclench his teeth. "No."

"Were you exaggerating, then?"

"No."

"Then listen to me. You made a mistake, but you were not responsible for that poor woman's death."

"It was a hell of a mistake," Braden retorted.

Logan rolled his eyes. "So you're not perfect. Welcome to the club, lad. Do you know how many years I blamed myself for my mistakes in the past, even for things I couldn't control? All that did was bring unnecessary pain to those I loved." He leaned forward again. "Braden, that bastard killed his wife, not you. He's responsible, not you. If you don't let go of this guilt and shame, *you'll* kill that great, grand spirit of yours. Please don't let Ritter take that away from you."

Braden rubbed his forehead, letting the words sink in. Finally, he sighed. "I was an idiot for not trusting all of you, and for keeping the whole ugly mess bottled up inside. I'm a doctor, so I should have known better."

"Frankly, you were so quiet and controlled about everything, it was hard for us to tell what was going on," Kade said.

He grimaced. "I'm sorry that I worried you all."

Logan pointed a finger at him. "I'm going to lock you in a room with Angus and his bagpipes if you don't stop apologizing. You need to focus on the problem—and the solution—in front of you."

"Samantha," Braden replied.

"Yes. She's a sweet, bonny lass, and she needs your help."

"She's also a bloody warrior," Braden wryly said. "She'll run you through with that blade of hers, if you're not careful."

Logan flashed a grin. "Sounds like my kind of woman. And I think she's your kind, too."

Braden drew in a deep breath, as if preparing to leap into the unknown. For such a long time, he'd been living in the past, unable to imagine a future beyond his work.

But now, finally, he could begin to envision something more, a future with Samantha. Still . . .

"I'm afraid of failing her," he admitted.

Kade shrugged. "So don't."

"As easy as that, is it?" he sarcastically asked.

"Do you love her?"

Surprisingly, he didn't even have to think about it. "I do. Although I can't say she loves me."

"I think she does," Logan replied. "She just doesn't fully realize it yet."

Braden eyed his brother. "So, what do you suggest as my next step?"

"Go and rescue the lass. And while you're at it, let her rescue you, too. She's more than a match for you, Braden. So, as Angus would say, quit sittin' around on yer arse and get the bloody job done."

CHAPTER 21

Samantha blearily tried to focus on the ledger in front of her. By all rights she should be working at the foundation today, following up with Mrs. Girvin and investigating Haxton's odd behavior. But given last night's debacle with Lord Beath and her subsequent sleepless night, she doubted that she'd be able to carry out her work with any semblance of success.

Besides, she was genuinely afraid to leave the house for fear that Beath would show up in her absence. Samantha wouldn't put it past the old goat to bring a constable along to help him enforce his rights to cart Felicity away to the country.

Sighing, she rested her aching head in her hands. She'd spent most of the night trying to think her way out of her problems, and the only answer she could arrive at went by the name of Braden Kendrick. But unless the man was a miracle worker, how could he change the equation?

She reached for the coffeepot perched on her desk then put it back down because it was empty. What she really wanted was a hefty dram of whisky, even though it was only ten in the morning.

Fortunately, before she could do something stupid, Mrs. Johnson came into the study. She picked up the coffeepot, clearly intending to pour Samantha a cup, but then put it down with a sigh.

"Ye drank the whole pot? Ye'll give yerself a headache, my lady."

"Actually, I was hoping the coffee would get rid of my headache. But no luck so far."

The housekeeper inspected her with a critical eye. "Ye didn't get a wink of sleep, and now yer trying to figure out those blasted figures. Why don't ye send that ledger over to Mr. Logan Kendrick? He'll figure things out."

Samantha had already reached that conclusion herself. "You're right as always, Mrs. Johnson. Have one of the maids run a package over to Heriot Row this morning."

Mrs. Johnson took the ledger from her. "At least ye had the presence of mind to remove it from yer office. Girvin or Mr. Haxton likely would have snatched it up if ye hadn't."

By the time the party ended, Samantha had been utterly frazzled. But before leaving with John and Bathsheba, she'd run up to fetch the ledger. Thankfully, it had still been in its usual place in the locked cabinet.

"I did ask the Kendrick's butler to keep a weather eye out in case anyone went upstairs," Samantha replied. "Macklin told me at the end of the evening that no one had made the attempt."

"That was a bit of luck. Now, speaking of the Kendricks, are ye expecting to see Dr. Kendrick today?"

"Probably not."

Not after the way she'd treated Braden. After that ugly scene with Beath, Samantha had avoided him for the rest of the night. She'd been too embarrassed to even look him in the eye, much less speak to him. And although it had felt necessary at the time in order to maintain any semblance of self-control, it had been horribly rude. Every time she thought about how she'd rebuffed the poor man, she wanted to sink through the floorboards in shame.

"I expect Dr. Kendrick would tell that nasty Lord Beath a thing or two."

"Which wouldn't help," Samantha ruefully replied.

Although Braden had managed the situation with an impressive degree of calm given the circumstances, his control *had* slipped a few times. An entirely different Braden had emerged then—an irate, growling Highlander who'd appeared more than willing to gut Lord Beath with a dirk. Underneath the urbane man of science lurked something more elemental that reached back to the old Highland ways. And while those ways were certainly useful when it came to a clan feud or facing down thugs in Old Town, they were unhelpful in dealing with fusty old snobs like Beath.

Mrs. Johnson crossed her arms at her waist, her brow wrinkled with worry. "What are ye going to do, my lady? We can't let that old poop take Miss Felicity away from us."

"I know. I'll figure out—"

A firm rap on the street door scattered her thoughts and sent Samantha's heart leaping like a frightened doe.

"Please tell me it's not Lord Beath," she said as Mrs. Johnson hurried over to the window to look.

"No, it's not Lord Muckety-muck. There's no carriage."

Samantha slumped back in her chair. "Thank God. But unless it's Bathsheba or John, please send them away. I'm not in any condition to receive callers."

Mrs. Johnson opened the study door, listened for several moments, and then hastily shut it.

"It's Dr. Kendrick, my lady. Sally's asking him to wait, but he's not taking no for an answer."

Samantha shot to her feet. "I can't see him, either. Not yet, anyway. I look like something the cat dragged in."

As if that should even matter right now, but for some reason it did.

Mrs. Johnson opened the door again. "I'm afraid ye've not much choice, because he's coming up the stairs."

"Oh, God." Samantha straightened her lace collar with trembling fingers. "I look like a complete hag. *Why* did he have to show up now?"

"You look neat as a pin, as always," Mrs. Johnson replied in a soothing voice. "And I expect he's come to help."

She stepped back, holding the door wide. "Good morning, Dr. Kendrick."

He smiled. "Good morning, Mrs. Johnson. I hope I find you well."

"Frankly, sir, we're at sixes and sevens, thanks to that nasty Lord Beath. I'm that glad ye've come to speak with my lady. She could use yer help."

Samantha sank into the desk chair and buried her face in her hands. The situation was now beyond mortifying.

"Not to worry, Mrs. Johnson," she heard Braden say. "We'll get it all sorted."

"Fat chance," Samantha muttered into her hands.

"Can I get ye some coffee, sir?"

"Don't bother yourself. I'll just finish what's left in the pot."

"Ye can't. Lady Samantha drank it all."

"Well, that's not good."

"Yer right about that, sir."

Samantha lifted her head to glare at her housekeeper. "That will be all, Mrs. Johnson."

With something resembling a smirk, the housekeeper retreated from the room. Of course, that left Samantha alone with Braden, without a clue as to what to say to him.

He walked over to the desk and lifted the empty pot. "Samantha, how many cups have you had this morning?"

She stared up at him, captured for a moment by his riveting green gaze. Then she noticed that despite his usual impeccable appearance, he, too, was looking pulled at the edges.

"I don't remember," she said. "But you certainly look like you could use a cup of coffee yourself."

His mouth kicked up in a wry smile. "I've already had

three. But no more for you today, all right? You look downright twitchy, sweetheart."

His endearment did little to calm her admittedly twitchy nerves.

"Can you blame me?" Then she immediately grimaced. "Sorry, I don't mean to bark at you."

"You can bark all you want," he said, coming around the desk. "I don't mind in the least."

Calm as you please, he took her hand and began checking her pulse.

She let out an aggrieved sigh. "You really must stop that, sir."

"And you really must stop drinking so much coffee."

"I had a headache. I was trying to get rid of it."

"Did it work?"

"No," she grumbled.

She knew she sounded like a petulant child.

He gently placed her hand down on the desk. "Sometimes coffee can help, but you obviously need something stronger. I'll send around some headache powders."

"Nothing with laudanum in it, though." When he frowned, she mustered a weak smile. "I cannot stand the taste of it."

"Nothing like that, I promise."

"Thank you."

"Did you get any sleep?"

She wrinkled her nose. "No, did you?"

He made a scoffing noise and then reached down and took her hand. "Come sit with me on the sofa. We can both be tired together."

She let him pull her up from the chair. She shouldn't allow it, since letting him get so close was the cause of her immediate troubles in the first place. But she couldn't help herself in that regard, either. Braden made her feel secure, and that was perhaps the most dangerous feeling of all. Just when one felt secure, disaster was sure to strike.

She plopped down on the overstuffed cushions, too weary to care about proper behavior.

Braden sat beside her and stretched out his long legs. He also extended an arm along the back of the sofa, just a whisper away from her shoulders. It was simply scandalous to sit with him like this, even if he was a doctor. Even more scandalous was her overwhelming desire to snuggle against him, taking shelter under that strong arm.

Ninny.

"I don't mean to pressure you, Samantha," he said in a quiet voice. "But we do need to talk about last night."

She sighed. "Do you mean about that ghastly scene with Lord Beath, or about how rude I was to you afterwards?"

"I have it on good authority that you weren't being rude, so not to worry on that account."

She twisted a bit so she could see his face. "I was positively dreadful to you, when you were simply being supportive. And who told you that I wasn't rude?"

"Kade. He's much better at reading people than I am."

"The fact that you even had to discuss it seems to suggest that I *was* rude to you."

And that was embarrassing, since other members of his family obviously had noticed her poor behavior, as well.

"I thought you were avoiding me because you were angry with me," he said.

She shot him a frown. "Why would I be angry with you?"

"Because I put you in a terrible spot."

"Truthfully, we both put ourselves in a terrible spot, and certainly the fault was more with me than you," she replied. "You told me to leave the blasted ledger for later, but I insisted on fetching it. If I hadn't, Beath never would have caught us in so awkward a position."

"He likely would have caught us coming out of your office or down the stairs anyway, which would have appeared almost as incriminating. Like we were sneaking back from a private rendezvous."

She huffed out an indignant breath. "As if I would ever dishonor Roger's memory in such a fashion."

Braden was silent for a few moments before answering. "Of course you would never do such a thing."

"Oh, by the way," she said, "I did fetch the ledger after the party. I have it right here. Quite honestly, though, I can't make heads or tails of it. Hopefully Logan will be able to do something with it."

When she made to stand, he wrapped a hand around her wrist and gently pulled her back down.

"No need to do that now, lass. We have other things to talk about."

She eyed him, disconcerted by his almost casual demeanor.

"All right," she cautiously said. "What else?"

His eyebrows ticked up.

She flapped a hand. "Yes, yes, I know. I'm ignoring the elephant in the room."

"Lord Beath. I take it he hasn't put in an appearance or sent around any threatening notes?"

"No, but he'll make his presence known sooner rather than later. It would not be good for you to be here when he does."

"I can always sneak out the back door. I know the way."

She twisted fully around to face him. "This is not a joking matter, Braden Kendrick."

As he studied her for a few moments, Samantha had the sense that he was carefully picking his way through the conversation, as if unsure of himself. That was interesting, since Braden was the epitome of confidence, even when facing down armed criminals.

"I know," he said. "It's anything but, and it's also hellishly complicated. Or it will be, if we don't come up with a plan."

"I'm aware. Aside from the immediate problem regarding Felicity—"

"Does she know?"

Samantha shook her head. "No, and I intend to keep it that way for as long as possible. But I'm also worried about the gossip. Lord Beath will likely spread damaging tales about both me and you."

"That's a certainty. Did John and Bathsheba have any suggestions as to how to handle things?"

"Not really. They did offer to speak to him about Felicity, but I advised against it. John isn't a favorite of Beath's at the best of times."

"And now is hardly the best of times."

She rubbed one of her aching temples. "Indeed, no."

Braden took her hand and let out an exasperated breath. "Your fingers are like ice, Samantha."

She grimaced. "Sorry. I suppose it's because I'm tired."

He began massaging her fingers and palm, which warmed both her hand *and* the rest of her quite quickly.

"I do have a suggestion for handling Beath," he said. "It would keep Felicity safe and effectively quell any gossip about us."

"Really? That would seem to require a miracle."

"Nothing so dramatic, although it will require a leap of faith on your part."

When he paused, apparently waiting for a response, Samantha huffed out an impatient breath. "And what would that leap of faith entail?"

"Marrying me."

Her brain stuttered. Was he joking again? He couldn't *possibly* be serious.

Anger flared as she snatched her hand away. "That is *not* amusing, Dr. Kendrick."

"I'm not trying to be amusing," he protested. "I'm completely serious. I think we should get married."

Samantha jumped to her feet and flapped her arms. "I don't even know why you'd suggest so outrageous a thing."

As she took a hasty step back, she collided with the table and caught her heel in the hem of her skirt. Braden leapt up, grabbing her shoulders before she toppled over in an undignified heap.

"Daft girl," he said with exasperation. "It's not necessary to break your neck to get away from me."

He steered her back to the sofa and gently pushed her down. He remained standing, crossing his arms over his chest as he studied her.

"I wasn't trying to get away from you," she replied, smoothing her skirts and trying to recover at least a shred of dignity.

"Looked to me like you were ready to flee the room."

"You just took me by, er, surprise. A perfectly understandable response to a . . . er, surprising suggestion."

When she winced at her bumbling response, his mouth twitched.

"If you laugh, I swear I'll run you through with my blade," she threatened.

He put up his hands. "I wouldn't dare."

She silently fumed at him because, really, she didn't know what else to do.

"Is it safe to sit down?" he finally asked.

"I suppose you'd better. If you're serious about this ridiculous proposal—"

"As I said, I am serious."

"Then we'd best discuss why it's ridiculous. Like two rational adults would."

He resumed his seat but leaned forward, propping his forearms on his thighs and frowning down at the floor, as if suddenly lost in thought.

Samantha poked him in the shoulder. "Well?"

He cut her a sideways glance. "It's not ridiculous at all, because our marriage could solve a number of serious problems."

She took a deep breath and marshaled her scattered wits. "You mean in terms of the gossip and nasty rumors."

"Correct. If we were married—or engaged to be married—Beath's accusation of scandalous behavior on our part would hold no weight."

That was not an inconsiderable point.

You cannot be truly considering this, can you, Braden?

Apparently, he was, which was a startling notion.

"All right," she said. "That would indeed be helpful, but what about Felicity? That's the most important thing. How could getting married solve that problem?"

Braden sat up straight. "Samantha, who do you think is more powerful, Lord Beath or me?"

"Lord Beath." She held up a hand. "I'm sorry to say."

"There's no need to apologize. But when you stack Beath against my entire family, who do you think would come out on top?"

She frowned. "Well . . ."

He started ticking down on his fingers. "My brother Nick is an earl, Logan is one of the richest men in the United Kingdom, Graeme is a magistrate knighted by the king himself, and all of my brothers are married to women with strong connections in the Scottish and British aristocracy. We don't like to puff ourselves up, but my family exercises many forms and degrees of power throughout the kingdom. If you were my wife, Clan Kendrick would fully exercise that power to protect both you and Felicity. Lord Beath would need to think very, very carefully before taking us on."

Anxiety, mingled with a fugitive hope, was making a wreck of her insides. She tried to think her way through all the implications of his most unexpected proposal, because keeping Felicity out of Beath's hands was that important.

"Beath is her legal guardian," she said. "All the power in the world can't change that fact."

He smiled. "True, but you haven't heard my trump card yet."

"Which is?"

"Nick's wife, Victoria, is the king's daughter. Born on the wrong side of the blanket, of course, but the king is fond of her and they maintain a regular correspondence. And Vicky's cousin, Alasdair Gilbride—who also happens to be Donella's cousin—is the natural son of the Duke of Kent. So, we have two royals in the immediate family, as it were."

Samantha blinked as she tried to absorb those stunning bits of information. "You're joking."

"I believe we have already ascertained that I'm not."

"I . . . I didn't know that." She twirled a hand. "About Lord Arnprior's wife, or Donella."

"It's not something we shout from the rooftops, but no one is ashamed of the connections, either. Just know that Clan Kendrick has deep ties to the royal family and wouldn't hesitate to exert as much influence as necessary."

"To control Lord Beath."

Braden nodded.

Samantha's breath went out of her lungs in one, big whoosh. "That is quite something."

"My family can be a wee bit brash and annoying at times, but they can also be very helpful."

"And they'd choose to help me?"

He nodded.

She studied his austere, handsome features, trying to get a read on his emotions. Why would he make such a life-changing offer, one that would affect him as deeply as her?

An ugly thought darted into her head.

"You must be proposing because you feel guilty about last night, like you dishonored me somehow." She pulled away from him. "I don't need your pity, Braden, and it would be a terrible reason to get married."

He frowned, as if genuinely perplexed. "Samantha, you're the strongest woman I know. Why the hell would I pity you?"

"Because you feel responsible for what happened last night. I know what an honorable man you are, but I will not allow you to be coerced into marriage over some misplaced sense of honor. That is simply not acceptable. I wouldn't want it, anyway."

In fact, it would break her heart. She had very strong feelings for the blasted man, more than she cared to admit. The idea of entering into a marriage devoid of affection, especially after her loving marriage with Roger, was utterly horrifying.

"Samantha, if I didn't wish to marry you," he said, "I would find another way to help you and Felicity. You can take that to the bloody bank. But I *do* wish to marry you. I wish it very much."

The fact that he now sounded irritated with her was reassuring in a deranged sort of way.

Still, she needed more. "Why though, truly? It can't just be about Beath."

"Because I think we would be splendid together. Our marriage would be a partnership of equals, based on affection, respect, and shared interests." He gave an apologetic shrug. "I'm sorry I didn't lead with that, Samantha. I brought out the big guns first, because I wanted to reassure you that I *could* protect you and Felicity."

"That's very sweet of you, Braden," she said, trying not to sound disappointed. "But I have to admit that it sounds rather . . ."

"Dry?" he finished for her in a dry tone.

She waggled a hand. "A bit."

He flashed her a rueful grin. "I'm a scientist, which means I'm not very good when it comes to expressing the emotions of the heart. In fact, it seems to be an occupational hazard."

"Not always. John's very romantic with Bathsheba."

"Right. Perhaps I should ask him for some lessons."

When she smiled, Braden took her hand, gently intertwining their fingers. Her heart jumped for a moment before slowing to a steady, quiet rhythm. His touch had the power to fluster her, but it also made her feel inexplicably safe, even cherished.

"I know how much you loved your husband," he continued. "I loved someone like that, once. She's gone now, but she will always be a part of me, even if that part is in the past. We don't need to forget those we cherished, Samantha. In fact, it's impossible to accomplish and we shouldn't even try."

There was a quiet sorrow in his voice that made her throat go tight. "She died?"

"Yes."

Samantha squeezed his hand. "Oh, Braden, I'm so sorry."

With his other hand, he gently cupped her cheek. His forest-green gaze held mysteries and hidden depths that she could get lost in for hours.

Or even a lifetime.

"Our past joys and sorrows will always be a part of us," he said. "And that's both good and appropriate. But it doesn't mean that we can't find happiness and even love again, and I'm hopeful that we can find that with each other."

His tender words brought a sting of tears to her eyes. She blinked them away.

"And you truly think you might love me someday?" she whispered.

She realized she was asking the question of herself as much as him.

He huffed out a quiet laugh. "Lass, in case you haven't noticed, I'm more than a little fond of you. Just this morning, Angus told me that I was smitten with you."

Well, that was embarrassing, but also rather lovely.

"And are you?" she shyly asked.

"I can say with scientific certainty that I am."

When she laughed, he gathered both of her hands up in his. "Samantha, I don't expect passionate declarations of love from you or even a definite answer, at least not yet."

"But you will at some point."

His gaze suddenly turned smoky. She had seen that look before, and her nerves promptly began dancing like butterflies in a spring meadow.

"Conclusively yes to both," he said in a deep, slightly rough tone.

That sounded promising, indeed.

Just then, the small casement clock on her desk sounded the hour. Braden glanced at it and gave a slight grimace.

"But time is not on our side," he said. "Right now, the most important thing is protecting Felicity. That means we must put Beath in his place, and soon."

Samantha's heart immediately thumped down to earth, where all the worries lived.

Reluctantly, she pulled her hands from his. "Yes, I know. Even now, he could be talking to his cronies and spreading gossip."

"Sweetheart, I hate to do this, but I must be off. I have a class, and then I'm due in surgery. I'll come by as soon as I'm finished and we'll talk some more, all right?"

She slowly nodded, reluctant to let him go with so many questions still whirling about her brain. When he started to stand, she couldn't help blurting one out.

"Braden, what would you expect from our marriage?"

He sat back down. "Could you be more specific?"

She fiddled with her cuff for a moment. "I suppose I'm asking how would we live together?"

"Ah. Well, of course I would move in with you, but you needn't fear that I would immediately claim my marital rights," he matter-of-factly replied. "There is no need to rush physical intimacies, obviously."

She felt a flush crawl up her neck. "Um, thank you for such a clear answer."

He smiled. "I'm a physician, love. We tend to be straight-forward about these things. As for the rest, we would go on as before. Working, taking care of Felicity, and searching for Roger's killer and for the children."

She perked up. "You would still help me with that?"

"Do you seriously think I would sit home by the fireside while you're out wandering the stews?" he sardonically replied.

"I could always take Donny with me."

"Daft girl." He took her hands and stood, pulling her up with him. "I'll be back later this afternoon. Promise me you'll think seriously about my proposal."

"I doubt I'll be able to think of anything else," she ruefully replied.

"Good. Now, I have a question for you."

"Yes?"

"May I kiss you?"

She took in the suddenly roguish gleam in his gaze, and something else—desire, strong enough to jumble her thoughts like a puzzle thrown askew.

Samantha tried to give the question the consideration it deserved.

Well, silly, what are you waiting for?

"You may," she replied.

Braden's smile flashed for a moment, but then his rogue's expression became tender. Carefully, as if she were a piece of porcelain, he cupped her chin. Samantha instinctively rested a hand on his chest, her fingers curling into the fine wool of his coat as if bracing herself. She hadn't been kissed in such a long time, and her insides fluttered with nerves and anticipation.

He bent his head and his warm, firm mouth touched hers, carefully at first, as if testing her response. Then he began to truly kiss her, slowly but possessively, with deliciously teasing caresses. His tongue flickered along the seam of her lips, not pushing or rushing her, but simply tasting.

Samantha found herself sighing as she leaned into the kiss.

His mouth on hers suddenly seemed like the most natural thing in the world.

As if sensing the change, Braden's other hand came up to cradle the back of her head, holding her gently as he deepened the kiss. Beneath the fabric of his coat, she felt the firm beat of his heart against her fingertips. Her senses sparked and desire rose, a sensation she'd thought buried forever.

Oh, how wrong she'd been.

His mouth moved in a seductive slide that made her tremble. And when his tongue slipped out to press open her lips, Samantha couldn't hold back a moan. He tasted of coffee and heat, and that heat surged through her body. It was like awakening from a long winter slumber and stumbling into the warmth of a bright summer day.

Braden murmured in response, a deep sound of pleasure that vibrated through her body. For several long moments he kissed her with a gentle passion, one she sensed was firmly leashed. She could feel the tension in his muscles and knew that he wanted more—much more.

And, as some dim part of her brain registered with astonishment, so did she.

After deep caresses that reduced her bones to water, Braden finally drew back. One last, gentle nuzzle of her mouth and then he straightened.

Samantha stared up at him. His green gaze glittered with hunger, and with an entirely masculine satisfaction that muddled her insides. She had to resist the deranged impulse to pull his head back down and take his lips in a demanding kiss of her own. Instead, she forced her hands down to her sides, clenching them into fists to regain a measure of self-control.

"That . . . that was quite something," she managed in a breathless voice.

"Indeed it was." Braden's tone, deliciously rough, made her shiver again.

Then he blinked, and a rueful smile curled up the corners of his wonderful mouth. "And now, as much as it kills me, I really must go. Get some rest, Samantha. Doctor's orders."

And then he was out the door, leaving her to navigate a world turned upside down.

CHAPTER 22

Once settled in the carriage, Samantha tapped Felicity's hand to get her attention.

"Are you warm enough?" she asked.

With a dramatic sigh, Felicity pointed to the woolen lap blanket swaddling around her waist. Then she gave an emphatic nod.

Yes.

In other words, stop fussing.

It was the first time Felicity had been out of the house in a week, as she was just getting over a heavy cold. Fortunately, she'd recovered well, and John had agreed that she could attend the Kendricks' party tonight. As it was an intimate family affair, it shouldn't be too taxing, and Felicity had been tremendously excited by the prospect of a little holiday fun.

Still, Samantha's nerves were on edge. Putting on a proper appearance tonight was vital, since the official guest of honor was Lord Beath. The *un*official purpose of the evening was, once again, to try to convince the old bugger that the Kendricks were eminently respectable and that Samantha was perfectly capable of moving in polite society *and* taking care of Felicity.

Fortunately, Felicity's illness had given them a bit of a reprieve and a chance to plan. Beath had difficulty dealing with his granddaughter at the best of times, so the thought of managing her when she was ill was more than he could bear. He'd grudgingly agreed to allow her to stay in Edinburgh until she'd fully recovered.

That was when the first step of Samantha's plan had come into effect. When Beath had come calling a few days later to discuss Felicity's potential move to the country, he'd found himself facing not just Samantha but Bathsheba and Donella, as well.

With her usual gentle warmth, Donella had engaged Beath in a discussion about mutual acquaintances that included the Earl of Riddick, who just happened to be Donella's uncle. Riddick held one of the most distinguished titles in Scotland and was also, although a kind man, a traditionalist and high stickler. Those qualities appealed to Beath, and accordingly he held Riddick in high esteem. So when Donella had mentioned that her uncle had made a point of asking her to pass on his regards to his *old and valued friend*, Beath had been greatly flattered.

"I hadn't actually written to Uncle about Beath," Donella had later confessed. "I just remembered that he and Lord Beath knew each other, so I thought it might help."

"But your uncle is a very good man," Bathsheba had protested. "I cannot believe that he would put up with Beath's nonsense for even a minute."

Donella's smile was wry. "Uncle thinks Beath is a pompous ass. But he also believes in the proprieties, so he would never be overtly rude to him. That being the case, I thought it was worth the risk."

As well as ruthlessly using her uncle to appeal to Beath's ego, Donella had, at Samantha's suggestion, made several casual references to their various connections to the royal family, including how Kade was a great favorite of the king himself. That bait had been sufficient to lure the old man into agreeing to Donella's invitation to attend their family party, despite his general dislike of all things Kendrick.

Marrying Braden was Samantha's trump card, one she preferred to hold for now. His proposal, although much more enticing than she cared to admit, had rattled her. There were a number of obstacles standing in their way—and some very significant secrets that Braden deserved to hear. Just the thought of telling him those secrets made her skin prickle with shame.

Felicity tapped Samantha's hand, pulling her out of her thoughts.

Nervous? the girl signed.

Samantha flashed her a rueful smile. "A bit."

Felicity tapped her chest and then touched her index fingers together. *Me too.*

Samantha turned fully to face her, so the girl could more easily read her lips by the light of the carriage lamp. "It will be fine, I promise. Just have fun."

When the coach pulled to a stop, Felicity lifted her eyebrows and tapped both thumbs to her chest. *Ready?*

"I am absolutely ready," Samantha stoutly replied.

If she could face down armed thugs and usually get the better of them, then she could survive a night with Lord Beath. And she now had the support of the Kendricks. Samantha was no longer alone in her battles, thanks to Braden. From the beginning, he'd taken up the role of champion before she'd even known he was doing it. Before she'd even known she needed one.

The door opened and one of the Kendrick footmen unfolded the steps and helped them out of the carriage.

She and Felicity paused on the sidewalk, gazing up at the Kendricks' mansion. Up close it was the picture of quiet and expensive elegance. With its four wide bays, it was the largest townhouse in the row and had splendid views over Old Town below.

A sense of unease rustled in her chest. While she knew the Kendricks were wealthy and powerful, she'd never stared it directly in the face before. Samantha had married into money and power, and even with Roger's help she had to struggle to fit in. Just a girl from the Highlands, she'd never wished for money, power, or the pressures of aristocratic life. And yet here she was, teetering on the verge of a decision that would catapult her into the ranks of one of the greatest families in the land.

The door flew open, and Donella appeared at the top of the steps.

"Why are you and Felicity lurking about on the pavement like a pair of footpads?" she asked in a humorous tone. "The neighbors are already convinced we're a houseful of loonies. You'll give them ideas if you don't come in."

Samantha's momentary panic evaporated like smoke. However wealthy and powerful they might be, there was nothing *fancy* about the Kendricks. And that suited her just fine.

She took Felicity's hand and went up the steps. "We were taking a moment to admire your lovely house. Felicity and I are rather country mice, you know. We're not used to such magnificence."

Donella hugged them both. "The Kendricks never do anything on a small scale. Of course, we need all this room, or we'd probably murder each other."

Samantha laughed. "That is a very practical approach to the situation."

As Macklin took their wraps, Samantha cast a discrete glance around the entrance hall, an impressive space with a gilt-painted ceiling above a black-and-white marble floor. Clearly, no expense had been spared in constructing the house, which should please Felicity's grandfather. Nothing impressed him more than displays of elegance and wealth.

"Has Lord Beath arrived?" she asked Donella.

"Not yet."

"Oh, good. What about John and Bathsheba? Felicity enjoys spending time with John, particularly. Perhaps they could find a quiet spot by the fire to have a chat."

She was hoping to keep Felicity well out of Beath's way for most of the evening.

Donella's eyes lit with understanding. "Yes, they're already here. And you're not to worry. There will be plenty of activities for the children, and we've planned a full campaign to keep Lord Beath occupied. You and Felicity are to enjoy yourselves and leave the rest to us."

Easier said than done, when it came to Beath.

Felicity touched her arm, looking concerned.

Samantha gave her a reassuring smile. "Everything is fine."

Donella turned to the girl. "You look lovely, Felicity. Your dress is beautiful."

Felicity gave her a shy smile. She touched two fingers to her lips and mouthed *thank you*.

The girl did look charming in a white muslin dress with lace trim on the sleeves and hem and a pink sash around the waist. Her glossy curls were simply coiffed, with an adornment of pink satin ribbons, and she wore a simple cross of gold around her neck. Even ever critical Beath shouldn't be able to find fault with his granddaughter's appearance.

"You look lovely too, Samantha," Donella added.

"I'm not a patch on you," she replied, casting an appreciative eye over her hostess.

Donella's hunter-green velvet gown, trimmed in Kendrick plaid, set off her vibrant auburn hair and creamy skin. She looked beautiful and festive, and Samantha felt rather underdressed by comparison. But she'd chosen to err on the side of caution, donning a dove-gray silk gown with a minimum of lace and trimmings. Suitable for a widow in half-mourning, the dress should also satisfy Beath.

"Neither of us is a patch on Bathsheba," Donella replied. "I'm afraid she'll give Lord Beath a heart attack."

"Hmm," Samantha said with a mock frown. "For some reason, his lordship seems to find Bathsheba very appealing. I'm not sure why."

"Well, he's not dead, so that probably explains it," Donella dryly replied.

They were both laughing when Macklin politely interrupted.

"Lord Beath's carriage has just pulled up, Mrs. Kendrick."

Samantha took Felicity's hand. "We'd best get out of the way."

Donella nodded to one of the footmen. "Ryan, will you—"

"I'll take them up," said a voice from above.

Samantha turned to see Braden descending the wide center staircase. Kitted out in stark black and white, he looked just as comfortable in formal gear as he did in breeches and boots, with his sleeves rolled up for work. Samantha was struck by how easily he moved between his worlds. Whether it was in a lecture hall, a society party, or a dangerous alley, he possessed a quiet confidence that was enormously appealing.

He also looked so handsome that it made her pulse quicken to double time.

"Good evening, ladies." His gaze tracked over Samantha, turning smoky. "You're both looking remarkably lovely."

She couldn't hold back a smile, since she looked more like a vicar's wife than the belle of the ball. "Thank you, sir. But if we could vacate the hall forthwith, I would be grateful."

"Ah, the dragon has arrived, I assume." He offered Felicity his arm. "Shall we?"

Felicity blinked, and then cast Samantha a startled glance.

"Go ahead, dear," she replied with a nod.

Felicity flashed a dazzling smile and took Braden's arm. When Samantha saw how pleased her sister-in-law was to be formally escorted up to the party, her heart all but melted into a silly little puddle. Dr. Braden Kendrick had a knack for making people feel special—especially those who weren't used to it—and it made Samantha love him even more.

Her brain staggered, and she came to a sudden halt halfway up the stairs.

Love him?

That seemed astonishing, and definitely too dramatic. Still, the revelation had all but nailed her to the carpeted staircase.

Braden glanced over his shoulder as he and Felicity reached the top of the stairs. He lifted an eyebrow. "Samantha?"

Almost at the same moment, she heard Beath's stentorian tones down in the hall. That spurred her to shake free and all but run up the staircase.

"Sorry," she said, joining them.

"All right, lass?" Braden murmured.

She nodded and then followed them down the hall, all the while trying to rein in her careening emotions. It didn't help that she hadn't been able to spend much time with Braden so as to discuss his proposal in a rational manner. Events—or emotions—kept overtaking her, and it seemed tonight would be no different.

He ushered them into a beautiful drawing room that had a high, molded ceiling and a parquet floor partly covered by thick carpeting in muted plaid. An impressive marble fireplace, topped with a landscape of a castle and a loch, dominated the room. A large pianoforte held pride of place in one of the two bays.

Despite its splendor, the room conveyed an air of lived-in coziness, with groupings of red velvet sofas and well-padded armchairs, along with polished round tables topped with bright bouquets of white roses and cheerfully glowing lamps.

It was also rather noisy, with Kendricks small and large carrying on various conversations. The children were clustered around a gigantic evergreen tree in a tub, strategically placed in the other bay window. Several boxes of ribbons and Christmas decorations were heaped around the base of the tree, and Angus was attempting to direct the children as they gleefully rifled through the boxes, dumping contents onto the floor.

Samantha blinked at the joyful mayhem. "That's a surprise."

"We thought a tree-decorating party might be a good idea to keep the children occupied," Braden said with amusement. "But looking at this chaos, I now have my doubts."

"I've never seen so big a Christmas tree," Samantha said.

Christmas was generally a quiet business in Scotland, with most of the holiday festivities occurring on Hogmanay and Twelfth Night.

"We have several *Sassenachs* in the family," Braden said. "So Christmas has become rather a thing with us."

"It seems like great fun."

He smiled down at her. "I think you'll find that Kendricks excel at fun."

"When you're not causing trouble," she wryly replied.

"Och, not us, ye ken," he teased back.

Angus, who'd been trying to untangle a ball of ribbon, straightened up and caught sight of them.

"Ho, lassie," he called. "Send yer sister over here. We're needin' help."

Felicity, who'd been gazing intently at the group around the tree, glanced at Samantha, her gaze shining with excitement. Clearly, she'd caught the gist of the request.

Please? she signed.

Samantha smiled. "Of course. Have fun."

As soon as Felicity hurried over, John and Bathsheba's daughter, Mary, immediately began signing with her. She then introduced her to Angus, who enveloped Felicity in a welcoming hug that she returned as if she'd known the old fellow forever.

Samantha was forced to rub away a wayward tear.

"None of that, lassie," Braden murmured. "It's a party, remember? You're supposed to have fun."

"I know, but Felicity so rarely has the chance to socialize. It's . . . well, I cannot thank you enough, all of you."

"It's our pleasure, sweetheart. Now, come sit and get settled before the dragon appears."

He led her to the group seated around the fireplace. Bathsheba jumped up to give her a quick embrace before John, Logan, and Kade could come to their feet.

"Good evening, Lady Samantha," said Logan. "You and your sister do us a great honor by joining us."

"Thank you, though you might not think it an honor after Lord Beath's arrival," she ruefully replied.

"Which is imminent," Braden said.

Logan held up a hand. "I will be on my best behavior tonight. Otherwise, my wife will run me through with a dirk."

"Angus has been warned, too," Kade added.

Samantha wrinkled her nose. "I'm sorry to put you all to such trouble."

"We're simply happy you could join us," Braden said, handing her into one of the comfortable armchairs.

Bathsheba threw an amused glance toward the tree. "I heard Angus wanted to dress up as Father Christmas, but I see he's looking entirely respectable in formal evening wear."

"Ah, I suggested that it might be best if he adopted a lower profile," Logan said. "For obvious reasons."

"Suggested? Yelling at the top of your lungs might be a more accurate description of that conversation," Kade noted.

Logan scoffed. "Nonsense. The yelling was Angus."

"You both raised your voices," Braden said. "To eardrum-shattering volumes. I was concerned a medical intervention might be necessary."

"How did you manage to convince Angus?" Samantha asked.

Logan snorted. "Braden had to bribe him."

"That's a novel approach," John said.

Braden's eye twitched. "I told him that he could help me at the clinic."

Bathsheba covered her mouth, trying not to laugh.

"Grandda used to doctor us when we were bairns," Kade explained. "The results were sometimes less than successful, but he remains convinced that he's a natural-born healer."

"I still remember that time he dosed us all with wormwood." Braden shook his head. "I thought that was the end of us."

Samantha pressed a hand to her lips, also trying not to laugh. Wormwood could have powerful effects on the digestive system.

"Such fond childhood memories," Logan sardonically said. "Lady Samantha, may I fetch you a drink? A sherry, or perhaps something stronger?"

"A small glass of sherry would probably be best."

Bathsheba scowled. "God forbid Lord Beath should see you drink of a glass of whisky. I honestly cannot wait until you are out from under that dreadful man's thumb, Samantha."

"Speaking of which," Braden said in a warning tone.

They all stood as Lord Beath entered the room with Donella. He paused for several moments, frowning at the noise of the children as they worked on the tree.

"Drat," Samantha said. "He's already in a bad mood."

Bathsheba winked at her. "I'll be sure to lean over him on a regular basis. My bosom seems to cheer him up."

"Yes, I've noticed that," John answered in a bone-dry tone.

She patted her husband's shoulder. "All in a good cause, my love."

Donella gently clapped her hands to draw everyone's

attention. "Children, Lord Beath has arrived. Please come and greet him."

"Excuse me," Samantha murmured.

She hurried over to Felicity, who hung back at the tree with Angus, clearly reluctant to greet her grandfather.

"The lass is a wee bit worried, ye ken," Angus murmured.

Samantha took Felicity's hand, squeezing it for courage. Then she led the girl over to Beath.

"Ah, there you are, Samantha," he intoned.

He cast a critical gaze over both her and Felicity, and then gave a slight nod. "My granddaughter is looking quite well. I'm pleased to see you both dressed as you should."

Donella, who was standing slightly behind Beath, rolled her eyes.

Biting her lip to keep from laughing, Samantha curtsied, as did Felicity. They'd been practicing, so Felicity's curtsy was, for once, on point.

"Thank you, sir," Samantha replied. "We're very pleased to see you."

Beath harrumphed. "So you should be. The weather is quite disgraceful tonight. I was most loath to go out."

"Lord Beath, you already know Miss Mary Blackmore, of course," Donella smoothly interjected. "May I introduce my son and daughter? This is Joseph, and Pippa."

Pippa looked like a little angel in a white cambric gown tied with a gold sash, and her hair trimmed with lacy ribbons.

"Good evening, Lord Beath," she said in her sweet little voice. "Mamma says it is a great honor to meet you. Thank you for coming to our party."

Beath actually unbent enough to smile. "You're welcome, child."

Although Pippa was a truly adorable bairn, Samantha couldn't help feeling resentful for Felicity's sake. Rarely did Beath so much as smile at his own granddaughter.

Joseph stepped forward and executed a faultless bow. "Good evening, Lord Beath. I've been looking forward to your visit. Mrs. Blackmore told me that you collect old coins, and I was hoping I would have the chance to ask you a few questions."

Beath's sparse gray eyebrows arched up. "You are interested in coins, young man?"

"I am, sir, especially those of ancient Rome."

Beath unbent even more. "Then we shall certainly have a chat. It's quite encouraging to see such interest in history in one so young."

"Mamma says that one is never too young to begin the study of history," Joseph smoothly replied.

"Your mamma is quite right," Beath said with approval.

Samantha could barely keep her mouth clamped shut. Clearly, the Kendricks had decided to launch a full-on charm offensive that even included the children.

"Lord Beath," Bathsheba exclaimed, her silk skirts rustling as she joined them. "I am *so* delighted to see you. Will you join me in that cozy little spot on the other side of the fireplace? We can have a nice chat, and John can fetch you a drink. Brandy, isn't it?"

As was expected, he couldn't resist Bathsheba's charm. Beath smiled at her—or, rather, at her bosom—and nodded.

"Thank you, Mrs. Blackmore. A brandy would be most welcome on such a cold night."

Bathsheba glanced over her shoulder. "John, fetch Lord Beath a brandy. And please be quick about it."

Her husband, clearly trying not to laugh, bowed and headed for a large drinks trolley with Logan.

"Mrs. Blackmore, may I join you?" Joseph politely asked. "Lord Beath has agreed to discuss coins with me."

"How delightful," Bathsheba enthused. She slipped a

hand through Beath's elbow. "Come along, dear sir. We'll get you out of the draft from the door."

With Joseph following behind, she led Beath to a conversation nook on the other side of the fireplace. It was set slightly apart from the rest of the room and would keep the old man out of the flow of commotion.

Samantha let out a ghost of a laugh. "That was much too easy."

Donella flashed her a wry smile before shooing the children back to the tree. Felicity went with them, clearly relieved to have passed her grandfather's inspection.

"We're quite adept at manipulation," Donella said. "Although Bathsheba puts us all to shame, I must say. She was the one who suggested that Joseph ask him about his coin collection."

"Beath loves talking about his coin collection, sadly at great length. I'll have to find a proper Christmas present to thank Joseph for falling on his sword."

Donella laughed. "He actually is quite interested in coins and Roman history, so I'm sure he'll get along fine with Beath."

"I noticed that the men are keeping out of the way," Samantha said.

They'd all given Beath respectful nods as he'd passed, but they'd made no effort to engage him in conversation.

"That's part of the plan," Donella replied. "And Angus will keep the children out of the way. We've also set up a buffet in the dining room. People can bring their plates back here, and then we'll have tea and cakes later in the evening. Lord Beath can hide away in his corner and ignore as many Kendricks as he wishes."

"You've thought of everything," Samantha ruefully said. "I don't know how to thank you."

Donella linked arms with her to lead her back to the men.

"You can say yes to Braden's marriage proposal. We would all be ever so grateful if you did."

Annoyingly, Samantha's brain stuttered again. "Oh, um . . ."

"Here we are," Donella gaily announced. "Everyone's settled, so we can all relax."

"And here's your sherry," Braden said, handing Samantha a delicate wineglass.

She flashed him a smile as she seated herself on one of the velvet sofas. When he sat down beside her and stretched an arm along the back of the sofa, she almost choked on her drink.

Braden ticked up an eyebrow. "All right?"

"You really shouldn't place your arm in so . . . so intimate a fashion. Lord Beath won't like it."

"Samantha, I'm simply resting my arm along the back of the sofa, not molesting you."

She did choke on that comment. Fortunately, Logan and Donella were already engaged in conversation with John and didn't hear him.

"Do you need me to pat your back?" Braden asked.

"I need you to behave in a less outrageous fashion."

She glanced over her shoulder to find Beath's eyes on her.

"He's already glaring at me," she hissed.

Braden removed his arm. "What a pompous ass. I take it that you've not told him about my proposal?"

"Since I have not yet made a decision about that, no," she tartly replied. "Nor is this the appropriate venue to discuss it."

"I stand corrected, my lady."

When she narrowed her gaze, he simply flashed her a roguish grin, the one that made her heart go pitty-pat in a most disgraceful fashion.

"Just relax and enjoy your drink, sweetheart," he murmured. "We'll talk later."

Then he switched his attention to the others and easily slipped into the conversation. Samantha did her best to keep up, but she was too flustered and too aware of Lord Beath to make a very good job of it.

When the handsome ormolu clock on the mantel chimed the hour, Angus herded the girls off to the buffet. Two footmen entered and went around the room, offering to make up plates for the adults.

"Thank you, but we'll fetch our own," Braden said.

He stood and offered his hand to Samantha. "Shall we?"

She glanced over at Beath. Fortunately, he was focused on Joseph, apparently fully engaged in one of his pedantic lectures about coins.

"All right," she replied.

She allowed him to lead her out of the room, but when he steered her past the dining room, Samantha cast him a startled glance. "We're not eating?"

"We've not had a chance to talk these last few days, and I wanted to catch up on a few things first."

"What things?" she cautiously asked.

"The foundation, and what we're doing about security for the orphanage."

"Oh, that's all right, I suppose."

He ushered her into a smaller room. "I promise not to make mad, passionate love to you, Samantha—unless you ask me to, of course."

She scowled at him, trying to ignore the flush heating her cheeks. "Now you're being ridiculous."

"A wee bit, perhaps."

He led her to a chaise in front of a marble fireplace, a smaller version of the one in the main drawing room. This room, while still lovely, had a more casual air. Books and journals were scattered on tabletops, and a large needlework frame stood on the other side of the fireplace.

"Is this your family's sitting room?" she asked.

"Yes. I thought we could be a little more private here. You

will note, however, that I left the door open. As you know, I'm a stickler for propriety."

"A paragon," she sardonically replied.

He arched his eyebrows in gentle mockery.

She sighed. "Yes, I know I'm not exactly a paragon, either."

"We'll have a brief chat and then rejoin the others," he said. "Beath will hardly know you're gone."

"I'm being a nervous ninny, aren't I?"

His gaze took on an expression that was growing increasingly familiar—the smoky look that muddled her insides.

"You're utterly delightful, is what you are," he said.

Well.

That compliment was certainly delightful, but since Beath was just down the hall, she had no intention of engaging in a flirtation with him.

Samantha smoothed down her skirts, trying to settle her nerves. "Thank you. But let's get to the matter at hand, sir. What did you wish to tell me?"

Braden noted the slight tremble in Samantha's fingers. Understandable that she would be twitchy since Beath was circling her like a vulture, waiting to strike. She was also, he knew, nervous about his marriage proposal. He'd not wanted to pressure her this week, but time was not on their side. They needed to reach a decision, and preferably tonight.

Her response to his proposal made it clear that she'd never expected to remarry. Braden suspected that she was afraid to love again, given the torment she'd suffered after Roger's death. He knew how gutting such a loss could be and how it affected one's vision of the future, especially when it came to matters of the heart.

At the same time, he was convinced that he and Samantha were perfectly suited. If he were the superstitious sort, he might even believe that fate had played a hand the night that she and Donny had rescued him. That event had catapulted him straight into an adventure, and into her life.

One *could* love again, he'd come to discover. Now, he needed to help Samantha realize that, too.

She tilted her head, looking slightly perplexed. "Sir, are you simply going to sit there and stare at me? Time does march on, and Beath will surely notice my absence."

Braden mentally shook himself. "Sorry, lass. I was just collecting my thoughts. Although you are well worth staring at, I assure you. You look lovely tonight."

Samantha scoffed. "I look like a vicar's wife, and you know it."

"If all vicars' wives looked like you, there would be legions of men storming into the profession."

"Braden, I *refuse* to flirt with you with Beath sitting in the next room. Now, you either tell me what it is you wish to discuss or take me to get something to eat."

He pressed a hand to his chest. "Apologies, my lady. I promise to behave, word of a Kendrick."

"I will hold you to that. Now, I presume you have some news about the various problems we're attempting to juggle?"

She was all business, his lass. That was something he hoped to change before the evening was out.

"As you know, Logan has some of his best men in Old Town, trying to scare up leads on the missing children."

"Any luck so far?" she hopefully asked.

"Lots of rumors, but nothing we haven't already heard."

She grimaced. "Drat. Emmy dropped me a note a few days ago. She's heard nothing new, either. What about the Hanging Judge? Have Logan's men made any inroads on that front?"

"Believe it or not, one of them managed to get into the place, although during the day."

Her eyebrows arched up. "Goodness, how did he manage it?"

"Very carefully. Even in the daylight hours, the place is

full of some fairly rough sorts. But Logan's man, Stevens, worked on the docks when he was a lad, so it was easy for him to fit in as an itinerant dockworker. He put it about that he was looking for a little extra work, shall we say."

"Criminal work."

Braden nodded. "He dropped a few hints that he'd be interested in a spot of thieving or swindling if anyone had need of an extra hand. Of course his offer was met with some degree of suspicion, but he's convinced that his cover was sound. Because they don't know him, the denizens of such an establishment would naturally be suspicious."

"Did he try a visit at night?" she asked.

"He did, but the guard stationed at the door made it very plain that outsiders weren't welcome."

She made an exasperated sound. "Then how are we ever going to get in there?"

When Braden took her hand, lacing their fingers together, Samantha shot him a fleeting, questioning glance.

"It's frustrating, I know," he said, "but Stevens's efforts tell us something."

She nodded. "They're protecting something valuable."

"Yes, or that a new gang is using the Hanging Judge as a hideout, and they're doing their best to keep their identities unknown. Fortunately, Stevens managed to assess the level of security on the perimeter. He spotted one man a block out who was watching the back of the place, while the guard at the door seemed to be the only one out front."

Samantha tapped her chin. "Hmm. That does confirm that the men who accosted us were actually out looking for us and not just guarding the perimeter."

"True," Braden said. "But security inside the place is bound to be tight. It won't be as easy as taking out the two guards, and then waltzing in and finding the children."

"I am aware of that, sir," she rather tartly replied. "Please remember that I've been doing this longer than you have."

Braden adopted a contrite look. "Yes, my lady. Sorry to offend."

She scoffed. "You're not fooling anyone, you know. Still, it's so frustrating, not being able to get in there when we so desperately need to."

He squeezed her hand. "Let's see how things develop with Stevens, since Logan plans to have him go back in a day or so. We just have to be patient."

"Braden, I'm responsible for those children. It's very hard to be patient when they are at risk," she exclaimed.

"Agreed," he quietly replied. "But they're already aware that we're looking for them, so we need to be very careful. Once we have something more to go on, we can plan our next steps."

She sighed. "I'm sorry. I don't mean to sound ungrateful. And it *is* incredibly comforting to know that your brother's men are guarding the orphanage."

Braden and Logan had decided last week to place men outside the foundation's buildings to keep a discrete watch. They'd debated placing guards inside the orphanage, too, but had decided it would risk tipping their hand. If anyone tried to abduct a child, they'd move in and catch the bastard. That might turn out to be their best chance to recover the missing bairns.

"Rest assured, the children at the orphanage are safe," he said.

"I know. It's just that it's driving me mad that I can't be out there looking, myself."

"I honestly don't think that would help, love."

As always, when he used an endearment, a pink blush colored her cheeks. It took all of Braden's discipline not to kiss her until she was rosy from head to toe.

Soon.

She briefly gripped his fingers and then withdrew her hand. Braden reluctantly let her go.

"I shall simply have to possess myself of some patience," she said. "And truly, Braden, I don't know what I would have done without your support. Your entire family has been splendid."

"I told you, lass. Clan Kendrick takes care of its own."

And Samantha was one of theirs, whether she fully realized it yet or not. Someday soon, he hoped, she would be a Kendrick in both name and heart.

"But for now," he added, "we stay the course. Something will break, sooner or later."

"From your mouth to God's ear. And I suppose I cannot afford to take risks while Beath is hanging over my head like a blasted sword of Damocles. One misstep and I'm cooked."

"And speaking of that situation—"

"Oh, I have something to tell you about Girvin," she hastily interrupted. "I finally spoke to her yesterday."

Braden mentally sighed. Trying to get Samantha to finally discuss his proposal was proving to be a challenge.

"And?" he said. "Is she still reluctant to talk?"

"The opposite. She was very forthcoming, which is most un-Girvinlike."

He smiled at her description. "I gather it was useful?"

"She's convinced that Haxton is colluding with at least two of our suppliers to skim funds. But she can't put her finger on how he's doing it. I told her to send those accounts to Logan as soon as she was finished with them."

Braden shook his head. "We're going to have to tackle Haxton at some point."

"Agreed, but I still fail to see how that matter is connected to the missing children."

"True, but stealing charitable funds could be a powerful motive for another sort of crime."

She was silent for a moment. "Roger's murder, you mean."

"I'm sorry," he quietly said.

"Don't be. We simply have to face it and figure out how

best to approach it. I was thinking that perhaps Arthur Baines and I might speak to Haxton—"

"No," Braden cut in, instantly annoyed by the suggestion. "We're keeping Baines out of this."

She looked perplexed. "Honestly, I don't know what you have against Arthur."

"Aside from the fact that he's a smarmy prig?"

Samantha held up an admonishing finger. "Really, Braden, one would think you were jealous of the man. That would be ridiculous."

He caught her hand and brought it down to his lap. "Actually, I *am* jealous, even though it makes me sound like an idiotic schoolboy."

So jealous that he hated to even hear her say the bastard's name. But beyond that, he didn't trust Baines, and neither did Logan. While Braden might be just a jealous fool, Logan was as canny as a fox. If he thought something was off with Baines, then it was.

"There is no need to be jealous of Arthur," she patiently said. "He has no interest in me other than friendship."

"And what about you?"

She pulled her hand away. "Oh, my God. Do you really think I would have let you kiss me if I was interested in any other man?"

"It's just that I would hate to think you were simply toying with me."

She narrowed her gaze. "Your grandfather is correct. You *are* a jinglebrains."

Braden had to laugh. "When did he call me that?"

"Never you mind. And you're rather mean, too, for making me walk right into your trap."

"I apologize, sweetheart, but you've been a bit hard to pin down in this regard. We do need to discuss my proposal before events overtake us."

She crossed her arms, which delightfully plumped up her

breasts. Braden could see the edge of her stays under the delicate silk of her gown, and he was tempted to trace it with his forefinger.

"I've been busy," she said a bit huffily. "As have you, I might add."

"You're right, but I don't think that's the only reason you've been dodging me."

"I don't know what you mean."

"Something's holding you back, Samantha. Something you're afraid to tell me."

When she flinched, he knew he'd landed a home hit. A moment later, he could feel her starting to build a mental wall, brick by brick. He slid off the sofa, getting down on one knee, so they were face to face.

Her eyes popped wide. "Braden, you've already proposed. There's no need to do it again."

"I'm not. I just want you to look at me. Whatever it is, there's no need to hide or be ashamed. You can tell me anything, and I will never judge you."

Samantha stared at him, her deep brown gaze swimming with a mix of turbulent emotions. Defiance was there, certainly, and even some anger, but underneath lurked sorrow and shame.

"Sweet lass, please trust me. Don't shut me out."

She blinked, likely trying to hold back tears. "I don't want to shut you out, but it's very hard to talk about."

"That means it's a burden, and one you've been carrying for much too long. You don't have to do that anymore. I'm here to carry it with you."

Her head dipped, and she breathed out a sad, gentle sigh that almost broke his heart. "It's about what happened when I lost my baby, after Roger died. I was very ill for a time."

He took her hands again. They were ice-cold, so he enfolded them within his. "Bathsheba told me, though she was very circumspect. I don't know the details."

Samantha managed a wobbly smile. "She's very loyal, as is John. I don't think I would have survived without them."

Anger and sorrow cinched his heart. It killed him that she'd suffered so much, but right now he needed to be calm and patient for her sake.

He settled back on his heels, intending to give her as much time as she needed.

"I was quite far along when I miscarried," she finally said. "Because I was already in a weakened emotional state, I struggled. It took a long time and there was quite a lot of blood. The physician who attended me at the time—Beath's doctor, as you recall—said that I suffered an injury."

While her voice was low and steady, her complexion had gone dead white. There was an almost hollow look to her gaze, as if she were staring at the horrors of that past event and not him.

Braden chafed her hands. "Did he give you any more detail than that?"

"Not much. Dr. Lane was not the sort of man to discuss such issues with the ladies, as he put it." She gave an angry little snort. "He is an awful person. I'd like nothing better than to bash him with the butt of my pistol, to tell you the truth."

He breathed a quiet sigh of relief. She was coming back to life, and she was angry—as she should be.

"I wouldn't trust a word Lane said," he replied. "But he obviously *did* tell you something, because it upset you."

She squarely met his gaze. "He said I would never be able to have children. That my insides were ruined."

"What?"

Samantha jumped in her seat. "Really, Braden, there is no need to shout. I am right here."

He squeezed her hands. "Sorry, sorry. I can barely believe Lane would say such a thing. I swear I'm going to kill the moron the next time I see him."

"Well, I wouldn't try to stop you."

"Did you tell John what he said?"

"Yes, and John's initial response was much the same as yours. Although his language was even more colorful."

Braden smiled. "What was his medical opinion, though?"

"After he examined me, John said that, contrary to Lane's opinion, it was impossible to make such a firm assessment." She paused, wrinkling her nose. "Really, this is rather embarrassing. I cannot believe I'm discussing this with you."

"Love, I'm a physician. I'm the perfect person to discuss it with."

"Yes, but you also wish to marry me."

"Another reason why we should be discussing it. Now, what else did John have to say?"

"He said I shouldn't make any assumptions, since there was no way to tell if I could bear a child until I tried to . . ." She twirled a hand. "You know."

"Become pregnant. That is excellent advice, and John is an excellent physician. You must listen to him."

"After a time, I didn't really think about it much," she confessed. "I wasn't looking to get married again."

"Then I came along and forced the issue."

"You rather did," she said.

He lifted her hand and briefly rubbed it against his cheek. "And I can't apologize for that."

"Braden, I might never be able to have a baby," she said. "You do realize that, now."

"And you think I won't want to marry you if you cannot?"

"Well, most men *do* want their wives to have children."

"Samantha, I would gladly welcome children, but the Kendrick family is hardly lacking in bairns. There are several we could borrow on a moment's notice, I assure you."

She shook her head. "Jinglebrains."

"Yes, but it's also the truth. We have many children to love in this family, and they would certainly love you back. My only real sorrow is that you had to endure such a terrible experience."

"Are you saying that it truly doesn't bother you?" she skeptically asked.

"Only for your sake does it bother me. It certainly doesn't change my feelings or my desire to marry you."

She blinked a few times. "Huh."

Braden pushed himself up. He took Samantha's hands and pulled her to her feet, so that she was leaning slightly into him. Sliding his hands down to her waist, he drew her closer. Silk skirts rustled, drifting around his legs.

"Would you like me to show you how much I still want to marry you?" he murmured.

She stared up at him, briefly pressing her lips together as if trying to stifle a smile. "Maybe."

Braden gazed into her beautiful eyes. They were now like polished amber, bright with relief and something so entrancing that it brought his head down until their lips softly touched.

Samantha breathed out an endearing little sigh that vibrated against his mouth. Her hands, which had curled into small fists, opened, and she grasped his coat as if to hold herself steady. Her lips trembled under his in a kiss so gentle that it made his heart ache. Braden longed to sweep her into his arms and shelter the darling lass from every bad thing that had ever touched her precious life.

But a moment later, she parted her lips and kissed him with such unexpected enthusiasm that it almost took him out at the knees. When he staggered a bit, she huffed out a chuckle. Then she slipped her hands around his neck, pressing close. Braden tightened his grip on her waist, relishing the feel of her soft breasts against him and her lithe body under his hands.

And she was so damn responsive, opening to him without hesitation when he slid his tongue between her lips. Samantha tasted of sherry and an innocent eagerness that made every muscle in his body strain to explore her luscious depths. It was a kiss as wild and sweet as spring in the Highlands. And now that her walls had finally tumbled, she gave not a hint of a retreat. Instead, she went up on her tiptoes, pushing her fingers through his hair as they tangled tongues in a delicious, sensual dance.

She was going to drive him completely insane, and he would happily let her. But somewhere in the back of his mind, a warning bell tolled. He should stop this. He should—

When Samantha sucked on his tongue, every rational thought dissolved in a massive surge of lust. Braden slid a hand to the curve of her backside, pulling her tight against him. She breathed out an entrancing moan and sensation bolted through him. His body went hard as iron, and his hand instinctively curled around her bottom. He nudged her against his—

"What is the meaning of this?" roared an all too familiar voice from the doorway.

Samantha immediately froze, as did Braden. Then she pushed against his chest to put space between them, and in her panic almost tripped over her skirts.

Mentally cursing, Braden eased her around to face Lord Beath, all the while keeping a protective hand on her waist.

The old bastard stood in the doorway with Bathsheba by his side, shaking her head. He was clearly spitting mad, but something besides fury gleamed in his hard gaze. It looked like triumph, knowing that he finally had Samantha exactly where he wanted her.

Not bloody likely.

"Samantha Penwith, have you no shame?" thundered Beath. "My granddaughter is in the other room, while you engage in—"

Bathsheba cut him off by hastily stepping in front of him.

"Let's not jump to conclusions, shall we? I'm sure there's a perfectly reasonable explanation, isn't there, Braden?"

Her tone clearly said *it's now or never.*

As if he needed the warning.

"There is, indeed," he said. "I was in the process of—"

"Dr. Kendrick just proposed marriage," Samantha blurted out. "I said yes, so he was just . . . just kissing me out of gratitude."

If the situation weren't so fraught, Braden might have laughed at her phrasing. As it was, he was stunned that she'd so readily grasped the bull by the horns.

Beath, too, was looking fairly stunned. "Er, what are you saying?"

Bathsheba hurried over to embrace Samantha, pulling her away from Braden. "That's wonderful news, dearest. Simply the best! And you're sure?" she quietly added to her in an undertone.

And didn't that make him feel like a nice bit of muck on a boot heel? Because he'd let his feelings get the best of him, Samantha had been forced into making this choice to protect her sister.

When Samantha glanced over her shoulder at him, Braden gave her a slight grimace. She simply shrugged.

"I am absolutely sure," she said. "I'm very happy to accept Dr. Kendrick's offer."

Then she reached back and took Braden's hand, all but yanking him forward to stand beside her. "I hope we have your approval and congratulations, Lord Beath," she said.

Braden frowned. "We don't really need his—"

Samantha squeezed his fingers—hard.

"Indeed, my lord," he hastily said. "Lady Samantha and I would be honored to have your approval and well wishes."

Beath looked as if he'd been struck into stone by Medusa's glare.

"This, this is most irregular," he finally blustered.

Donella appeared in the doorway, wariness in her gaze. "Is something wrong?"

"Quite the opposite," Bathsheba enthusiastically announced. "Samantha has accepted a proposal of marriage from Braden!"

Donella clapped her hands. "Oh, my goodness, that is simply splendid news. Congratulations, my dears. We've been so hoping for you both."

"Thank you," Samantha replied. "As you can imagine, I'm very happy."

Actually, Braden thought she sounded a bit annoyed. But clearly this was now the ladies' show.

When he didn't say anything, Samantha again squeezed his fingers.

"And I am delirious with joy, as you can imagine," he said. "Absolutely delirious."

"Oh, God," she muttered.

"I actually am," he muttered back.

Or at least he thought he was. It was hard to tell, given the awkwardness of the situation.

"Well, this is just *too* terribly exciting," Donella enthused. "We must go tell the others. And I'll have Macklin bring out our best champagne to celebrate."

"I suppose," said Beath, obviously unsure.

Donella pressed the old man's arm. "My uncle, Lord Riddick, will be over the moon. Braden is a great favorite of his, and the king will be so delighted. His Majesty and Braden had the loveliest chat during the royal visit to Edinburgh a few years back. Isn't that right, Braden?"

"Oh, yes. Lovely chat. Splendid." Of course, he'd never actually met the king.

"Come along, everyone. We must go tell the others." Donella whisked herself out of the room.

Bathsheba took Beath's arm, nudging him toward the hall. "Dear Lord Beath, you must be *so* delighted to see Samantha finally settled. This is so wonderful for everyone." She glanced over her shoulder at them, a clear warning in her gaze. "Are you two coming, or shall we wait?"

"No, we're coming," said Samantha. She took Braden by the elbow and started to propel him toward the door.

"I do love a masterful lass," he said, trying to lighten the moment.

Samantha's chocolate eyes narrowed to irate slits. "You're an idiot."

"Yes, but I'm now your idiot."

"Lucky me," she muttered as she hurried him out of the room.

CHAPTER 23

Samantha stared at her reflection in the mirror over her dressing table. It was her wedding night, and she looked positively ghastly.

The last three days had been hurried and stressful. Braden had been busy with work, while she'd been reorganizing her household to accommodate his arrival. Surprisingly, he had few possessions beyond his clothing, books, and materials from his study. Although her new husband was a complex man, he led a simple, efficient life.

"You'll barely notice me, I promise," he'd said as he lugged books up to her study just yesterday. "Some days, you'll probably forget I'm even here."

Forget him? She could barely go five minutes without thinking about him, a fact she found both annoying and nerve wracking. Thankfully, for the time being, physical intimacies were not a concern. Although she was wildly attracted to the man, she was far from ready to share his bed. She would remain in possession of the master suite, while Braden had the spare room down the hall.

Essentially, they'd contracted a marriage of convenience. How ironic, given the passionate kiss that had led to this state of affairs.

What choice had been left to her? When she'd seen the

look of horror on Beath's face, Samantha had instantly known what she needed to do. In order to save Felicity from her grandfather's clutches, she'd taken the leap of faith that Braden had talked about when he'd proposed to her. And she'd done it without a second thought or a qualm.

Those had come later.

Braden had taken it all in stride and had even seemed mildly amused as he'd also done his best to keep to a minimum the resulting uproar over their precipitous engagement. He'd held her hand through the worst of the Kendrick family fussing, agreed to one champagne toast, then directed the focus back to the Christmas activities.

Discussions with Lord Beath that night had also been kept to a minimum. Braden, supported by Bathsheba, had managed to convince his mighty lordship that the best situation for Felicity was to remain in Edinburgh. He later told her that Beath had grumbled and put up some resistance, but had finally capitulated in the face of their combined persuasions.

As for Felicity, she was initially stunned by the news but also tremendously relieved to be out from under her grandfather's thumb. The girl liked Braden a great deal and seemed content to accept him into their little household.

While all that was splendid, it meant that Samantha now had a husband she didn't quite know what to do with.

She finished braiding her hair after she dismissed her maid, preferring to be alone. Then she contemplated pinching her pale cheeks to give them some color, not that it would matter. Braden had already deduced after their wedding dinner at Heriot Row that she was fighting a headache, and he'd promised to bring her some headache powders.

When the clock in the bedroom chimed the hour, she made a face at her reflection and stood, retying the sash of her dressing gown. A woolen plaid designed for warmth rather than style, it left much to be desired as wedding night garb. But prancing about in a frilly night thing would surely send the wrong message, though the fact that she owned no frilly night things suddenly struck her as rather sad.

She left the small dressing room and was crossing to her bedroom's fireplace when a soft knock sounded on her door.

"Enter."

Braden opened the door, balancing two glasses in one hand. "Ready for your powders?"

Samantha's heart skipped a beat at the sight of him. He'd discarded his coat and cravat, but was still in the waistcoat and trousers he'd worn for dinner. He was also wearing his spectacles, which suggested he'd been reading.

And his feet were bare. They were very nice feet, she noticed, long and well shaped, and proportionately as big as the rest of him. An old wives' tale she'd once heard about husbands with big hands and feet and what that said about—

Slamming the door on that thought, she dredged up a smile. "Why are you wandering around in bare feet? You'll catch a chill."

He closed the door behind him. "Och, your house is as snug as a tea cosy. No chance of me getting a chill."

"It's not that snug," she replied as she picked up the small fireplace shovel. "Mrs. Johnson scolds me constantly for letting the fires go out."

Placing the glasses on the round table between the two needlepointed armchairs, Braden took the shovel from her hand.

"Let me do that."

He crouched down and added a generous shovelful into the coal grate to build up the blaze.

Samantha eyed how much coal was left in the bucket, making a mental calculation. "That much should certainly keep your toes warm."

"Samantha, have you been stinting on coal to save money?" he asked as he put the tool back in the bucket.

"Maybe a bit."

"Then please stop. I have a generous income as well as substantial savings. What's mine is yours. We're one household now, remember?"

She gave him a sheepish smile. "Sorry, I hadn't really thought that far ahead."

"Believe me, I understand," he wryly responded. "It's not as if we've had time to discuss any of this."

Beath had insisted they marry before he returned to his country estate at the end of the week. He'd wanted the deed done quickly and quietly to avoid any scurrilous gossip. The fact that *he* was one of the sources of the gossip didn't seem to bother him. And while that was annoying, Samantha didn't see any point in objecting to a hasty wedding. They might as well crack on with as little fuss as possible.

Of course, there'd been *quite* a bit of fuss these last three days. Angus had insisted on a proper ceremony in the cathedral, Bathsheba had insisted on a new dress for Samantha, and Donella had insisted on a celebratory wedding dinner at Heriot Row. Samantha would have been happy with a quiet ceremony at a small church, but for Beath's sake, appearances had to be maintained. In the end, they'd pulled it off to everyone's satisfaction, even to Beath's exacting standards.

When the old curmudgeon had finally departed Heriot Row this evening, Samantha had all but collapsed with relief. By then, her stupid head was roaring because the accumulated stresses had caught up with her, producing a thundering headache. She hadn't put up a peep of resistance when Braden took one look at her face and bundled her and Felicity back home.

"I'm sorry everything's been such a mad dash," she said, gratefully taking a seat in front of the blazing fire. "It must feel very odd to you."

"You don't need to apologize, sweetheart. Just rest and

take these powders. Then we can chat for a few minutes before it's off to bed for you."

"It's not much of a wedding night, is it? What a terrible cliché—that I've come down with a headache."

"Samantha, we already discussed this," he firmly said. "It's fine. Do you have some water, or should I ring for Mrs. Johnson?"

She pointed to her dressing room. "There's a pitcher in there."

He disappeared for a minute, then came back with a glass of water and handed it to her.

Samantha raised it to her nose and sniffed. "There are no laudanum powders in this mix, are there?"

He frowned. "Of course not. I know you don't like the stuff, and I try not to use it unless it's absolutely necessary."

She mentally winced. He must think her a complete ninny.

"Bottoms up, Samantha," he gently admonished. "And make sure you finish it."

"Dr. Kendrick, are you going to be a bossy husband?"

"Only when it comes to taking care of you."

She rolled her eyes then swallowed it in one go. The potion had a tart, medicinal taste, but wasn't too awful.

"Thank you." She handed the glass back to him.

He exchanged it for one of the wineglasses he'd brought in with him. "Here's a little sherry to get rid of the taste and help you sleep."

"You've thought of everything."

"It's now my job, Samantha. To take care of you and Felicity."

She sighed. "Our marriage rather sounds like a one-way bargain. What are you getting out of this arrangement?"

"You." He subsided into the other chair, stretching his long legs toward the fire. "That is ample compensation, sweetheart, I assure you."

That made her blush, but in a nice way.

"I hope you'll let us take care of you on occasion," she replied.

He flashed her a sideways smile. "I'm counting on it, Mrs. Kendrick."

Hearing her new name on his lips sent a frisson rippling along her nerves. It was the same sensation she'd felt in the cathedral today when he slipped the wedding ring on her finger. Until that point, none of it had truly seemed real. But the simple weight of that slim gold band, and his hand holding hers, had produced a sensation rather like missing the bottom step of a staircase. One didn't fall or lose one's footing but experienced a considerable jolt.

"It's all going to take some getting used to," she quietly said.

"For me as well," he replied. "But we'll go slow. You've nothing to be anxious about."

Clearly, he thought her something of a wet goose, and that was not how she wanted him to think of her.

Time to rally and face your future, old girl.

"Braden, I want to thank you for all you've done. And your family has been so kind and supportive. No one uttered a word of complaint about what a dreadful commotion we caused."

"My family was happy to support us, for your sake as well as mine. Though I do believe one person voiced a few objections to the arrangements."

"Angus," she ruefully replied. "And I feel bad about that. He wanted all the trimmings and for your entire family to attend. I'm sorry for his sake and yours that we weren't able to do that."

"Rest assured that no one but Angus was thrilled by the idea of traveling to Kinglas in December for a full-blown clan celebration."

"So, you really don't mind that we were wed in such a havey-cavey fashion?"

He snorted. "Heard that conversation, did you?"

"Your grandfather speaks rather loudly when he's fashed."

"That's one way of putting it. He was just annoyed because Grant is the only one who had what Grandda would deem a proper wedding. The rest of us were married quickly and with little fanfare. Donella and Logan all but married over the anvil—in secret, no less."

"Really? That sounds very exciting."

"The yelling that ensued when the rest of us found out was not very exciting."

She laughed.

"I think our wedding was perfect," he added. "We were married in a grand cathedral in the presence of family and friends, and the bride looked absolutely beautiful. I wouldn't have changed a thing."

Samantha suddenly felt shy. "I'm glad you think so."

He raised his glass to her and then settled back in his chair with what sounded like a contented sigh.

"I will admit, however," he said, pushing his spectacles up onto his head, "that I'm even happier to be sitting quietly with my wife, enjoying a whisky in front of a good fire."

"I do want you to be able to relax. And consider this house as your own, of course."

"Thank you."

After several moments of what felt like awkward silence, she snuck a peek at her husband. He was staring into the fire, his brow marked with a slight frown. Despite what he claimed, he had to be feeling some disorientation. In many ways, the impact of the sudden change in life was greater for him that it was for her.

"How is your room?" she finally ventured. "I hope you're finding it comfortable."

He glanced over with a quizzical smile. "Yes, I do. I like

your house, Samantha. It's elegant and well designed. This bedroom seems very comfortable, too."

Yes, a bedroom that included a large four-poster bed, which loomed behind them, was impossible to ignore. The thought of what they might do in that bed brought another blush to her cheeks.

"It's not nearly as grand as Heriot Row," she said.

"That house was much too grand for me and too noisy, as well. I love my family, but sometimes living with them is akin to being in the middle of a small riot."

"You won't find any rioting around here," she wryly replied. "We live a very quiet and peaceable life."

"Except for the occasional midnight excursion into the stews, of course."

She winced. "Except for that. Sorry."

"Don't be. I know what I've signed up for, and I don't regret it."

That sounded rather depressing. "I didn't mean to pull you into any of this, Braden. It's not fair to you."

He reached across and took her hand. "As I recall, I rather thrust myself into the situation—over your firmly stated objections."

She toyed with his wedding ring. When Braden had insisted on wearing one, it had touched her more than she cared to admit. Her first husband had never worn a wedding band. At the time, it hadn't bothered her. Now, though, she realized how much Braden's gesture meant to her.

Are you saying Roger is now simply your first husband, already relegated to the past?

Samantha closed her eyes, feeling the burn of remorse deep in her chest.

Braden gave her hand a gentle tug. "Sweetheart, what's wrong?"

She opened her eyes to see nothing but acceptance in his extraordinary jade-colored gaze.

"It's just that I feel Roger's ghost everywhere," she burst

out, "and I don't know what to do about that. I do know that it's an utterly horrible thing to say to you."

"There's nothing horrible about it. You need to stop feeling so guilty, Samantha."

She sighed. Her emotions were in such a tangle.

"From what I know of Roger Penwith," Braden added, "he would want you to be happy, would he not?"

More than anything, Roger had always wanted her to be happy.

"Yes, and I do want to be happy in our marriage, Braden. But I need to find Roger's killers. I don't think I'll be able to move on fully until I do."

He squeezed her hand before letting it go. She immediately missed his touch.

"We'll do that together," he said, "and we'll find the children, too."

She mustered a smile. "I believe you, and I want you to know how grateful I am."

"It's my pleasure." His expression grew thoughtful. "There are a few things I need you to know, too. The first is that I love you."

His simple declaration hit her squarely in the chest. She drew in a deep breath as a lovely warmth cascaded through her.

"You do?" she whispered.

He smiled. "Yes, and because I love you, I'm prepared to wait until you know what you need from me. And until you're ready to love me back."

Her eyes began to prickle. He was the most *ridiculously* wonderful man.

"I'm already at least halfway there," she admitted.

"I want you to be all the way there and to arrive in your own time. Until then, we carry on as always, taking care of those who need us. All right?"

"Yes." She crinkled her nose. "I am sorry it's so awkward, though. Ours is not exactly a conventional marriage."

"You'll find that we Kendricks manage awkward and

unconventional quite well." He settled back in his chair, once more facing the fire. "And that leads me to my second point. I am not without a past, either. I don't believe in ghosts, but I've found that memories can haunt you just as effectively."

"The woman you loved and lost?" she hesitantly asked.

"Yes."

Samantha wasn't quite sure she wanted to know about that woman. But because she'd already dumped so many of her burdens on him, she wanted to share his burdens, too, as painful as it might be to hear.

"Can you tell me about her?"

He breathed out a weary sigh that sounded like he might be letting something go.

"Her name was Annalise, and I met her in Hanover when I attended university there. I was entirely focused on my work at the time, and thought myself impervious to women." He flashed her a rueful smile. "I was stupidly naïve."

"How old were you?"

"Twenty-four when I first met her, but we didn't become involved until I returned to Hanover two years later."

"And before that you'd never had any . . ." She twirled a hand. "You know."

He cut her an amused glance. "Relationships? No. I lagged behind my brothers in that respect—although they were not quite the rakes the gossips made them out to be. Honestly, I never had much interest in women. I liked them, of course, but work and family took up all my time."

"Until you met Annalise."

"She was my first love," he quietly said.

"As Roger was mine."

Something that felt like sorrow and regret—for both of them—stirred in her chest. And just a tiny bit of jealousy that Braden had loved another woman before her. She wondered if he felt the same about Roger.

For a minute or so, they listened to the gentle hiss of the coals in the hearth as the night settled deeply around them.

"So, after you became involved," Samantha finally prompted, "did you ask her to marry you?"

"I did. I wanted her to move back to Scotland with me."

"Did she love you?"

"Yes."

Samantha frowned. "Then why didn't she accept your offer?"

He hesitated briefly. "Because she was already married."

She almost knocked over her glass. "You fell in love with a married woman?"

He winced. "I'm not proud of it, I assure you."

She flapped a hand. "Sorry, I didn't mean to screech at you. It just seems so unlike you."

Samantha had known many honorable men in her life, including Roger. And she knew in the depths of her bones that Braden Kendrick was a man of honor, too.

She touched his arm. "I know you would never intentionally hurt or dishonor anyone. If you became involved with Annalise, you had your reasons."

He looked at her then, and her heart broke a little at the sadness and shame that lurked in his gaze.

"You're much too kind, sweetheart."

She waggled a hand. "You might want to ask some of the villains I've encountered in the stews if they agree."

A small smile tipped up a corner of his mouth. "They deserved everything you gave them."

"You, however, deserve everything good. To echo what you've told me on more than one occasion, I won't judge you, Braden."

"It's not a pretty story."

"Well, my life has certainly been no fairy tale, so you needn't worry about scaring me off."

He reached over and took her hand, raising it to his lips for a brief kiss. "I'm so lucky to have found you, sweet lass."

That rather choked her up, but over the next few minutes he told a tale that dried up any tears. She found herself wanting to kill Annalise's brute of a husband for the murderous deed, one that had left Braden grief stricken and harrowed with guilt.

"I am so, so sorry," she said when he'd finished. "What a complete travesty of justice."

He scrubbed a hand through his hair, as if trying to get rid of the awful memories. "Yes. Annalise deserved justice, at least, and I could not give that to her."

"You tried, though."

"And failed."

"That was *not* your fault, Braden."

He gave a slow nod. "It's still a burden, though, even if I've learned to live with it."

Samantha propped her chin on her hands, staring into the fire. On a very deep level, they shared more than she'd ever imagined. In her mind's eye, she could see two lonely gravestones, and she wondered if she and Braden could ever rise above the sorrows of the past.

"We're quite the pair, aren't we?" she said with a sigh.

"Aye, that."

"It's terrible that you weren't able to find justice for Annalise."

"Some crimes can only be left to divine justice." He turned to look at her, his gaze now calm and determined. "I'm convinced, however, that we *can* find justice for Roger Penwith. He was a good man and deserves nothing less. You deserve nothing less."

His words carried the tone of a solemn vow, and she suddenly realized that Braden needed to find Roger's killer almost as much as she did. For both of them, it could mean redemption and a chance to start over again.

She reached for his hand. "Thank you for telling me."

"You're my wife, Samantha. I don't want there to be secrets between us."

"There have been quite a lot, haven't there?" she ruefully replied.

There was at least one more she should share with him— but not tonight. The poor man was looking ragged around the edges, and she was teetering on the brink of emotional exhaustion.

When he cocked his head, she could see the change come over him. Dr. Kendrick had just reappeared.

"How is your headache?" he asked.

Samantha blinked. "It's gone, actually."

And wasn't that a surprise? Her headaches normally lasted for hours and were conquered only by sleep.

He smiled. "Good. Think you can sleep, now?"

She nodded.

"Even better." He stood and then reached down to pull her up from the chair. "Off to bed with you, lass."

She stared up at him, getting lost in the depths of his gaze. Braden tipped up her chin and brushed a soft kiss across her lips. Barely a touch, it sent shivers rippling along her nerves.

But when she rested a hand on his chest, instinctively wanting to deepen the caress, he pulled back.

"Good night, love." He gently tapped her nose. "I'll see you in the morning."

Then he picked up his glass and strolled from the room, leaving her fighting the impulse to run after him. She wanted to pull him close and give him all the comfort her body could offer.

Clearly, though, and despite his harrowing tale, Braden was a very self-sufficient man who exerted iron control over his feelings.

He said he loved her, but he obviously didn't need her.

At least not yet.

CHAPTER 24

Braden was finishing up his notes when he heard a murmur of voices from the front room of the clinic. Another patient would mean a drink with Samantha before dinner would have to wait.

Sadly, his absence might not even bother her, given her mixed feelings about their marriage. There'd been some hopeful signs last night, but *thinking* one might be in love with one's husband was far from *being* in love.

He, however, was now decisively in love with his wife, and that had made their wedding night a bout of mental and physical torture. Sitting only feet away from her cozy-looking bed had only amplified the torment. He'd spent most of last night battling visions of torrid pleasures, and of the fun they could have in that bed.

Their fireside discussion had taken a very serious turn that didn't lend itself to even a gentle wooing. He'd done his best to open his heart to her, but it seemed clear that until they made more progress on finding Roger's killers, Samantha would struggle to move forward into their new life.

Braden took off his spectacles and rubbed his eyes. These last few weeks had been a whirlwind that had spun his life one hundred and eighty degrees on its axis. He'd not been expecting marriage, and certainly not like this.

Even with all its challenges, he didn't regret anything. At the end of it, he had a chance to win the heart of the fairest lady in Scotland. And that was worth fighting his way through any number of thugs, murderers, and evil grandfathers that stood in his way.

Mrs. Culp tapped on his door. "Ye have a visitor, sir."

He frowned. "Not a patient?"

Logan loomed up behind her. "No, it's your big brother, come to drag you away from work. It's going on six, Braden."

Mrs. Culp nodded. "A very good point ye make, sir. Dr. Kendrick has been working all day with nary a break."

"I was just about to pack up before this annoying person appeared," Braden sardonically replied. "And I did take a break for lunch."

"A pasty and a cup of tea while sittin' at yer desk writin' a lecture," Mrs. Culp replied. "That is no break."

Logan made a disgusted noise. "What in God's name am I going to do with you, man?"

"You could start by getting to the point of this visit, so I can go home," he sardonically replied.

Logan flicked a warning glance at Braden's assistant.

So, trouble.

"Mrs. Culp, that's it for today," Braden said. "If you would lock up on your way out, please."

"Aye, sir." She nodded to Logan. "A pleasure to see you, sir."

"Likewise, Mrs. Culp. Have a good evening."

They waited until the front door closed and locked behind her.

Logan grabbed a stool from the corner. "I hope you pay that woman a good salary. She obviously keeps you in line."

"You mean she nags me, just like the rest of you."

"Och, we just make wee suggestions."

Braden opened his eyes at him. "Is that what you call it?"

"You could use a spot of nagging, lad. You're looking worn around the edges."

Braden rolled his shoulders, working out the kinks. "It's been a long day. Besides, you don't need to scold me. I have a wife to do that now."

"Samantha doesn't strike me as the scolding type."

Braden smiled. "She can be bossy, though. I like that about her."

"If you like her so much, then why are you at work— literally the day after you got married, I might note."

"It's complicated."

Logan snorted. "A Kendrick specialty."

"True, but you didn't come down here to discuss my marriage. What's amiss?"

"The Penwith Foundation ledgers. I think I've finally cracked the damn things."

Braden expelled a relieved breath. "Thank God. Samantha's been a bundle of nerves, waiting for something to break. Have you got names?"

Logan waggled a hand. "I'll get to that. Right now, it's the how that I'm most interested in, not the who."

"Which means?"

"Someone has devised a rather elaborate system for washing money through the foundation and skimming it off, too."

"Ah, so my fellow board member, Mr. Haxton, is skimming?"

"Probably," Logan replied. "That's been happening from the daily accounts for some time, although not in huge amounts, and it's been carefully done."

"So Mrs. Girvin suggested."

"The real problem, however, lies in the foundation's main operating account, the one holding the bulk of donor contributions. There's a smaller account for minor donations, but that one is fine. It's that operating account that's gone sideways."

Logan shook his head. "I had to go back three years to find the bloody pattern."

Braden frowned. "Before Roger Penwith was murdered."

"Yes."

He leaned forward. "Explain."

"For three years, a growing number of anonymous contributions have been made to the operating account. Some of the more recent donations are significant, while others are small enough that I wondered why they weren't placed in the minor account set up for that."

Braden shook his head. "I've reviewed the foundation's contributor lists. We don't have any anonymous donors, and certainly not ones who've made significant contributions."

"I asked Samantha that question last week," Logan said. "Didn't give her any details, since I wasn't yet sure what was going on. She confirmed your point."

Braden crossed his arms and leaned back in his chair. "Isn't that interesting?"

"Indeed, especially when you look at what happens to those donations."

"And that is?"

"Some of it flows into the daily expense accounts." Logan twirled a hand. "You know, clothing for the boys, school supplies, food, mercantile goods, and so on."

"And that's where the skimming occurs?"

"Indeed. But the bulk of the anonymous contributions are, over time, siphoned off from the operating account. As far as I can tell, those funds are never utilized by the foundation."

Braden snorted with disgust. "Haxton."

"It does all happen through the bank where Haxton is a director. Probably keeps two sets of books to cover it up."

Braden pondered this new information before shaking his head. "This sounds like a complicated rig, much too complicated for Haxton. The man's afraid of his own shadow. It's hard to imagine him as the head of a criminal scheme like this, much less murdering Roger Penwith—because right now I'm going to assume that Penwith was starting to figure this out, and that's what got him murdered."

"I agree on both counts. I know Haxton, and I'm not impressed. He holds his position because his father was one of the original founders of the bank. So, if it's him, I suspect he's got an accomplice, and possibly more than one."

Braden frowned. "Mrs. Girvin? She would be a likely candidate, but for the fact that Samantha trusts her."

"I don't know. But even if she was involved, it's unlikely that the two of them could manage something this big. My gut tells me someone else is behind this—someone who could run very good interference for them."

"Another board member?"

"Maybe, but that brings me to my next point. Or, rather, to the next question that needs to be asked."

Braden mentally flipped back through their conversation. "Where are the extra funds coming from in the first place?"

"On the nose, little brother. Someone is acquiring funds, and is using the foundation to move them in increasing numbers."

Braden's mind caught on a thread and pulled it. "Do these increases parallel the disappearances of the children, by any chance?"

Logan frowned for a few moments, as if reviewing the information in his head. "Actually, yes."

Braden felt a piece of the puzzle settle into place with the satisfying *snick* that told him he was on the right track. "That's the connection. Someone is kidnapping or recruiting the children into their gang, using them for the kind of thefts where children are helpful, and *then* utilizing the foundation to both hide and move the proceeds. And because the jobs are getting bigger over time, they require more resources."

Logan blew out a breath. "If that's true, that is one hell of a rig."

"Yes, but it feels right to me. And if Roger Penwith had discovered this, whoever was running the rig would be well motivated to kill him."

It was coming together with the same degree of confidence he felt when he'd made a difficult diagnosis. Random pieces of evidence suddenly fell into place, like a mathematical equation that finally made sense.

Logan grimaced. "This suggests a very talented and dangerous gang at work."

"That was Samantha's conclusion some weeks ago. And that brings us to the Hanging Judge. Any news?"

"Yes, and it fits with your hypothesis. Stevens, my fellow who's been trying to infiltrate the place, is convinced it's a flash house with a new gang. He's made a few visits during the day, putting it about that he was looking for work from the occasional break-in or snatch and grab."

"Any response?"

"Yes. A few regulars told Stevens that he was to cease visits to the Hanging Judge, or they would stop his claret," Logan dryly replied.

"They threatened to kill him?"

"They did."

"Seems rather brash, not to mention foolhardy."

Logan shrugged. "According to Stevens, they didn't even bother to tell him to keep quiet about it. Just said that if he showed up anywhere near the place again, he'd end up with a slit throat."

Braden pondered that information. "That suggests they feel secure in their position. That no one would dare take them on."

"Because someone with power and influence is protecting them?"

"Someone on the inside, who stands to profit."

"Again, that brings us back to Haxton," Logan said. "But he's a well-to-do banker. Why would he get involved in something like this?"

"Good question." Braden intended to ask Haxton, sooner rather than later.

"I'll tell you something else," Logan said. "This group of bastards is definitely getting bolder. My men keeping watch at the Hanging Judge have had a few close calls with some very unsavory characters. I've pulled them back a bit, just to be safe."

Braden frowned. "Why didn't you tell me?"

"Because you were getting married?" Logan incredulously replied. "Did you really think I was going to bother you with this on your wedding day?"

"Yes, actually."

"Don't be daft."

When Braden started to object, Logan held up a hand. "My men are guarding the orphanage, and still keeping watch on the Hanging Judge. Nothing will happen that we don't know about, I promise."

Braden scrubbed a frustrated hand over his head. "There are children in harm's way. Samantha is not the patient sort when it comes to that."

"You'll just have to keep her in check, because we don't have enough proof yet to take to the law. I need to nail down a few more details before I feel confident accusing Haxton of outright fraud. His family is both well regarded and well established in the financial community."

"Then maybe it's time you and I made a little sortie down to the Hanging Judge. Just to see what we can see."

"And maybe that's a bad idea," his brother retorted. "They know you, remember? You can't be seen. You need to trust me on that."

Braden grimaced. "I do trust you, but it's damn hard waiting around for something to happen. What do you suggest I do in the meantime?"

"Go home to your wife. And, by the way, why *are* you working on the day after your wedding? Seriously, Braden, that's just . . . odd."

"I think you mean sad," he ruefully replied.

"You said it, not me." His brother sat, calmly waiting, and clearly expecting an answer.

Braden sighed. "We had a rather difficult discussion last night."

"Oh, what fun for a wedding night. What was it about?"

"Annalise."

Logan snorted. "Och, lad."

"I know, but it had to be done."

"Samantha probably thinks you're still in love with her."

Braden held up his hands. "In my defense, she brought up Roger Penwith first. All this has happened too quickly for her. I don't think she really sees me as her husband. More a friend and companion in arms at this point."

"Spending all your time at work isn't going to do much to change that opinion." Logan clapped him on the shoulder. "You've got to woo her, lad, and do it properly."

"It's hard to concentrate on wooing when one is also trying to solve a murder and various criminal schemes."

"Look, you're not alone in this. You've got me and you've got my men. Something will break fairly soon. In the meantime, discuss what you must with Samantha. Then, for the love of God, have some fun."

Braden eyed his brother. As always, Logan made a great deal of sense.

"All right, oh wise one," he said. "Any suggestions for the fun part?"

"Definitely. Show Samantha that you're a true family man," Logan said. "Take her and Felicity for an outing and bring Pippa and Joseph with you. Make her part of your family.

From what I can tell, Samantha is a woman who longs for family. The lassie needs to belong, so show her that she *does* belong—to you."

"You know, for such a big lummox, you're actually quite smart," Braden replied with a wry smile.

Logan snorted. "Smart enough to know that my wife will have my head if I don't get myself home soon. And you have a wife waiting for you, too. Show her that you're worth the wait."

CHAPTER 25

Despite Samantha's dodge, Donny still caught her a glancing blow on the shoulder. "Och, sorry, my lady. Didna mean to give ye such a hit."

She shook out her arm. "It's fine. Anyway, I'm terribly rusty, so it's good to keep me on my toes."

"The doctor won't be happy if I give ye a bruise, though. He'll give me a right dressin' down."

"He'll do no such thing, and you know it. And you should call me Mrs. Kendrick, not my lady. I don't want Dr. Kendrick to feel like he's playing second fiddle to me."

Or to Roger.

Donny shrugged. "He's nae fashed about it. He said I should call ye whatever I liked."

Samantha couldn't hold back a smile. "He's a very nice man, isn't he?"

"Aye, he's a good one." Donny wistfully sighed. "The master would have approved of him."

Samantha mentally grimaced. As well as Braden had adapted to their household, it was still a difficult change for the staff, especially for Donny, who had cared for Roger since he was a little boy. Having a new master took some getting used to.

It was true that Braden didn't seem fashed about any of the

living arrangements, including the fact that he was essentially banished to the spare bedroom. He was so accommodating, and so willing to stay out of everyone's way, that Samantha was beginning to feel guilty. For a man supposedly in love with her, he had the patience of Job. Except for a goodnight peck on her cheek, he'd not made one move in the direction of sexual intimacy.

And that, she had to admit, was beginning to annoy her.

"Shall we go again, my lady? Er, Mrs. Kendrick?" Donny asked.

"Yes, but only if you feel able. You mustn't overdo it, Donny, or the doctor will have *my* head."

He scoffed. "I'm that sick of sittin' around twiddlin' my thumbs. And we have the chance to practice in the daylight, what with young miss off visitin'."

Usually, they held their practice session, fighting with wooden blades, at night after Felicity had retired. Today, though, the girl was visiting with the Blackmores and wouldn't return home till after dinner.

Samantha retucked her linen shirt into the waistband of her plain black skirt and resumed the stance. Donny engaged and for several minutes stick clattered against stick as they parried and thrust, sliding back and forth across the floor in their stocking feet. Despite her rustiness, she felt confidence flowing through her body as her training reasserted itself.

Their mission had been too long delayed due to Donny's injury, Beath's infernal meddling, and the commotion of her marriage. Thankfully, the Kendricks had stepped into the gap. She was immensely grateful for their help, but no one knew the situation better than she did, and it was time to get back into the game.

She saw an opening and slid her faux blade under Donny's point, jabbing him in the armpit. He retreated, shaking his head in disgust.

"Ye got me there, missus."

She grinned. "I certainly did. It's good to get back to it, I must say."

Panting a bit, Donny picked up a towel from the back of a chair and scrubbed the sweat off his flushed face.

"Perhaps we'd best call it quits," she said. "We don't want to push it, now that your ankle is finally better."

"I'm just a little out of shape. It's all that sittin' around for so long."

"Why don't you rest for a minute and let me fetch you a glass of water?"

He nodded and sank gratefully into the chair.

Mentally kicking herself, Samantha went to the pitcher on the sideboard. Donny was getting older, probably too old for this work. While he'd always been her valuable right hand, she had another champion now—her husband. Braden had vowed that he would see this through to the end. She also had the entire Kendrick family on her side. Because of them, she was closer to cracking the case than ever before.

For the first time in ages, Samantha felt hope. Still, a fierce battle lay ahead of them, and her greatest fear was that one of those she most cherished, including Braden, could be hurt, or even killed. She would take a bullet herself before she allowed that to happen again.

She would not lose another man she loved.

After she brought Donny his water, she covertly studied him. Yes, he was showing his years. To keep putting him in harm's way—

Donny interrupted that thought by scowling at her. "Just ye stop it, my lady. I'm damn capable of takin' care of myself, as is Dr. Kendrick."

Sometimes Samantha wished her servants didn't know her quite so well.

"I can't help worrying, Donny. You're not getting any younger, and I think we're in for a tough fight before we get to the end of it."

"And ye'll not be cuttin' me out. I've gone this far with ye, and I intend to see it through to the end—for Master Roger's sake. It's what he would have wanted. Me by yer side, as always, lookin' out for ye. I ken I'm just a servant, but—"

She cut him off. "You're much more than that, and you know it. I do realize that you need this resolution as much as I do, and I promise you'll be there with me, right to the end. But we must be careful, all right?"

"Yes, my lady," he gruffly replied. "Now, are ye up for another round before we quit?"

"Are you?"

He snorted. "I ain't the one who got yanked off his feet the last time we was out in Old Town."

She wrinkled her nose. "How ungentlemanly of you to remind me."

He picked up his faux blade. "If I remind ye, maybe ye won't make that mistake again."

"Well, then prepare to—"

"Prepare to explain exactly what's happening in here," said the stern voice she knew so well.

Oh, blast.

Braden was standing in the doorway, arms crossed, with a decidedly irritated expression on his face.

"Oh, hallo," she said rather sheepishly. "I didn't hear you come in."

"Obviously."

She flashed him a bright smile. "I didn't expect you so early. Are you finished work?"

"I thought to come home and spend a little time with my wife. Instead, I find the drawing room furniture pushed back, the carpets rolled up, *and* my patient hopping about on an ankle that's barely healed."

"My ankle feels fine," Donny protested.

Braden stalked over and held out his hand. "I'll be the judge of that."

Grumbling, Donny handed over the sword.

"Sit," Braden ordered.

When Donny looked mutinous, Samantha decided it was time to intervene.

"It's not a bad idea for Dr. Kendrick to check your ankle," she said. "We don't want you going down in the midst of a fight, do we?"

Braden shot her an irate glance. "It might be best to avoid fights, if at all possible."

She wrinkled her nose in silent apology.

Muttering, Donny subsided into the chair.

Braden crouched down and conducted a quick examination, flexing Donny's foot and pressing around the ankle. "No pain?"

"Nae, just a little stiffness. That's why I need to work it out."

Braden stood. "Agreed. But you do need to take it by degrees, or you'll reinjure it. We cannot afford for you to be out of commission again. We need you, Donny."

"Yes, sir," Donny replied in a slightly mollified tone.

"Good. Now, I want you to go down and rest for a bit. Elevate your foot and ice the ankle, all right? I'll finish the practice session with Mrs. Kendrick."

"You?" Samantha and Donny exclaimed at the same time.

Braden started to shrug off his coat. "I am a Highlander, in case you've forgotten. I'm familiar with a variety of weapons, including the blade."

Donny studied him for a moment and then nodded. "I'll leave ye to it, sir. My lady is a bit rusty with her footwork, just so ye ken."

"I am not," Samantha muttered.

Braden tried to hide a smile. "How unfortunate. We'll be sure to work on that."

"You really are an annoying man," she said after Donny left the room.

Braden draped his coat over the sofa and began rolling up

his sleeves. "I suspect that I'm the least annoying person you know."

"Well, you must admit that you can be a fussbudget."

He flashed her the roguish smile that never failed to make her heart skip a beat. "Someone needs to fuss over you, love."

"My staff fusses over me just fine. Besides, I don't like to bother you when you're already so busy."

"Samantha, I'm your husband. You can always bother me." He studied her for a moment. "Now, why don't you tell me what this is truly about? Why the sudden urge to drag Donny into a workout? You know we've got everything covered. Nothing will happen without us knowing about it."

"I have to be ready, Braden. We've never been this close before, and I just know something is going to happen soon."

"Very likely it will. But I'm hoping that when it does, my wife will not be in the middle of a knife fight, or worse."

Samantha couldn't help bristling. "You're not to keep me away from this, Braden. I'm perfectly capable of taking care of myself."

"I haven't kept you away," he protested. "Everything that Logan has uncovered, I've shared with you, have I not?"

She expelled an irritated breath, though her irritation was with herself more than him. "Yes."

Not that she'd responded particularly well to what he'd told her. When she'd learned about Haxton's certain involvement in defrauding the foundation, she'd wanted to storm over to the blighter's townhouse and hold a pistol to his head. Braden had finally convinced her that it would be unwise to show their cards this early.

"And you trust me, don't you, love?" Braden quietly asked.

Whenever he used that endearment, Samantha's heart melted into a puddle. Still, she could hear the note of quiet dismay in his voice, as if he feared she didn't trust him.

She sighed and flopped down on the sofa. "Of course I trust you. I'm sorry for being so difficult."

He sat beside her, taking her hand and raising it briefly to his lips. The tender gesture made her heart ache with longing.

"Please tell me how I can help you," he said.

"It's all this sitting around," she burst out. "It's driving me mad, if you must know."

He gave her a quizzical smile. "Seems to me we've done very little sitting around, lately."

She had to admit that was true. In the past week they'd spent considerable time Christmas shopping with Felicity, purchasing gifts for the Kendrick family and various friends. While Samantha would rather die than admit it, she'd thoroughly enjoyed spending money on presents and treats without worrying if she'd have to stretch the food bill to the end of the month.

They'd had several other outings, too. Since there'd been snow, Braden had arranged a sleigh ride for the children, taking Angus along to tell his hilarious stories about the Kendrick brothers. As well, they'd had lovely suppers at Heriot Row and visits with John and Bathsheba.

Braden had also taken her to one of his lectures. It was brilliant, as she could have anticipated, and she'd been immensely proud of him. Finally, they'd spent time at his clinic, where she'd seen firsthand how good he was with his patients. He treated all of them with compassion and courtesy, be it a worried young mother with a sick child or a rough-edged dockhand.

Clearly, she'd married an extraordinary man. Even more clearly, Samantha now realized she was thoroughly in love with Braden, but she didn't quite know what to do about that. To simply blurt out such a declaration, especially in light of their wedding night discussion, seemed rather absurd. He'd insisted on giving her time and yet here she was, barely ten days later, madly in love. The poor man would think her daft.

And, of course, there was still the matter of—

Braden gently tapped her on the nose. "What's going on in that beautiful head of yours?"

"Um, not much." She winced when he chuckled. "Sorry, what was the question again?"

"Never mind." He started yanking off his boots.

"What are you doing?" she asked.

"Donny said your footwork was rusty."

"You're really going to practice with me?"

He cocked an eyebrow. "Are you worried that I'll best you?"

"Is that a challenge, Dr. Kendrick?"

"Sounds like it, doesn't it?"

Samantha rose and picked up her practice blade. "Then may the better man win."

He snorted and came to his feet to test the weight of Donny's blade. "This is an excellent substitute, but don't you ever practice with the real thing? Capped, of course."

"My tip fell off once when we were practicing. Let's just say that Donny couldn't sit down for a week."

"That does sound alarming. I'd best be on my guard."

She flashed him a smile as they both assumed their stances. Blade met blade with a satisfying crack.

For several minutes, they danced and slid across the floor, parry meeting thrust. Braden was clearly an accomplished fencer, which made her wonder if there was anything he couldn't do exceptionally well.

Perhaps he's as adept in bed as he is with a blade?

As a physician, he should certainly know his way around a woman's body.

He suddenly passed under her guard to press his tip against her shoulder.

"Oh, blast," she muttered.

He disengaged and stepped back. "Lucky on my part, but I think you're flagging."

She shook her head. "I just let my mind wander. Five more minutes, all right?"

"Samantha—"

She pointed her blade at him. "And no more holding back. I can tell you're doing that."

"Och, lass, I'd never—"

She lunged, catching him off guard. He twisted aside, then he pressed forward with his attack. It was clear now that he had been holding back, because he was *very* good. Samantha had to call up all her skill and reserves of energy, dancing around him as he steadily forced her to give ground.

Suddenly, she saw an opening. She sidestepped his blade and ducked under his arm, forcing him to turn. When his heel caught the edge of the partially rolled up carpet, Braden pinwheeled his arms to try to recover his balance, but his stocking feet went out from under him.

He landed on the floor with a thud.

Samantha dropped to her knees and put a hand on his chest. "Did you hurt yourself? Are you all right?"

He stared up at her, momentarily stunned. Then mischief flashed through his eyes. He reached for her waist and, in one swift move, lifted her right off her knees and onto his body.

Gasping, she grabbed his shoulders. She now straddled him and her skirts were hiked high, exposing her garters and the tops of her stockings. Braden's hand slid down to rest on her naked thigh.

"At the moment, I am more than all right," he murmured.

Samantha stared down at him, her heart thundering with excitement and shock.

A faint smile lifted his oh-so-tempting mouth. His hand rested lightly on her thigh, barely caressing her, and the roughened tips of his fingers sent shivers cascading over her skin. But he made no other move. He simply waited.

Even in the dark days of the past, Samantha had never

thought of herself as a coward, but this moment filled her with trepidation. At the same time, she felt a longing for Braden so fierce that her heart could barely contain it. Her new life patiently waited, right in front of her. All she had to do was reach for it. It *would* be a kind of surrender—not to Braden, but to herself.

She wanted that surrender with every fiber of her being.

Her husband lifted an eyebrow, as if to say, *Well, lass?*

"Challenge accepted," she whispered.

His faint smile flashed into a grin, and then he brought his other hand to the back of her neck, urging her head down to his. Samantha felt her eyes drift shut, and then their lips met.

Braden's mouth took her with sensual sweetness, nuzzling her lips and then slipping inside. It was a beautiful plundering, passionate and yet infinitely tender, so tender that tears gathered behind her eyelids.

With a murmured sigh, Samantha let her body relax, melting into him. His hands moved to her hips, cradling her against him. Braden was tall and lean, but muscular for all that. She nestled against his chest, relishing the feel of him. There was so much latent strength in his powerful body, always carefully leashed and under control.

Braden unleashed.

It was a ravishing thought. All that masculine strength let loose, all focused on her. Instinctively, Samantha deepened the kiss, snuggling closer, tangling her tongue with his.

He groaned, a low rumble that vibrated between them. She had to resist the temptation to rub her breasts against his muscled chest, because they were on the floor of their drawing room, and to behave in so—

But when Braden nipped her lower lip and then sucked it into his mouth, rational thought went up in smoke. She whimpered and dug her hands into his shoulders, eagerly opening to his now ravenous exploration. The world disappeared, leaving her oblivious to everything but the feel of his body, and his hands as they moved back to her thighs, caressing her naked skin.

Their kiss grew so hot and wet that she started to tremble. A lovely ache began to build between her thighs, one she hadn't felt in a very long time. Kisses flowed one into another, as his mouth teased hers with languid sensuality and an unspoken promise of more to come.

When his hand moved to her backside, clamping her tight, Samantha gasped. His erection, formidably hard, rubbed against her sex. Her body lit up, and she went boneless with desire, wanting more—so much more.

When he flexed his hips, pressing hard between her thighs, she couldn't hold back a moan. She squirmed, fighting a driving need to let him do whatever he wanted, right here and right now.

Then what are you waiting for?

Braden suddenly broke the kiss, and Samantha came up for air with a shattered breath.

"God, sweetheart," he growled, his brogue as deep as night. "I've wanted this for so long. I want you, Samantha. All of you."

She tried to focus through the sensual haze clouding her brain. She wanted it, too, but something was tugging at the back of her brain, holding her back. It was that final secret, the one that *needed* to be told. But the idea of sharing it with anyone, much less Braden, filled her with shame.

His gaze suddenly grew sharp. "What's wrong, Samantha?"

"I . . . I . . . nothing," she stuttered.

Braden grimaced. "No, I'm pushing you before you're ready. Forgive me, sweetheart, I'm an idiot."

When he started to shift, as if to lift her off, Samantha clamped her hands onto his shoulders. She couldn't bear the look of guilt on his face. He'd done nothing but love and protect her, always putting her needs before his.

"No, it's not that," she managed in a shaky voice. "It's something else. Something I need to tell you."

His stark expression eased as he gently stroked the tumbled hair back from her brow. "You can tell me anything, love. Nothing can change the way I feel about you."

She hoped so, but anxiety twisted her insides. She was caught between the desperate need to tell him and the fear that he would think less of her if she did.

"Whatever it is," he said in a soothing tone, "it's all right."

"I know," she said, trying to really believe that.

"Do you want to get up?"

"No. I want you to keep holding me."

"I'll never let go," he said. "I promise."

And Kendricks never break their promises.

She couldn't help but smile at the memory of the first time he'd said it to her.

"Go on, brave lass," he quietly prompted.

Sighing, she rested her forehead on his shoulder. "All right. It's an awful thing, but I was addicted to laudanum. It controlled my life for a long time after Roger died and I lost the baby."

Just saying it made her feel ill. Those horrible months had passed by in a dark, drug-induced haze. The laudanum had made everything worse, dulling her senses and yet seeming to trap her in a spiral of grief. Even though she'd been desperate to escape that nightmare, she couldn't. She'd grown too dependent on the drug, and began craving it more than she craved the will to live.

Braden stroked a soothing hand down her back. "I know. It's all right. It wasn't your fault."

Samantha jerked up her head. "What do you mean, you know?" She couldn't help scowling. "Did John tell you?"

"Of course not. He would never betray a patient's confidence."

"Then how do you know?" she said sharply.

"It wasn't that hard to figure out, sweetheart. More than once, you stated your strong aversion to laudanum, which was a bit unusual. Then I put together the bits and pieces of information I knew about your condition after the miscarriage and came to the conclusion that someone—probably your idiot of a doctor at the time—must have put you on laudanum."

"Oh, well, that makes perfect sense." She grimaced. "I'm sorry I yelled."

"It's fine. Yelling is generally a daily occurrence in my family."

"Still . . ." She sighed. "It's just that I hate talking about it."

Braden shifted, gently rolling her onto the carpet. Then he reached over and swiped a pillow from the nearby sofa, slipping it under her head. Then he settled back and tucked her against him. Samantha snuggled close, and immediately felt some of the tension drain from her muscles.

"I know, but do you think you could tell me more?" he asked.

She nodded. "Dr. Lane first gave it right after my miscarriage. I was in pain, but I was also emotionally agitated. I . . . I didn't even think to say no."

"Love, your husband had been murdered and you'd just lost your baby. You were in deep grief."

She had been indeed harrowed with grief, but it had been more than that. "I was also furious. I kept trying to tell Beath and the police that Roger wasn't a victim of some random robbery, but no one would listen. Dr. Lane said I was becoming too agitated, and that I needed the laudanum to calm me down."

"In other words, he and Beath wanted to keep you quiet."

"I suppose. Beath wished for the whole thing to just go away, and I was insistent that there be a proper investigation."

Braden held her close. "I'd like nothing better than to throttle that old fool. And I *will* throttle Lane the next time I see him—or toss him off the nearest bridge. God knows his patients would greatly benefit."

"That is a lovely thought, but I would prefer not to have to visit my new husband in a jail cell."

"Who says anyone would find out?"

She let out a watery chuckle. "Spoken like a true Kendrick. In all fairness, I did develop terrible migraines during that time. The laudanum was the only thing that helped."

"How much did he give you?"

"I don't remember the details, but by the end of it, it seemed Lane was practically pouring it down my throat."

Braden muttered a surprisingly vicious curse. Not that it bothered her.

"Eventually, John took over my care," she added. "Things got much better after that."

"Not right away, though, I'll wager," he grimly stated. "Not with a laudanum addiction."

He would of course know better than anyone how hard it was to overcome it.

"It took several weeks to wean me off it," she said. "I won't pretend it was pleasant."

The first few weeks had been hellish. John, Bathsheba, and Mrs. Johnson had nursed her through the worst of it, with one of them always by her side.

"I imagine it also took some time to get your strength back, after so many traumas."

"The better part of a year, I'm afraid."

He cupped her chin, making her look at him. "You suffered two devastating losses, Samantha. Even without the addiction, it likely would have taken you months to recover. Again, you are entirely blameless."

She grimaced. "John and Bathsheba said that, too. Still, I felt terribly weak and stupid for allowing myself to become so dependent."

"That's nonsense," he replied. "It took incredible courage

to get off the damn stuff. I've known men—strong men—who couldn't overcome it. What you did was absolutely heroic."

She eyed him. "You're not just saying that to make me feel better?"

He gave her a stern look. "Have I ever lied to you?"

She waggled a hand. "A few lies of omission."

"Och, lass."

"No," she admitted. "You never have lied to me."

"Then listen well, Samantha Kendrick. You have no cause to feel ashamed. In fact, you should feel nothing but pride. In the space of one year, you overcame a series of tragedies that could have destroyed you or practically anyone else. Instead, you fought back—you literally fought back. You're a true heroine, my love. Trust me when I say I'm utterly humbled by you."

She had to rub her nose. "Drat, you're going to make me cry. But thank you. It's very sweet of you to say such nice things."

"They're the truth, Samantha, and I'll keep on telling the truth until you believe it. All right?"

She smiled at his rather stern expression. "Yes."

He pressed a kiss to her forehead. "Good. Now, I think we've had enough activity for one afternoon. You need a nice cup of tea and a rest before dinner."

When he started to get up, Samantha hooked a hand in his waistcoat and pulled him back down with a thump.

"You're not going anywhere, Dr. Kendrick."

He frowned. "Samantha, do you want to lie on the floor? It's not very comfortable."

She slipped her hands around his neck. "What I want is for you to make love to me."

His eyebrows shot up. "Now?"

"Of course now, you ninny. Why do you think I told you that awful story in the first place? No secrets between us, remember? Well, that was the last secret."

Heat instantly flared in his gaze. But a moment later, caution mingled with it. "Are you certain?"

Samantha had never been more certain in her life. She'd married an incredible man, one who would always protect her heart. And she was ready to give that heart to him, just as he'd given his heart to her.

She craned up and pressed a kiss to his lips. "I am absolutely certain."

A sensual smile curled up the edges of his wonderful mouth. Just thinking about how that mouth would feel on her body made her toes curl with anticipation.

"Then might I suggest we retire to the bedroom?" he replied in a husky tone.

She shook her head. "Too far. The floor will do just fine."

Braden practically choked. "Truly?"

"Yes, and you'd best crack on before I lose interest."

He laughed. "At your command, my lady. And how delightfully unconventional of you, I must say."

Samantha felt the warmth of his laugh—and his love—fizz through her body like champagne. She wanted to laugh, too—or cry out of sheer relief and gratitude for the chance to love again.

"Dr. Kendrick, when have we ever been conventional?"

"True, that."

He suddenly rolled away and scrambled to his feet.

"Where are you going?" she demanded.

"To lock the door. I don't want Donny or Mrs. Johnson walking in us."

"That would be rather dreadful."

"Indeed."

A moment later, he was back and taking her into his arms. He loomed over her, his gaze a thrilling mix of love and desire. "Are you quite ready, my darling girl?"

She slipped her arms around his neck. "More than ready."

His smile—the roguish one she'd come to love—flashed bright and quick. "Thank God."

Then his mouth came down to hers, and Samantha gave herself up to love.

CHAPTER 26

As the fading day cast the shadows of dusk across her desk, Samantha paused to light the Argand lamp before returning her attention to the notebook in front of her. After an entire afternoon at the foundation pouring over board meeting minutes, she was practically cross-eyed. The work was beginning to feel like a waste of time.

Something had niggled at her these last few days, the sense that she'd missed a small but vital clue hidden deep in the books. So, she'd started at the beginning, reading through all the minutes of the Penwith Foundation board from its inception. Thanks to Logan, she now had a better idea of where to look for anomalies. But it was tedious work, and so far she'd found nothing.

She reached for her cup of tea and took a swallow of the tepid and rather bitter brew, hoping it would jolt her brain.

Mrs. Girvin appeared in the open doorway to Samantha's office. "Mrs. Kendrick, can I get you a fresh pot?"

"Thank you, Mrs. Girvin, but I'm fine."

The housekeeper came closer. "You've been working steady on those records for hours, ma'am. Are you sure I can't help?"

Samantha put down her pencil with a sigh. "I'm not really

sure what I'm looking for, to tell you the truth. Hopefully, it'll jump out at me at some point."

Girvin pulled an unhappy face. "I apologize for not coming to you sooner with my concerns. I should have."

"There's no need to keep apologizing, Mrs. Girvin. I likely would have done the same in your shoes." She smiled. "I'm glad we finally had the chance to have a good talk about it."

Samantha hadn't been to the foundation for several days, due to the recent turmoil in her life. But she'd resolved to come in today, both to catch up on work and to dig deeper into the books.

She'd also been determined to quiz Girvin about Haxton and any other concerns the housekeeper might have about the foundation. Though Haxton would naturally deny any accusations Girvin made against him, everything the housekeeper had detailed in their discussion squared with what Samantha already knew about the ongoing fraud and Haxton's role in it.

Girvin had been one of Roger's first hires, and he'd always trusted her. She performed her job with rigorous competence, and Samantha saw no reason not to trust her, too.

"You're very kind, ma'am," said Girvin. "I'm grateful for your trust in me."

"You're welcome."

Samantha returned to her work, but the housekeeper hovered in the doorway. "Is there something else, Mrs. Girvin?"

"I must ask you if you're sure I can't help you, Mrs. Kendrick. You seem fatigued today, which is quite understandable, given all that close work."

"I'm just going to work a bit longer, and then pack up the rest and take it home with me."

Girvin nodded. "Then I will leave you to it. Just ring if you need me."

"Thank you. Oh, by the way, Felicity and Donny will be joining me shortly after a bit of shopping. When they arrive, please send them up to my office."

"Dr. Kendrick will not be escorting you home tonight?"

Samantha frowned, thinking it a rather odd question. "Dr. Kendrick will be working late, so Donny and Felicity will take me home."

"Very good, ma'am. I'll send them up as soon as they arrive. Please ring if you need anything."

She gave the housekeeper a quizzical smile. "Yes, as you already mentioned."

"Oh, yes, of course. Well, I'll be down the hall in my office."

She left in something of a rush, which was also rather odd. It wasn't like Girvin to appear so . . . distracted. Then again, the situation with Haxton was bound to produce disquiet. Girvin was also looking a bit pulled around the edges, as if she were tired as well.

Of course, Samantha had an additional reason beyond work for her fatigue—her husband. For the last two nights, Braden had kept her up *quite* late, making love to her. Ever since their thrilling and highly improper encounter on the drawing room floor, Braden had been almost solely focused on her. The man was insatiable, and had a rather astounding degree of energy.

Not that Samantha minded one bit. Braden was a wonderful lover, both generous and inventive. Being married to a physician certainly had its advantages, especially one who had such a precise knowledge of female anatomy.

Even better, though, was the tenderness and love he poured out on her. She felt utterly cherished and safe in his arms. To be loved and to love again, to have this second chance, was a blessing beyond measure.

Well, she'd have plenty of time to daydream about Braden in the years to come. For now, she had work to do.

Samantha turned back to a record from a board meeting held a month before Roger's death. The regular business seemed perfectly normal, so she focused on the financial committee. If she was going to stumble across anything new, that was where it would be.

Suddenly, she froze, staring at the page.

Staring at the name of the board member who'd presented the financial committee report.

It couldn't be.

She flipped back to the foundation's first official minutes. It was the same name, the new head of the finance committee.

And it wasn't Haxton.

Impatiently, she flipped forward, scanning the reports for the name. After a few minutes, she shoved the book away and pressed her palms over her eyes, trying to think through the roar of consternation and disbelief in her head. Could such a heinous betrayal be possible?

She placed her hands flat on the desk, trying to keep them from trembling. From the first, they'd assumed it was Haxton managing the flow of money, probably with assistance from another quarter. Since Samantha had joined the board, Haxton had kept the books and thus controlled the flow of funds into and out of the foundation.

But Haxton hadn't even been on the board while Roger was alive. Because Samantha hadn't been involved with the foundation at the time, she'd never realized that the banker's appointment had only come later. She'd never once thought to look back to the very beginning, to the other person who'd been working with Roger right from the start. She'd never dreamed that the person who might be at the bottom of it all could be the one she'd never suspect.

Arthur Baines.

Arthur had recommended Haxton as the new finance chair—insistently and over other candidates. Before that, Arthur had managed the books and handled the funds. *He* was the one in charge when Roger had begun to suspect financial misdeeds.

And when that first boy had disappeared from the orphanage? Arthur had been in the thick of it then, too. He'd been the one to discuss matters with the police and manage investigations, just as he'd done with every subsequent disappearance.

All had the same result—nothing.

Samantha pressed a clenched fist over her heart, which felt ready to pound through her chest. Guilt and rage swamped her in equal waves, clouding her brain. She needed to think, and she needed to know if her suspicions were justified.

You need Braden.

If she'd ever needed her husband's brilliant mind and calm clarity it was now.

She reached for a sheet of paper. Twice she blotted the short missive, but urgency drove her, like a whip between her shoulder blades. She sealed the note and scrawled Braden's name across the front. Then she bolted out of her chair and out to the hall.

Stop. Think.

Pointing a finger at Baines was an enormous accusation to make. She had to be sure, or the consequences could be devastating. She couldn't afford even the slightest niggle of suspicion or gossip to circulate at this point anywhere, starting with the foundation staff.

She took a deep breath and then strode down to Girvin's office. The housekeeper was at her desk, doing paperwork. She glanced up with surprise before rising.

"Mrs. Kendrick, are you unwell? You look quite pale."

Samantha dredged up a smile. "I'm perfectly fine."

Girvin studied her for a moment. "Is there something I can do for you now?"

"Actually, I need one of the older boys to take a message to Dr. Kendrick's clinic. Could you please arrange for that?"

"Of course. Their final class for the day should be ending shortly—"

"No, I need it done now," Samantha sharply interrupted.

Girvin looked startled. "As you wish, Mrs. Kendrick."

Samantha mentally cursed her lack of self-control. "I apologize for snapping at you, but I need to get this message to my husband sooner rather than later. It's regarding a family matter."

Girvin came around her desk. "I'll pull one of the older boys out of the classroom right now."

"Thank you."

Samantha started back to her office but then turned back. "Oh, I know Felicity likes to visit with the kitchen staff, but she mustn't dawdle today. Please send her and Donny right up when they arrive."

"Of course, ma'am."

Samantha strode back to her office and closed the door behind her. She tried to catch her breath as emotion battered her from every direction. If her suspicions were true, she'd been criminally stupid in missing it.

Arthur had been her friend when she'd had almost no one else. The idea that he could have so thoroughly betrayed her— betrayed Roger—made her stomach churn.

She forced herself to once more start combing through more minutes and records. As the minutes passed, her conviction— and horror—grew. Now that she knew what to look for, she could spot Arthur's hand behind so much. With the exception of Braden and John Blackmore, Arthur had recommended the appointment of every other board member in the year following Roger's death.

When the casement clock on the mantel sounded the time, Samantha jerked up her head. Almost an hour had passed since she'd handed Girvin the note. Braden should be here by now, as should Donny and Felicity.

She rose and started for the door, then breathed a sigh of

relief when she heard heavy footsteps. Donny and Felicity, no doubt.

"Goodness, you're late," she said as she opened the door. "Where have you—"

Samantha gasped as Donny staggered toward her, blood smeared on one side of his face. Shocked, she quickly braced her hands against his shoulders.

"Donny, what happened? Where's Felicity?"

"That she-devil must have taken her," he rasped out.

"What? Who?"

"Girvin. She coshed me on the head when I wasn't lookin,' and when I came to, Felicity was gone." His face contorted. "I'm sorry, my lady."

Samantha helped him to a chair. Donny thumped down, looking like he was going to faint.

"Where did this happen?" she asked, fighting a rising tide of panic.

"Girvin met us in the front hall. Said ye were in one of the classrooms, and we should go there. Felicity ran ahead and went in. When I followed, Girvin hit me from behind. When I went down, she hit me again and put me out."

Samantha pressed a hand to her roiling stomach. "My God."

Not only had she trusted the bloody woman, she'd delivered Felicity right into her hands.

"How long ago were you out?"

"About twenty minutes, I think." He gazed up at her, his eyes bloodshot and furious. "I canna believe she got the drop on me."

"No, it was my fault." She grabbed her reticule, pulled out a handkerchief, and handed it to him. "Catch your breath. One of Mr. Logan's men is keeping watch from the tavern across the street. I'm going to ask if he saw anything."

She ran out of the room and down to the central staircase. Panic chased her like a demon from hell. Girvin was obviously involved, but why would she take Felicity, and why now? Even in her note, which Girvin had obviously read, Samantha hadn't mentioned Arthur's name. She'd simply said she had new evidence that Braden needed to see.

Braden.

He would never have gotten that note.

As she pelted down the stairs, the front door opened and Braden stepped into the entrance hall. He took off his hat and glanced up at her, starting to smile as he dropped his hat on the side table.

Then his smile instantly vanished as he took in her face. He rushed to meet her, and Samantha threw herself into his arms.

"Love, what's wrong?"

"It's Girvin," she gasped out. "She hit Donny and took Felicity."

"What?" he exclaimed. "Why?"

"She's in on the entire thing, Braden. So she coshed Donny and took Felicity. But I'll explain later." She started to struggle out of his arms. "Right now I've got to find Logan's man and ask him if he saw anything."

"Is Donny badly hurt? Does he need my help?"

"I . . . I don't think so. Braden, we really need to get Logan's man."

"I'll fetch him. Go take care of Donny."

She grabbed him by the sleeves and shook him. "Braden, she *took* Felicity."

"And I promise we'll get her back."

"But—"

His gloved hand cupped her cheek. "Samantha, it's understandable that you're shocked and scared, but you cannot fall apart. Felicity needs you. We all need you, all right?"

As Samantha stared into his grim but calmly set features, she felt her panic ease. "Yes, you go."

He turned and stalked out the door, his greatcoat swirling around his legs like a cloak.

She ran back upstairs, gasping for breath. Terrible visions of Felicity in the hands of those monsters swam through her brain. If anything happened to her—

Stop.

Braden was right. She'd be no good to Felicity if she fell apart. She'd done that after Roger died, and she'd be damned to hell if she did it again.

She hurried into her office. Donny had wiped off the blood, and she saw that he had a cut over his temple and his face was starting to purple. Yanking open one of her desk drawers, she pulled out a bottle of whisky and a glass. She never drank the stuff but kept it on hand if one of the board members, like Arthur . . .

Her mind stuttered on his name, then a cold fury rushed in. They would find Felicity, and then *she* would find Baines. And when she did, she just might bloody well kill him.

She poured out a dram and thrust the glass into Donny's hand. "Here, drink this."

He shot down the whisky with a grimace.

"Donny, are you dizzy or having trouble with your vision?"

"Nae, my head's just ringin' like a bell. The bitch gave me a good whack, excusin' the language."

"I'll be calling her worse before the night is out," Samantha grimly replied. "Did Girvin say anything else before she hit you?"

"Nae. It all happened fast. Felicity had her back to us, so she wouldna have heard anything." He swallowed hard. "That poor lass . . ."

Samantha pressed a hand to his shoulders. "We'll get her back, I promise."

"So, Girvin's in on it. With that Haxton bastard."

"And Arthur Baines, most likely."

Donny stared at her, his mouth gaping. "What? He was the master's good friend. He's been workin' on the foundation since the beginning."

"Which made him perfectly placed to control everything."

"Bloody hell," Donny whispered. "Do ye think he killed the master, too?"

She'd been fighting that dreadful thought, but of course it could be true. "I intend to find out."

When footsteps sounded in the hall, Samantha rushed to the doorway to see Braden and Logan's man striding toward her. Braden put an arm around her waist and swept her into the room.

Then he went to examine Donny, who waved him off. "I'm fine, sir. What did yon fella see?"

Braden nodded to his companion. "Go ahead, Max."

Max, a sturdy young man with blunt features and a sharp, intelligent gaze, doffed his cap. "I'm sorry, Mrs. Kendrick. I didn't know it was yer sister who left with Mrs. Girvin."

Even though the confirmation wasn't a surprise, the room tilted on a sickening slant.

"Steady on, love," Braden murmured, putting his arm around her shoulders.

She nodded. "I'm all right. Max, tell us everything."

"The young miss and Donny, here, arrived by hackney coach." Max glanced at Donny. "The coach didn't leave, so I'm thinkin' ye asked it to wait."

Donny nodded. "We were pickin' up Mrs. Kendrick to take her home."

"Aye, well about ten minutes later, Mrs. Girvin came out with what I thought was one of the schoolgirls. She gave the driver a direction, and then she and the girl got in the carriage and it drove off."

"My sister was dressed like a schoolgirl?" Samantha asked.

"The schoolgirls wear those gray cloaks and bonnets, and

the young lass were wearing those. So I thought she was one of them. Seemed a bit odd that they were takin' the coach, but because Mrs. Girvin goes in and out several times a day, I didn't think anythin' of it."

Samantha rubbed her head. "She made Felicity change, so you wouldn't recognize her."

Max grimaced. "If I'd known, I would've stopped her."

"Samantha, what's going on here?" Braden asked. "Why the hell would Girvin kidnap Felicity?"

"It's because of the note I sent you."

He frowned. "What note?"

"You never got it because Girvin kept it." She frowned. "But then why are you here?"

"I had to see a patient a few blocks over, so I thought I'd drop in to see you before heading back to the clinic. Samantha, what was in that note?"

"That I know who's behind the fraud. Arthur Baines."

Braden's face grew hard as iron. "Tell me everything."

Samantha summarized what she'd discovered and how she'd accidentally tipped off Girvin. "It was incredibly stupid of me, even though I didn't even put any details in the note. Clearly she was already suspicious."

"I'll kill them all, I will," Donny growled.

Samantha touched Braden's arm. "I'm assuming they took her to the Hanging Judge. That's where we should go, right now."

She went to fetch her cloak, but Braden reeled her back in.

"No, we can't rush off," he said.

Her temper flared. "I'm not sitting around while my sister is in danger."

"She'll be in greater danger if we burst in and startle them," he replied. "It seems obvious that Girvin is spooked and figured Felicity would be a good hostage. That being the case, Felicity will be safe for the time being."

Frustrated, Samantha shook her head. "We can't be sure of that."

"I see no other reason to take her."

"Braden, we *need* to get down there."

"I agree, love. But we also need both a plan and some reinforcements."

He took her face between his hands. His gaze, focused and intent, was utterly determined. She knew that he would do whatever it took to rescue Felicity, including putting himself squarely in the line of fire.

"Samantha," he quietly said, "please trust me."

When tears gathered at the corners of her eyes, she blinked them away. She needed him, but he also needed her trust and support to do what must be done.

"I do, my love," she whispered back.

He pressed a quick kiss to her forehead. "That's my brave lady."

"So, what's the plan, then?" Donny asked in a gruff voice.

"Should we go to the coppers, Dr. Kendrick?" Max put in.

"I doubt they'd believe us," Braden replied. "Baines is too well respected by the legal community. Right now, I don't want to waste time trying to convince the police of his guilt."

Samantha's mind was already leaping over that obstacle. "We need Haxton. He's the key to all this. If we can get him to give up Baines, the police would have to believe us. Plus, he'll likely know where Felicity and the children are being held."

Braden's quick smile flashed with approval. "And I would bet a bob that Girvin wouldn't bother to warn him that you've blown their cover. She obviously can't stand the man. I'm guessing that Baines would think Haxton expendable, too, so he'll try to pin the blame on him."

Samantha nodded. "We need to find out where Arthur is. If we can catch him in time—"

"You're right." Braden faced the others. "Max, you head

down to the Hanging Judge and find Stevens. If Girvin went there with Felicity, Stevens will have seen them. Then report back to me at our townhouse. You know where it is?"

"Aye, sir. I'm off." Max hurried out.

"Donny, you take Mrs. Kendrick home," Braden said. "Put some ice on your head and rest while you can. We'll be going back out soon enough."

"What are you going to do?" Samantha asked.

"I'm going to see if Baines is at home."

Samantha grabbed his sleeve. "You can't go there alone."

He pressed her hand. "I'll get Logan first. If Baines is home, we'll send you word. If he's not, we'll meet you back at the house. I'll rustle up Kade and Grandda, too. We're going to need all hands on deck for this one."

"Promise me you'll be careful."

The thought of anything happening to him was too much to bear.

"Och, I'm a Kendrick," he said. "We're all but indestructible, ye ken."

"Well, I'm a Kendrick now, too, and I still want you to be careful."

"We'll *all* be careful."

He grabbed her cloak from its hook and flung it around her shoulders. Then he took her hand and led her out the door, with Donny following close behind.

"This needs to end," Samantha said, more to herself than to him. "Once and for all."

"Aye," Braden grimly replied. "It ends tonight."

CHAPTER 27

Braden kept his arm around Samantha as the carriage rattled around the corner, once more going over everything in his head. They'd spent the last few hours planning for a raid on the Hanging Judge—hopefully with help from the police, if Haxton cooperated.

Baines was already in the wind. Braden and Logan had tried to track him down at both his office and home, only to be informed by the man's butler that his master had gone out of town for several days. Logan had then made a quick foray to Old Town to get a report from his men watching the Hanging Judge before meeting up with Braden and Samantha at their townhouse.

Now, their best hope was getting to Haxton before he could also flee the scene.

Kade, who was sitting next to Logan, rechecked his pistol before slipping it back into his pocket. "Your men were absolutely certain they'd not seen Baines go into the tavern today?"

"No, just Girvin and Felicity," Logan replied.

Girvin had arrived by carriage at the Hanging Judge, shortly after she would have left the orphanage, accompanied by a girl dressed in a gray cloak and bonnet. That news had assuaged Samantha's fear that Girvin would transport Felicity out of the city and beyond their reach.

"That's not to say that Baines might not have slipped in another way," Logan added. "There might be an entry that we don't know about, given that Old Town is a rabbit warren. This bloody fog isn't helping either."

Edinburgh's infamous haar had descended a few hours ago and covered the city in a dense blanket of mist. But at least it might allow them to get closer to the Hanging Judge undetected.

"How many guards do they have stationed outside the tavern?" Samantha asked.

"Stevens counted three. That's why I told Max to stay with him. I didn't want him out there by himself."

"They'll know we're coming for them," Samantha grimly said. "They'll be prepared."

Braden took her gloved hand and held it in his lap. She clutched his tightly, as if it were a lifeline in stormy seas.

"We'll be better prepared," Braden said. "By the way, that was good thinking to send Donny on ahead to back up Stevens and Max. Nothing will get past those three."

"I couldn't stop him," she ruefully replied. "He barely paused to change clothes and arm himself before he was out the door. I hope he's all right."

"Donny will be fine. He showed no signs of a concussion."

Actually Braden wasn't entirely sure about that, but the last thing Samantha needed was another cause for anxiety.

"And speaking of trying to stop someone," he said to Kade. "I'm guessing that Angus wasn't best pleased when you decided he should stay home at Heriot Row."

Kade snorted. "That's putting it mildly. But he's getting too old for this kind of work. It's too dangerous for him."

Logan twisted around to stare at his younger brother. "I hope you didn't tell him that."

"God, no. Otherwise, he would have waited until I left the house and then snuck after me, just to prove he isn't too old."

"How did you manage to convince him to stay put?" Braden asked.

"Donella made it clear that she needed him to help guard the house in case the thugs tried to come after us, too."

"Well done, Donella," Braden said with a smile.

"Having once been kidnapped herself," Logan dryly noted, "my wife has a nose for these sorts of things."

"Donella was kidnapped?" Samantha exclaimed. "How awful."

"We got her back, and everything was fine," Braden said. "Just like we'll get Felicity back, and she'll be fine, too."

"Still, I'm so sorry to bring such danger to your family's doorstep. It's dreadful."

Logan patted her knee. "Samantha, you and Felicity are part of our family, too. Besides, we have a great deal of experience managing dangerous situations. We'll come right again, never fear."

Samantha let out a suspicious little sniffle. "You're all so wonderful. I don't know how I got to be so lucky."

Braden ducked down and kissed her cheek, knocking her hat slightly askew. "I'm the lucky one. I don't know what I would have done if you hadn't come into my life."

She rubbed the tip of her nose, before giving another little endearing sniff. "You would have been taking care of people, as you always do."

"And cutting up gruesome objects and then endlessly relating the details," Logan said, obviously trying to lighten the atmosphere.

"Not to mention giving lectures on disgusting ailments," Kade added. "Really, Samantha, the Kendricks owe you a tremendous debt for taking the old boy off our hands."

"Now if only we could find someone to take Kade off our

hands," Logan quipped. "If I have to listen to Handel's *Messiah* one more time, I might throw myself out a window."

"Philistine," Kade replied. "People empty their pockets to hear me play."

Logan elbowed him. "Especially the ladies, eh? I bet they'd pay *quite* a lot for a private concert."

"Donella's right," Kade replied. "You are a Highland barbarian."

"Why do you think she married me?"

When Samantha huffed out a watery laugh, Braden bit back a smile. His poor wife had been vibrating with anxiety, but his brothers' ridiculous banter had lightened the tension.

When the carriage slowed, Braden glanced out the window.

"We're here." He glanced at Samantha. "Ready, love?"

"I am."

They climbed out in front of an old but impressive-looking mansion. Unlike most of the business class, Haxton still resided in Old Town, near the palace. The house had several potential exits that their prey could use to escape, so they sent their groom around the back, while the coachman was to keep watch out front.

Logan drew out his pistol. "Haxton might have guards."

Braden waggled a hand. "Maybe, but—"

The boom of a gun from inside the house startled them. Recovering, Braden ran up the front steps, Samantha close on his heels.

When a second shot echoed from inside, Braden drew out his pistol. "Samantha, I think you should stay out here until—"

She stopped him by pulling her blade from its sheath, its steel glinting in the light from the streetlamps. "You were saying?"

He snorted. "All right, but stay behind me."

The door, of course, was locked. Logan rattled the knob,

and then ordered them to stand back. He unleashed a mighty kick at the lock with his boot heel and the door flew open.

He moved into a long, narrow corridor, his weapon at the ready. "I can't see a thing, it's so bloody dark."

Right behind him, Braden pointed. "At the end of the hall. There's light coming from under that door."

"Kade, hang back here for a moment," Logan said. "Make sure no one gets out."

"Got it," Kade replied.

Logan stalked down the hall, Braden and Samantha close behind. Just as they reached the door, it opened and a man stumbled out. He took one look at them, then let out a shriek and retreated.

"Don't . . . don't kill me," he begged in a quavering voice.

From his garb, he was obviously the butler.

"I'm Dr. Kendrick, and we're not killing anyone," Braden said.

"Maybe," Samantha muttered.

"Where's Haxton?" Logan barked.

The butler cringed against the doorframe. "In here, in the study. Some . . . someone tried to kill him."

Braden shoved past him.

A scene of carnage met his eyes. Haxton was slumped in an armchair, moaning as he clutched his shoulder. Blood stained his dressing gown and the white shirt underneath. A pistol was on the floor, right in front of him.

Several feet away, in front of the fireplace, lay a man on his back. Where his eye had been there was a hole, and blood and brain matter were spattered on the fireplace surround.

Samantha stalked over and nudged the inert body.

"He's definitely dead," Braden said.

"Clearly." She began rifling through the man's pockets.

"Your lassie has a strong stomach." Logan nodded at the butler, quivering in the doorway. "Unlike that fellow."

"Put him in a chair and stick his head between his knees," Braden said as he went to Haxton.

When he pulled the banker gently upright, the banker moaned and opened his eyes.

"Kendrick, what are you doing here?" he asked in a faint voice.

"Saving your life, apparently." He pushed aside the dressing gown to examine the wound.

Samantha came over to join them.

Braden glanced at her. "Find anything?"

She shook her head. "Haxton, where is my sister?"

The banker let out a yelp as Braden carefully pulled the blood-soaked fabric of his shirt from the wound. While the bleeding was slowing, the man had blanched as white as old bones.

Haxton blearily focused on Samantha. "Felicity? How should I know where she is?"

She crowded over Braden's shoulder. "If you don't tell me where she is, I *will* kill you."

"Love, you need to let me work," Braden said. "He won't be able to tell us anything if he faints from blood loss."

She made an impatient sound but stepped back.

Braden pulled out his kerchief and pressed it against Haxton's shoulder, then eased him forward to get a look at his back. The blood on the sofa confirmed his suspicions.

"The shot went right through. You're lucky, Haxton."

"He was going to kill me," the banker faintly replied.

Samantha whirled an impatient hand. "Again, clearly, but why?"

Logan joined them. "The butler says Haxton's assailant arrived shortly before we did. Haxton seemed frightened but agreed to see the man in his study. Only a few minutes passed before the gunshots were fired." He bent and picked up Haxton's gun. "The old bastard was expecting trouble."

"Have the butler fetch me clean cloths. The wound isn't

that bad, so once I bind it up we can question him." Braden glanced at Samantha. "Can you find some whisky or brandy and pour him a glass?"

She nodded, and turned to search the room.

"Och, this bloody butler is no good," Logan said, casting a disgusted glance at the man, still with his head between his knees. "I'll find some cloths."

Moments after he stalked out, Samantha returned with a glass of whisky.

Braden held it to Haxton's lips. "Drink this."

The man spluttered at first but managed a healthy swallow before subsiding back in his chair.

"Ho, you. Sit up," Samantha called to the butler. "Where is the rest of the staff?"

The man slowly pulled himself upright, took out a kerchief, and mopped his face before answering. "There's no one but me and—"

Logan came back into the room, followed by Kade.

"Kade found a maid hiding in the pantry," Logan said, handing a stack of cloths to Braden. "I told her to stay where she was, for now."

Braden went to work binding up the wound, ignoring Haxton's moans.

"Do you want me to check upstairs?" Kade asked.

"The kitchen maid and I are the only servants," the butler interjected. "The master was to leave tomorrow for the family estate near Dumfries. The other staff have already gone ahead or been given holiday."

Logan glanced around the room. "If this little tableau is any indication, I'd say Haxton knew he had to get the hell out of town."

Braden propped Haxton up on some pillows and then rose to his feet. "I'd say he's ready to talk."

The banker peered up at them, fright lingering in his

watery gaze. "I . . . I don't feel up to talking. I need a doctor. I must go to bed."

"You just saw a doctor," Braden said. "And my medical assessment is that you're perfectly capable of talking."

"But the shock—"

Samantha brought the tip of her blade to inches from Haxton's nose. "Will this help you get over the shock?"

"The lassie's a true Kendrick," Logan said with approval.

Braden pointed to the dead body on the floor. "Haxton, who is this man? Why did he want to kill you?"

"And *where* is my sister?" Samantha asked through clenched teeth.

Haxton lifted a trembling hand to his perspiring forehead. "I know nothing about your sister, Lady Samantha. That is the God's honest truth."

Samantha brought the lethally sharp point to a hair's breadth from his nose.

"I swear it!" Haxton yelped.

She whipped down her blade to rest against her skirt. "Unfortunately, I believe you."

"Then let's return to the man you shot," Braden said. "Who is he?"

Haxton visibly swallowed. "One of MacGowan's men. He was sent to kill me because I no longer wanted to be a part of their schemes."

Braden and Samantha exchanged perplexed glances.

"Who the hell is MacGowan?" Braden asked.

"A gang leader. The one at the Hanging Judge."

"And he kidnapped the children, too?" Samantha asked.

"Yes, he and his sister have been organizing the disappearances."

Logan frowned. "What sister?"

"Mrs. Girvin."

Braden felt his jaw sag at that revelation.

"You're joking," Logan exclaimed.

"I am not."

Samantha pressed a hand to her stomach, looking ill. "Oh, my God. Girvin has been with the foundation since the beginning. How could I not have seen this?"

Braden put his arm around her shoulders before narrowing his gaze on Haxton. "And Baines? Where does he come into this?"

"He's Girvin's lover."

That stunned all of them into silence for several long moments.

Braden mentally shook himself free. "You'd best start at the beginning, Haxton. Who came up with the idea to run a criminal rig out of the foundation?"

Haxton took another swig from his glass, fortifying himself. "Girvin did. Then Arthur formulated the mechanics of the plan with MacGowan."

"How the bloody hell did Baines and Girvin even meet?" Logan asked.

"It was about ten years ago, when Arthur represented her in a criminal case for theft. They became lovers shortly thereafter."

"But Roger vetted her so carefully before he hired her," Samantha exclaimed. "How could he have missed that?"

"She changed her name," Haxton replied. "With Arthur's help, she created a new identity."

Samantha sank into a nearby armchair, as if the stuffing had been knocked from her. "And Arthur recommended her to Roger. *He* vouched for Girvin."

Haxton nodded. "But I didn't know about any of that until after Arthur brought me onto the board."

"Specifically with the intention of helping to defraud the organization," Samantha bitterly said.

"I didn't know that until later, too."

"Then why the hell did you agree to any of this, Haxton?"

Braden exclaimed. "You're a respectable banker from a distinguished family. Surely you didn't need the money."

Haxton shrank into himself, looking even more pitiful. "It wasn't the money."

"Then again, why?"

The man rolled his lips inward, refusing to meet Braden's gaze.

Logan snapped his fingers. "He's got something on you, doesn't he? Baines is blackmailing you."

Haxton's whisper was barely audible. "Yes."

"What is it?" Braden asked.

The banker's gaze darted nervously around the room and landed on his butler.

"Nevins, what are you still doing here?" he snapped, apparently just becoming aware of his presence. "Get out."

The butler started to scurry from the room, but Logan stopped him. "Wait in the kitchen with the maid, in case we have need of you."

"Yes, sir," he said, and he escaped out the door.

"So, what does Baines have on you?" Braden asked again.

"He . . . he represented me in a delicate legal matter, some years back," he replied.

Kade, who'd been standing quietly by the window, scoffed. "Delicate legal matter. That sounds like a euphemism to me."

Haxton glared at him. "It's none of your damned business."

"So Arthur used it against you," Samantha said. "To get your cooperation."

An intense hatred suddenly flashed across the banker's face. "He left me no choice."

"There's always a choice," she said sharply. "You could have come to me."

Haxton's laugh was bitter. "Really? Perhaps you've failed to notice the dead man on the carpet? If they'd caught a whiff of betrayal, they would have killed the both of us."

Samantha came to her feet. "Like they killed Roger?"

Haxton's momentary show of defiance bled away. "Yes."

Her hand curled around the handle of her blade, her eyes glittering with rage. Braden had to resist the urge to sweep her away and shelter her from all the ugliness in the room and in her life. But this was Samantha's quest, and he knew she needed to see it to the end, and in her own way.

"Who actually killed Roger?" she gritted out.

"MacGowan," Haxton replied. "Penwith was beginning to suspect that Arthur was stealing money from the foundation, and . . . and was involved in other things, too."

"Like kidnapping children and working with crime lords?" Braden sardonically asked.

Samantha took a step forward, pinning Haxton with her gaze. "Did Arthur order MacGowan to kill Roger?"

Haxton shrank back against the sofa cushions. "I don't know."

Samantha leaned over him. "Tell me the truth, Haxton."

"Arthur never told me, I swear! It's possible that Mac-Gowan made the decision. The bastard is utterly ruthless."

"As the dead body on the floor would indicate." Braden said. "So, they decide to kill you and . . . what, try to pin the blame on you for most of this?"

Samantha shook her head. "That doesn't make sense, though. Girvin already knows that I know. That's why she kidnapped Felicity."

"They did want to pin the blame on me," Haxton spat out. "I could tell by the way Arthur and Girvin were acting. They didn't trust me anymore. That's why I was leaving town, to get away from them."

"But why would a gang leader need to run his ill-gotten gains through an entity like the Penwith Foundation?" Logan asked. "Why not just employ the usual methods, like using pawnbrokers or moving goods out of the city to sell somewhere else."

"Because MacGowan's ambitious. He wasn't just stealing

pocket watches and bill clips. His gang has been going after ever-larger hauls. Warehouses, jewelry shops . . . he even robbed a factory of its payroll last month. Crime like that produces large amounts of cash or goods, which are not easily moved."

"And is that why he needed so many of my children?" Samantha asked. "For those jobs?"

"Children are small and agile, and quite adept at breaking into buildings once properly trained. Little ones and girls can also serve as lookouts. No one notices the girls."

Samantha again whipped up her blade to an inch from Haxton's right eye. "If any of those children have been harmed, you won't live to see another day. I swear it."

The banker shrank even farther into the cushions, terrified.

Braden placed his hand on Samantha's arm and brought it down. "Haxton won't get away with it, I promise. But there's no point in frightening him. He'll just clam up."

She darted a look at him, her gaze looking almost feverish with fury and bone-deep pain that made his heart ache. He forced himself to be calm, for her sake.

"We need to focus, Samantha," he said. "We have a long night ahead of us and much to do."

She stared at him for a few moments longer, as if barely seeing him. Then she blew out a long, slow breath.

"You're right. Sorry."

"Sweetheart, you have nothing to apologize for." Then he looked at Haxton. "What does a man like Baines get out of this? He'll likely go to the gallows if he's caught."

Haxton winced as he eased his shoulder onto the cushion. Some of his color had come back, now that Samantha was no longer threatening him.

"Arthur made some very bad investments and lost almost everything he had. If anyone found out, he'd lose his reputation and his business, too. He needed the money."

"So he teamed up with his mistress and her crime lord

brother to kidnap children and defraud a charity," Logan said, incredulous with disgust.

"I never would have gone near the damned foundation if I'd known," Haxton bitterly replied.

"That night you were arguing with Girvin at the charity gala," Samantha said. "Was that when you refused to be part of their schemes?"

"Yes. What they wanted to do next was too big, too dangerous."

Logan twirled a hand after the man fell silent. "And?"

"MacGowan and Arthur want to rob a bank," Haxton reluctantly replied.

Braden thought for a moment and then shook his head. "They want to rob *your* bank, don't they?"

Haxton gave a miserable nod.

"So, they rob your bank, run the funds through the Penwith Foundation, and then redeposit them back into your bank," Samantha said.

Haxton nodded. "Yes, into the capital account."

She frowned. "But we don't have a capital account."

"You've had one for three years. You just didn't know it."

"Let me guess," said Logan in a sarcastic voice. "You and Baines were the signing authorities on that account."

Haxton's grimace was his admission.

Braden glanced at Logan. "That capital account must have kept both Baines and MacGowan well-supplied with funds."

Logan nodded. "It's why I couldn't figure out that last piece of the puzzle. I didn't know about the secret capital account."

"Where's Arthur now?" Samantha asked Haxton.

"I'm not sure. Probably with Girvin."

She looked at Braden. "At the Hanging Judge."

He nodded. "No doubt. Haxton, do you know where they keep the children?"

The banker opened his mouth but then closed it. His watery gaze suddenly turned shifty.

"I'm a victim, too, you know," he said. "They blackmailed me and then tried to kill me. I won't utter another word about any of this until I talk to my solicitor."

"Oh, that is *not* going to wash," said Samantha as she took a step forward.

Braden pulled out his pistol. "Allow me."

He leaned down and pressed the tip of the barrel against Haxton's temple. The banker let out a strangled cry as he tried to squirm away.

"Tell me where the children are, or I'll blow your brains out," Braden growled.

"You . . . you'll never get away with it," Haxton said in a trembling voice. "You'll never be able to explain it."

"You could say Haxton couldn't live with the shame and decided to off himself," Logan helpfully supplied.

"Sad turn of affairs," Kade said. "Too bad we couldn't stop him in time. God knows we tried."

"Exactly what I was thinking," Braden said, keeping his gaze steady on Haxton's sweating, horrified face. "And since we're Kendricks, everyone will take us at our word."

"Haxton," Samantha softly said, "if you wish to live, you'd better tell us where the children are."

The banker gave way in a puddle of nerves and sweat. "The underground vaults, below the South Bridge. There's an entrance behind the Hanging Judge. That's where MacGowan has his hideout, and where he's keeping the children."

Samantha muttered a curse. "Of course, the old vaults and tunnels. Donny and I searched a few of them but never found any evidence of the children."

When the bridges connecting New Town to Old Town had been built, some were constructed right over existing houses or shops, creating a bizarre, subterranean complex of tunnels, rooms, and vaults. These days, only the poorest of the poor lived in some of the grim recesses. The rest were abandoned.

They were the perfect boltholes for criminals to hide almost anything, including children.

Logan shook his head. "It's not surprising this gang has been so hard to track down. No one in his right mind would go into those vaults."

Braden looked at him. "We will, though."

"Whoever said we were in our right minds?" Kade dryly put in.

Samantha nodded. "We need to get to those vaults as soon as possible. I doubt Baines and MacGowan will sit around much longer, and God knows what they'll do with the children at that point."

"Yes, but perhaps now is the time to bring in the police," Braden said. "It's a bloody maze down there, and very dangerous."

"You've been in them?" Samantha asked, clearly surprised.

"Some of my most indigent patients have the misfortune of living down there."

"Well, we can't wait any longer," she said. "It would take too long to explain the situation to the police. We need to go *now.*"

Braden grimaced. His gut told him that she was right.

"Very well, this is what I propose. You, Logan, and I will head to the Hanging Judge and meet up with Logan's men. Kade will take Haxton to the police and explain the situation." Braden pinned Haxton with his gaze. "You will help my brother, understand? If you do so, we'll make it clear to the police that you cooperated. If you don't, things will go very, very badly for you. My word as a Kendrick."

Haxton, thoroughly crushed, simply nodded.

"Do we know how many men MacGowan has?" Logan asked the banker.

"I don't know. I've never been to the vaults."

Samantha nodded toward the dead body. "There's one less now."

"True, that," Logan wryly replied. "Well, we've faced bad odds before, and it's never stopped us."

"And they won't be expecting us to find them in the vaults," Samantha pointed out. "They think Haxton is dead."

"Yes, but they'll start to wonder when their man doesn't return," Braden warned.

Samantha slipped her blade back into its sheath. "Another reason why we'd best move now."

Braden reached down and hauled Haxton to his feet, ignoring the fool's protesting yelp.

"Here, I'll take him," Kade said, striding forward. "And I'll get the coppers to the vaults as soon as I can."

"Send a message to Blackmore, too. We'll need his help with the children." Then Braden took Samantha's hand. "Are you ready, love?"

She looked up at him, her fearless gaze shimmering with determination. "Yes, always."

CHAPTER 28

A rat scampered over the toe of Samantha's boot, brushing under her skirt before disappearing. She shivered, more from cold than from the vermin rustling in the dark. After only twenty minutes in the nightmare maze of tunnels and chambers beneath South Bridge, the dank atmosphere had already leached into her bones.

Braden made a disgusted noise. "Splendid, more rats. Are you all right, Samantha?"

She mustered a smile. "I'm fine. What's one more rat, at this point?"

"I had no idea it would be this bad down here," Logan said. "How do people survive it?"

"Sadly, most don't." Braden grimly replied.

They set off again as quickly as they could. Still, their progress was cautious, since the interconnected tunnels and chambers were like the grave, the darkness broken only by the lanterns carried by Logan and his man, Stevens. The stone floors beneath their feet sloped unevenly and were slick with damp and mold. Moisture dripped down the surrounding walls.

The deeper they went, the colder it became. The atmosphere was so fetid and close that Samantha wondered if she would ever get the stench out of her nostrils.

"What do you think, Braden?" Logan quietly asked after they'd traversed yet another vaulted chamber. "Should be getting close now, don't you think?"

"Yes, if we can depend on what that idiot told us."

Leaving Kade to deal with Haxton, Samantha, Braden, and Logan had made their way to the Hanging Judge on foot. Given the dense fog, it was quicker than taking a hackney. They met up with Donny and Logan's men at the rendezvous point, an alley near the tavern. MacGowan still had three men guarding the place, but Donny had already pinpointed their locations. He and Stevens had then disappeared into the fog, returning a few minutes later with the news that the guards were no longer a threat. Samantha hadn't been sure if it meant they were incapacitated or dead, and thought it best not to ask.

Logan, meanwhile, had gone around to the back of the tavern. According to Donny, there was only one man standing watch at the hidden entrance to the vaults. They needed that man alive and conscious, so he could tell them where to find MacGowan's lair.

The guard had proved no challenge to Logan, though he'd been reluctant to reveal his leader's location. That momentary reticence ended when Logan lifted him off his feet and slammed him into the brick wall behind him, before shaking him like a rag doll.

"You'd best tell us where to locate your boss," Braden had then said in a casual tone. "Or my brother will happily throttle you."

Obviously convinced, the man gave up the location of the lair and how to get there. Logan had then delivered a punishing blow to the lout's face, knocking him out.

After a short debate on whether they should wait for backup in the form of Kade and the police, they'd decided not to lose any more time. Felicity and the children were at too great a risk, since Girvin would have alerted her brother that their cover was blown.

Leaving Max behind to guide Kade and the police to MacGowan's lair, they'd quickly descended several narrow, stony staircases into the tangle of tunnels and chambers under South Bridge.

Now, if their directions were accurate, they should be getting close.

Samantha peered forward and then blinked to adjust her vision. "There's a light up ahead."

Logan and Stevens instantly closed the shutters on their lanterns. Sure enough, a faint light glimmered around the next bend in the tunnel. They waited as the crushing silence settled around them.

"I think I hear voices," Braden finally murmured.

"I can't hear anything," she whispered back. "Are you sure?"

By now, her eyes had adjusted to the dark, and she could see him nod.

"Yes, but we need to get closer."

He took her hand and led her forward, while the others fell in silent step behind them. For such big men, they moved like the ghosts that supposedly haunted the vaults beneath the bridge.

As they came to the curve in the tunnel, Braden held up a hand to bring them to a halt.

"I definitely hear voices," he whispered. "Three, possibly four. They're arguing."

Samantha again strained to hear, but heard nothing but low, indistinct sounds. "Are you sure?"

Logan leaned in close. "Braden has ears like a bat. He was always able to overhear whatever insane plot the rest of us were cooking up, without even trying."

"Unfortunately," Braden absently replied, as he cocked his head, listening.

"That squares with what that whiny little bastard told us before Mr. Logan knocked him out," Donny muttered. "Baines, MacGowan, Girvin, and two or three men to stand guard over the bairns."

The thug—if he was to be believed—hadn't been sure about who else might be with MacGowan. Samantha prayed that the numbers would be on their side, since they could hardly charge in, pistols blazing, until they knew exactly where the children were located.

Braden inched forward and took a quick glance around the bend.

"Can you see anything?" Samantha whispered.

"More tunnel up ahead, with what looks like a big chamber off it. One well lit."

"They'd need a larger room to hold the children and store all their goods," Logan said.

Braden glanced up. The tunnel had widened in the last few hundred feet or so. It now arched over their heads in a high stone vault, the top of which disappeared into inky blackness.

"We're about a third of the way under South Bridge, where the large chambers are," he said. "So that squares, too."

Logan set down his lantern. "Final check of your weapons, lads and lady."

They were, in fact, bristling with weaponry. Logan had insisted they be well prepared, with knives in boots, a cudgel for Stevens, and pistols for all of them. Samantha intended to rely mostly on her blade. In her hands, it was both lethal and accurate, and much less risky for bystanders.

Braden put an arm around her shoulder and pulled her in.

"Ready?" he whispered.

"Absolutely."

"Just get a fast look, and then pull back as quick as you can."

She craned up to give him a quick kiss on the cheek. "Don't worry. I know what I'm doing."

"I trust you, sweet lass."

Since they had no idea what they might be facing, they needed to know the layout of the chamber, the numbers of men, and where, exactly, the children were stowed. It was the only way to proceed with any confidence that the bairns wouldn't be harmed or grabbed as hostages during a fight. Samantha had argued that it made sense for her to conduct the initial reconnaissance. If, by chance, she could catch Felicity's eye, she could sign for her to try to keep the children out of the way. Samantha was also quicker and smaller, and thus less likely to be spotted than one of the men.

Braden had struggled with the idea, knowing how dangerous it was for her, but he'd finally agreed. And that simple act of trust meant more to Samantha than he would ever know.

They ghosted forward around the curve in the tunnel. The chamber was about thirty feet ahead, light streaming out from its wide entrance. Once she stepped out from the shelter of the tunnel wall, she'd be fully visible if anyone glanced her way. All Samantha could do at this point was hope that luck was on her side.

She and Braden advanced to the edge of the opening.

And her husband had been correct—people inside *were* arguing, vociferously. From this vantage point, she couldn't see them but could make out a portion of the interior chamber. Crates were shoved up against the rough walls and a few dozen barrels of what appeared to be whisky were stacked on top of each other.

"No one on the right side," she whispered over her shoulder.

The voices were coming from near the entrance to the chamber. One was Arthur's.

"And what the hell are we supposed to do now?" he angrily exclaimed. "This whole night has been a spectacular cock-up."

Samantha closed her eyes and sucked in a calming breath.

Roger's best friend had betrayed him, a fact she still could hardly believe. But hearing his voice made it all too real. It harrowed her with sorrow but also made her want to carve him into bits.

When Braden gently squeezed her shoulder in silent support, she forced herself to focus completely on the voices instead of her fury.

"What the hell did ye expect Becky to do?" came another male voice. "The Penwith bitch obviously figured it out. And that's because ye and that moron Haxton didn't cover yer bleedin' tracks."

Samantha felt Braden tense behind her. He recognized that voice, as did she. It was one of the men who'd confronted them that night in the slums, when they'd first tried to get to the Hanging Judge.

MacGowan.

"I didn't expect her to kidnap Felicity," Arthur snapped back. "Rebecca, what the hell were you thinking? Why do such a criminally stupid thing?"

"Dinna ye be blastin' my sister like that, ye bloody ponce. I'll slit yer feckin' throat."

"Oh, I'm shaking in my boots," Arthur replied. "Whatever you think, the fact remains that Rebecca's foolish actions have put us all in mortal danger. Abducting the girl will bring the entire Kendrick clan down on our heads."

"I was trying to protect you and my brother," Girvin said in freezing tones. "It was obvious that Mrs. Kendrick had the scent."

"So you kidnapped her bloody sister?" Arthur snapped. "Just brilliant. Why didn't you bring the entire Edinburgh Constabulary after us while you were at it?"

"It was yer bloody job to keep the law off our backs," MacGowan butted in. "Yer doin' a piss-poor job of it."

"As usual, you don't know a damn thing," Arthur replied.

"Just stop this," Girvin said. "Right now, we need a plan to get out of Edinburgh. We have Felicity for leverage, and the Kendricks don't yet know where we are. Time is still on our side."

"Do you really think we're safe down here?" Arthur said. "Why hasn't the man you sent to kill Haxton returned? They're onto us, I tell you."

Arthur's pertinent observation led to a few moments of silence.

"Boss," said a new voice. "Do ye want me to go to Haxton's and find out what happened to Billy?"

Braden and Samantha flattened themselves against the tunnel wall. If MacGowan sent someone out—

"Don't be a fool," Arthur exclaimed. "If Billy didn't come back, he failed to kill Haxton. Sending someone else then will make matters worse."

"Oy, don't be tellin' me what I can do, ye bloody bastard," MacGowan barked.

That set off a vigorous round of yelling, with Girvin, from the sounds of it, trying to intervene.

"Now's your chance, love," Braden whispered.

Samantha inched forward and popped her head around the corner.

She caught a glimpse of a high, wide chamber with corners shrouded in darkness, but the center lit with multiple oil lamps. A few coal braziers, obviously intended more for heat than light, imparted a smoky haze over the room. More crates and barrels were haphazardly stacked around the chamber, and a number of cots were shoved against the wall.

Huddled on those cots were Felicity and four of the orphanage children. Their gazes were tense as they listened to the arguing adults who were clustered around a table in the center of the room.

Swallowing a gasp of relief, Samantha pulled back and leaned for a moment against Braden.

His arm circled her waist, and his mouth was close to her ear. "Did you see her?"

She nodded, taking a moment for her heartbeat to steady. The children were safe. But she needed a better look, and she had to get Felicity's attention.

She patted Braden's hand before removing it from her waist. Then she peeked out again, focusing her attention on the kidnappers.

Girvin stood with her back to the doorway, between Arthur and MacGowan, who were at opposite ends of a large table. A hulking brute stood behind MacGowan, glaring daggers at Arthur. Another man lingered closer to the children. Like everyone else, his attention was fixed on the argument.

"We need to cut our losses," Baines said. "If we stay here much longer, they'll find us."

"We'll have plenty of warning from up top," MacGowan said. "Besides, like Becky said, we got the girl for protection. No one'll try anything as long as we have her."

"The Kendricks won't wait," Arthur warned. "And they won't hesitate to kill the lot of us, I assure you."

MacGowan sneered. "Yer a coward, Baines. I could never ken what my sister saw in ye."

Since that precipitated yet more yelling, Samantha took a chance. When she reached back and tapped Braden on the thigh, she heard him quietly cock his pistol. Then, sending up a silent prayer, she stepped out fully into the light.

Felicity caught the movement, her gaze darting over to Samantha. She jerked with surprise and leaned forward, as if to leap off the cot.

Samantha rapidly signed. *Wait.*

Felicity subsided, her eyes wide and fixed on her. Samantha flattened her hands, moving down, up, and then out to the side. Then she pointed to the floor.

Children. Stay down.

Felicity nodded and started to sign back, but Samantha felt

Braden's arm go around her waist, yanking her back from the entrance.

"Where are the children?" he whispered.

"Against the back wall. Felicity will keep them down as best she can."

They retreated several feet as Logan and the others came forward into a huddle.

"The children are against the back wall," Samantha whispered. "The adults are clustered in the center of the room around a table, Arthur at one end and MacGowan at the other. He's got a man behind him, but they're all distracted."

In fact, the shouting was getting louder, and Girvin had now joined in.

"Let's crack on," Logan said.

"Donny, there's a guard on the children," Samantha whispered.

"I'm in first and to MacGowan," Logan murmured. "Then Donny." He glanced at his brother. "No Marquess of Queensbury rules this time, lad."

Braden rolled his eyes. Then he looked at Samantha. "Ready, my brave heart?"

She nodded. "I'll take Girvin. You and Stevens go for Arthur and MacGowan's other man."

If they moved quickly enough, it should be over in moments. If not . . .

Logan, now poised at the edge of the chamber, held up a hand. He counted three, two, one, and then charged into the room, Donny right on his heels.

"Hands up," Logan barked, pistol extended as he went straight for MacGowan.

The gang leader whirled, reaching into his greatcoat, but Logan was too quick and slammed into MacGowan, taking him down.

Donny rushed for the guard near the children. But from his left darted another man, one Samantha hadn't seen. He barreled straight into Donny, who staggered but quickly recovered and wheeled about to deliver a punishing blow to his attacker's face. Incredibly, the man shook it off and lunged in, throwing desperate punches at Donny. The children shrieked and cowered behind Felicity, who had dragged them down to the floor.

By now, the man guarding the children had fumbled in his coat pocket and pulled out a gun. He cocked it and aimed at Donny, trying to find a clear shot in the midst of the fight.

Samantha jerked forward. "Donny, watch—"

A boom echoed through the chamber, and the guard dropped to the floor, shot squarely in the chest. Braden tossed his smoking pistol aside and charged toward Arthur, who was still motionless at the table, his face contorted in shock.

Suddenly, Arthur came to life. He shoved Girvin out of his way, sending her flying into Stevens, who was fighting Mac-Gowan's other man. The three went down to the floor in a tangle of arms and legs.

The chamber had now descended into a melee, punctuated by the screaming of the children.

Samantha couldn't get to them, but she *could* get to Arthur.

She darted sideways, just as Arthur rounded the table and flung himself toward the chamber entrance in a desperate attempt to escape. She slashed him across the face. With a cry of pain, he stumbled backwards until he fell against the table.

Samantha brought the tip of her bloody blade near his throat.

"Don't move," she snarled, "or I'll run you through."

He sagged against the table, holding a trembling hand to his bloodied cheek. "S . . . Samantha, I can explain. None of this was my idea. They forced me to do it."

"Save your lies, Arthur. You betrayed Roger. You were his best friend, and you *killed* him."

"Never! It was MacGowan and Girvin who killed Roger,"

he babbled. "They were blackmailing me. I . . . I was going to tell you."

When she pressed the tip of her blade right against his throat, drawing a trickle of blood, Arthur whimpered and fell silent.

"Stop talking," she gritted out. "Haxton told us everything."

Her mind was black with rage, darker than midnight. Inside, she shook with the effort to hold back the urge to push her blade right through his throat.

Braden's firm voice cut through the roar in her head. "Samantha, stop. We have a problem."

At the sound of his voice, her fury receded a bit. Her husband was now standing right next to her, his features grim and tense. Then she noticed that, except for the muffled sobbing of the children, the room had fallen eerily silent. MacGowan was out cold on the floor, and Donny and Stevens held the other gang members at gunpoint. As for Girvin—

Samantha let out a strangled cry. "Felicity!"

Girvin had managed to get out of the fight and make it across the room to the children. She now stood behind Felicity, one hand dug securely into her hair, the other holding a knife to the girl's throat.

Panic rose in a choking tide, robbing Samantha of breath.

Braden took her arm. "Steady on, lass. She won't hurt Felicity."

"Oh, won't I? I'll kill her without a second thought if you get in my way," Girvin snapped.

When she tugged on Felicity's hair, the girl whimpered, her wide gaze fastened desperately on Samantha.

Logan took a few steps forward, his empty hands facing up. "You'll never get away with it, Girvin. Best give it up now."

She scoffed. "And end up on the gallows with this lot? No bloody way."

"It's your brother who's responsible for most of this,"

Logan replied. "And Baines. If you just let Felicity go, we can help you."

"As if you would help the likes of me," she answered with contempt. "Now, step back and get out of my way."

"What are you going to do with Felicity?" Samantha asked, trying to keep her voice steady.

Girvin's attention flickered to her. "I'm not going to keep her, if that's what you're asking. Even though you're a fool, you've always treated me with respect. So, once I'm clear and safe, I'll leave the girl behind. I won't hurt her unless you make me."

"And I'm just supposed to believe that?" Samantha asked, her heart thudding. "After everything you've done?"

"Seems like you don't have a choice." She shoved Felicity forward a step, keeping the knife at her throat.

Samantha knew they couldn't let Girvin escape. The woman was desperate and capable of anything, including murder.

"Girvin, if you don't let my sister go," she said, "I'll kill Arthur. I swear it. I'll run him through right now."

Arthur moaned, but Girvin simply laughed, a chilling sound that bounced around stone floors and walls.

"Do you think I care? He wouldn't even marry me, after all the years I gave him. He used me, and now he wants to pin all this on me and my brother." Girvin's lovely features suddenly contorted with fury. "Kill the bastard and be done with it, I say. Makes no matter to me."

Despair filled Samantha as Arthur moaned again and slumped down on the table. She'd played her last card.

Braden squeezed her arm, then went to stand beside Logan.

"If you hurt Felicity, you'll never escape us," Braden calmly said. "No matter how far you run, we'll find you. Samantha will never stop looking for you, and neither will the

Kendricks. You should give up while you still have the chance for some mercy."

Girvin seemed to waver for a moment before her features went cold and hard as flint. "I'll take my chances. Now get out of my—"

Suddenly, rapid footsteps could be heard out in the tunnel.

"That'll be the police," Braden said. "There's no escaping, Girvin."

"No," she barked. "Make them—"

She let out a startled cry, dropping her hand from Felicity's throat as she stumbled. Instantly, Logan was on her, knocking the knife from her hand and pushing her down to the floor.

As Kade and several constables appeared in the doorway, Samantha dashed across the room. Felicity threw herself into her arms, burrowing against her chest. Relief almost took Samantha out at the knees as she held the girl in a fierce embrace.

"What . . . what just happened?" Samantha asked Logan.

Logan, down on one knee and pinning Girvin's arms behind her back, smiled.

"Look at her leg."

Blood was flowing from a nasty cut on Girvin's calf. Standing a few feet away was one of the orphanage boys, holding a sharp and bloodied piece of glass.

"Got yourself a nice little weapon there, eh?" Logan said. "Well done, laddie."

"I picked it up when one of them bastards knocked over a lantern," the little boy said. "I couldn't let that mean lady hurt anyone else."

Samantha let out a watery chuckle as she hugged Felicity. "Very well done, indeed. Logan, this is one of my boys, Jimmy McGrath."

Braden came to join them. "Jimmy is the hero of the day, now isn't he?"

"Had to do something, sir." His small face scrunched up in a fierce scowl. "Scabby goats were hurtin' everyone."

Felicity slipped out of Samantha's embrace and went down on her knees to hug the boy. Another child snuggled against her, while the remaining two ran to Samantha and wrapped their arms around her legs, sniffling away the last bit of their tears.

She bent over the little ones. "There, now, darlings. You're safe. We'll take you home very soon."

Braden rubbed her back. "Are you all right, my love?"

She glanced up. "Yes, although I feel rather upside down and in a muddle. It's a bit hard to absorb what just happened."

"Shock will do that to you. It takes some time for one's brain to catch up with events."

Samantha almost laughed. His brief analysis was so wonderfully Braden-like.

Kade strode up to them. "Sorry to be so late. Haxton went squirrely again at the station. Took some persuading to get him to open up again."

"Well, better late than never." Logan hauled Girvin to her feet, and she cursed him in protest.

"I'd better look at her leg," Braden said. "You don't want to have to carry her all the way through the tunnels."

"Och, it's not so bad. I'll give her my handkerchief to bind it up." Logan nodded toward Felicity and the children. "You and Samantha should get the bairns to the orphanage. Kade and I will help the police clean up this lot, then we'll meet you back at your house."

Four constables and a sergeant were now busy handcuffing MacGowan, his men, and Arthur.

"John will be waiting for you at the orphanage," Kade added. "He and Bathsheba will look after the children tonight, so you can take Felicity home and get some rest."

Samantha smiled at him. "Thank you for arranging that. John and Bathsheba will know just what to do."

Felicity stood and came back to her, slipping her arm through Samantha's and cuddling close. She smiled at Braden and Kade, tapped her lips, and mouthed *thank you.*

"Och, you're welcome, lass," Braden replied.

Then he pulled both Samantha and Felicity in for a long hug, cradling them in the shelter of his strong arms. The last dregs of Samantha's fear slipped away, replaced by a sense of relief and gratitude almost too big to contain.

"It's finally over," she murmured, rubbing her cheek against the soft wool of his coat.

Braden dropped a kiss on the top of her head. Somewhere in the commotion, she'd managed to lose her hat.

"Yes," he replied. "Felicity's safe. We're *all* safe. And I've got you, my bonny lass, and I'm never letting you go."

As Samantha closed the door to Felicity's bedroom, she heard quiet voices drift up from the front of the house. It seemed Logan was finally going home.

Braden extended a hand as she came down the stairs to join them. "Here's my brave, beautiful wife. How are you, love?"

She swallowed a yawn. "Feeling neither brave nor beautiful at the moment, although I thank you for the compliment."

"Lassie, you're a true heroine," said Logan as he pulled on his gloves. "The rest of us could barely keep up with you."

"I think you mean to say that I tend to be a trifle impetuous," she ruefully replied.

"That's more or less a requirement in our family."

"With at least one exception, I hope," said Braden.

Logan scoffed. "Oh, yes, you're a veritable sobersides. As

evidenced by the way you plugged that thug right in the chest. Excellent shot, by the way."

"It certainly was," Samantha said, patting her husband's waistcoat. "I wouldn't have had the nerve to take it, given the chaos."

Braden shrugged. "I would have preferred to avoid violence, but it was the only way to save Donny."

"I'm sorry you were forced to make such a decision," she replied with a sympathetic grimace. "I, on the other hand, seem to have a regrettably bloodthirsty nature. If not for you, I probably *would* have killed Arthur."

When Braden and Logan exchanged a swift glance, Samantha's heart sank. While she'd spent the last few hours with Felicity, talking to her about her ordeal and getting her settled, Braden and Logan had been dealing with the aftermath of the evening's events. Clearly, they'd learned a few things from the police, likely including the precise circumstances of Roger's death.

"Well, I'm off," Logan said. "Donella will hunt me down if I don't get myself home."

Samantha glanced at the longcase clock. "Goodness, yes. It's ridiculously late. I apologize for keeping you waiting, Logan."

"No worries, lass. How is Felicity, by the way? Sleeping, I hope?"

"Yes. Mrs. Johnson is going to stay with her tonight. Felicity is remarkably brave, I must say. Even when that villainous woman held that knife to her throat, she was more infuriated than frightened."

"She has a good role model," Braden said with a smile.

Logan clapped on his hat and opened his arms. "Give us a hug, Samantha, and then get this brother of mine off to bed. You both need a good night's sleep."

With a smile, she gratefully entered her brother-in-law's

embrace. He hugged her tight and dropped a kiss on the top of her head before letting her go.

"Thank you, Logan," she quietly said. "I don't know how I can ever repay you—all of you. The Kendricks truly saved the day."

"Nonsense. You've repaid us a hundred times over by marrying my scapegrace little brother."

Braden snorted. "Scapegrace? I believe you're referring to yourself."

"True, that," Logan replied. "But you've made our lad happy, Samantha, and that's worth its weight in gold. We're so grateful that you and Felicity are now part of our slightly deranged family."

She was forced to rub her nose. "You'd best leave before I burst into tears. I don't want you to think I'm a sentimental watering pot."

"No chance of that, now that I've seen how you handle your blade."

Then, with a wave, Logan was out the door and into the cold night.

Braden shut the door and leaned against it, studying her. "I'm thinking you're not quite ready for bed."

"Do you mind? I want to hear what you found out from the police, about . . ."

"About Roger's death," he quietly finished.

She nodded.

He took her hand and led her upstairs to the drawing room. There was a cheerful blaze burning in the hearth, and a decanter and several glasses were set on the low table between the armchairs.

"How about a brandy?" he asked as she sank into one of the chairs.

"I'd love one—to chase away the last bit of the chill."

He cast her a concerned glance. "Are you still cold?"

"Just a bit of lingering shock, I suppose." She shook her head. "I hope we never have to go through anything like that again."

He poured her a brandy and handed her the glass before sitting opposite her. "Well, MacGowan and his gang are thoroughly rolled up, and Haxton, Girvin, and Baines are all safely behind bars. They'll pay for what they've done, all of it."

She took a sip, hoping the beverage would fortify her nerves. "Braden, two of the older boys weren't with the others tonight, and neither was Betsy McNair, the girl who disappeared from my school. Do you know what happened to them?"

"Yes." He propped his booted feet against one of the firedogs. "The oldest of the two boys, Timmy, was a willing accomplice."

"He was the first to disappear from the orphanage. So, that means he did run away."

"Apparently. Girvin said he was holed up at the Hanging Judge with a few other pickpockets. Betsy was there, too. She was abducted primarily to take care of the little ones, but usually slept at the tavern. Several constables were already making a final sweep of the tavern when Logan and I left the jail to come home, so Betsy should be safe by now."

She breathed out a sigh of relief. "Thank God. And what about the other boy? Johnny Campbell."

"Ah, it seems that lad ran away from the gang the first chance he got. Girvin had no idea where he went."

Samantha grimaced. "I wish he'd come to me. I would have helped him."

"Too scared, I imagine. But Logan's men will look for the lad, and we'll work our contacts, too."

They fell silent for a minute or so, absorbing the welcome heat pouring out from the hearth.

"Do you want to hear about Baines?" Braden finally asked.

"I've been trying to work up the courage to ask."

He put down his glass and reached out a hand. "Come here, sweet lass."

She stood and went to him, and he gently pulled her down onto his lap. Samantha settled against his broad chest, resting her head on his shoulder. Almost instantly, her nervous energy began to drift away, replaced by a sense of . . . coming home.

"All right," she said. "Go ahead."

He held her close, a steady shelter in the storm.

"Although it was MacGowan who pulled the trigger, Baines was ultimately responsible."

She'd instinctively known that would be the case. Still, that didn't make the final cut of betrayal any less painful. "Because Roger figured it out."

"Yes."

"Did he finally admit to it?"

"No, Girvin told us. She's hoping that if she provides enough useful information, she'll be transported instead of going to the gallows. Apparently, she was quite forthcoming."

"That's fortunate, I suppose. What else did she say?"

"Roger discovered that Baines was the mastermind behind the plan to defraud the foundation. He confronted Baines and demanded that he return the money."

"What about the abductions? Did Roger know about that, as well?"

"It sounded like he hadn't figured that out, yet. It was early days."

Her heart hurt when she thought of how alone Roger must have felt, carrying the heavy burden of such a betrayal.

"How did Arthur respond when Roger told him to return the money?"

"Baines told him that he was too far in debt, but that if

Roger would keep his secret he would eventually repay all the funds. He needed time, though, and he needed Roger to maintain the fiction that he was still an upstanding member of the legal community. For appearances sake, Baines also wanted to remain on the board."

Samantha shook her head. "Roger would have none of that."

"No. He gave Baines three weeks to return the money and demanded his resignation from the board. From what Girvin said, Baines made a pretense of agreeing but then went straight to MacGowan. Events . . . proceeded quickly after that."

Pain twisted through her as the memories of that heart-wrenching day surfaced in her tired mind.

"His murder," she whispered.

Braden hugged her close. "I'm so sorry, Samantha."

"I wish Roger had told me. I could have helped."

"I'm sure he was trying to protect you."

"But I don't need protecting!"

"I know," he quietly replied.

Samantha closed her eyes, resting against him. Braden simply held her, letting her work through the terrible implications of it all—the loss of her first love, the pain over lives destroyed.

Yet she'd been grieving for so long. It was now time for the past to be the past, joys and sorrows both. Roger would always be a part of her, but now that she had the answers she'd sought, she could finally allow him to rest in peace.

"Logan was right, you know," Braden finally said.

She shifted on his lap so she could see his face. "About what?"

He brushed an errant curl away from her forehead. "That you're a true heroine. None of this would have happened without you, Samantha. You found the children, and you found justice for Roger. And that justice *will* be served, thanks to you."

His praise brought a prickle of tears to her eyes. Apparently, she *was* turning into a watering pot.

"I did have a wee bit of help," she said, trying to lighten the mood. "You Kendricks proved occasionally useful."

He grinned. "Yes, the family does have its good points, when we're not making a ruckus."

"I like a good ruckus, now and again."

Braden settled her back in his arms. "I'm hoping our days of ruckusing are over."

She chuckled. "Is that even a word?"

"If not, it should be. But what's important is that a great injustice has been rectified. You have prevailed, my love. You can put down your sword now and rest."

She sighed. "I can hardly believe it."

"Because you've been living it for a very long time. But it *is* truly over, and do you know what that means?"

Samantha sat up again so she could see his handsome, wonderful face. His extraordinary gaze was filled with love—a miraculous love for her.

"It means we get to begin again," he said. "It means we get to have a life, a good life with Felicity, our family, our work. It means that we finally have a future together."

She craned up to press a tender kiss on his lips. His arms tightened around her, and he lingered over the caress.

When Braden finally let her go, she gave him a misty smile. "Aye, that, as the Kendricks would say."

"Well, this Kendrick would also say that it's time for us to be off to bed. If we sit here much longer, we'll be seeing in the dawn."

She snuggled back against him. "Soon. I just want to sit here for a few minutes and let the future sink in a bit."

"All right, but if you fall asleep, I'll have to carry you up to bed."

"Oh, dear. Would that be a terrible imposition?"

He chuckled, the warmth of it vibrating through her. "Not in the least."

Samantha settled into the security of his embrace, letting his strong and yet gentle love surround her. Sorrow had finally been replaced by joy. It was a quiet joy, to be sure, almost too new to feel real. But there it was, along with the promise of a future warm and bright.

Epilogue

Christmas Eve, 1827

Braden leaned against the door of their bedroom, pausing to take in the peaceful scene. The gratitude that filled his heart was mingled with a joy so profound it defied words.

Samantha was propped up in bed on a mound of pillows, dressed in a warm flannel wrapper and with her hair pulled back in a soft braid. Snuggled against her side on top of the coverlet, Felicity was fast asleep, worn out from the excitement of the day.

Cradled in Samantha's arms was John Kade, the newest addition to Clan Kendrick.

His wife glanced over, a smile lighting up her face when she saw him. "How long have you been standing there?"

"Just a few moments." He walked over to join her. "You were absorbed in studying that handsome little fellow. I trust all is still in order?"

She gently patted the swaddled babe in her arms, now fast asleep. "I checked only a few minutes ago, and he's still perfect."

Braden caressed his son's wee head, covered in silky black hair. Then he leaned down and brushed a kiss across Samantha's lips. Her hand fluttered up to his cheek, resting there as she sweetly kissed him back.

"You need a shave," she said. "You're as bristly as a hedgehog."

He rubbed his chin. "Not quite, but it's been a busy day, ye ken. No time for shaving."

After a few false starts over the last two weeks, Samantha's contractions had begun in earnest last night. Because she'd had a relatively trouble-free pregnancy, Braden had been mostly confident she'd have a healthy delivery. Still, he was unwilling to take the slightest risk, especially given her medical history, so he'd immediately sent a note around to John. His friend had assisted hundreds of mothers in giving birth and could be relied upon to skillfully manage any complications. Thankfully, none had occurred, and Samantha had carried it off with her usual grit.

She'd even apologized to Braden for squeezing his hand so hard during a particularly intense contraction.

"Sorry," she'd gasped as he'd blotted her damp forehead with a cloth. "But you're the one who got me into this situation in the first place."

John had glanced up from his position at the foot of the bed. "Feel free to give your husband a good wallop if the pain becomes too much. I find that often helps during labor."

"No wonder the husbands stay out of the room, if that's the sort of advice you give their wives," Braden had joked.

"Do many husbands actually stay in the room when their wives give birth?" Samantha had asked once she caught her breath.

"No, they're squeamish," John had replied. "Most would faint dead away from fright."

"Not my husband," she'd said with more than a hint of pride. "Nothing frightens him."

"I wouldn't do my patients much good if I fainted at the first sight of blood," Braden had said. "Terrible precedent to set."

Her laugh had turned into more of a strangled yelp when another contraction started to roll over her. Braden held her hand through the worst of it, and only a few minutes later their son entered the world by setting up his own vigorous cry.

When Braden had held the babe in his arms, it had been the most astounding moment of his life. He'd felt transfused with love for the little creature in his arms and even more so for his incredible wife. All the troubles and anxieties that had led up to this—including his secret fears for Samantha's health—had disappeared like wisps of fog on the wind. Only love remained, and the abiding sense that he'd been blessed far beyond what he deserved.

Samantha patted the coverlet. "You must be exhausted. Why don't you take off your boots and get on the bed with me. I don't think you'll wake the baby, or Felicity for that matter. Poor dear is worn out."

He glanced at Felicity. "She doesn't look very comfortable, though. She'll end up with a crick in her neck in that position."

"I suppose you're right. And it is late. She should really be asleep in her own bed by now."

Braden went around to the other side of the bed and gently shook Felicity's arm. She opened her eyes and sat up, yawning.

Time for bed, he signed.

She gave him a nod, and then leaned over to softly kiss the top of the baby's head before giving Samantha a hug.

"Good night, sweetheart," Samantha said.

Felicity rolled off the bed, looking rather rumpled.

Good night she signed to Braden with a sleepy smile.

He gave her a quick hug before she left the room, closing the door behind her. Then Braden removed his boots and carefully joined his wife. He wrapped an arm around her shoulders, cuddling her, and she subsided against him with a happy sigh.

"And how are you truly feeling, sweet lass?"

"Sleepy and rather sore, but quite grand for all that."

"All to be expected. You'll feel quite a bit better after a good night's sleep."

She rested a gentle hand on their son's tiny chest. "If this little fellow cooperates."

"I'll stay up with him. When he needs to feed, I'll wake you, but I want you to get some rest."

The nursemaid they'd hired would start tomorrow. For tonight, Braden was happy to take her place.

Samantha craned a bit to look at him. "Dr. Kendrick, you also need your rest. You've been up as long as I have."

"But you did all the work. I just hung about, making a fuss over you."

"I like it when you fuss over me. And you made the entire experience infinitely more bearable."

"Does that experience include putting up with my deranged family?"

She started to laugh but choked it off. "Don't make me laugh, you brute. It hurts."

"Sorry about that. But I'm also sorry you had to put up with my family all day. They were so ridiculously excited, though, that I didn't have the heart to kick them out to the street."

"It was lovely that they could be here," she said. "And it's not as if you let them swarm in all at once. Nor did you allow anyone to stay very long. I swear you were timing their visits."

"I was timing them," he admitted.

She pressed a hand to her lips, trying not to laugh.

"Well, there were quite a lot of them popping in and out," he explained. "I didn't want them to wear you out. Besides, it's not good for the baby to be around so many people, so soon after the birth."

It had been quite the Kendrick mob scene. Nick, Victoria, and their children had arrived from Glasgow last week, and Graeme and Sabrina had come for a visit from their estate up north. They'd all piled into Heriot Row, leaving Logan and Donella with a full house.

Samantha scoffed. "You barely let them look at the poor little thing. I thought Angus was going to cry when you took the baby away from him."

"The old fellow would carry wee Johnny off if we let him. You know how he loves babies. Anyway, Logan managed to console Grandda with several tots of whisky. In fact, they practically had to roll him out to the carriage when they departed. He was exceedingly full of good cheer by that point."

She patted his arm. "There's quite a lot to cheer about, after all. So I take it that everyone has now gone home?"

"They left about an hour ago. And I gave them strict orders not to come back until tomorrow afternoon. You do need your rest."

"I know, but tomorrow is Christmas. And we have a Christmas baby. Braden it is *too* terribly exciting, isn't it?"

He rested his cheek on top of her head. "It's a bloody miracle. I never thought I could be this happy."

She nestled closer. "It's a Christmas miracle."

It was *all* a miracle—the fact that fate had brought them together, the storms they'd weathered, and now the quiet joys of family life. He'd never thought such a life would be his, but Samantha had given him that gift. For that, he would be grateful for the rest of his days.

The clock in the hall chimed the midnight hour, echoed moments later by the tower bells of the nearby church.

Samantha stirred. "Goodness, midnight already? I had no idea it was so late."

"It's now officially Christmas."

"Happy Christmas, Dr. Kendrick," she said, smiling up at him.

"Happy Christmas, Mrs. Kendrick. Thank you for being my wife, and thank you for the most splendid gift a man could ever wish to have."

For unto them, against so many odds, a child had been born. Love had been restored.

Visit us online at
KensingtonBooks.com
to read more from your favorite authors,
see books by series, view reading group guides, and more.

BOOK CLUB
BETWEEN THE CHAPTERS

Visit us online for sneak peeks, exclusive giveaways,
special discounts, author content, and engaging
discussions with your fellow readers.

Betweenthechapters.net

Sign up for our newsletters and be the first to get exciting news
and announcements about your favorite authors!
Kensingtonbooks.com/newsletter